Martin, Crook,

By Donna Nitz Muller

Dedicated to Sarah and Bonnie

Martin, Crook, and Bill

A casket in the bedroom
A wake in the parlor
A lone oak tree as sentinel
On a rolling rise of pasture
Guarding the burning ember
Who will step from the ashes
Wrapped in a great coat
Carrying the secret of life

Martin, Crook, & Bill

Part One

Chapter One

Martin watched the tall, skinny kid with loose jeans and a long navy colored shirt turn past the bus driver. He watched the kid pass the first rows of empty seats, and mumbled, "Do not sit here. I repeat, not here."

Refusing to even glance at the seat beside him for fear of giving the space some psychic power of attraction, Martin said, "No, no, no, no."

The young man walked toward him, appeared to count the rows, and squeezed in the space beside Martin. Despite the empty rows, despite Martin's long legs filling every centimeter of leg space, the kid sat down, adjusted his body to fit around Martin's elbow and looked straight ahead.

"Why did you sit here?" Martin asked him.

"Seven rows, left side," the kid said.

"What does that mean?" Martin tried to appear completely calm, the whole of him calm and easy.

"Lucky for me," the kid answered without turning his eyes from the front.

Martin had thought it was him, something in his own manner or appearance that attracted the passenger to sit beside him. Relieved that he had not attracted the kid he asked, "How is it lucky?"

This time the young man did turn to face Martin. He had to look up to meet Martin's eyes. "You are one tall dude," the kid said, and then continued. "It is lucky because seven is a lucky number, but it is a double lucky number on the left side in rows." The young man smiled, showing even teeth and a charismatic face.

Martin nodded and turned back to the window. He watched the jagged lightning flash through the sky above the squat buildings. The bus lumbered through the Sioux Falls streets, brakes screeching and frame moaning while turning west on Interstate 90. In the open country the storm raged outside Martin's window. The wind rocked the bus and sometimes the gusts spit bits of rain around the aging window frame. What should have been August dusk was coal black night.

"Scary," the young man said, sitting slightly forward on his seat.

"What?" Martin asked.

"The weather," he said. He gestured with his head toward the window.

"Oh." Martin looked again toward the window. "I thought you meant me."

The young man laughed, and Martin liked the sound of his laughter. Martin smiled, and the kid talked. "I'm heading to Rapid City to be a dealer in a casino. I start on Tuesday at Uptown Joe's. Not exactly the top of the trade, but everybody starts somewhere."

Martin did not know what to say to that information, so he said nothing.

"What about you?"

"I'm going home," Martin said.

"What do you do, for a living, I mean?" the kid asked Martin with a genuine glint of curiosity in his lively brown eyes.

"Guess," Martin turned to look at the kid. In the dim bus light, he could see the kid's focused expression, trying to guess a riddle.

"Not sales or banking," the kid said. "Maybe a farmer, maybe a musician. I cannot guess." He shrugged and waited for the answer.

"I'm mental. I mean I am seriously whacked, dysfunctional, but cured enough to go home to my farm." Martin had to be careful not to get too excited. He hated when his stomach churned and his mind raced ahead of him.

"Be quiet now," Martin told the young man. He had nothing to lean his head against, so he hunched down and bowed his head and closed his eyes.

"You look like a man on a mission," the kid said quietly.

"I do?"

"Yes," the kid said. "I met a guy at a carnival once who looked like you with the long, shaggy black hair and the haunted looking eyes. He walked around on stilts trying to scare people. He sang stuff in this soft voice."

"What did he sing?"

The kid put his hands out full beside his ears, closed his eyes, and wiggled his fingers. "I see murder and mayhem."

The kid spoke in a sing-song voice like a carnival act. When he opened his eyes and looked at Martin he quickly added, "Joking, just joking."

Martin said, "Did I murder someone?"

The kid gaped at him but did not move away or answer the question so Martin asked, "Does the murder come after the mayhem or before?"

The kid beside him had turned away. When Martin did not move or talk for several minutes, the kid finally settled deeper into his seat. Martin could feel the young man's energy.

"Not far now," Martin said. "I'm almost home."

He was a young man once, but even then he did not ride the bus. He flew to places, first class. Now, at age thirty-nine and one half, he rode the bus. There would be no high school band or waving pom-poms to welcome him, just an old, empty farm house. He forced calmness through his veins like dye for a cardiogram. And he thought of Crook. The cragged, tough, enigmatic visage of Crook provided peace and motivation.

The old Greyhound crawled west on I-90 into a vast and empty cavern as though some crazy wizard had put the bus into an alternate universe. Nothing was visible through the sheets of rain, and Martin said, "Welcome to the *Twilight Zone*." The bus sliced through the deep South Dakota darkness.

Looking across the row to his right, Martin watched the green interstate signs loom out of the darkness as the bus lights moved across them. He saw Buffalo Ridge and Hartford, Humboldt and Montrose and Canistota. As the Canistota sign passed, Martin stood and indicated for the kid to let him pass.

"We aren't anywhere," the kid told him, annoyed, but he slid his feet into the aisle and made himself small.

Martin, pulling his gym bag from under the seat, squeezed past the kid, and then turned back, "Remember the house always wins." A stupid thing to say, Martin thought, but he was sure he had said it out loud and that was satisfying.

7

Martin stood, very tall, behind the driver. Due to the confined space, Martin found it necessary to bend his head forward and lean into the driver's space. "Do not miss the Wheaton exit," he said, his soft measured voice almost menacing. Martin noted the fear that passed across the driver's expression, and Martin wondered at it.

The Wheaton town stop was better than three miles from the exit, so the driver asked Martin to sit down. It was not easy for Martin to explain things, so he kept standing. His hands began to wave at his sides as though pushing through water. The gym bag hit soft against the iron railing. When the bus sloshed and creaked to a halt at the stop sign, Martin stepped down and faced the door. "Here," he said. The door split in two and opened.

Martin faced the thick, wet darkness and yelled, "Kid!"

He heard the steps stop behind him. Martin remained looking straight ahead, through the open door, "Remind the driver that I have a chest in the luggage compartment. He might drive off with it when I step out."

Martin's tall body filled the doorway. He braced himself with his right hand and held the gym bag in his left. He could neither step out nor turn around.

"He heard ya," the kid's voice rising above the weather. The driver squeaked in his chair, and pulled out plastic rain gear. Martin nodded and said, hopefully out loud, "Thank you."

Martin heard the driver's cough, held his breath and stepped into the black night.

Protected by the bus from the wind and driving rain, it took both men to heave Martin's trunk onto the road. The driver shut the baggage area door, glanced from Martin to the trunk, shrugged, and climbed back to his seat. Then Martin watched the taillights of the bus cross the highway to the interstate on-ramp and disappear, carrying the young man with his new job further west.

The tool chest was two feet by four feet. Martin pulled a flashlight from a side pocket, held it in his mouth, and detached the dolly from the top of the chest. It was all his design. Martin recalled guiding the hand of Tobias, the welder. He saw the blue flame and the thin line of silver like hot glue, attaching the retractable wheels. He could not remember how long ago that was. Crook told him many times not to dwell backwards in time.

Martin braced the dolly with his feet. It took several tries at full strength, but Martin finally heard the click that meant the box was firmly fixed onto the wheels. Distant lightening flashes provided a neon light. The wind and rain could not maintain such ferocious energy; still gusty, still dark and wet, but less threatening and more embracing. He pulled the handle from its place, attached it, found his sopping wet gym bag and plopped it on top.

It was twenty years since he left home, but Martin did not need light to walk this mile, half on highway, half on gravel, to the house of his father. Many visits of course, but this time there would be no one to greet him. This time, he thought, he would not leave. It was time to heal or die. The kid had said murder and mayhem. Then Martin remembered, the kid was joking.

Martin felt the slight downgrade of the gravel road beneath his feat and, looking up, he saw the white light from the kitchen windows of his neighbor's farm house. Bill Bendix lived in that house along with his wife, Tillie. As far as Martin knew, they had always lived there, were born there. Martin waved his hands at his sides as though paddling his way through the night, moving the night behind him. It was the familiar bitter-sweet recognition of Bill's farm house, lighted in the night, which caused Martin's lapse into deep unrecognizable thoughts.

He rubbed his eyes and shook his arms and picked up the handle to his toolbox and started down the road. The road beneath his feet was so familiar to him that the final quarter mile to his own driveway slipped beneath him quickly and smoothly. He knew the driveway was there despite the weeds growing down the middle and leaving a barely visible two-wheel track that led to the old, abandoned house. He knew it in the dark as he would know it in the light.

Martin considered leaving the chest at the end of the driveway until morning. As he was thinking about that, his legs kept moving and his body kept pulling until he was looking into the dark windows of the porch. The row of sagging porch windows looked like eyes into a black hole. This house was like no other Martin had seen or built.

It was after midnight and Martin was tired. Exhaustion weighed him down and he could only think of sleep. How wonderful to feel so tired. Most people, he thought, did not know what a wonderful thing it was to feel tired, to want to sleep. It felt so good in fact that it gave him new energy.

Leaving the chest at the bottom of the three cement steps, Martin climbed, one foot up and then the other. His breathing rasped and a chill played down his spine. When he pulled at the screen door, the whole door came off in his hand, swung by the handle and flopped lengthwise against the siding. "Jesus!" Martin gasped. He set the door against the siding and stepped onto the porch floor. The floor felt mushy under his feet; rotten wood.

Martin crossed the eight feet to the door leading into the kitchen. When he opened the kitchen door, he was greeted with a sudden scurrying sound. He recognized the quick, rushing scamper of rats. His hands again fluttered at his sides. It took a long time to push his way past the scampering sounds.

After awhile, he slowly pulled the flashlight from his pocket, feeling it in the utter darkness, heavy in his big hand. Silence now and darkness and a dizzy loss of direction until the flashlight worked under his thumb. With the flashlight he found his father's stash of lanterns.

The lanterns on the pantry shelf clanked and fell under his clumsy grasp, but he caught them. The wicks were dry but the kerosene in its small spouted can stood at the end of the shelf.

He worked quickly, standing at the small, wood table in the pantry. He talked in a constant, soft flow of words. The sound of his own voice kept him company. A rat crossed his shoe and he sent it flying with a tiny scream that sounded a lot like the sound of the rat. He talked louder and heard the fear in his voice. He could not allow the darkness any closer. "Too long a day. Go to bed. Too long a ride. Find a bed," he said into the circle of light around the flashlight which stood on end on the table.

Carrying the lighted lantern, he moved cautiously through the long kitchen and the dining room and into the living room. He remembered a huge stuffed horsehair chair with arms as large as fat logs, its rounded edges several inches over the side of the chair. He sought it.

Martin knew what happened as soon as the light fell into the room. Kids used the living room to party. Beer cans were stacked in pyramids along one wall. The light outlined cobwebs flowing from the beer cans like lines of frost on thin wires. Only the huge, stuffed chair remained of the furniture. The chair appeared to have drunk all the beer. It sat crooked and sloppy drunk. Martin did not approach it. Anything could inhabit the chair.

Retracing his steps, Martin realized the claw-footed dining room table was gone and the window was missing. The lead glass dining room window with the colored pieces at the top was completely gone. Someone had put cardboard over the opening. The other window facing the porch was broken. He felt moist air on his cheeks and heard the crunch of glass and garbage and the suck of slippery stuff under his work boots. Still, the hardwood floor was solid beneath. He held the lantern down to double check.

The furniture, strangely, did not matter to him, but the disrepair of the magnificently built house hurt like stabbing needles between his shoulder blades. Martin had not felt that kind of hurt for long months, even years. It reminded him both that he was alive and that it might not be a good thing.

There was emotional release in pounding the dining room wall and feeling the old plaster give beneath his fist, and satisfaction in solid lathe beneath the plaster. "It can be fixed," he told himself. "Nothing broken here that cannot be fixed better than ever."

Martin knew houses as he knew how to breathe. Knowing things was not the problem. In fact, his knowledge of design and structure was stronger than ever. Functioning was the problem, getting up in the morning, talking sentences, keeping the blackness away; that was the problem.

He slowly found his way to the small room off the kitchen with linoleum flooring worn through to the black. His mother once used this room for washing both clothes and children. The room was turned into storage after indoor plumbing in 1962. But the ancient high-legged, sprawling bathtub stood where it had always been. It was easier to put stuff into it than to move it. Martin lowered the lantern into the tub and checked carefully for animal droppings or nests, at least animals big enough to see. Nothing but his mother's canning equipment, strainers and pressure cooker, jar lids, and a cone shaped apparatus with a wooden tool used to squeeze every molecule of apple juice from the crab apples.

Moving quickly now, Martin took the stairs three at a time. He used the back stairs to reach the winter closet which held his father's greatcoat. His father wore this heavy, long, double-breasted coat over his barrel chest when he stepped from the ship. The cleaning label was printed in German. On his father, this coat flapped about his ankles when he strode the winter sidewalk to church. The coat commanded respect. So it was with respect Martin separated the coat from the other clothes on the rack. He pulled and lifted the heavy wooden hanger from the closet and tore the rotting plastic cover from the coat.

Ignoring the scampers of feet, ignoring the raindrops plopping in the hallway, ignoring cobwebs and grime that tasted on his tongue, Martin carried the coat down the stairs like the body of a beautiful woman. He set the lantern on a bench and laid the coat into the tub. It filled the bottom. In the poor light and deep shadows the coat seemed to float. He resisted diving into it.

Before rest, he had to find his gym bag. The wet thing lay where it was dropped on the kitchen floor. Martin put it into the bathtub. Next he pulled and tugged and lifted his tool chest up the steps and across the porch and through the kitchen door. He shut the door hard and tight, pushing one more time with his backside. The darkness instantly closed in.

"Don't panic, Jim Bob," he muttered as he yanked the door open and snatched his lantern from the porch floor. Again, he shut the door. No longer heeding the squeaks and scuffles he caused among the rodents, he stepped into the bathtub while holding the lantern above his head. He lay down still holding the lantern with one raised arm. Only then did the sensation of wet reach him.

His hair was wet, his clothes and shoes were wet, and the gym bag was sodden. Standing up in the tub, he removed his socks and shoes and jeans. He molded the gym bag into a pillow and put it beneath the coat. He reached to extinguish the lantern and decided to let it burn out. Lying down and wrapping himself into the coat, he shut his eyes.

"Goodnight Nancy, goodnight Carmen and Christie, goodnight Crook. Sounds like the Walton's in here."

Martin was home.

Chapter Two

With his determined strides away from the house, the long coat slapped against Martin's bare calves, causing a swishing sound. He focused downward, careful to follow the old path visible like a pencil line between thistles and pigeon grass gone to seed. His untied work boots slipped on his feet, and the sun was hot through the black coat.

Martin noted the furious hammering of his heart. "Overslept, overslept," he said as he rushed along the thin path. "Running on a tight rope," he said. "Running a damn tight rope."

Breathing hard inside the heavy coat on an August morning, he reached the well with the once-red steel pump jack. His fingers worked in quick, deft motions over the belt and wheel, following the wiring to the box. The well would work. Martin nodded in satisfaction and moved on.

He passed the barn, deliberately not looking at it. He turned his head away like a soldier on parade, looking sharp and straight toward the tangled apple trees. Judging that he had passed the barn, Martin straightened his head, searching for the tree. The tree stood on a mild rise, a huge oak with roots visible above the earth like fat snakes. The place they called "the bench" was still barren of bark. Martin bent to gently pat the cool, sun-bleached wood.

Standing completely still, he arched his head to listen to the echo of his dad. "Son," his dad called. "What are you doing? Waiting for cows to come home?" His father's voice was strong and clear in the morning air.

"Yes, I am," Martin answered.

It was their joke, and even now as Martin looked to the sky, he smiled. This was a good memory, a good selection. He remembered the old wood silverware box used to hide his drawing. It probably still lay between those roots. Martin did not look.

It wasn't the box that mattered. Martin caught the memory of that boy hiding his work. Even in his hurry, the boy was careful not to bend the sheets of paper before running to see what his father wanted. Martin studied that boy with great care from thirty years distance. He had been a good boy, then. He touched the memory with tenderness. Yes, it was all right. He felt no fear trying to suffocate him.

When Martin sat on the bench, he faced the decaying farm buildings. Even in abandonment, Martin saw the beauty and balance in the scene. The thistles topped with bright pink flowers were in fact noxious weeds. From this distance, they looked like small pink splashes on the gray boards of the granary. The old building was shot through the heart and bleeding blue sky.

Martin worked hard to look everywhere but at the barn. This was difficult because the barn was central to the scene before him. It stood down the rise, huge between the tree and the house. His eyes had to curve around it to study the granary or the chicken coops or the old garden spot and the orchard. He caught a glimpse from the corner of his eye, and fear crawled with cold fingers on his spine. "No," he whispered, throat tight.

Martin heard the loud laughter coming from the haymound. Joseph and Maureen and himself swung on the pulleys used to haul hay into the barn. They swung out of the haymound door until their arms were nearly pulled from their sockets and their hands had no skin left, swinging into the night and back, grasping with their toes for the ledge.

Maureen, the last one to surrender, went to the house with her bare legs and feet a mass of scratches from the dry alfalfa. The fun was over. Joseph swung the pulleys back and tied the ropes. Was it Joe? Yes, it was all right to remember Joe at the time. It was all right to remember the laughter that always leaked from Joe no matter what the rest of his body was doing.

He thought for several minutes, sitting as still as the hot air around him. "If I am very, very careful, I can look at the barn," he said with some wonder.

It was for Maureen that he waited. He had to be sure that all the business of things was correct: the taxes, the title, whatever had to be done to assure him that he could live here without problems. He presumed Maureen took care of everything even though the farm was left to him.

Martin knew the farm was his because the lawyer read the will after his father's funeral. In his father's own words, the lawyer read, "The farm goes to Martin. Take care of it, son." The lawyer did not call his father's document a will. He called it a "legacy." Martin's legacy was the farm.

Sitting in the lawyer's office, Martin turned to Maureen and asked what Joseph was to inherit. That was the exact moment he knew he was sick. Maureen jerked toward him, her eyes shocked. Then she could not look at him at all. Now he asked the blue sky for the thousandth time, "Why?" And he heard his answer, "Joe is dead."

At the time of his father's funeral eight years ago he did not care about the farm. He never returned after that, allowing the place to crumble and hoping that his father could not see it. He scorned the old farm because he was a Golden Boy with work and money and potential for more money. Now, in a sarcastic twist of fate, it was all he had. His survival was here, his final hope.

Martin's head was just beginning the throb at his temples when he heard the car. Maureen drove right past the barn on the almost invisible dirt track. She drove a small, red Mustang, and she drove with confidence. The weeds slid under the bumper as the car leveled itself over the uneven ground. She stopped just short of the tree roots and got out.

"Hello, Martin," she called, waving her arm high in the air as she stood beside her gleaming car like a picture out of *Great Gatsby*.

"Maureen," Martin yelled, surprised at his own excitement.

"Brings back old memories, doesn't it?" She sounded oddly cheerful as she climbed the rolling ascent to the bench. Her feet moved in white sandals and she wore a flowered sundress. Her red-blond hair gleamed and melted into the sunlight like smeared crayon.

His mouth flopped open in amazement. When, he wondered, did Maureen turn sexy? He remembered strong, wholesome, loud, even abrasive and aggressive, but he did not remember the woman who approached on long, slim legs. Her shape had lost its wonderful power and seemed vulnerable and soft. Her cheerfulness alarmed him.

Her fine fingers felt cool on his forehead as she lightly brushed his hair aside. Except for the smile that continued on his lips, Martin could not respond. He was painstakingly careful in his speech. He pleaded inside his head for his voice to work, for his thoughts to work.

"Why haven't you gotten married?" he asked her and she listened carefully. His two daughters were the only grandchildren.

"Well," she said, that ridiculous smile glued to her peach lips, "I met the right man, but he was already taken." She sat beside him on the bench and gazed at the decaying farm buildings and the weeds and the grass gone to seed just as he had. She also avoided looking long at the barn. Sighing, she put her hand lightly on Martin's shoulder.

"The farm is mine." Martin intended this as a question, but it sounded like a child claiming a toy. He looked down at his boots and bare shins and wished he had put his pants on.

Maureen nodded slightly, but did not shift her gaze from the devastated property. "It was so beautiful once, Martin. It was like a picture. Now look at this. We couldn't even sell it for half of its old value."

Martin wanted to tell her in no uncertain terms that he intended to live here. He reached with his hand to her chin and turned her face to look at him. He wanted her to know everything just by looking at him.

"I know," she whispered.

After a long pause, she added, "You left the hospital against everyone's wishes, even mine. But I have decided to trust you."

Martin was relieved. "Crook knows," he told her.

"Oh, God, yes, Mr. Crook knows!" The anger rose in a hot flash though her eyes. Martin looked away from her anger because she worked so hard to keep it hidden.

This time a long silence, several minutes before either Martin or Maureen could look at each other. Tears ran freely down her freckled cheeks. "See how you can talk, Martin?" She was determined to be positive and Martin smiled at the old stubborn-willed sister he always knew. He nodded.

"The farm?" he asked her.

"I've talked with our lawyer. The farm is yours. Maybe while you reconstruct yourself, you can do some work on this place." This time her smile was genuine.

"Can you tell me?" That was all he could say, but she understood.

"No," she answered, laying her hand on his coat over his knee. "I've been told by every doctor you have ever seen that I must not say anything unless I want to risk a trip of no return, if you know what I mean." He nodded, he knew.

"Would I rather die than remember?" Halting words, but clear.

"I would rather take a scissors and cut this disgusting hair of yours, and then I could reach your neck and choke sense into you, but I can't do that either. Patience, patience and more patience." She stood and faced him, bent and hugged him, fiercely.

Martin said, "Don't go." He held her hand so that she could not turn away.

She sighed and tugged her hand; he tightened his grip. At last, looking down at him, she said, "You never cried, Martin. Not for Joe, not for Mom and not for Dad. Not a single tear. It is hard for me to understand."

Martin nodded. Before releasing her hand, he said, "Crook understands." Since she rolled her eyes he knew he said the words aloud. She walked with care in her tall shoes down the slope to her car.

Martin stood suddenly, waved his arms above his head. She finally noticed him and turned to look at him while standing inside the car door. "REA," he yelled. He had to have the power turned on. She nodded. "Groceries," he yelled. Again she nodded.

Before Martin stood to retrace his steps, he thought about Crook. Inside that hospital, Crook was everything. He owed his life to Crook. Furthermore, he promised to get Crook out. Maureen did not know, nor did his ex-wife Nancy, but getting Crook out of that hospital was the necessary force driving him forward.

Planning Crook's exit from the Nebraska State Mental Hospital for the Criminally Insane in Lincoln, Nebraska was the only reason Martin had to get well. Even his children were not reason enough, love them as he did. Crook needed him, though Crook did not know it. Crook saved him and that Crook did know.

Crook told him that the workers dying in the construction of the Milwaukee Brewers stadium triggered something repressed in Martin. The fall and the death of those construction workers triggered something Martin did not remember. Martin did remember opening the St. Paul paper and reading about that accident. He remembered looking at the picture. A chill had run through him and his mind turned to ice.

The thick leaves above his head caught his thoughts and lifted as a green mass turning a thousand different shades, twirling. Martin watched them, listened to the sound of brittle rustling. This spot had always been the conference room and it served well indeed.

Rain noisy on the barn roof. The smell of damp hay. Anger crushing his chest.

The glimpse into the past was gone and he could not force it. He started toward the house, stopping again to check the pump. In the house, he waited for Maureen to bring groceries, and he waited for the lights to come on. While he waited he went into the laundry room to dress and discovered that his blue work shirt was missing. He had worn it home; he took it off before he lay down and hung it across the side of the tub to dry. Carefully he re-enacted every action including the buttons sticking in wet button holes. Rats would not carry away his blue work shirt.

Hallucinating and blank periods were not part of his problem, at least they had not been. Flashbacks were not hallucinations. Shrugging, he reached for the gym bag with the red TWINS logo across the side. He pulled out the tan Dockers shirt. "No one does tan like Dockers," he muttered as he buttoned the shirt and rubbed his hands down the front to iron it.

His fingers ran over the square bulge in the pocket created from the folded, washed, dried, and washed again letter from Christie. His hand over the pocket, he recited the letter like saying the Pledge of Allegiance.

Dear Daddy,

I am starting third grade this year. Mom is mad that you are leaving the hospital. I am happy for you to get out. I love you. Carmen says hi.

Love Christie

PS. Say hello to Mr. Crook for me.

Then he tied his shoes.

Maureen returned with a fair supply of groceries, and the old Hot Point refrigerator hummed loud. He pulled his notebook from his gym bag and made notes, carefully numbered notes regarding wiring and plumbing. The now-dry pages crinkled as he turned them on the spiral.

Maureen told him that the town was already buzzing about his return. He did not care.

He told her his blue shirt was missing. She had no response for that.

"I have money," he said.

"Nancy controls your money, remember. But, yes, you have money. You have to submit duplicate accounting to your accountant and to Nancy." Maureen stood at the door like the pet dog needing to pee.

He nodded. "Goodbye," he said. Then he walked with her to the car. "Drop me off at Bill's."

Chapter Three

Martin knew Bill Bendix's habit of pushing the bill of his cap together with his hands in prayer formation when things would not fix. He wore a specific cap for repair jobs that was already so black with grease and stiff with grime it was no longer a cap. It was like an ancient head ornament.

As Martin strode around the slight curve of Bill's gravel driveway, Bill's cap sat high and pointed. The older man focused on his tractor as though looking mean would make it run. At sixty-five, Bill looked fit as a fiddle, lean and strong. Tools lay scattered at his feet, and the sun glimmered hot off the metal. Bill was the neighbor down the road all of Martin's life. He was as much a part of life as the creek rising in the spring thaw or church on Sunday morning.

Bill appeared unaware of Martin striding past the house. Martin assumed Bill felt him because like most farmers, Bill had a sixth sense of atmosphere and movement. So, when Martin said, "Hot out," he was amazed to see the older man jump two full inches into the air.

Bill's glance went immediately past Martin. He checked for a vehicle, saw none. He gripped his wrench tighter. "What can I do for you?" he said to Martin, but his tone was not friendly, not like Martin expected.

"I don't know," Martin stammered.

Bill stepped closer, studied Martin, looking up into his face. "You look like shit," Bill said. He dropped the tool and took Martin's hand and pumped it with vigor. "I didn't recognize you at first there, Martin. Sorry about that. Didn't mean to hurt your feelings." His straight white teeth gleamed behind the black grease on his cheeks. Gray hair poked from under the cap.

Martin did that quick check for sarcasm that was habitual to him in recent years. If Crook was here, Crook could tell with a glance if the man was being sarcastic. As Crook was not here, Martin had to make his own judgment. He decided to believe Bill as being the same Bill. What you saw was what you got with Bill Bendix.

Bill glanced at the great coat with a questioning expression.

"Security blanket," Martin told him.

"You fixing up your dad's place?" Bill said. His gaze moved up and down Martin's tall form. Bill sized him up, checking the damage so to speak. Martin felt Bill's inspection, silently. He thought Bill looked at him exactly the same way as he looked at his tractor. Then Bill bent down and retrieved his wrench.

"I am fixing the place, and that wrench is wrongo."

Bill walked with deliberate casualness toward the tractor and tossed the wrench on the scattered pile. He bent and plucked a grease rag from the tool chest and wiped his hands, carefully. Martin knew what Bill was doing, he allowed it.

Martin walked to the side of the once bright green John Deer, patting it. Bill moved quickly to stack tools within Martin's reach. Bill leaned against the big tractor tire, waiting. He handed, wiped, held, and jumped whichever way Martin pointed. Martin paused long enough to watch Bill fold the coat and lay it carefully inside the pick-up cab.

Martin worked without stop for over two hours. At last he climbed up and sat on the hot steel seat. The cover and the padding had long ago worn away and only the holes in the bare steel remained. In the sun, as today, it was hot enough to fry an egg.

The engine clunked and then purred. Martin made three circles around the yard, his ear cocked toward the engine. When Martin climbed down, he smiled and pumped his fist.

"How long?" Bill asked.

"Until the piston locks up again. You need to unfold some of your moldy money and buy parts," Martin said. For a minute they sounded and looked as though ten years could fall away like snow melt. Martin smiled.

Tillie's thick, energetic form crossed the yard toward them. She looked like a tug boat. She carried lemonade in big plastic glasses. She held a glass toward her husband and then toward Martin. He continued to smile though she did not recognize him.

Her hand froze midway as she saw Martin's face. He watched her stout German features register shock and surprise like light across a prism. He took the glass from her shaking fingers.

"I thought we had a helper from the Colony." She looked pointedly at Martin's hair. "Come to the house. I will get my clippers." Since Martin saw no secret exchanges between Bill and Tillie, he nodded.

That was that. Martin did not clench his hands together behind his head, fully prepared to lose a finger before one strand of hair. Martin did not lie down on the ground and refuse to walk even one step toward the clippers. No, he did not. He followed, a lamb to the shearer.

By the time Bill entered the kitchen, hair lay like a miniature haystack on the kitchen floor. Bill was obviously not pleased. "Good grief, Tillie, you have it all the same length like a girl's. Cut that away, that part right there." Bill frowned and winced and walked in a circle around the chair.

Tillie stood on a step stool behind the seated Martin. When Bill was about to cross behind her, she jabbed Bill with her elbow hard enough to hurt.

Martin said, "Ouch, Tillie."

The flesh on Tillie's arms vibrated with the humming clippers, and her hands worked through Martin's hair again and again. In her day, Tillie had cut many heads of hair, all exactly the same. For the boys it was a crew cut and for the girls a single length page boy. Martin's hair appeared to cause her some confusion. Martin saw in the mirror a cut that left Martin's natural curls waving around his head like a child's wool cap.

Both Tillie and Bill faced Martin, looking at him, hands on hips and lips pursed. They nodded simultaneously in a positive manner. Bill fetched the shaving kit.

An hour later, well past lunch time, Martin's neighbors were done with him. Their work was complete. He was good as new. The good citizens of Wheaton, South Dakota would be able to walk the streets safely.

"Good," Martin told them, "now we can fix the well."

Bill had to eat first. He ate on a schedule like every decent man and ate now while Martin watched him and Tillie vacuumed Martin like a lumpy sofa. Bill also informed Martin that the REA truck passed by while he was still outside. Tillie touched Martin's shoulder when he started to stand. She glanced toward his plate, and he obediently gulped the sandwich.

Climbing into the passenger side of Bill's pick-up, Martin tied the rope that held the passenger door shut in a gesture as routine and familiar as putting his elbow out the window. The rope crossed his knees, running from the gearshift to the door handle. He waited.

Because the window refused to crank shut, he or Joe could rest their elbow out the open window in winter as well as summer. The boys rode in that '56 Chevy pick-up with their arm on the window ledge as though they wanted it that way. They were tough. Memories of Joe's suntanned face creased in wide laughter flittered through Martin's mind. These were soft memories and not the paralyzing kind.

"Where is Joe?" Martin asked himself.

"Joe is dead," he answered, but he didn't really believe it.

"Stop talking to yourself," Bill said as he pulled himself behind the steering wheel. "You sound like a fruit loop."

At Martin's farm, three men stood at the open side door of the REA van. They greeted Bill with obvious relief. "Where do we start? This place is a mess." The older man spoke quietly to Bill as though Martin could not hear them.

Martin pulled a folded sheet of paper from his shirt pocket, being careful not to disturb Christy's letter in the process. He gestured for the men to gather around and told them exactly and with detail down to the type of wire, the volts for the outlets, and the type of outlet, where to install, and how to run the wire. While Martin pointed and gestured and instructed the REA crew, he saw that Bill was pleased. It mattered that Bill was pleased. Martin felt good.

The initial mistrust and hesitancy on the part of the REA men faded from their eyes. Martin saw respect. His objective abilities were the last to leave and the first to come back. His vision was fine; his confusion was clearing like smoke from a dead fire. What he knew, he knew.

Bill nodded to Martin. "We got that hair cut just in time," Bill said, smiling. "Not to mention the coat. Mighty glad you took off the coat."

"Do you think you cured me with a hair cut?" Martin said. He saw Bill's stunned look. He moved away a few steps.

"No," Bill said, "but you look better, that matters."

"I can do this. Please, God, help me to do this." He turned toward the house.

With Bill at his heels and the crew chief following Bill, Martin crossed the kitchen en route to the basement fuse box. Mid-stride, Martin froze. He stopped, absolutely still and stared toward the counter, mouth open.

"What?" Bill asked, his eyes following Martin's gaze.

Martin saw an open jar of peanut butter and a loaf of bread. One slice lay on the counter with the knife full of peanut butter on top. He had not started to make a sandwich and then left it, had he? Was there something new wrong with him? His chest tightened, and his mouth went dry.

"Forgot to finish your sandwich? It's okay," Bill said to Martin with a definite command to his voice. With his body, Bill blocked Martin's view of the crew chief while he pinched Martin on the flesh above his elbow and on the inside of his arm, the old parent in church pinch. "It is okay, Martin. Let's get this done."

Martin rushed to the counter. In quick motions, he put the lid on the peanut butter and put the jar in the cupboard. He closed the bread wrapper with the blue plastic tie and put it in the fridge. He threw out the bread slice from the counter and washed the knife from the bottled water, putting it away. Then he wiped the counter several times with hard motions. He was breathing hard.

Bill started toward the basement stairs, the electrician in tow. "Wait," Martin yelled. "I'm coming." In long, fast strides Martin passed Bill and led the trio down the dark steps into the old, rock basement.

First he would do this. Then he would examine what had happened. He inhaled and forced himself to focus on the task at hand. He was able to, and for that he felt gratitude to God.

Later, as the crew worked, Martin walked outside. He walked across the overgrown lawn and back, leaving behind a swath of broken grass. With head bent to his chest, he missed his beard. He ran through every single moment of the day, including that open jar of peanut butter. His diagnosis was latent trauma reaction.

Perhaps he was blacking out. He took out his notebook and wrote down every single action of his day. He was not missing time, nor did rats run off with blue work shirts or make peanut butter sandwiches. After several minutes, he put the notebook back into his shirt pocket. He joined the crew chief, Thomas, and Bill who stood together in front of the house, chatting.

Tom was saying, "Strange things come in threes, you know," as Martin joined them. Tom told of another strange event in the small farm town of Wheaton. Martin assumed one of the strange events concerned his own return.

Bill leaned against the box of his pick-up, his casual stance in sharp contrast to the worry clouding his features. Tom faced Bill, but he stepped to one side to form a triangle that included Martin. Martin stepped forward into the group and tried to hide his sudden, intense interest behind a dull expression.

"She's been missing for five days, and Sheriff Hauk doesn't have a clue." Tom hooked his thumbs in his pants pockets.

Bill told Martin about Cassandra Peters. "Sandra's the star of the girl's basketball team. She is big time popular at school. Her parents woke up Saturday morning, and Sandra was gone. There seems to be no explanation." Bill looked at Martin and added, "She reminds me of you at that same age with the basketball."

Martin said, "What is the third strange thing?"

"Don't know yet," Tom said. "Something will happen. It always does."

It was near dusk, and the electrical workers began to gather around the REA trucks, their work completed. Martin checked everything. He ran his fingers over outlets and switches and wires until satisfied. Then he returned to stand by Bill and Tom. "It is all good," he said.

The work crew left, and Bill opened his pick-up and looked to be planning on heading home himself. Martin grabbed Bill's elbow. "The well," he said, alarmed.

"Tomorrow will work," Bill answered. "I'm tired. I have work of my own to do, and it's getting late."

"No." Martin looked directly at Bill and then turned sharply and headed toward the well. He marched across the farm yard and toward the barn without looking back. He knew Bill was behind him. He knew the grumpy scowl on Bill's face and didn't need to see it.

When the two men reached the well, Bill said, "If damn stubbornness fixes things, you'll be right as rain in about three minutes."

The motor hummed, but the pump-jack wouldn't move. Martin tried a quick turn on the belt with his hand. The rubber that stretched tight between the two wheels nearly caught his fingers between the belt and the wheel as it tried to turn. Within seconds it smelled like burning rubber. The pump-jack was stuck solid. Martin ran to turn the switch off.

Bill sprayed rust remover on all the moving parts and greased the bearings. The two of them each took a side of the rusty red steel pump-jack, shaped like hollow rectangles, and tried forcing it. They pushed up with all their brute strength, and on the third try the rectangles jerked loose, throwing Bill back three steps and cutting an inch into Martin's palm.

Martin ran to turn the power on. The motor ran, and the belt turned, and the pump-jack cranked very slowly up and down. Then it took off, whoosh, pumping like a resuscitated heart.

Bill shouted, "All right!" He raised his arms and danced in a slow circle. Martin walked slowly to the nozzle end of the pipe and waited for the water to shoot out. Within minutes water was pouring from the nozzle, and Martin put some in his cupped hands to clean his cut and wash his face.

Looking at him, Bill chuckled. "You have rust on your cheeks like smeared paint. You better let that water run for awhile."

The two men silently watched the water run onto ground already damp from last night's storm. It was dark and the newly-wired yard lights flicked on, one by the garage and one by the barn. Mosquitoes buzzed around their sweaty heads. Finally Martin was satisfied that the water ran clean and he connected the pipe from the well to the underground storage tank that fed the house.

The men walked toward the house. On each side of the path and in every spot where the gravel had thinned the weeds stood waist high. Trodden patches stood darker than the dusk where the REA guys drove their vehicle and walked around the buildings.

On the other side of the house, the once immaculate yard stretched to the road in a sea of grass with bulbs of seed rocking gently in the mild breeze. Bill shook his head. "A lot of work."

Martin nodded.

Martin's father, the only man in the county who had money, built the huge house in 1936. It was inherited money from a grandfather in Germany, money the grandfather wanted out of Germany. The house was huge even in an area where all of the houses boasted spacious, square rooms. It was almost two houses connected by a foyer, staircase, and landings. The two sides were identical in design but for different purposes. On the farm side of the staircase was the kitchen and laundry room, the informal dining room, and the downstairs bedroom. On the road side of the house was a formal dining room and living room big enough to hold a small dance or a good-sized funeral.

Upstairs, three rooms lined each side of the curricular landing. A back staircase went from the landing to the kitchen. The same builders who ignored closets downstairs compensated for that error upstairs. Each room had a closet the size of a small bedroom. The front bedrooms had their own closets; the back bedrooms shared their closets.

The formal rooms downstairs featured window seats. At one time the windows featured colored mosaic glass, but a man didn't raise three athletic children without sacrificing something. The colored mosaics were gone from all but the living room window.

The front porch faced east and ran the length of the house with two doors to enter the house. The door they used entered the kitchen. The door to the foyer was only used on rare, formal occasions.

On the south side, which faced the road, was a smaller porch. This porch actually housed what was considered the front door, which opened into the formal dining room. This door was used on New Year's Eve, baptisms, first communions, confirmation, and graduations. Those were the good times. His mother's wake was one of the bad times.

Other than his sister, Bill was the only person who crossed that threshold every time the door was opened. Bill was like a brother to Martin's father. Martin thought about his brother's wake as he slowed his pace to allow Bill to walk easily beside him.

A casket in the living room, blue silk along the lid. The face in the casket was Joe.

Martin stopped, his arms straight at his sides and his hands waving side as though pushing water. His heart pounded. He shut his eyes hard and tight, breathing in and out. It passed.

When he opened his eyes, Bill was not looking at him. Bill looked toward his truck. He was pretending not to see.

"Thank you," Martin said. He wanted Bill to know they could move forward.

"No problem," Bill answered. "I just hope Tillie kept the food warm. I might faint from hunger."

The crickets started their continuous whine, and a cool breeze felt cold on Martin's damp neck. A sense of tragedy hung about like a fog. Bill moved adroitly to hand Martin his great coat. Then he drove away.

Bill was gone, and Martin entered the kitchen. The light switch turned on one old bulb, but it was enough. Martin began running water down the dirt-black sink. He threw water with his hands across the floor trying to hit a brave rat with the spray. The sound of the splattering water across the floor brought the memory. Not a real, actual memory: a cloudy awareness that a memory should be there. "It rained that day," Martin said.

"Not tonight, not yet," he mumbled and shut off the water. He turned his back to the sink and slid down to sit on the floor, his legs sprawled in front of him. His strength drained, he felt like a rag doll. Still, he had to eat something and sleep.

Finally, he rose and made coffee and found the bread and sliced ham Maureen put into the frig. He walked through the house, cutting a path through the cobwebs and leaving tracks in the dust on the hardwood floors. The dust was so thick it folded above his shoes in a thick, condensed layer.

Martin made mental notes of what had to be done first in the restoration process. He turned on lights, most of which did not work or sparked and went out. Did Maureen remember light bulbs?

He would start with cleaning the mess. Crook would not like a mess and then new windows, roof and shingles. At first he thought the noise he heard was a cricket. He wasn't sure and stopped dead still, barely breathing, to listen. Then he heard a light padding sound coming through the ceiling. He tracked the noise and it led across the room. Someone was walking across the upstairs bedroom to the bathroom. The bathroom was not functional, but the steps entered the bathroom anyway and stopped.

Martin reached for a beard that was no longer there, hand landing on bare chin. As far as he knew, rats still didn't get up and walk on two feet. As Martin did not want to scare anyone, he stood on the middle landing of the staircase and called softly, "Who is there?"

No answer.

"The toilet doesn't work yet," he called up to the upstairs octagon shaped hall. The bathroom was a converted closet with a doorway cut into the hallway. The original door still opened into what always was Joe's room. Joe had to trade his private closet for a private entrance to the bathroom. So, their father bought Joe a giant wardrobe. Not a single piece of clothing hung in that wardrobe because it was full from top to bottom with athletic equipment. Joe's clothes hung in Martin's closet. Martin smiled.

"I won't hurt you," he called into the dark silence. He switched on the light and amazingly the bulb worked and shadows flittered on the hallway ceiling. "This is my house, and I won't hurt you." He spoke from the top step and lifted his voice, but spoke calmly like calling a stray calf. It was hot as Hades upstairs even with the windows broken and a breeze beginning to flow.

"I'm coming up," he called though he was already up. It was a warning to the intruder. He stepped closer to the closed bathroom door and noticed a light coming and going from under the door, a flashlight. Rats scurried in confusion around the upstairs hall. They were unnerved by the light, dim as it was. There were so many rats that Martin was stunned by it. He could not imagine a worse infestation.

"Don't be afraid," Martin called again from near the door, "but the toilet doesn't work. I'm going to fix it right now." He took a step, waited, took a step.

"The light might work in there," he said, now at the door. "Try it," he said, keeping his voice soothing. "Go ahead, try it."

A line of light appeared full across the bottom of the door. Martin stepped back, amazed. "That was the bulb we always had to change," he told the unknown person behind the door. "And now it works!"

Nothing from behind the door, so Martin said, "I'm relieved you are not deaf." He meant it sincerely. "Are you a man or a woman? Are you Sandra Peters?" This seemed logical to him. The rats had quieted, hiding.

Martin had no fear of the down-and-out unless it was an addict. The ones he knew where all in one stage or another of recovery, forced or unforced. It was the stories they told and the calm way they told them that chilled him. They all hid from their guilt, denied it, afraid to face it. He thought no addict would wander into rural South Dakota. Nothing here to beg, borrow, or steal. But someone who wanted to hide could do that for a long time.

Something else occurred to him. His voice raised an octave. "How was the peanut butter sandwich?"

"I didn't get to eat it," a raspy female voice answered, not a meek voice, actually quite voice. However, the door remained shut.

"I'm going to check the room you've been sleeping in," he told the occupant behind the door. Martin crossed the hall. He reached into the doorway and tried the light switch. Nothing. Just then the bathroom door opened to his back and light filtered over his shoulder and through his legs to reveal the steel frame bed with its bare, striped mattress.

An odd sensation began to squeeze his mid-section, and he had to examine it. Am I afraid? he wondered. No, I think it is the stink and the upstairs' heat. The squeezing passed, so he turned to see who was occupying his house and wearing his shirt.

The shirt pulled tight around her stomach. She was not obviously pregnant, but Martin knew. Her hair was shoulder length and tangled all over her head. She was a big girl, tall and well-proportioned in her shoulders and hips. She looked strong like an athlete in gray track warm-up pants.

Martin took a step toward her, but she held up her hands to stop him. The odor was tangible and stung his nose and burnt in his throat.

"Did you hear me last night? I came up here for my coat." Martin tried to be gentle. He didn't want to spook the girl.

She nodded.

He remembered the hot summer nights when they slept on the porch roof outside the windows. Now, the heat boiled the stench, and it was overpowering. How had he walked through here last night and not smelled or heard a thing? "I was tired, too tired to smell," he decided aloud. When the nausea brought specks of light dancing in his eyes, he ran for the bedroom window.

The window was completely gone and the screen hung from one top corner. Gulping in the night air and feeling the breeze on his cheeks revived him. He heard the night sounds in the trees and looked up to a clear sky and quarter moon. It would be much better to sleep outside.

"I couldn't flush it and I had to go," Sandra told him, somewhat defensively, a natural rasp to her voice that Martin liked.

"Try it now," he told her over his shoulder, not turning away from the window. "We fixed the water."

"Doesn't work," she answered.

"You might have to prime it with water from the kitchen. There is a bucket under the sink." He did not move, still wondering if he was going to faint. The young lady did not move.

"Do it now." He had not heard that edge to his voice since Christie ran into the street after her cat. Finally he turned into the room and listened to her plodding steps descending the stairs. He heard the water splashing into the bucket and followed her return. He wondered why she wasn't sick.

When she stood in the hallway, holding the bucket of water, there was defiance in every muscle and a tremble in her features. She looked lumpy and vulnerable in the pathetic hallway light. A stubborn young lady, Martin thought.

"Jesus, help us," he moaned. He moved slowly, like a drunk, toward her. His balance was out of whack, and he pitched a bit from side to side. He took the bucket in one hand and covered his nose and mouth with the other. It had to be well over a hundred degrees up here. He and Joe slept on the porch roof on nights like this.

"Lift the lid and I will pour." His voice was muffled by his hand, but clear enough. The toilet flushed, but no new water came into the tank. The water must be shut off. What had the girl used for drinking water? In this heat, she had to have water. He was sure Tom said she was missing for five days. Saturday morning, Bill said, and this was Thursday. Six days up here: how had she survived?

Martin tried the faucet on the sink for water and it broke off in his hand. He tried the bathtub; nothing there either. He would fix that later. He returned to the window and the girl followed him.

"How do you know who I am?" she asked in a snotty tone that did not hide her desperation. It was Martin's turn not to answer. He couldn't talk any more. As soon as he brought his head inside he felt a clamp of heat cover his face and burn in his eyes.

Instead of trying to talk, he looked at the old, stuffed mattress and thought it must be home to countless numbers of creatures both big and tiny. A sleeping bag lay across the top of the mattress. Between the bed and the wall were bundles of supplies and camping equipment. He couldn't tell what was in the cloth bag bundles, but it satisfied his curiosity as to how she survived.

The hideout was planned. The supplies were stashed. She probably had not realized the stifling upstairs heat in the summer or given proper thought to the lack of hygiene, or understood the rat infestation.

"Hauk is probably searching every camp ground in the whole state, maybe Minnesota and Iowa and Nebraska," Martin commented, softly, thoughtfully.

To this comment, Sandy covered her face and turned away. "Jesus, Jesus, Jesus," she said into her hands.

A sudden brisk breeze lifted the siege of heat. "Twenty-four hours ago I was riding the bus in a storm. Weren't you afraid of the storm?" Martin asked this because he could not understand her sudden change of emotion.

"I was more afraid of the rats," she answered, again facing him in the near darkness. "I almost went home and told my parents everything, but I couldn't. So, I kept my flashlight on all night. I remembered to bring batteries." She smiled. Anyway, Martin thought it was a smile.

"How did you manage?" Martin asked with such a genuine concern that Sandra looked at him, hard.

"I thought I would die and hoped I would, except basketball practice starts in three weeks," she finally answered. She stood still as a statue, not a muscle moved. Martin thought of bad actors in a play. Neither of them could move. Neither of them knew what to do with their next minute of time.

"Basketball starts in three weeks," Martin repeated. That struck a chord in him. He remembered counting the days and hours until official practice started. Not an odd thing to say; of course a person could not die with basketball starting in three weeks.

"Joe and I played basketball," he told her. "Joe didn't play his senior year. Where was Joe? Joe was dead."

Sandra took two steps backward, preparing to run. Martin saw her movement, and he forced away his thought of Joe. Not now, not now. "I've had a nervous breakdown," he told her. "But I'm not psycho, and I won't hurt you."

He passed by her and started down the steps. She followed him, slowly, tentatively. "I forgot the girls play basketball in the fall in South Dakota." He tried to make up for his earlier lapse into stress with trivia, but realized he couldn't and said nothing more.

He pulled the peanut butter and jelly from the refrigerator. Neither said a word while Martin made sandwiches. Sandra went upstairs and returned with a liter bottle of 7-Up. They sat crossed legged on the floor, passing the warm soda back and forth, and eating without saying a single word.

Chapter Four

Bill was not pleased to see Martin at his front door before the sunrise was more than a vague line of light along the horizon. Still Bill opened the door and gestured for his neighbor to come inside. The gesture may have been a little sharp, but nothing that appeared to disturb Martin.

"Hurry up, Bill." Martin sounded frantic. He had the look of a man who had not slept or showered or changed clothes. "We have things to get." Martin pulled a sheet of folded paper from his coat pocket. He began to read from the list.

Martin's voice followed Bill into his bedroom. As Bill tied his shoes, he heard, "Three pounds of six-inch nails, eight window panes each measuring . . ."

Bill tiptoed in the darkness, trying not to wake Tillie, and then decided that Tillie should be awake to get some clue as to what he was forced to tolerate. Share his misery. He dropped his wallet, banged a drawer, and shut the bathroom door with a bang. When he emerged Tillie had slid her feet to the floor. "I'll make coffee," she said.

When Bill returned to the living room, Martin remained standing inches inside the front door. The living room was separated from the kitchen by an L-shaped counter, and Tillie stood behind the counter. Bill did not like that Tillie smiled at Martin. He wasn't sure why he was bothered by Tillie's pasted-on smile. The phoniness annoyed him. He said, "Coffee ready?"

Martin had on his coat which was unbuttoned and hung open to expose the wrinkled tan pants. Martin appeared edgy and ready to go, every minute a torture.

Tillie said, "You look good, better even than one day ago." Apparently she looked past the wrinkled pants and dark circles under his eyes. Bill looked again. He thought it must be lovely to have Tillie's rose-colored vision. Though on second look, Martin's skin was tighter on his face. He was not so slack along his jaw.

"Relax, Martin," Tillie told him. She poured coffee into mugs and pulled toast from the toaster with her finger-tips.

"Cassandra is pregnant," Martin answered.

Bill, who had moved to stand at the counter and wait for his toast, clenched his teeth. He felt his muscles tighten. "Damn, Martin," he said. "I'm willing and even glad to help. I owe your family a lot. But I will not tolerate any of your hallucinations. I absolutely cannot and will not handle that."

Martin cast his eyes down. The only sound was Bill swallowing his coffee in gulps. He stood at the counter with his back to Martin.

Tillie said, "No one has mentioned that thought before. I'm sure she cannot be pregnant. It would be impossible to be pregnant in a town like Wheaton, especially in the summer, without people knowing it. A girl cannot hide a thing like that for long, not the way kids talk."

Bill told himself he could not be angry at Martin. Martin had an excuse. He was nuts. However, he could be angry with Tillie for her foolish and false encouragement. He tried to catch her eye, but she knew not to look at him.

Tillie said, "That would be the first thing everyone would be whispering about if it were a possibility."

With deliberate slowness, Bill put his cup down on the counter. "Don't encourage him, Tillie. The girl is not pregnant and that is the end to it. Martin could not possibly know a thing like that. It is ridiculous!" Bill looked long and hard at his wife. She did not know the necessity of denying Martin his ramblings. It just got Martin into a big depression.

"Sandra can't be pregnant." Martin said with his eyes still downcast. Then he looked up. He looked straight and square at Bill. "Sorry, Bill. I won't mention it again. Sandra is not pregnant, but Joe is dead."

"See what you've done." Bill directed his words to his wife, but he forced his voice to be calm because tears were already gathering around her eyes.

Turning to Martin, forcing his shoulders to relax, Bill said, "Martin, do you have money to buy what you need? Let me see your list." Martin looked up, pulled the folded sheet from his coat pocket.

"Nancy sent me money, and she sent my credit card." He pulled the credit card from his pocket. A piece of folded paper came with it. Martin smiled as he picked the paper up from the floor. "It's my instructions from Nancy. She made a list of what I can use the credit card for. I cannot use the credit card for anything that is not on this list."

Bill staunchly ignored Martin's regression into child-like speech. He chose rather to take the list from Martin's hand. While Martin's thoughts appeared to ramble in a fantasy world, his list was absolutely clean and precise but equally fantastic. "It will take a semi for this stuff, Martin."

"They deliver," Martin said.

Bill was aware through Maureen of the weeks that Martin had not spoken at all, not a word. Martin was a long way from weeks of utter silence. Bill decided to accept progress where he could. He returned the list and went for his jacket. The mornings were already cool.

Martin carefully folded the list around the credit card and put it deep in his pocket. "I can get whatever I need for the house. House is on the list. Nancy knows that I know what I need for the house."

"Nice of her," Tillie said with some sarcasm in her tone. "After all, it was you who made Nancy a rich woman."

Bill glanced at his wife, relieved that she had dropped the phony chit-chat and annoying smile. Martin did not appear to have heard her. Instead he accepted a buttered toast on a napkin from Tillie's outstretched hand.

They would have to take the pick-up to bring home even some of the stuff on Martin's list. Bill stepped toward the door. He said, "Since Nancy sent you money, you can buy lunch."

Bill relaxed his muscles to show no sign of tension. He managed what he considered to be a cheerful expression. Dealing with Martin was like the stress of a cattle auction. He had to maintain his auction face. He just wished he had not waked Tillie.

Martin stood studying the list and not moving while cold air rushed through the door Bill held open. "Lunch is not on the list," Martin said. "I will have to use the cash. I know you like lunch. All you have to do is remind me when it is time."

Bill could no more help the surge of affection that tightened his chest than he could deny his responsibility before God to help this man. Martin's dad had once saved him from financial ruin, a long time ago but not forgotten. He told Martin's dad at the time he would look out for those boys. He didn't know what made him say it, but those words came from his heart.

"Someday," he told Mr. Webster, "those boys might need me and I'll help them like you helped me." He could not help Joe and the grief of that boy's death still tightened his throat. He would do what he could and all he could for Martin.

Just as Bill thought they were leaving, Tillie decided to try conversation again. She could not help herself. Tillie moved toward the door saying, "Has Sheriff Hauk been to your place yet? He seems to be everywhere, even drove down this road."

For a second, raw fear crossed Martin's eyes. She looked questioningly from Martin to Bill and back to Martin. Bill said, "It's okay, Martin. Tillie just did not want you to be surprised if a sheriff car pulls into your driveway." He now regretted waking up his wife as much as anything he ever did.

"Don't worry about Sheriff Hauk." Bill was now trying to shut the door behind himself and Martin. "He won't be stopping at your place. He scratched off his list the places Sandra would not be at. Your place is not on his list." He checked Martin to see if Martin caught his meaning. Bill saw a slight smile of understanding. Martin understood that his house was not on Sheriff Hauk's list. The Sheriff would not find Sandra there.

"I think she ran off with some man," Bill prattled on. "No matter what her dad says, parents do not always know, do they?"

"No," Martin shaking his head almost violently. "Basketball starts in three weeks."

"The town has never seen a search like it," Tillie said from the top step. The woman was relentless. "The Sheriff and Carl and volunteers are searching house to house, field by field. I hope they find her, and find her alive. I'm going into town this morning to help with coffee and sandwiches. Is there gas in the car?" Bill nodded.

"Leave your coat here, Martin," Bill told him.

"No," Martin answered. He started for the pick-up. By the time Bill climbed into the driver's seat, Martin was settled in, rope tied. They headed down I-90 to Sioux Falls.

Martin did not tire in his pursuit of each item on his list. Bill stepped in only when Martin had problems communicating. He watched Martin measure each window before it was loaded, and weigh items in his hands, mimicking the scales of justice. He counted 2x4's and scheduled deliveries and made notes. He left indelible marks on the psyches of lumberyard workers who had never encountered such precision.

The one thing Martin did not do was check the prices. He barely glanced at the charge receipts before he signed them. Bill checked it all for him. Martin was spending a lot of money, but the clarity and precision of Martin's buying could not be denied. He was a fish in water.

"Past time to eat," Bill told him.

"I need to stop at Sunshine," Martin answered.

Bill went into the café to order their food while Martin pushed his cart through the aisles of the market. Bill had never followed Tillie through a grocery store, and he wasn't about to follow Martin. At last, Bill saw Martin counting out cash to the clerk. Food must not be on the list, he thought.

Back in the cab of Bill's pick-up, two grocery sacks squeezed between Martin's feet. Martin adjusted himself without taking his eyes from his list. With one hand he lifted the rope; with the other he held the worn piece of paper. He nodded at each check mark.

As Bill turned the key, he glanced toward the sacks. On top of one of the sacks was a box of Newborn Pampers. Bill felt sick at seeing it. He struggled with himself to just let it go. But he couldn't. It was too much like seeing birth control pills in his daughter's purse.

"Martin." He made his voice as calm as possible while talking through clenched teeth. "Why did you buy diapers?"

"You don't want to know," Martin said, even more absorbed in checking his list.

"Yes, I do." Bill blindly hoped that Martin's daughter had a Cabbage Patch Kid.

"I bought them because basketball practice starts in three weeks." Martin put the list in his pocket and looked straight forward. The wind through the window muffled Martin's words, but Bill heard him. He could not let it go even though he knew he should.

"How is basketball practice related to those Pampers in that sack?" Bill pointed at the Pampers with a stiff, forceful finger.

"You won't believe me." Martin sat stiff and stubborn.

"I might not believe the facts as you see them, but I believe you. I mean, you are not lying." Bill frowned. He hated conversations like this.

Martin said, "Sandra wants to play basketball, and she'll need the Pampers. Joe did not get to play basketball his senior year. That was somehow my fault. Every day I know more about it. I remember more about it. It was my fault Joe didn't play basketball that last season. So, I want to help Cassandra." His hands rested still on his knees. He appeared to have made up his mind. He appeared to be at peace with it.

Now Bill dropped it. He regretted telling Martin about Sandra Peters. The crazy fool had somehow linked Sandra to his brother. Bill could tell Martin what he knew about Joe's accident. But the truth was, Martin and Joe were alone at the time. Only Martin knew exactly what happened in that barn.

Bill was not big on praying, but he prayed now. When he was utterly helpless, he prayed. The words memorized in his childhood always came back when he wanted them. The wind swirling through the cab, the back-end weighing down too far on his tires, Bill drove slowly, and he prayed.

It was after six in the evening when Martin and Bill finished unloading the pick-up. "That should do it," Bill said, meaning that Martin would not need anything more today.

"Just about," Martin answered.

To Bill, that was the single largest symptom that Martin was out of whack. The man didn't notice mealtime. There was nothing more unsettling to Bill's internal clock than unscheduled meals.

"What?" Bill asked and the frustration showed in his voice. Martin asked for the old dining room table and chairs stored in Bill's chicken coop. The old dining room set in Martin's house was no longer there. Bill told Martin to walk over after supper. They would load the table and bring it to Martin's.

Then to his astonishment, Martin walked behind him almost on his heels. Bill turned to face him trying with near desperation to stay calm. "What?"

When Martin only looked abashed Bill again went for his truck and climbed into the driver's seat and considered rolling up the window. Martin ran after him, he put his hands on the window and looked in at his neighbor like a big puppy.

"On Saturday, we need to get Crook," Martin told him. "Crook is on the list right after electricity and water." Bill knew Martin was aware of his pending explosion. He could see it in Martin's eyes. Martin was aware and pretending not to be. Bill felt conflicted about this. On one hand he was pleased that Martin had already gained understanding. On the other hand it was not a good thing that Martin was manipulating him.

He could not let it matter right now. Even Tillie knew to back off once Bill reached his limit. His jaw hurt from clenching his teeth. "You are a stubborn man, Martin. I think you will be all right. I have only one rule and that is that you never again pretend not to know when I have reached my limit."

Martin nodded and smiled. He had enough sense to look sheepish. Bill felt the power of Martin's intellect and Martin's relentless pursuit of a goal. It was power few recognized. Bill's anger vanished, and he laughed his silent, farmer laugh.

"We'll get your friend. Is he coming to Sioux Falls?"

"Nope," Martin answered. "We have to go to Lincoln. You'll need to drive your car. Crook wouldn't like to be crunched up in the pick-up."

Without asking if there was anything else, Bill drove off.

After dinner, when the table sat in Martin's kitchen, Bill noted with satisfaction the clean cupboards and sink, and the scrubbed floor. Martin apparently had not slept last night, and that's why he looked the way he did.

Martin ran his fingers down the grooves on the table legs which turned into bird claws with rounded bottoms. It would be a lot of work to refinish, fix the table legs and fix the chairs. The six-inch side pieces on the table had the same groove lines. Not as nice as the claw footed round table missing from Martin's dining room, but a lovely piece all the same. Martin talked while writing in his notebook. "Stain and varnish, wood filler for the torn nail holes and glue."

Bill watched the younger man finish writing and then stand silent, waiting. Now Martin wanted him to leave. Sorely tempted to pull up a chair and sit down, Bill resisted. He was too tired.

Bill said, "Good night." Only at the last minute did he think to look about for signs of a teenage runaway girl in the house. Of course there was nothing. Why did he even give it a glance?

Then as Bill drove home in the deep darkness of a cloudy night, he comprehended what Martin had earlier asked him to do. Maureen had mentioned that Martin pointed out a man named Crook when she visited, but she thought Martin was confused. The man named Crook never spoke to Martin or introduced himself to her. Crook did not appear to know Martin.

A knot tightened in his stomach. What had he agreed to? If Crook was real that meant he would be living down the road less than a quarter mile. If he was a fantasy, what would Martin do once they reached the hospital? Will I have to open the car door for an imaginary friend?

Bill was not at ease with bringing Crook to Martin's house. His joints hurt and that always meant trouble was on the horizon.

Chapter Five

Martin listened as Bill's footsteps squished across the porch floor. He heard the sound of the porch door being pushed shut and the sound of the pick-up engine. Then he sighed, slumped his shoulders and leaned on the back of a chair. His wired energy had burned all available fuel and was shutting down for the night.

He could not allow himself to stop, not yet. As the scratching in the bottom row of kitchen cupboards reminded him, he had one more task that had to be done before he could rest. He dreaded it as much as anything he ever had to do. Could the task wait one more night? Would it be cheating to ask Bill to go to the barn for him? With regret, Martin accepted that the job had to be done now, and only he could do it.

He squared his shoulders and lifted his chin, grabbed the big red flashlight, and stepped outside into the night. He faced the barn with an almost military turn. In one of the rooms intended for calving, his father stored rat poison. He planned his route as he walked: the side door, run a few steps to his right, avoid the milking stanchions and the ladder to the hayloft. Martin inhaled the cooler night air, eyes cast toward dark night sky, treading the path to the well. Once at the well, he inhaled another deep breath like a swimmer going underwater.

Joe, his features consumed with unabashed joy danced backwards along the hay mound-floor. Martin's heart pounded. The tension in his body about to burst.

Martin, recognizing the flashback for what it was, stood quiet. He gathered the quiet about him and put his hand firmly on the cold steel of the pump. He gave a moment's thought to pursuing this memory of Joe. This memory was important, but it was gone.

Holding his breath, he left the pump and ran. His coat flapped loud on his jeans. Once at the side door, he stopped and turned his back to the door. He looked again at the cloudy-black night sky, gathered himself, and turned to face the barn. Using his flash light to focus on the steps he had to take, he ran to the calving room.

The ten-pound cloth sacks, marked with a large X, were covered with dirt, but exactly where they belonged inside a steel bin. Martin grabbed one and ran. He did not stop running until he reached the door. He paused only to kick the door shut behind him. His heart pounded and his hand shook the flashlight so much that the light bounced around in front of him. He dropped both bag and flashlight. Putting both hands on the pump nozzle he said, "I'm on base, no touch backs."

He gulped air. He waited for his heartbeat to slow and his breath to come easier before picking up the flashlight and bag of poison. Slowly he treaded the dark line of the path to the house.

He thought about the weeds, and borrowing Bill's tractor and mower. But with Sandra and her baby squeezed into the picture, that pushed lawn and yard work into late fall. When he entered the kitchen it felt good to see the white lacquered cupboards clean, and the worn butcher block countertop shinning. Sandra had a busy day.

He would not replace the cupboards, but he would need to remove and repair them in order to redo the plaster wall. "In its time," he said as he carefully put his bundle down by the door.

Sandra walked in from the foyer as he filled a glass of water.

"Hello," she said, tentative and almost shy. She startled him.

"May I touch your arm?" he asked.

"Why?" she said, squinting her eyes with suspicion.

"My friend thinks you are a hallucination," Martin said. His eyes fixed on her until he saw her cheeks turn crimson. He did not move toward her, so she walked to him and put out her forearm. He gingerly touched the firm muscle. It certainly felt real enough.

"Tell me something about you that I wouldn't know," he said, his face inches from hers. He read fear and desperation in her eyes, but controlled for right now, at bay.

"My father's name is Jarvis," she told him.

He shook his head. "I might have known that."

"We went fifteen and six last year." She was obviously trying to cooperate.

Martin bunched his face in concentration. He said, "I probably read that somewhere. We get the local paper. Think of something I could not possibly know if I were making you up." His eyes never wavered. She had a summer tan and newly washed hair. He thought she must have heated water on the old stove.

"How would you know what I looked like?" she asked.

"I saw your picture in the paper," he answered.

"Close your eyes and see if you can make my eyes blue," Sandra suggested. Martin shut his eyes and visualized Sandra with blue eyes. When he looked at her, she looked back with large, clear brown eyes. He sighed with relief.

"My middle name is Jean," she added. "I have a music box on a table in my bedroom. Does that help?"

"How did you keep anyone from knowing you were pregnant?" He sounded more forceful and demanding than he intended. He was not an inquisitor, nor judge or jury. He needed to find some understanding of how Sandra had reached this place.

"First and foremost I did not have a boyfriend, no one obvious to be the responsible party. Secondly, I didn't show hardly at all for a long time. I ran every day to stay strong. I wore jogging pants and sweatshirts no matter how hot it was." She stated the facts like reciting a school assignment.

"I never went swimming. My friends all asked me about that because I'm big on swimming, but I told them I had a babysitting job every afternoon. That worked." Her face, her voice, and her words all seemed real enough. "I had to volunteer to baby sit my niece just to make it real. Yuk, what a brat."

Martin said, "Don't call your niece a brat."

He looked carefully at her stomach. He could believe she wasn't pregnant if she were wearing big clothes instead of his lean cut shirt. She sat down on one of the newly arrived maple wood ladder chairs. She put her hands under her belly and rocked slowly back and forth. "It won't be long," she told Martin. "My due date as I figured it was two days ago. And I know when I got pregnant to the second."

Martin heard this with his usual acceptance of things that happen. Nothing seemed real enough to cause alarm. She did not look anywhere near to that time. He recalled Nancy's large body when it was her time. How Nancy hated being big!

"Did you see a doctor?" Martin reached to rub his chin and felt whiskers.

Sandra rolled her eyes. "I don't dare see a doctor. I'm fine. I'm ready for natural childbirth. Like I said before, I ran every day. I did all of the exercises in my sister's pregnancy book. I made my plan. He is not going to change my life."

Martin said, "Really. You can stop your life from changing?"

Sandra looked up at him. Her clear, brown eyes looked hard and unafraid. Martin saw her hands twist on her lap. He noted the hard lines of her face and understood that hardness. That was how Crook looked sometimes. She was forced to deny fear even existed.

Martin, standing three feet from where Sandra sat, looked down at her. "You were going to have a baby all by yourself? Out here, without lights or water." He almost added, "Are you crazy?" but he did not.

"My plan has some flaws," she said. "But it's all I have. If I give in, then he wins." Martin could see that whoever she referred to was not going to win. Her body was taut. Martin recognized petrifying fear.

Running toward the house, clutching his chest, his plaid shirt tearing in his fingers.

Martin's hands waved at his side. His hands moving at his wrist waved the vision away. He pulled out a chair and set it beside Sandra. He did not look at her. He did not want to see her face. She knew to be still. They sat side by side, legs out in front of them. A rat scurried under the counter ledge. The rat didn't like the clean and scuttled quickly into the laundry room.

Martin's shoes reached several inches past Sandra's. She wore Nike tennis shoes and no socks. Her gray sweat pants stopped at her knees. From the sweat pants to the shoes stretched long, well shaped legs that had not been shaved for quite some time.

"I'll tell you my plan," she whispered. "I was going to kill it and bury it out here where no one would ever know. Then I was going to go back home with a story about camping by myself in the State Park by Lake Vermillion. That was my plan."

Martin had to strain to hear her, but he did hear her.

Neither of them spoke again for a long time.

At last Martin said, "Could you do that?"

Sandra said, "No."

"So what was plan B?" Martin said.

"Now you are plan B."

For the first time, Martin believed that Sandra was real. He would never in a million years create the words that just came out of her mouth. He thought he knew desperation, but now he understood he did not know desperation like this girl. He remembered the blind grip on his legs like steel clamps. He could not remember what caused it.

"Oh, my God," he whispered.

Martin wiped his face and realized he had tears on his cheeks. Sandra stared straight ahead. Her eyes were dry. She would not allow herself to feel anything. Martin understood that as he understood many things. Mostly he understood imperfection.

He put his arm around her stiff and unyielding shoulders. "Who did this to you?" he asked, thinking there had to be one other person who knew the possibility, who carried some responsibility. Why was she here alone?

"I had a flat tire one night last winter, before Christmas. A man stopped to help me. I didn't even know what was going on until it was too late. He was so strong. I fought and screamed and cried. That is until I realized it was the screaming that turned him on. So, I quit fighting." She shrugged. "I was only two miles from town. I took my friend home after a basketball game. The same as I have done a lot of times." She sounded puzzled as though she was still trying to understand what happened to her.

Martin realized she felt safe in telling him what she had never spoken. He was too crazy to judge her. What could he do? A rush of sympathy for this child beside him simply filled him like raging flood water. Sandra was raped and pregnant and refusing to allow it to make a difference. Basketball practice started in three weeks.

"It will hurt to cry," Martin said. "But you should do it anyway."

She shook her head. "I don't want this baby. I want to play basketball." Her voice sounded squeezed through a closed throat. "This is the first time I've been able to call it a baby." Her face lost all color. She looked like a ghost in the pale kitchen light. Her hands were fists at her sides.

Martin held her, his arms around her shoulders. He thought of his own daughters. Would they tell him if something like this happened to them? He wondered if he would be open to hear it. He said, "I will hold you. You are allowed to cry."

Someone once said that to him. It had not worked. To this day he had not cried for his lost loved ones. So he was surprised when Sandra lowered her head of auburn tangles and rested it on his shoulder. Her body heaved with the depth of her tears.

When the tears subsided, Sandra hunched with exhaustion. Martin told her, "On Sunday you can have the baby. On Saturday we are going after Crook. You can't have the baby on Saturday. On Sunday, after church, would be fine. I bought new sheets, but you really need a new mattress and springs. I bought some Pampers and t-shirts for the baby. It isn't the baby's fault. Try not to blame him or her."

He could not stop talking. He saw himself and felt this to be an extraordinary reaction, but he could not stop. "Maybe we should walk over to Bill's in the morning. He would give you a ride home. Your parents are worried." Words and more words filled the space around them. He struggled to fill a void in their hearts, and to fill the sudden, thick loneliness in the room.

"The baby knows that he is not loved," Martin said. He felt bad about that.

At last his voice stopped and the silence settled about them.

"I can't go home." Her voice was almost gone. "I want to go home, but I can't. It's not how angry they will be. I could probably face that. My dad will make me tell him who the father is. I can never tell that."

"Who is the father?" Martin asked again.

"Sheriff Hauk." Her voice was a bare sound. Martin felt the answer in his chest more than he heard it in his ears.

"Oh," he said.

"Hauk will kill me if I tell, and don't think for a minute that he wouldn't. He would kill me without so much as a thought if he knew I was pregnant, and if I told." Sandra was very matter of fact about this, and Martin believed her.

"We have to presume that he has an idea since you disappeared at this time, and he was present nine months ago." Martin had to fight to stay calm and objective. He remembered the rule of thumb for shrinks: the more emotional the topic, the calmer and objective the shrink.

This unjust, horrible thing happened to her, and now she had to deal with it. He felt angry for her. He would not make a good shrink.

"He won't care as long as I don't come back with a baby, and I never tell." She sounded sure about this.

"Why not just tell. Tell everything. The pig should go to jail." Martin felt hot with emotion. He didn't want his feelings mixing in with hers. For the most part he didn't know his own feelings. He cautioned himself to be objective even as he smelled a sweet scent in her hair. She had used his shampoo.

"He would never go to jail, and he would kill me."

Martin nodded. "Thank you for cleaning the kitchen today." Martin said.

"Your welcome," Sandra answered.

Martin got up slowly. He was so very tired. He exhaled a long breath as he reached for the bag of rat poison. "I'm going to put this around the house, inside and outside. It is very toxic, so don't touch it and don't breathe it. Make sure you stay away from it and keep your clothes away from it. Don't even smell it. I want you to wait outside while I do this. The smell will make you sick." He worked at opening the bag.

"You shouldn't open it in the kitchen then," Sandra said as she backed toward the porch door.

"Okay," he said. "I have a fold-out tent in my trunk. We will sleep outside tonight." It took another hour to set up the tent in the tall grass behind the house where passersby could not see it from the road. Sandra opened the new bedding amongst the sacks and sacks of stuff Martin bought that day. Then she carried out bottles of water and a box of donuts along with the peanut butter and remaining bread.

"Okay," he said. "Go to sleep."

Martin returned to the kitchen. He found the box of containers he had earlier filled. He put on gloves and tied a new towel around his face. With flashlight in hand he did the outside of the house first, placing a small container in sheltered spots about every three or four yards along the foundation. He had already carefully examined the foundation of the house, so he knew where the rats entered. By the narrow basement windows, he carefully placed the containers in the casement corners.

Entering the porch, Martin paused. The entire south end was filled with his purchases from the day. He saw the empty packaging where Sandra had rummaged and found the blankets. He would have to leave that area alone for now.

Working methodically, Martin filled his containers and placed them about the house, in every room, along the walls, in the corners, under the stairs and in the closets. In several instances the rats were at his feet, tussling to reach the container while he still held onto it. The smell was intended to attract them.

At last he stopped. He did not remove either his gloves or his mask until he was back in the kitchen. Then he sat down his flashlight, carefully shut and tied the nearly empty cloth sack. He removed the towel and gloves and scrubbed his hands and arms and face.

He took his last clean pants and shirt out to the porch and changed his clothes. He would sleep in them. Again with flashlight in hand, he walked carefully through the tall grass to the tent. Checking inside, he saw Sandra sound asleep on the air-filled tent bottom, wrapped in a flowered blanket, head on a new pillow with a white pillow case. Her flashlight poked between her elbow and side, still on, casting light on the tent top.

He saw that she had made a spot for him. The tent was close quarters, but she had folded his blankets in a highly defined separation. Without questioning anything, Martin lay down on his spot and was asleep in less than a minute.

Chapter Six

For Bill Bendix, Friday was a long day. Bill did not see Martin all day, except for Martin using his phone early in the morning and then leaving again. Bill missed him. He spent some time guessing what Martin might be doing. He watched from his tractor seat, the trucks zooming by, lifting the dust from the road.

A furniture truck, the lumber yard crew each driving their own pick-up, the cement plant truck loaded with crushed rock, and a semi-load of lumber passed within an hour, early in the morning. With difficulty, Bill resisted quitting his work to go see what was up.

When he had to call the lumber yard, or the cement plant for one of his projects it took days to get what he wanted. When Martin called, they could not get there fast enough. "Nosy bastards," he said. But he kept to his own work. He would see whatever was happening at Martin's in the morning. Saturday would likely be two days worth of Martin.

On Saturday morning Bill ate his bacon and eggs while sitting across the table from Tillie. She looked pretty this morning. He thought perhaps she had a new perm but always better not to ask if he should already know. Instead he said, "I am a little concerned about bringing this Crook fella to Martin's."

"It will be fine," Tillie said. "You have to trust Martin's judgment on this."

Bill choked and coughed and spit out his coffee. Wiping his mouth, he said, "Of course I can't trust Martin's judgment. That's why I have to judge for him."

At 7:30 AM, Bill aimed his big Lincoln car toward Martin's place. Lincoln was a five-hour drive and Crook was scheduled to be released at 2:00 PM on Saturday afternoon.

This Crook fellow might be all right and he might not be. No matter, it was sure to raise hell in the little farm town of Wheaton, him being from a mental hospital and all. He and Tillie knew Maureen's feelings on the matter. She didn't like Crook or she didn't like what Crook meant to Martin, even though the man befriended Martin when in most need. She thought if Martin was able to leave the hospital then he should leave Crook behind as well – a clean break so to speak.

Martin would not do that.

So in the early morning light, a few clouds remaining on the horizon, Bill drove to Martin's place and prepared to bring Crook home. Bill hoped this was not a big mistake. He knew it was going to make a difference, somehow, in his life. He was afraid, and he was going to do it anyway.

First Bill saw the new mailbox with the red flag up. Martin was mailing some letters. Then as he drove the curve of the driveway he saw stacks of wood, siding, windows, shingles, and assorted boxes set in perfect rows on Martin's yard. Scaffolding lined the south side of the house in preparation for the lumberyard crew to install windows, siding, and roof.

As he pulled to a stop near the porch, he thought, "The lumberyard crew was a busy little beehive yesterday." The porch sported a new gray shingled roof. Twelve new windows lined the porch and a new combination screen door fit into a new doorjamb. Forms for cement steps led to the door. The siding was gone and new wood waited for new siding. Martin had scathed away the weeds and grass for several feet on the lawn side of the house plus he had dug all the weeds and saplings from the foundation around the porch

The old porch siding was tossed in a broken pile to one side of the steps. Bill thought, Martin needs to add dumpster to his list.

It was a big house to re-side and re-roof. Bill walked around the house and looked it over. He shook a scaffolding bar to make sure it was solid. Martin did know how to motivate workers. He saw that with the electrical crew. "Amazing," he said aloud. All this work confirmed Bill's belief that Martin was a genius.

He knocked several times on the new screen door and then opened it and entered. Under his feet, he felt a solid floor. Rolls of blue-green indoor-outdoor carpet sat against the wall. The ceiling and walls were also waiting for sheetrock. Only as Bill turned to his left did his chest tighten. Three new bed frames leaned against the wall. What good did it do Martin to be a genius if he imagined people? Sandra Peters was not inside this house.

He heard Martin in the kitchen and called to him, "They must have had everything on your list."

Martin opened the kitchen door. "No," he answered. "I wanted hanging plants."

"It will be nice, Martin, real nice, once it is done," Bill said, though he could not look at the three bed frames.

"Bill," Martin said in his soft, quiet voice, "sit down a minute. We have time."

Bill thought something had gone wrong with Crook's release. Then when Martin continued to block his entry into the kitchen, he thought maybe Martin had damaged the table.

Martin gestured toward three table chairs. They sat along the far south side of the porch next to the bed frames. Bill walked to the chairs and sat down. Martin carried three coffee mugs in his big hands. Bill could not speak because behind Martin, Sandra Peters carried the coffee pot, and she was pregnant.

Bill found his voice. "Is crazy contagious?"

Then, composing himself, he said, "Sandra, we have to get you home right now! The whole town is looking for you."

Neither Martin nor Sandra said a word. Bill couldn't understand it. They had to get the girl home right now. Finally Sandra moved forward and poured them all a cup of coffee in a slow-motion, stiff movement.

"I can't go home, Mr. Bendix," Sandra said. Her voice allowed no argument.

"Your parents will understand. I know they will," Bill said. "I faced the same situation with my daughter. It was not easy, but we loved her all the same."

"It's more than facing my parents," Sandra said. Her tone held the stone calmness of a decision that could not be changed.

Bill forced his mouth to close. He studied her face. She had a hard face and hard eyes. He saw eyes like that only once before in his life and that was in Korea.

She said, "Martin told me to tell you what happened."

Bill's heart raced. All he could think was to get the child home, but he couldn't move from his chair.

"Nine months ago I was raped," Sandra said.

Bill said nothing. He listened, unable to look away from her face.

"Sheriff Hauk raped me. Now three people know that, four counting Hauk. I will not say it again. I can only say it now because I've switched to plan B. For plan B I need help." Her words squeezed through stiff lips like forcing solids through a sieve.

Bill felt a shock like a physical blow. He looked at Martin who looked back with this sad sympathy in his eyes. "I can't believe it," Bill said. "I can't believe that you are here in Martin's house. I can't believe any of it. Not that you are lying. There has to be some mistake."

Martin said, "See now why I had to buy Pampers."

Bill nodded. "Martin found you hiding here?" Bill looked at Sandra but he thought about Martin. He had to force his hands not to shake.

"I told Martin because when he found me, he did not run screaming to the nearest phone. He didn't say it was my own fault. I had to say what happened to someone while I still could. I mean before anything happened to me."

She looked very young to Bill. She did not look fragile or vulnerable. Bill thought that Sheriff Hauk would regret his actions. Cassandra Peters was no one's victim.

"We need to take you home all the same," Bill said.

Sandra shook her head. "I'm not the first."

When Bill could only gape at her, she continued. She adjusted her chair slightly to include Martin in the circle though Martin kept sidling his chair further away. Bill thought Martin was trying to escape, to hide from this horror.

"Do you remember two summers ago when that other teenager disappeared?" Sandra's eyes looked huge in her pale face.

"I remember her picture in the paper. She had black bangs in her eyes," Bill said. "I remember that no one searched for her. Hauk completely ignored that disappearance."

"That was Allyson. Some of her teachers and classmates organized kind of a search, but that was it." Sandra's coffee cup shook.

Bill thought about this. "Everyone presumed she ran away from a broken home. How is it that no one is remembering her? Really, it was a similar situation except Alyson was not you."

"Hauk knew Ally was dead," Sandra said. "No need to search for her."

"There is likely no connection at all," said Bill. "If Hauk hurt her as he did you that would have come out. He would not have gotten away with it." Even so the memory of that girl planted doubt in Bill's mind. He wondered, had Hauk hurt these girls? A knot of fear clutched his chest.

"He got away with it the same as he will get away with killing me," Sandra said.

Martin leaned forward and said, "This man will never hurt you or anyone again."

Martin's words did not shock Bill as much as the manner in which he said them. He spoke without doubt.

Bill said, "How can you know that, Martin?"

"I will tell Crook," Martin said.

Bill looked from Martin to Sandra. Suddenly overwhelmed, he put his head in his hands. "My God, help us in this vale of tears." The words sprang unbidden from his mouth. For a minute the world had stopped.

"Well," Bill said. "Well," he said again. "We have to do what we have to do."

"I know," Sandra said, "that my mom and dad are sick with worry. I'm sorry for that." She looked more determined than sorry, but there was sorrow in her eyes. Bill felt better at seeing it.

Reluctantly, Bill accepted that Sandra's parents would have to suffer a little longer. Short of physical force, the teenager was not going home. This was the only thing about which he was sure.

"Hauk is a jerk and a bully, but rape and murder? What are we even thinking here?" It was too difficult to grasp.

"Look, Mr. Bendix, doubt all you want. I'm living it." Sandra turned burning eyes to Martin.

Bill saw Martin acknowledged her pain with a nod as though to say, "He's old, give him more time." Bill felt helpless.

Martin sat ashen faced and tight lipped. Then he spoke. "I remember looking at Allyson's picture in the paper. I read that Ted Peppe found the body in the spring in a low spot along his fence line. The coroner ruled it death by exposure."

Bill said, "There were whispers at the time that Alyson was pregnant, but they came and went quickly. She had not been a part of people's lives. Not like Sandra is a part of life in Wheaton."

"We could call the cops in Sioux Falls," Martin said. "But we can't, too many questions."

"My plan may not be sensible, but it is the best one. By a miracle from God, no one knows I'm pregnant. I have to keep it that way."

Bill understood that Sandra would have her way. "What is the plan?"

"I will have this baby in secret and go home like it never happened," Sandra said.

"Tomorrow," Martin said. "Today we have to get Crook."

Bill suggested she spend the day with Tillie. He believed Tillie could convince Sandra to go home by noon. Sandra refused.

Bill sighed. What did it take for a child not to run home crying after one night alone in this house as it was then?

"Time to get Crook," Martin said.

Sandra said, "I'll lay down and die before I admit to anyone that this is Hauk's baby."

"Adoption," Bill said. Where would she have the baby? He didn't know. He couldn't think.

"Must be on our way." Martin started toward the door.

"Martin." Bill's voice was urgent. "We can't take Sandra across state lines. She is only seventeen. We are not relatives. Do you know the trouble we could be in?"

"We won't be in trouble," Martin said. "No one will notice us."

"I can stay here," Sandra said. "Nothing happening today."

"No, you can't," Martin insisted. Turning to Bill, Martin said, "Work men will be here today, in and out. Sandra is safer with us. What if Hauk decides to search here today? That is much more likely to happen than someone stopping us on the road."

Bill felt himself relenting and could not believe it. "Hauk likely has been informed that you're bringing Crook here today as a resident. He might have plans to check on that, but I doubt it. He's too wrapped up in this search to read his mail." Still it was too strong of a possibility to ignore.

The mention of Hauk checking on Crook's arrival turned Martin's skin ashen gray. His dark hair looked like a picture frame around white paper. Bill turned to Sandra. The decision was hers. If she wanted to come along, he would take her.

The color on her lips was startlingly bright. Her hair looked like a floating halo, and her skin was flawless.

"I don't want to be alone today," she answered.

And Bill thought it was a better risk to take her than to leave her. He would keep an eye on her until he took her home.

Martin said, "Let's go. Crook will be waiting."

Bill repeated, "Let's go then," with far less bravado. He felt exactly like this in Korea. The reluctant heaviness came back to him the same as standing in the mud facing his soldiers. "Move out. Let's go."

Sandra sat in the front so she wouldn't get car sick. Martin sat in the back behind the driver's seat. As they turned south on Highway 81, Sandra found a Golden Oldie station on the radio. For sixty miles barely a word was said. Bill sang with Tina Turner, *What's Love got to do with it, got to do with it.*

Only when Martin began poking his hand in and out of the front seat while attempting to walk like an Egyptian did Bill reach for the volume button. They crossed the James River Bridge and passed the scenic hills outside of Yankton, still in South Dakota; so far, no problem.

Bill's Lincoln moved with the Saturday morning traffic through Yankton. No one pointed at them or shouted for them to halt. At any second he expected sirens to blast, or the Special Forces Unit to line the street. Nothing happened. It was just another sunny Saturday along the Missouri River in Yankton, South Dakota.

At the bridge crossing into Nebraska, Bill's Lincoln stood apart in the line of campers and sport vehicles pulling boats. Lewis and Clark Lake beckoned to everyone trying to hold onto summer. No one cared about Martin, Bill or Sandra. They could just as well be law abiding citizens, not kidnappers.

As Bill inched his vehicle forward, he gave some thought to driving to the police station, going inside and turning himself in. He trusted the police to protect Sandra. He gave her a side long glance. She was tapping her fingers on her knees to a quiet Elvis Presley doing a jail house rock. Her head rested on the back of the seat and her eyes were closed. She appeared vulnerable. He drove on. Let's get there and get back, he decided.

Bill moved forward across the old, historic bridge. The water far below looked ragged and deep even as the sun danced on the waves. His fellow passengers perked up to see the water, the traffic, and the huge, U-shaped steel girders.

"We are crossing the state line, Sandra," Martin said.

"Yeah."

Even on low volume, the radio music was clear - *Every breath you take, every move you make, I'll be watching you.* No other sound conflicted with the words as the bridge slid foot by foot beneath the car.

Sandra said, "I feel a little spooked."

Bill said, "We can't go back now." Bill was thinking of the one lane, bumper-to-bumper traffic. He meant they would have to wait to turn around.

Martin said, "We are at the point of no return." Martin leaned forward on the front seat. His elbows touched Sandra on one end and Bill on the other.

Bill, who considered himself the least prone of all people to the horrors of imagination, felt a tingle on his neck. "You are right, Martin, we are at the point of no return." A line had been crossed other than the state line into Nebraska. He thought, I am one of four people who know what Hauk did. Now what?

Martin sat back, and Sandra turned her face toward the window. The Nebraska farm land rolled by, cows grazing, the houses prosperous and clean: the landscape turned boring.

"What did you do while the workmen where there on Friday?" Bill asked Sandra, his voice shattering the silence.

"I hid upstairs in one of the back bedrooms." Sandra shifted her position so she could look at Bill.

Martin returned to lean his chin on his hands on the front seat between Bill and Sandra. "I gave her a book to read and some food." He sounded defensive.

"Oh, yeah." Sandra rolled her eyes. "*Basic Design*, I couldn't put it down."

"And if the baby decided to arrive in the midst of all that pounding?" Bill asked.

Martin answered, "That's tomorrow."

Then as the miles miraculously slid beneath the Lincoln, Martin explained to Bill how he scrubbed the upstairs bedroom sterile before he allowed Sandra inside. He used his hands to describe, and nearly hit his fellow travelers several times, as he talked.

"The cobwebs are gone. The dust is gone. All rat bodies, all bugs, all creatures of any kind or size are not only gone but scrubbed away."

Bill listened, absorbing the gigantic improvement in Martin's speech. He wondered how that happened. He decided being home was good for Martin. Thinking of someone other than himself was good for Martin.

Sandra leaned against the car window out of reach of Martin's gestures. Bill caught a sad smile holding the corners of her mouth.

Bill wondered about her. She had said nothing of those nights alone in the house with the scratching in the walls and scampering feet under her bed and the merciless heat. She said nothing of planning carefully. Obviously, she stowed stuff for several weeks. She must have approached the house from the west so that she did not pass his house. He likely would have seen her. Early Saturday morning, she must have walked the three miles across the fields.

"Sandra had her sleeping bag and pillow, ice water, cookies and apples and books to campout for the day. The room gets hot in the late afternoon sun, but not too bad. She couldn't walk around. She could tiptoe in bare feet if she had to use the bathroom, but no flushing. If some nosy carpenter wanted to look through the house, I instructed her to duck into the closet. She stored her supplies inside the closet door in preparation. Fortunately, no one walked past the bathroom. The scaffolding is not on that side. In comparison to her recent days and nights, she was in the lap of luxury."

Sandra added nothing for several minutes. Bill was adjusting to the quiet, considering finding a news station when Sandra's raspy voice surprised him.

"I wanted to go home," she said. "I almost left all the stuff behind and went home, but I couldn't. No matter how hot it was or hideous, the one thing I could not do was go home. I would see Hauk's ugly face or feel movement inside of me and just hunker down."

Bill glanced; no tears. Martin moved his hand toward her shoulder but he did not touch her.

"I read *Harry Potter,* all of *Harry Potter*. I looked around the closets. I didn't walk around downstairs. I was afraid of the rats down there. The upstairs rats didn't seem to notice me much. I walked outside everyday, in the pasture or the apple trees where I couldn't be seen from the road. I just waited for it to end."

"What about the bathroom?" Martin asked.

"I thought of water, but I didn't think of the toilet. I went outside. That is until you came. I heard you downstairs. I heard you talking to yourself. Then you came right through my bedroom and took something from the closet. A rat ran over my sleeping bag, and I didn't move a muscle. You know what I thought about?"

They looked at her, waiting.

"I pretended I was Anne Frank hiding from the Nazis."

For the last few miles into Lincoln, Martin's head and shoulders filled the space between Bill and Sandra. He could just as well sit up front with them. He provided perfect instructions right to the red brick, sprawling government hospital on vast acres of immaculate lawn. Martin reached for his coat and then changed his mind, giving it a pat like leaving a pet in the car.

Bill felt stiff from driving and anxious for what was to come. He silently prayed, "Let this be easy, in and out." After that he would deal with the new guy. After that he would take Sandra home and deal with Hauk.

He did not know why his thoughts reverted back to Korea. He rarely thought of those hard years any longer. But his mind went there. Bill lifted his hand and held two fingers aloft.

"Forward, march," he said.

Chapter Seven

This morning, Martin cared how he looked. Martin wore his tan pants and shirt. He appeared trim and neat. His hair was now too short for a pony tail and too long to leave alone. He parted the natural curls straight down the middle right to his forehead. He looked like a tidy mystic. The hard square of Christy's letter still left a worn square image on his pocket. His fingers traced the shape of the letter while invisible pliers squeezed tight around his middle.

As the three of them walked the curving sidewalk to the front door of the hospital. Bill looked as he was, a dressed-up farmer. He walked like a no-nonsense, take-care-of-business man. He had farmer hands, brown and a little gnarled and newly scrubbed.

Sandra looked like a plump, big girl, but her carriage and self-possessed step and cold, distant aura reminded Martin of royalty though he had never seen royalty. Martin knew it was never the reality that mattered; it was the impression that mattered.

Martin noticed that Sandra did not look well. She looked hot and blotchy, occasionally putting her hand to her back. "Tomorrow is for the baby, today is for Crook," he said quietly to himself.

The three of them entered the new glass and chrome entry built onto the old brick front. Martin was preoccupied, checking in his mind the list of forms and signatures required for Crook's release. This was Saturday, and if there was a problem, Crook would not like waiting until Monday. So Martin, with his head bent down in thought, was the last of the three to see Crook, who stood less than six feet away.

Crook stood in the middle of the lobby, waiting. His body had the tension, flexibility and wiry strength of a dancer. He resembled Yule Brenner. More than his build, Crook's continence gave pause. Martin heard Bill's sharp intake of breath which was why he looked up.

Crook looked like a Pac-Man when he smiled, it cut his face almost in half, but his smile was rare. His head was completely bald. If it were not for the hard, cold expression on his face and in his bearing, Crook would be comical.

Crook was a small man, maybe five feet, seven inches tall. Sandra was taller. He was trim and smooth and fluid, maybe fifty years old. He was ageless. Martin and Crook did not hug or even shake hands. They nodded.

"You need to do the paper thing," Crook told Martin. His manner had the feel of telling secrets. He nodded toward a doorway set inside a miniature entrance. The door had a window above it and a placard to the side that read "Administration."

Martin went white. His eyes fogged over. His hands flapped limply at his sides. All he saw in a narrowing tunnel was Crook. Crook's expression never changed. Martin was going under, and he wanted Crook to help him stay up. He tried to reach out but couldn't.

Bill said, and Martin heard the panic, "Martin was fine this morning. In fact he was so coherent that I almost forgot that Martin was sick. This change is crazy."

"Quick, Sandra." Bill sounded as though he struggled to get the words around his tongue. "Run to the car, get his coat." Bill produced the keys without looking at his hands. Sandra ran for the door. Martin could see Bill's scared eyes looking at Crook as Bill stepped closer.

"It's a stress attack." Crook's expression remained unchanged, no panic in his controlled voice or manner.

Martin fought. He fought hard. Suddenly Bill grasped his hand to either stop the motion of his hands at his side or help him push faster. Martin felt the heat in Bill's hand until Bill released Martin's fingers to move on their own.

"Tough watching a battle you can't see, ain't it?" Crook's eyes held the slightest flash of concern, but Martin had to look fast to see it. Crook was inscrutable. For the first time Martin dimly wondered if Bill would get along with Crook. He would ask Crook later not to hurt Bill.

Sandra ran to them, producing the coat. Martin noticed that Sandra looked drained and flushed. He saw things in circles as though that spot alone was illuminated by a stage light. Considering the run down the steps, to the car and back, her appearance was not striking. Still, the skin around her eyes and mouth was drawn tight. Sandra was in pain.

She lifted Martin's arm to slide the coat onto his shoulder. Bill grabbed the other side and shoved Martin's arm through the sleeve. "It's your coat, Martin. Feel it." Bill took Martin's hand and rubbed it on the coat. Martin stroked the coat front with a heavy, sloppy gesture.

Martin noticed the receptionist who sat watching with cold detachment. "This man is going to puke," Crook told her. His voice sounded with the slightest echo, as though in a tunnel.

Martin puked. He bent his head and opened his mouth.

"Now, we'll know." Crook directed his quiet voice at Bill. "Within the next few minutes he will either pull himself out of it, or he won't. Any longer and you'll be going home without him." He paused. "Or me."

"Come on, Martin!" Sandra pumped his hand as she talked. Martin felt her strength as she pumped his hand like priming a well.

Martin raised his head and turned around to follow Crook's gaze. He looked through the big, square windows lining the front of the entry. He looked at the heat coming off the parking lot pavement. He looked at the playground equipment, sitting on worn grass with bare ground beneath the swings and in a circle around the merry-go-round.

Crook whispered to Martin, speaking close to his face, "I did not allow a look outside while I still had hope of seeing it from the other side of the door." Crook turned his head to Martin. "I was this close." He gestured with his thumb and forefinger touching. Martin heard him but could not answer.

An orderly with a mop and bucket came running out of the elevator like a code blue heart doctor. Behind him were two white clad men, ageless and faceless. They stood on each side of Martin. Crook turned toward them, slowly, gracefully. He put his face within an inch of the man on Martin's right.

"He is not a patient and don't touch him." Crook's voice was calm and his face was blank. Martin felt the white clad men step back. Crook elicited raw fear. Martin saw it but it was as he expected. Unlike the shock he saw on Bill's face, even Sandra's, he felt nothing.

"Martin, please," Sandra whispered to him.

Martin thought she sounded like his ex-wife. Sandra did not realize that her plea added weight to the heaviness already enclosing Martin, just as Nancy never realized how her pleas made everything worse.

Due more to Crook's piercing calm than to Sandra's pleas or Bill's agitation, Martin began to focus. Crook had a way of lifting the weight by not adding to it. Crook did not lay any emotion on Martin. Martin thought how hard and ugly his friend, Crook, must seem to outsiders. Crook knew how it was as they never could. At least Martin hoped they never would.

Sandra was crying, but it was a natural crying, no commotion, no fuss. Even in his frozen fear, Martin saw that Crook liked Sandra and did not dislike Bill. Martin saw this in Crook's eyes.

Martin focused on his friend, Crook. He smiled just as a "suit" walked up to the gathering. Martin noticed the prim receptionist at her desk as he looked over the shoulder of the new man. "A problem here, gentleman?" The suit had a voice.

"Not at all, Dr. Durksen, I was just on my way to your office," Martin answered with calm authority and clear diction. He appeared unaware of vomit on his chin.

Martin's three friends, even Crook, could not completely hide their amazement. Bill recovered from his surprise quickly. He helped Martin remove his putrid coat, and Sandra wiped his face. Crook gave the newcomer an odd, sloppy smile not at all consistent with his manner only a minute earlier.

Martin did not look back at his friends as he followed the shorter doctor toward the door marked Administration. He felt stronger. He could do this.

Chapter Eight

Sandra walked behind Bill and Crook as they moved to the other side of the hospital lobby and sat down on orange plastic chairs that encircled a round coffee table covered with magazines. She felt miserable, but she could not allow her misery to matter. Ever since Hauk attacked her, she had refused to feel it. He could not hurt her. She sat on her hard plastic chair and watched Bill as he pointed toward the vending machines with a questioning expression.

Crook said, "Coke."

Sandra said, "I'll have a coke also."

She watched Bill stride toward the machines. She wondered why these men were trying to help her when she did not need help. Well, she did need help, but not as they expected, not as a victim. She would return to her life just as it was, and she would make Hauk pay.

When Bill returned he handed Crook a coke. He offered to Sandra a fruit punch. She frowned at him and indicated with her hand for him to set the drink on the table. Her mouth was dry enough to drink anything but her stomach was too hard and tight to allow for food. She watched Crook accept his drink without comment, just a slight nod. Crook frightened her, and she wished for Martin's quick return. She had liked how Crook smiled at the doctor, that phony smile, but she would keep her distance from the man.

Bill smiled at the receptionist and glanced at the spot where Martin had stood. Sandra followed his look. Clean as a whistle. Only a lingering odor of antiseptic remained. The receptionist reached out with a lawn and leaf sized garbage bag. Bill walked over and took the bag. "Thank you, ma'am," he said.

Sandra liked the old farmer. What you saw was what you got with Bill Bendix. He was kind, but not stupid. Now he was here, in her life. She felt Crook studying her. She thought as long as I am with Martin, I will get through this. Martin was a life preserver in a stormy sea. Plus Martin played basketball. Plus Martin was handsome.

Bill's soft soled shoes made a muted echo as he walked back to his friends. Smiling, Bill held the garbage bag full length in front of himself. He snapped the bag open with a flourish and a loud crack of plastic. The snap echoed through the entrance hall. Sandra enjoyed the sound of Bill's show of rebellion to such a place as this. With tentative fingers, Sandra reached from where she sat to deposit the coat into the garbage bag. Martin would undoubtedly want it cleaned. The three of them each found something to read.

In all this time not another person entered the front door. Saturday, obviously, wasn't a big visiting day. They began the wait. Not a trace of concern showed on Crook's face. Crook looked over his *Money* magazine and said, "I will believe I am outside of those doors when I see my feet on the outside steps."

"We will be in and out of here like a covert special forces mission. We have to trust Martin." Bill looked stiff and uptight. Sandra did not want to add her problems to the situation, so she did not tell Bill of the constant, hard pain in her lower back. The pain was reaching intolerable. She could not stand or drink. She hunkered down to wait it out.

She thought it could not be the baby hurting in her back. She must have pulled a muscle cleaning and lifting stuff. Sandra believed contractions should come and go. This was solid. The fast walk to the car and the return trip up the steps relieved the pain a little. Still, she felt as though a rubber band stretched around her mid-section. She glanced toward Bill. He was reading a *Field & Stream*. He was actually reading.

"Ever been fishing?" Bill asked Crook.

"Nope," Crook answered.

"Want to go?" Bill looked over the top of his magazine.

Sandra saw excitement in Crook's eyes, but only for a second.

"Yup," Crook answered. His voice was toneless and flat.

If excitement in Crook sounded like that, Sandra wondered if he talked at all if he were bored.

"I'll take you tomorrow," Bill told him. "By then you'll want to get away from Martin. He'll work you to death."

Sandra leaned her head back on her chair. She closed her eyes and laid her hands across her tight stomach. It is not the baby, she told herself.

Chapter Nine

Martin sat on the visitor side of the doctor's clean desk. In a neat stack in the middle of the large varnished surface were the papers Martin signed. There was not a pen or a calendar or a clock or a picture. Martin wanted to put something on the desk. He dug in his pocket and found some change. He lined two quarters and a dime and a penny across his edge of the grained wood surface. The papers didn't look so intimidating with something else on the desk.

Then he sat calmly listening to the doctor, focusing on the man's words. It was important to understand what he was being told, what the words actually meant for himself and for Crook. He knew there were always two sides to the words, what was said and what was meant.

"I know," Dr. Durkson was saying, "that people who sign the checks think I'm in charge around here. Well, you and I both know that isn't true. Crook's been in charge around here since before I even knew this hospital existed. He's done a good job. I even reached the point where I watched him before I did my employee evaluations. If he treated the employee with respect, so did I. If he did his senile smile routine like what we just saw him give to me, I knew that employee was a shithead. Fortunately, my own superiors do not know this secret."

The doctor paused, sucking in his lips. He was a big man, football scholarship type. He had the look, the broad shoulders and the square chin and the game face. Martin knew that Dr. Durkson talked to him as most people did because he was like a universal receiver.

"Crook is a lifer, Martin. He could tear you apart in seconds both emotionally and physically if he chose to. His crime was before we had our computer system, and I had to dig in boxes of paper files to find it. He's been lost in the system. Just before his eighteenth birthday he was convicted of killing a man in Chicago. His lawyer got him off on temporary insanity which leads me to believe there was something in the case the judge considered mitigating."

Dr. Durkson took a breath and looked at Martin. He seemed to want Martin to say something. Martin focused on the doctor's face. His eyes watched his lips. When Dr. Durkson at last understood that Martin had nothing to say, he smiled at him.

"I know the whole thing with you and Crook as house-mates is hopeless for both of you, totally hopeless, but the paper work is correct. I have no reason to prevent Crook's departure, unless you give me one."

Martin nodded his understanding of these words. Generally he accepted what he was told, but he had to disagree with the good doctor. He felt hope. Crook gave him hope.

Dr. Durkson inhaled, folded his hands on his desk, and continued. "The law has changed. Back in 1968 if the criminal was sent to a mental hospital and determined to be cured, he was released. Now he would have to finish the sentence in prison; back then he didn't. The law was not retroactive, so Crook actually could have been out of here years ago. He just didn't have anybody to do the paperwork. He didn't have family or a lawyer on the outside pushing for him, no place to go, until now."

Martin's fingers adjusted the change on the desk, but he never moved his eyes from the Doctor's face. He listened. He did not know Crook's crime. He felt no need to know. He trusted that whatever Crook did, he had good reason to do it.

"Crook has befriended you, so I believe you will be fine. I know no one else will harm you. That is a fact. You may not need that kind of protection, but you'll have it."

The doctor paused and cracked his knuckles. Martin returned his straight-eyed look, and waited.

"I've assigned a doctor at the hospital in Yankton to provide outpatient care. I thought that would be easier than reporting to the Sheriff's office in McCook County even though Yankton is a long drive and transportation may be a problem. What do you think?" He looked at Martin.

"Yankton is best," Martin answered. He tried not to look blank. He tried to look thoughtful.

"Good," Dr. Durkson pushed his palms against his desk and stood up.

"You talked to the Sheriff's office in Wheaton?" Martin did not stand.

The doctor exchanged a quick glance with Martin and then he laughed a big football guy laugh. "No," he answered. "I know how it can be in rural counties. I don't want to set Crook up for harassment. I talked with the hospital personnel in Yankton. I sent the required letters to the McCook County Sheriff's Office. McCook County did not have the facilities for professional counseling. It would not hurt you to seek some counseling at the same time. Make the trip worth your while."

Martin nodded. He knew the rules: no trouble and check in once a month to the assigned doctor. Only Crook was required to go. But Martin should. He moved his change around, looking at his fingers. Martin heard and he understood. When words were not required, do not speak. Extra words only prolonged the lecture.

Dr. Durkson came around the desk and reached out his hand. "That's all there is to it. The papers are in order. Crook is free to go with you."

Martin shook the doctor's hand, but he didn't get up. "Do you mean that you personally could have released Crook years ago?" Martin intently moved the quarters to stand as guards for the dime.

"Yes, I could have, but he had no place to go. All I needed was an outside address and a signature on the release forms." The doctor shrugged. "Crook hasn't been receiving any actual therapy or drugs for years, ever since he asked to stop attending the sessions. He isn't diagnosed with any mental illness. He was labeled 'Criminally Insane' thirty years ago. I had to dig to find his real name for the forms. Anyway, the papers I found suggested Crook was a perpetrator in an unfortunate situation. The 60's were a time when anyone could sign anything and it was so. I suspect that route was taken by some lawyer and a humane judge to save Crook's life."

Dr. Durkson abruptly turned and walked to the bare window behind his desk, his back to Martin.

Martin understood the doctor had nothing more to say. He unfolded from the chair and stood six inches taller than the beefy doctor. Now Martin sensed an advantage. Dr. Durkson had to look up to address him. That is if he bothered to look at him at all.

"So why are you willing to do this?" Martin felt compelled to ask despite the nagging feeling that he should leave now. "You got everything ready. You filed the reports and made the call, and cleared the way. Why?" Martin with his soft tones and straight bearing felt strong. He felt good.

"The truth, Martin? For years I've watched Crook run this place on the inside. He did a superb job. He made life easy for me. No hassles, no fusses. I like Crook. I believe he deserves a chance on the outside. He's already lost a lot of years. Besides, the man coming to replace me is a hard-nosed, by-the-book asshole. Once you made the first move, I decided to get Crook out. Save Crook from breaking in the new man."

He finally turned from the window with a new hard look covering his face. The game face vanished. "Do not make me regret it."

Martin said, "Thank you," and started for the door. As Martin reached for the door handle, the doctor said, "Your change." He handed the money to Martin. As Martin closed his hand on the change, his heart beat fast. He had done it. Crook was free to go. It was all he could do to resist hugging Doctor Durksen.

Sandra, Crook and Bill sat in their circle. Bill was showing Crook pictures in a magazine, and Sandra looked pinched and uncomfortable. Her hands clutched the sides of her chair, and she did not even pretend to be looking at the open pages on her knees. As Martin approached, all three faces looked at him, judging him, their anxiety showing various degrees. He deliberately tried to look dumb, which he couldn't do when he wanted to.

"I can go?" Crook could not keep the fear from his eyes.

Martin knew Crook had prepared to be denied this chance. He also knew hope still fed some corner of Crook's hard heart. For that reason Martin could not play any guessing game. He nodded like a child, and clapped his hands, and danced for joy.

"I can go," Crook told Bill, and Crook did not even try to hide his excitement. How many years since Crook had shown his true emotions? Martin, recognizing the depth of his friend's emotion, felt tears on his cheeks.

Crook sprinted to the receptionist's desk. He had one bag, a tan suitcase with one thick brown stripe down the center on each side. He looked at the receptionist until she handed the bag to him. The suitcase was older than its owner. Crook had to sign a form placed before him by the prissy woman. He did this, took his suitcase by the handle like it held gold bars, and moved with his graceful stride to stand at the glass door. Bill held the door open and then both men turned to find Martin and Sandra.

Martin stood beside Sandra. He watched Bill and Crook. He heard Crook say, "I got to two inches from the door. Do you see that Bill? I can feel the outside air." Then he lowered his head and sighed. "Not yet."

Bill let the door shut.

Martin bent over Sandra. Her face was streaked with tears. The floor beneath her chair puddled with water. Unable to speak, she lowered her head and looked down at herself.

"When did your water break?" Martin asked her in an infinitely gentle voice. She could not answer.

"Are you in pain right now?" he asked. She shook her head no.

"Can you walk?" he asked. She nodded.

Martin straightened and looked at Crook. Bill and Crook stood beside Martin and formed a protective circle around the girl. "The hospital personnel will remember your departure, first puke and then a baby," Martin said to Crook.

"Sandra is only seventeen," Bill said quietly.

"They can't know," Sandra said.

Martin knelt before the girl and said softly, "It will be all right. Crook will take care of everything."

Martin stood and saw Crook's questioning look. He was asking without words, "Who is this girl?"

"Sandra is with Martin. He has emotionally adopted her," said Bill.

Crook said under his breath into Martin's ear, "Was this rape or incest? It makes a difference on our survival chances. If we lose either the mother or the baby, I can not keep it under the radar."

Martin was stunned first at Crook's perception and then at the thought of anyone not surviving. Of course they would all survive. "Rape," he mouthed. Crook nodded.

He said to Martin, "Go, stand in front of the receptionist and ask for my bag like you don't know that I already have it. Make sure you block her view of the elevators." Crook paused, looking Martin full in the face and speaking soft and slow. "This is no time to stress out. Keep it together."

Confidence surging from his recent success signing Crook out, Martin strode to the desk even as he felt the odds of Crook's escape into the world plummeting out of reach. Martin stood in front of the woman and addressed her.

He tilted his head to read her name tag. "Tamara," he said, "Crook expected his freedom would slip away at the very moment he believed he had freedom. That is what he expects. We won't let it slip away, will we?" He tried to smile at the woman who allowed none of it.

Martin counted to five by tapping his fingers on the counter. He assumed Crook, Bill and Sandra waited for the elevator. He adjusted his body to block the woman's gaze as she moved with her chair on wheels. Some skills come back and defensive feet were one of them.

When he heard the elevator door open, he said, "I need Crook's suitcase." He stepped two inches to his left following her head and eyes.

Martin refused to step away even when the receptionist told him that Crook had his bag. He refused to shrivel before the badly hidden look of disgust in her saucy expression. With her painted nails, she moved the form signed by Crook so Martin could see Crook's signature. Still

Martin did not move away. He shuffled back and forth always blocking her line of vision until she finally stood and glared at him.

When Martin heard the whoosh of the elevator door closing, he said, "Well, Crook forgot his carving piece." He turned quickly to the elevator, and pretended not to hear her say, "You are not allowed."

Martin waited for the elevator while ignoring the receptionist behind him. It took a few minutes for the elevator to return. Once inside he pushed third floor. He wanted the sixth floor, but the third floor was Crook's sleeping quarters. That was where the receptionist/detective would expect him to find a carving piece.

At the third floor he went to a different elevator and pushed six. He did not have time to plan, he just moved. Crook would take Sandra to the sixth floor where the medical rooms were located and a surgery room that wasn't used for much more than temporary patch ups.

When the elevator stopped and the door opened at the sixth floor, Martin poked his head out expecting to find some type of activity. The hallway was deserted. Lit only by the small square night lights along the floorboard, the space was eerily silent. Martin tried walking lightly down the echoing hallway to the last room. He was so afraid for Sandra and for Crook he felt stiff and cold. Only his confidence that Crook was in charge prevented the fear from turning into blackness. "No time to stress out," he mumbled several times.

Though no light showed beneath the door or through the small square window near the top, Martin knew they were in there. He knocked lightly with a shaking fist. "Merciful Jesus. Merciful Jesus." That was his prayer.

An orderly Martin recognized opened the door and replaced the towel along the bottom of the door to cover the light. The square glass above the door was covered with black construction paper saved in a drawer for just this purpose. The people in the room were silent specters under fluorescent light.

Clandestine surgery had not happened often, but it had happened, and the long timers knew the routine. Most secret surgeries were in the line of wounds. Martin was sure that this was the first baby. If there was an expectant mother, she would normally be moved to a medical hospital.

Crook controlled the room. He picked the helpers -- all people who owed him favors. Crook whispered between his teeth, "We all know this situation never happened, right fellas?"

Another orderly from the medical ward stood by a high table on which Sandra lay. Bill stood by Sandra. The area above the table was so brightly lit that it felt to Martin like a stage. And it was silent, the only sound Sandra, breathing in and out with deep breaths. Martin's gut wrenched when he looked at her. He knew to show no emotion, not now. Now she had to survive.

Never having participated in anything clandestine while he was a patient, Martin had not actually believed Crook's stories. Now he believed the knife wounds and broken fingers. Everything was synchronized; everything moved to Crook's command as though he conducted a small but elite orchestra. Martin could not help his smile.

Crook left to fetch a woman named Clara. Martin moved to Sandra's side. He took her hand. She looked white, her eyes glazed and nearly rolling into her head. "Sandra," Martin called her name. "You will be all right. Sandra, can you hear me?"

The girl focused her eyes toward him and nodded. "I want my mom," she said.

"You all have to be quiet," an orderly hissed. Martin glared.

The black orderly took Sandra's blood pressure and felt her stomach, but he didn't write anything down. "Doing fine," he told Sandra.

"Your blood pressure is good," Martin repeated to Sandra in a whisper. She grimaced. Martin considered pointing out that she was not having this baby by herself in an abandoned farmhouse. He did not say his thought because the sushing police stood across from him, and Sandra was in enough pain. He held her hand.

"You must not talk." The orderly's face contorted with urgency. Sandra nodded. Martin made no response though it was Martin who was guilty of talking. The guards did walk this hallway every now and then in the afternoon. Twenty minutes passed without a sound in the room but Sandra's controlled breathing and occasional moan.

Martin watched her. Her stomach stretched like a drum. He watched her eyes grow large. "I want my mom," she repeated.

A light tap sounded on the door. Crook entered, followed by Clara, the obese, crazy midwife. Clara had blond tufts of hair that looked like a badly burned home perm surrounding fat cheeks and small features. Clara was the only one in the room who actually looked crazy. The group assembled nodded to her.

Sandra's body was so tight that Martin thought her arm would break off if he moved it. She was literally paralyzed with fear. She gagged and swallowed.

"Don't tighten up like that," Martin whispered to her. He was present in the room when his daughters were born.

"I want my mom now," Sandra whispered.

"SShh," Bill whispered to her, "we will call your mom when we get home."

Martin noticed Bill for the first time since entering the room when he stood by Sandra. Bill looked miserable, ready to have a stroke. His face was blotchy red. His hands kept going to his head as though he wore a cap. He stood close to Martin, nearly touching him. His eyes shifted from the teenager to Martin.

Martin exchanged a look with the old farmer, but Bill was too tense to speak. He patted Sandra's arm and looked steady at her face. If Sandra felt uncomfortable with all these men around her, she made no mention of it.

Bill must have thought of that as well because he whispered to her, "Would you rather I leave?"

Sandra made no answer, so Bill stayed.

The black orderly stood across the bed from Martin and Bill. He kept his fingers on Sandra's wrist. Crook and Clara stood at her feet. The second orderly was really a guard at the door.

"No mommy, no mommy," Clara sang back to Sandra. Everyone tensed and averted their eyes from the woman, everyone except Crook

Martin, who watched Crook's face, saw Crook as much as he heard him say to Clara, under his breath and in her ear so Sandra could not hear. "Give the baby to me right away," he told her. His eyes and expression were as cold and hard as lifeless stone. "Now tell her what to do. You will not hurt her. Do you understand? I am standing right here, and I will cut your eyes out."

"All right," Clara snarled back. Then she smiled at Sandra, showing teeth with several black fillings. "She's lost her water and there ain't nothing I can do about that. And she's all tensed up. That'll make her bleed a lot. There's nothing here to give her for the pain and besides it's too late. Anything now would slow the labor."

Martin knew who Clara was through hospital scuttlebutt, but he had never spoken to her. He could see from the excitement in her eyes that she relished pain, asking Sandra about it as she put Sandra's feet in the stirrups. The orderly covered her with a sheet like a tent.

Bill looked sharply at Crook and made a gesture with his hand for Crook to move away, at least look away to give the girl some privacy.

"He has to watch Clara," Martin said to Bill.

"Try to relax," Martin said to Sandra, rubbing her hands and arms.

Sandra's eyes were wild with fear so Martin told her, "No choice now, Sandra. Go for it."

"I see Hauk," she whispered.

Martin put his hand gently over her eyes. Then he bent to within inches of her face. "Hauk will pay someday. Think now of breathing in and out. Don't fight the pain. I learned that in pre-natal daddy class. Not for me, but for you."

Sandra stuck her tongue out at him while one hand gripped his and her other hand gripped the bed. Martin lifted his hand from her eyes. Determination began to turn the brown color dark. For a second Martin glanced away. He thought he saw hate in Sandy's eyes. He didn't like it. Bill continued to stand at Martin's elbow.

Clara nodded to the orderly and the orderly said to Sandra, "You are doing fine. Keep breathing like I told you. When we tell you to push, push hard. Push with the pain. Then it won't hurt so much. Try not to scream."

Martin saw the blood. Quickly he looked away. "You are safe. You are all right. Scream if you want."

He could see only Sandra but he said the name, "Crook, Crook, Crook." God worked in the world. Crook worked in the hospital.

Bill touched Martin's elbow and gestured to Crook. The bald, wiry man focused on Clara with burning intensity. Bill was showing Martin the knife in the palm of Crook's hand.

Martin said, "Only Clara can see that."

"Push," Clara sang.

"We can see the head," the orderly reported.

"Once more, once more, push with the pain," and on it went. And then it was sudden and total relief and over.

"It's a boy," the orderly whispered while he wiped Sandra's face with a cold wash cloth.

Clara completed a few stitches. "We need paper," Crook said to the obese woman. She rolled her eyes.

The guard brought over a hospital form. He gave the form and a pen to Clara.

"Father's name," Clara asked.

"Martin Webster," Crook answered.

Martin felt the guard gape at him.

"Mother's name," Clara looked at Crook. Crook looked at Sandra. Sandra shook her head. She didn't know what to say.

Crook answered, "Put Loretta for the first name, unknown for the last name. List her as deceased, died in child birth." Crook's expression never changed, nor did his tone. Clara wrote as she was told. Clara signed as the attending midwife. Crook signed as a witness.

"We need a name for the baby," Clara sounded tired.

All eyes turned to Martin. Martin barely noticed them as he was wiping Sandra's neck and arms with a cool cloth.

"A name," Crook ordered, looking at Martin.

"Kirby Puckett," Martin answered, quickly, first thing that came to mind.

"Kirby Puckett Webster," the orderly smiled at Sandra. "That is a fine name."

Sandra's eyes were glazed so Martin gently pinched her arm. She nodded at the orderly.

Clara said to Martin, looking directly at him, "Take this form to the court house in Lincoln County and get it filed. They will register the birth and give you a birth certificate, and then you have to get a social security card. Understand?"

Martin nodded. He understood. He had to swallow the bile that rose in his throat merely from looking at Clara. She was hideous. He again covered Sandra's eyes.

"I want money," Clara said to Crook.

"Money, Martin," Crook said to him.

He pulled out his credit card.

Bill said to him, "Use your cash, Martin. That's for stuff not on the credit card list."

Everyone shuffled nervously. Crook moved away from Clara and snatched the wallet from Martin's pocket. Martin saw that he gave Clara a twenty. Clara frowned, and Crook shook his head.

Without another word, or even a sound, she opened the door, put her head into the hallway and her bulk followed her head with amazing agility. All Martin could see was her fingertips as she held the door from clicking shut. She was gone.

The orderly gave Kirby a fast scrubbing, running water on a towel to muffle the sound. Kirby wailed a baby wail that was both quiet and piercing. The orderly dressed the tiny baby in an adult-sized t-shirt that he wrapped back around his body. Kirby looked like a tiny mummy. The young man weighed him and measured him and printed the information on the form. Then he handed Kirby to Sandra.

Sandra in turn handed the baby to Martin.

"He has to eat," Martin told her. He knew he sounded stern. At this moment, Sandra was no longer the child. Shock showed in her eyes as she looked at Martin, but she did not resist as Martin helped her to feed Kirby.

Martin said, "He is a handsome lad."

Sandra turned her face away.

Martin did not care that Crook handed out money from Martin's wallet to his helpers. Bill found a hoarse whisper in which to say, "Add that to your cash list, Martin. Miscellaneous health."

When Martin noticed a white-green line around Bill's mouth, he clutched Bill's upper arm with one hand. He hoped to comfort Bill but he couldn't speak. Both men turned away while the orderly helped Sandra. Martin gazed at the baby curled inside his elbow.

A wheelchair appeared beside Sandra's bed. Bill and Crook gently helped her into the chair. They used a white square bed pad with blue plastic backing as a pillow beneath her. Martin held Kirby. Kirby weighed six pounds and eleven ounces and nearly disappeared in Martin's hands. Martin was at ease with Kirby, and Kirby blessedly did not cry.

Chapter Ten

Sandra felt relief, tremendous relief and exhaustion. In a week she would be home and back at practice with no one the wiser. She struggled to hold her head upright as the guard whispered hurried instructions to Bill on how to drive to the back entrance. Bill walked quickly from the room, and tears gathered in Sandra's eyes as she watched him. These men helped her. They were with her, and she was with them.

As Crook wheeled Sandra to the service elevator, she glanced briefly to verify that Martin followed with Kirby. It shocked her how much it mattered that the baby was okay, that he was with Martin. That was all. She felt no need to hold him or care for him, only that he was safe and cared for.

The service elevator was beyond the regular elevators around a corner and down another hallway. It was a wood platform without sides used to haul heavy supplies and equipment. About four inches of air outlined the platform from the elevator shaft, and the pulleys and cables were also open.

The platform was obviously not intended for human cargo, but this elevator would take them to the back loading docks and not to the front lobby. Onto this platform Crook wheeled Sandra, carefully lifting the wheels across the open space. She watched Martin overcome a reluctance to step over. He covered Kirby with his hand to protect the baby. Cool air drafted over them as they descended.

The noise and metallic rattle startled them all. "Oh, man!" Crook gripped the wheel-chair and cursed under his breath.

"Uncle Crook forgot about the noise," Martin whispered to Kirby.

"So did daddy," Crook said over the noise. "The elevator running at this time on a Saturday will raise alarms."

Sandra wondered what that would mean. Even if she was discovered, they couldn't keep her. Then she gasped as she realized they could keep Crook, maybe even Martin. They would call her parents. Her parents would know she had a baby. Her fingers clutched the sides of her chair as she struggled to breath.

And it was slow, the elevator lurched down at a snail's pace. It was too late to go back, so they descended. She glanced up at Martin. He was frozen like a statue. Still he looked at her and said, "Don't worry." He nodded his head toward Crook. His balance appeared precarious, and his bundle was held with utmost care.

Finally the platform halted about six inches above the cement dock. Martin had to use one hand to help Crook lift the wheelchair from the elevator. For a second Sandra felt herself pitch forward but she balanced her own weight and held on.

Crook pushed the wheelchair to the platform steps located a few yards away. She stared into the dusk for Bill while clutching Martin's shirt. "I can walk," she said.

So Crook helped Sandra to descend step by step while Martin lifted the wheelchair off the side with one hand. He stepped past his friends, and righted the chair. Sandra sat back down, breathing heavily, and Martin carefully moved her hair from her face.

Security lights were not on in the early evening dusk. The three of them moved like thieves into the dusk with hesitant steps. Her mouth was dry, and she kept swallowing. Where were Bill and the car?

He appeared like a spook in the dim light, apparently too traumatized to talk. He gestured toward the Lincoln, idling along a bend in the delivery road, nearly invisible from where they stood. In minutes, Sandra rested in the back seat, leaving room for Crook. Martin sat in front with Kirby, and Bill sat behind the wheel.

They would make it undiscovered. They would make it. She heard Bill sigh and Martin talk softly to Kirby. She closed her eyes. Then Crook said something that stopped everything, Sandra's heart and Sandra's hope. Leaning into the back passenger side door, Crook said. "I have to go back. Pick me up at the front door." He was gone.

Chapter Eleven

Crook re-entered the hospital by a seldom-used maintenance entrance. Inside he glanced at the big, white-faced clock. It was 6:40 PM. He had twenty minutes until lock down and lockdown was tight. Even he could not move around after lockdown. Two things propelled him up six flights of stairs: he would walk out the front door or he would not walk out at all, but he had forgotten his suitcase in the surgery, and his carving piece was in that suitcase.

He thought about the baby. Now there were two lost souls who knew no other life than inside these walls. Not exactly a silver spoon for the kid, but a false identity was better than no identity. Martin would take care of the baby, Crook knew that. His mother couldn't love him, Crook saw that.

Rape, he thought. A mother who could not even look at her newborn had suffered beyond forgiveness. He would find out how she came to be in Martin's care, but it helped Martin, pushed him to work harder to be well.

At last he saw the large number "6" painted on the door at the top of the steps. The stairs stopped here. Crook pushed open the door into a dimly lit, deserted hallway. No one waited there. He soundlessly ran the corridor, passed the regular elevators, and ran for the surgery room. In front of the locked surgery room door sat his suitcase.

The security people would be in the dining room counting heads. They would not be counting his anymore. Bag in hand, Crook strode to the elevator that would take him to the lobby. The elevator landed gently and quietly and the doors swooshed open and there stood Dr. Durkson, facing him, arms crossed.

Crook's heart raced and his hands were wet, but nothing showed in his expression, nothing flickered in his eyes. "Forgot my suitcase," Crook said. He noted the empty receptionist desk and the glass doors across the entrance way. Since the doctor did not move or speak, Crook started to go around him. He would not run.

"Crook," Dr. Durkson called him. Crook turned. Obviously the receptionist reported to Dr. Durkson that Martin went upstairs. So, likely he waited for Martin to come down. "I am here well past my time to be home on a Saturday. I told my wife this morning that I might be late. I just knew that your exit would not be routine."

To Crook, the doctor looked reconciled, almost sad. Crook forced himself to hold his bag loose in his hand, no clutching. Two janitors emerged from a side door with bucket and mops. They began moving the chairs and mopping the floor where Sandra sat.

"Why are you here?" the doctor asked him, still without moving and in his calm doctor voice. Crook saw in the man's eyes that he hoped for a lie good enough to be believed. He did not want to investigate anything. He did not want to know why Martin went up and Crook came down.

For a second Crook thought the place was a science fiction novel where zombies awoke to come out at night and do their mopping and then return to some invisible, unknown hideout. To the doctor, he repeated, "I forgot my suitcase."

From the doctor's glance to the elevator lights, Crook knew the doctor was waiting for help. Had he expected Crook, he would have had Security in place in the hallway. "I asked Martin to get it for me, but he couldn't find it. So, I had to come back inside and get it."

Dr. Durkson pondered this answer for several seconds. He glanced toward the sitting area where the janitors were finishing their work. One man pushed the large, wringer bucket by the handle of his mop. He pushed it on squeaky wheels towards the maintenance door. Then Dr. Durkson let it go. Crook saw it, the release of control, like a physical cloud in the atmosphere vaporizing.

"Good answer," the doctor said.

The elevator doors opened and two security guards stepped through. They shook their heads at Dr. Durkson, indicating that no one was missing, nothing out of place. Crook gave no more indication of relief upon observing that report than he registered alarm at seeing the doctor.

Again, they waited while the Doctor thought about it. He said, "I called security to check on a Saturday service delivery. Nothing was scheduled." He sighed. "I should ask you if you have any knowledge of why the service elevator was used. I am interested in what you would say about that. However, my curiosity is outweighed by my reluctance to open that can of worms. I guess that Martin left the building via the service elevator for some unknown reason and you used the elevator so he could exit out the front door."

He looked hard at Crook. "Don't say anything," he said.

Crook had no intention of saying anything.

"Goodbye, Crook," Dr. Durkson said and turned to his office, dismissing the guards with a wave of his hands. Then he turned back; the guards again stood still. "May I check your bag, Crook?" he asked.

Crook wondered why he had never liked Dr. Durkson. He liked him now. He handed his suitcase to the security guard who opened it and held it for the doctor to look through the humble contents.

"Another chess piece," Dr. Durksen asked while turning a six-inch square piece of wood in his hands. "How you can carve without knives allowed is thought for another day." He used his hands carefully. Crook thought he did not want to dig too deep.

"A Queen," Crook said.

"I could use one for my new desk. A whole set would be nice." Dr. Durkson snapped the bag shut and returned it to Crook. This time Crook sprinted toward the door, grabbed the garbage bag containing Martin's coat, came to a complete stop, looked outside for several seconds and then slowly, head high, he stepped through.

In less than a minute he sat in the back seat of Bill's Lincoln. Bill sped away as fast as he could without causing suspicion. They did not stop, or talk, or move until the hospital was well behind them, and then the city.

Chapter Twelve

Inside the big Lincoln, silence reigned. Only the sound of Sandra's deep sleep could be heard, a rhythmic sighing in the far distance. In the rear-view mirror Bill saw that her knees bent and her feet rested on Crook's thigh. Bill adjusted to the experience, testing it for reality. Kirby snuggled in Martin's arms. A small sucking sound came from the baby at intervals and verified that he lived.

The headlights bent through the deepening dusk. Bill's grip on the steering wheel relaxed and he eased back in his seat, sighing. As the last vestiges of city drifted past, no one spoke of what just happened. Certainly Bill had no words, not even for himself.

At last, Martin said, "K-mart," gesturing to the right as a final, almost isolated, shopping center emerged. Bill nodded. As the car halted, rocking gently when Bill jammed the gear shift into park, Martin placed Kirby in Bill's arms. Martin moved around, jerking his large frame in the cramped space.

Bill as well as Crook observed Martin's movements, waiting, watching. Martin pulled Nancy's list for his credit card from his pocket and held it aloft. Bill rolled his eyes, and Crook sat back. Martin then rooted in the glove compartment until he found a pen and carefully printed at the bottom of the list the word "Items." They needed some items.

Sandra, still sleeping, bled through her jogging pants. She did not look comfortable with her head at an awkward angle against the door and her body across the seat with her long, bent legs nearly to Crook's door. In a sudden image flitting through Bill's mind, he recalled scolding his own daughter for spilling soda on the upholstered seat. He shook himself, realizing how much it did not matter. He did not care about the seat. What he felt was an overpowering surge of protectiveness. That and exhaustion.

He was not accustomed to plodding through life's underside. He laid his head back to rest while Martin went to shop, but could not close his eyes. Kirby whimpered against his chest. Then he felt wetness on his shirt. "Of course," he thought. "What else is there?"

It took Martin a long time. Crook was preparing to go in after him when they heard cart wheels rattling across the black top, and Martin's bulk emerged under the parking lot lights.

Not an inch of space remained unused. Not even an aspirin could fit inside the car or in the trunk. Sandra woke to feed the baby. She fumbled around for awhile, embarrassed even in the darkness, but eventually Kirby sucked. She said nothing about the uncomfortable wetness of Kirby's make-shift wrap. Bill wondered if she did not notice or if she did not care.

After Sandra returned the infant to Martin's outstretched hands, she again slept and Bill drove through the darkness. In Norfolk they found an all night diner and Bill went inside to buy food, damp shirt and all. When he returned, on his seat was a basketball that had fallen there when he got out.

"For Christ sake, Martin," he said. "why did you buy a basketball? Couldn't Kirby wait until after we got home?"

"It's not for Kirby," Martin answered, taking the ball from the seat and waiting to position it until Bill was sitting.

Bill had no answer for that. He began handing out food. He said, "Sandra has to go home. Her parents will want to help her through this. God willing that we get home. You can do nothing more for her."

Crook, leaning forward to take his soda from Bill's hand, said quietly, almost in a whisper, "Who did this to her?"

Kirby began to cry as though in answer to Crook. Martin opened his car door and with the dome light he began to arrange a diaper and wipes, a blue sleeper and three blankets. He opened the new packages with precise care and carefully took what he needed. He positioned the infant on his lap with almost comic softness in contrast to his own strength.

Bill said, "Come on, Norton!"

Martin said, "It was a man named Hauk."

"We need a plan," Crook said. No more words were spoken. No more words were needed. In that instant, all three men clicked on a single cylinder.

Martin completed his task and handed the big eyed infant to Bill while he again adjusted his body into his space. He reached one arm for Kirby and pulled the baby into himself.

"Sandra will want to help," Martin said.

"Whatever it takes," Bill said.

Bill drove on. The lights along the Missouri Bridge greeted them like a warm embrace. The dashboard was littered with containers, opened plastic packages, baby wipes and assorted Martin things.

Bill's only thought was to get home. He would clean the car another day. He had to get home, and the miles passed beneath the car in an exhaustive blur. Crook sat silent in the back while Martin held Kirby and talked to him. Martin spilled more words in his chatter to the baby than Bill had heard since Martin's return.

Martin dressed Kirby in a Bart Simpson diaper and blue baby t-shirt under the sleeper. He wrapped him again in new blankets. The radio emitted: *You have to walk that lonesome valley; you have to walk it by yourself.* Bill drove in such cramped quarters that he feared he would never walk again.

At last, after midnight, Bill parked in front of Martin's house. Inside the car all was silent though no one slept. He felt Sandra shuffling around in the back seat. He saw Crook in the rear-view mirror looking across Sandra toward the house. Beside Bill, Martin sat still as a statue while holding Kirby on his shoulder. Bill knew the beds were not put together, but he could not stay to help.

On his way home, Bill decided that he could not tell even Tillie about this day, certainly not about Kirby, maybe not about Sandra. Tillie was still up when he walked inside the kitchen door.

"How did it go today?" Tillie asked. "Tell me the highlights for now."

"I'm guessing you want a brief reply so you can go back to sleep. Well, forget that," Bill said. Before either of them slept again, Bill told his wife every detail of the longest day of his life.

Chapter Thirteen

Two weeks later on a breezy, warm Saturday morning, Martin worked alone. He wore a mask and swung a large hammer into the plaster walls of the downstairs master bedroom. After some internal debate he admitted the necessity of removing the wood work and clearing the walls and ceiling to the lathe and replacing it with studs and sheetrock.

He felt peaceful working by himself. Bill had left his cornfields to take Crook to the state park fishing. Sandra returned to her parents' home last Thursday in time to begin basketball practice, late but not too late. He would see her at their Wednesday meeting of the Revenge Club.

Anxious as he was to hear how her homecoming went -- what was said, what was believed -- he could wait. An earplug sat snug inside his ear. The cord ran in a lazy line from his ear to the baby monitor attached to Kirby's portable crib. The crib sat in the kitchen beneath a net tent and on Kirby's nose nestled a tiny oxygen mask to protect the baby from the plaster dust.

Even with the precautions, Martin knew he would be wiping fine plaster dust from Kirby's ears and hair. This made Martin smile. At two weeks of age, Kirby loved his bath. Swinging his hammer, stepping, swinging, listening to baby breaths and slurps he did not hear the pounding on his front door until a strong, male voice shouted from the kitchen. "I know you are here."

Martin stopped dead still, set his hammer down and followed the black cord through the short hallway, passed the small family room with the bricked up fireplace and into the kitchen. Kirby fussed in his ear as he walked in long, quick strides with his heart thumping because Kirby was in the kitchen.

Once inside the kitchen, seeing Kirby as he had left him, Martin checked the big shouldered, thick-necked man in uniform who stood with his legs apart. One hand rested on his firearm. Martin thought with relief, You do not scare me.

Martin made no effort to hide his surprise though he did hide his disgust. Not time yet to warn the sheriff that he was in serious trouble.

"What do you want, Sheriff?" he asked as he bent to look at Kirby.

"I heard you brought your baby to church," Hauk said. He pulled a chair from the table and sat down.

Martin said nothing.

At the door stood a deputy who looked so much like Barney Fife that Martin did a double-take. He stood with his arms across his chest, guarding the door as though Martin would run from his own house. Upon his narrow face sat such a smug, arrogant expression that Martin did what he immediately knew was the wrong thing. Martin laughed out loud. He wiped his laughter away with his hand when he saw the surge of rage cross the deputy's face. Apparently the deputy did not see any humor in himself, the sheriff, or the task at hand.

Hauk ignored this. He allowed a near minute of silence. Martin assumed the silence was intended to put fear into Martin's heart. Martin felt no fear. It wasn't there. He waited through the silent treatment. Martin stood a few feet from where Hauk sat.

"Do you know why I am here?" Hauk asked with a slight, thin-lipped smile.

Martin thought it could be Sandra. It could be Crook. It could be Kirby. So he answered, "Extortion."

Hauk laughed but his eyes were mean.

Martin removed the earphone. It was Kirby in stereo and annoying. He waited both for Hauk to say what he wanted and for the thin black circle to form in his peripheral vision. Stress still caused the blackness to gather. As neither happened for a few seconds he used the time to consider telling this big bully that he knew about him. He resisted because Kirby was too close and he did not want to stir up any biological vibes. The big, bulky man appeared totally unconcerned about the infant other than as leverage for his evil plans.

When Martin said nothing even though Hauk tapped his weapon with his fingers, Hauk said, "I heard you are plum crazy and I don't think you should be caring for a baby. I think I will start paperwork with social services to have this baby removed from this filthy house."

Martin's chest tightened. He pulled his notebook from his pocket and printed the word "lawyer." Even as he felt a hovering fear for his son, he thought with relief, He does not know about Crook. As long as Hauk did not know about Crook then Hauk would not bother Crook and Crook would not have to hurt the bastard. Plus it felt good to have Crook as a secret weapon. Martin smiled.

Then Martin focused on the brute sitting on Bill's chair and in his kitchen. He wanted to ask him if he had not received his notification from Dr. Durksen. Instead he shut his lips tight and put his fingers to his lips to lock them. He had to be careful not to give any hint of Hauk's impending doom.

"Nothing to say, you dumb ass?" Hauk's face was turning pink.

"No," Martin said.

Hauk kept drumming his weapon. He turned his menacing stare toward Kirby. Martin wished he had left the oxygen mask on Kirby's little face because the infant bore a remarkable resemblance to his father. Now Martin couldn't speak even if he wanted to, even if he had words. Outright fear froze his tongue.

Abruptly Hauk stood. He knocked his chair backward with a crash to the floor which startled Kirby and the baby began to wail. Martin bent down to lift the infant into his arms with tenderness. Hauk sneered.

"Five hundred dollars a month will keep that paperwork in the drawer. Carl will be out to collect on the first of every month." Hauk's voice was contempt defined.

"Can't," Martin said.

Hauk unhooked the flap from his holster and circled the grip with his beefy fingers. "I think you will," he said. "I will shoot you and no one will be the wiser."

In that second Martin understood what Sandra had heard and believed. Martin looked down at his spiral notebook lying in Kirby's bed. He wanted to write something but he couldn't think of any words. Then he thought that he could add extortion to his list, but he could not reach his notebook.

His hold on Kirby tightened and the black circle began to form. Hauk was framed like an old-fashioned oval picture. Martin said the only words that came, "Get out."

Hauk reached over and grabbed another refinished chair belonging to Bill. He threw the chair, flinging it across the room. Martin watched the chair hit the wall and bounce on the floor and roll one time. He was relieved when the chair did not break.

"Good workmanship on that chair," Martin said though his stomach churned, and he felt vomit in his throat.

Veins stood out on Hauk's neck as he shook his pistol toward Martin in silent rage. Martin knew the safety was on. If Hauk's fore-finger released the safety he would have to drop Kirby. He turned his body while his eyes watched Hauk's finger.

Finally, Hauk said, "Be ready with cash on the first. I think I will collect personally from you." He then called Martin some vicious names not fit for infant ears and stomped out followed by Carl who had remained silent and motionless throughout.

Martin carefully laid Kirby in his bed. Then he ran up the back stairs and into Crook's room where he grabbed a book from Crook's shelf. He could not unsay the harsh words used in anger by Hauk. He could not undo the ugliness Hauk radiated. All he could do was dilute them among other words spoken with loving intent. Martin again picked up Kirby and began to read. *Big Bird sat on the steps of 123 Sesame Street.*

He babbled as he fed Kirby. He babbled as he changed him. When Kirby slept so soundly that his little head lolled on Martin's arm, Martin finally returned him to his bed. Calmness returned to Martin. The blackness had retreated to invisibility. He was quiet on the inside. "We will have to do something about Hauk," he told the sleeping baby, "sooner rather than later."

Then he hooked up the baby monitor and the oxygen mask, put the earphone in his ear, layered the fine net over Kirby's bed and returned to work. He thought, Only if all else fails will I tell Crook. I will not tell Crook that Hauk called his immaculate kitchen filthy or that he threatened to take Kirby, not unless I am prepared for what Crook would do.

Martin sang softly as he worked, *I shot the sheriff but I did not shoot the deputy.*

Chapter Fourteen

On the following Wednesday night, Martin presided over the third weekly meeting of the Revenge Club. Martin sat at the beautifully varnished table in his kitchen. He faced Sandra and could not keep from looking at her. She was home with her parents, back in school and back at practice, but she did not look happy. If anything the lines around her eyes were tighter, her full mouth set in a tight edge.

Wednesday nights were Church nights. No school activities were scheduled on Wednesday, not even basketball practice. Most students went to religious education class. So Wednesday worked perfectly for the four of them to meet and plan revenge. Tillie sent cookies with Bill. He munched on one now.

Kirby lay tummy down on Martin's knee. Martin jiggled his leg in a nearly constant motion until Bill told him to stop. So he gently patted Kirby's back as he tried to focus on the meeting. He was finding it difficult to concentrate. The truth was he had begun a bathroom project to create a master suite and had run into difficulties. The old house was not square. Should he custom build a vanity to fit or level the wall? He could not quite force his thoughts away from his work.

Bill said, "The trouble with you, Martin, is you have no judgment." He sounded annoyed with Martin about something that Martin had not heard.

Crook said, "He has judgment. He doesn't judge other people. There is a difference. That's why Sandra could tell him her secret. That's why he has Kirby. He isn't normal that way."

"I am right here," Martin said. "Stop talking about me."

Sandra looked at him, tilting her head, examining him. She said, "As I was saying before, Martin, you do not understand." It was not panic in her voice as much as urgency. "He will kill me. He absolutely, positively will. I am sick of nightmares and looking over my shoulder and living a lie with my parents."

Martin said, "I understand exactly what you mean."

Sandra rolled her eyes.

"Why?" Crook asked her. "Why would he risk killing you?"

"There's no risk to him at all to kill me. He told me he would, and I believe him." Sandra turned her hard gaze on Crook.

Bill said, "Do you believe Hauk murdered Allyson or that her death was a suicide? It is important to know how far he has escalated in order to predict his behavior. We need to know his history." Bill addressed Crook to bring him up to speed so to speak. "Hauk didn't look for Allyson so much. She was not like Sandra. I mean, she was not important to the community like Sandra is. People whispered at the time about foul play, but it was ruled accidental exposure by our county coroner."

Martin said, "I don't think he intended for Allyson to die but once it happened he felt all right about it. I believe he believes the same thing could work on Sandra if she became a problem." He looked up and saw eyes staring at him. "What?" he said.

Crook said, "Priors. Hauk's done this before. He's hurt women before. He did not turn lethal overnight."

Sandra said, "We need a plan tonight."

Bill said, "We just don't know how to do this."

Martin nodded. "We need to know more about him, about Hauk. We need to find his weak spot." He reached to tug his hair and discovered again that his barbershop hair cut, which seemed out of place on his head, did not allow for tugging or twisting. His friends nodded.

Over the three Wednesdays since Lincoln, this suggestion to research Hauk had been said before along with other suggestions. Now it felt more tangible, but still not concrete. How exactly did they research Hauk?

Crook said, "We know two weak spots and that is enough to work with."

Now all eyes were on Crook. "He has a weak spot with power, specifically power over Sandra. He has a weak spot with greed, specifically extortion. We need a plan to draw him to a trap."

Bill did not like that idea. He again suggested going to the law in Sioux Falls. To this oft-repeated suggestion Crook again stated how the law in Sioux Falls would want to know about Bill. It was Bill, not Hauk, they would investigate. How did Bill know about Hauk? What had he done? Where was the baby?

Bill looked crestfallen. Martin said, "Not easy is it, Bill. When we most need the law, it is of no help."

When Crook suggested outright killing the bastard, Martin and Bill backed off. It was not in them. Martin said, "To do that we need immediate pressure." He thought of Hauk threatening to take Kirby. The way his gut tightened he thought that could be immediate pressure if it came down to it.

Sandra said, "When he tries to kill me that will be immediate pressure." Her tone was dry.

No one answered her, but Martin caught a slight smile on Crook's lips. Not a happy smile but a cunning smile.

Martin said, "We must be careful. Our first priority is to allow nothing more to happen to Sandra," he paused, "or Kirby."

Upstairs in his locked box lay an envelope containing a birth certificate and a social security card. Kirby was real. Kirby was his. It said so on the birth certificate. Martin saw a look of surprise in Bill's eyes. The older man turned in his chair to look at Martin. Martin looked at his hands.

"Martin, has Hauk threatened Kirby?" Bill asked.

"His existence is a threat to Kirby," Sandra said.

Since Sandra answered Martin felt that he did not need to. He was not willing to share his worry. He said, "We have to find if Hauk's other victims and gather a body of evidence."

Crook said, "We have all we need."

But again Sandra answered, "We do not have time for evidence gathering, unless you want to hold a town meeting and ask everybody, 'Has Hauk assaulted you? Do you pay protection money to your local fat and ugly sheriff? Are the streets quiet enough for you?'" The natural rasp of her voice combined with the urgency she exuded made her sound angry.

"We all want to help," Bill assured her.

Crook looked at her closely. "Sandra, if something happens, bring him out here to the barn."

"I won't have time for that." She spoke in a tone of hopeless acceptance that sent chills around the table.

"You will." Crook's voice held an edge, an excitement. "He will want to see fear. He will toy with you. When he does, do not show fear. Mention the money."

Silence. No one wanted to ask what money. They waited for Crook to explain. When Crook did not appear to know an explanation was required, Martin finally asked, "What money?"

"The make-believe money Sandra saw in the barn," Crook answered.

Bill nodded his understanding. "If it comes right down to it, Sandra, that is something to do," he told her. "Not that Hauk will actually try to kill you. He is crazy evil but not self-destructive. We will protect you."

No one asked how. The four of them remained silent until Martin said, "When Hauk tries to hurt Sandra, she will lead Hauk to the barn, and Crook will ambush Hauk."

Sandra said, "If I disappear it will not be as shocking as you think. No big search this time. What happens if Hauk doesn't care about the money, or he decides he doesn't need me to find it?"

Bill said, "We are assuming that Hauk will at some point try to harm Sandra."

Martin said, "Yes, he will. He hasn't conquered her yet."

"What does she do once she gets Hauk to the barn?" Bill asked.

"Stall until I get there," Crook said.

"He doesn't know that you exist," Martin said. "

That could be useful."

Bill nodded. "I think you are right with that, Martin. If he knew, Hauk and his buddy Carl would have been for a social call." He paused. "Have they been for a social call, Crook?"

Crook shook his head.

Martin said nothing. The social call had not been about Crook. He had until his first scheduled payment on October 1st to decide what he had to do. He would wait and see what happened between now and then.

That was it. The informal revenge meeting adjourned. Martin wanted to research and plan and compile. Crook wanted lethal. Bill wanted legal. Sandra wanted quick. Martin walked with Sandra through the cool September night to her car. He asked about school and her mom and her dad.

"Fine," Sandra said.

Then Martin took a few minutes to show her how to use her feet under the basket on defense and on offense. Under the yard light with hovering, buzzing insects, Martin moved with an invisible basketball. For the first time, Martin caught a genuine smile from the girl. He stopped and handed her the pretend ball. She copied him.

"You have to practice that move," Martin told her, "but it always works."

Sandra nodded.

"Drive careful," he said as Sandra shut her car door. She drove an old black Mazda. Hauk knew this car.

Crook approached the car until he stood three feet away. He gestured for Sandra to roll down her window. "Martin has a big social gathering on Saturday."

"I forgot about it," Martin said. "Come out on Saturday and meet Carmen and Christy. Christy is coming for her birthday."

Crook added, "And the ex-wife and the sister."

"Awkward," Sandra answered. She almost laughed. "No thanks."

Then Crook stepped closer. He said, "If Hauk operates on an internal clock like most rapists, he will be back to see you soon. Do not be afraid. He will want the money, and he will want you to bring him to it. Can you do that?"

Martin watched Sandra think this through. After a few minutes, she looked at Crook and said, "Yes, I can do that."

Chapter Fifteen

Vehicles of every make and model filled with teenagers drove slowly up and down Main Street while Sandra waited at a side street stop sign. Religious Education was over and they would risk a few turns before going home. Watching the kids she knew go past was annoying. Why was this fun? What did they know? They were all stupid kids.

Then her throat tightened. She knew she would never have fun again. She spent her Wednesday night with three old men planning revenge. She stopped short of hating her schoolmates. She stopped herself. It was not Kirby's fault that he existed and it was not their fault that she feared for her life. She had to stay calm.

The street cleared and Sandra crossed. Sandra took side streets to her fastidious white, two story house on the corner. She entered into the kitchen from the garage. Her mom and dad watched the ten o'clock news and Sandra heard the familiar voice from the TV as she opened the kitchen door. She considered taking the stairs directly to her room to avoid but it crossed her mind that she should say goodbye, no, not goodbye just goodnight.

She went to sit on the footstool in front of her mother's chair. She had no words to say, but she allowed herself to soak in the warmth. Her mom reached out her hand and stroked her hair.

"Your teacher called that you did not attend class tonight. She mentioned that you have not attended since your return. Your father and I were wondering if you have an explanation for that."

Sandra stiffened. Her whole body turned into a taut wire ready to snap. She answered without looking at her dad who leaned forward in his chair and went so far as to turn the TV off. She did not look at her mother either though she wanted to shake her mom's fingers from her hair. She said, "I have better things to do on Wednesday night. I hang out with friends."

She knew her mother was trying not to cry. "Why are you crying, Mom?" she asked and the anger spilled out in her voice.

Her dad, always so defensive, said, "We are trying to understand."

"Don't," Sandra told him. "You can't understand. Give it up and leave me alone."

Her mother dropped her hand as though burned. Sandra reached for the remote and turned the TV back on. She stood. At the doorway, she turned and said, "Goodnight."

As she brushed her teeth, she considered how little her parents had actually nagged her. She considered how desperately they were trying to understand. Well, she told herself in the mirror. They can't. They can not ever, not ever know anything about it.

As she lay in the darkness, she thought about the baby. Only as long as no one suspected a baby was she safe and how could they not? How could her mom and dad not suspect a baby? How could Hauk not suspect a baby? He just didn't care unless he could extort something. Did Hauk know Crook was at the farm?

Did her parents believe her story of camping, of falling down the rocks where Bill Bendix found her? Yes, Sandra thought, they choose to believe her. Deputy Carl wrote down the story. His shoulders all hunched and his lips pursed like some freaking bird ready to pounce. The search ended.

She thought perhaps when the time was right, she would tell her mom. Then she thought no. She would never tell. It would go away if Hauk were dead. Hauk would protect himself by getting rid of her if he could. She needed a preemptive strike. Would he hurt the baby? Was Kirby a threat? Sandra decided he did not give a rat's ass about the baby, only her.

Her thoughts ran in circles as the hours ticked by in the dark stillness of her room. She watched the morning light fill in the spaces around her furniture until the light rested on her quilt in a long rectangle. It was time to get up and go to school. Only at basketball practice did she forget for a few blessed hours.

Meanwhile, she stayed low-key and quiet. She talked sparingly with friends, and avoided all social activities. Everyone knew she did not have a steady boyfriend. That might partially explain why they did not put two and two together. The change in her was not obvious because the change had actually begun last fall. Her friends already adjusted to the shake of her head. No, she would not go. Even her best friends accepted that Sandra wanted to be left alone.

Her religion boiled down to a single constant low rumble of desperation. Sometimes she felt close to slipping, to giving up, telling that Hauk had touched her. Then on the very verge of cracking, she crawled back from the precipice while gripping the rosary in her pocket.

As she showered and dressed, dried her hair, she heard her mom downstairs. She wished for the old days when she ran the steps and gulped breakfast and talked with her mother in the natural chatter that now was absolutely impossible.

Well, she thought, nothing bad is going to happen today. I have a plan. I will be the bait and Crook will be the hook. When Hauk was gone her life would be normal again.

Chapter Sixteen

Late Saturday morning the words, "Daddy, you're better!" rang through the kitchen as Christie ran for Martin's leg. Christie's birthday cake with seven candles sat on a lace cloth in the middle of the table. Carmen was two steps behind Christie and was forced to shove her sister in order to get her own spot at Martin's waist. Carmen would not be five until November.

When Martin turned from the stove, adjusted his children and looked up, he looked square into the deep green eyes of Nancy. His stomach lurched and his mouth went dry. Nancy held her lethal stare and the angry set to her jaw.

What had he done? He forced himself to carefully set the potato masher on the stove. Then he jerked his eyes away from the gravitational pull of his ex-wife. Martin bent down to lift both girls in his arms. Carmen grabbed his hair for support. "Daddy is some better, but not all better," Martin told Christie.

"You can talk," Carmen commented on this fact with eyes showing an awareness that cracked Martin's heart.

Martin struggled to a kitchen chair and sat down, adjusting his daughters onto his knees. He asked Christie about pee-wee softball and Christie informed him that it was T-ball.

"I am the best player. You will not want to miss seeing me next year." Her expression and tone were both admonishing and wounded. He held the sturdy, strong little girls for several minutes without talking, and they allowed this.

Maureen entered the kitchen, arms full of bags and boxes. She chatted quietly, like in a hospital wing, as Nancy helped to sort things and place a salad here and dessert there. Then the two women sat on chairs at the kitchen table, and looked at the renovated white cupboards and butcher block countertop, the level crème walls, and new sink and appliances.

Even a brown and yellow-stripped curtain with tie backs hung on the new kitchen window. "The kitchen looks very nice," Maureen said.

Christie wanted to look at the house, and Martin released her. Carmen was happy where she sat, but Christie ordered her to come along.

"Stay off the scaffolding," Martin warned them and found his voice choked. Since Wednesday evening after the Revenge Club meeting, he had been emotional, almost weepy. In comparison to months of struggle to find any feelings at all, this sudden turn baffled him.

He was close to his memory now: the memory that paralyzed him. He felt it hovering. He could almost touch it, but when he reached out, it moved away. He was afraid of his memories and glad to focus on other things.

He smiled at the two women in his life. Nearly the same age, both women were strongly attractive. All resemblance ended there. Though Nancy graduated cum laude from Minnesota State University with a degree in economics, she never held a job in her life. Her work was house, home, and family, and second to that was being beautiful and perfect in all things.

In stark contrast, Maureen started working at age twelve as a waitress and had never stopped working. Maureen's degree was in Computer System Management from South Dakota State, and she was an expert in her field. She never married, nor did she have any children.

Martin knew while Nancy discussed fashion and flower arrangements and went to yoga class, Maureen went to work in the school gymnasium as a statatician.

Still, the women got along well when they had to be together. His sister made concessions to get along with Nancy because Maureen loved him. Nancy made no concessions and was blissfully unaware that concessions existed. At one time he loved that about her.

The two women sat like vultures. He had written to Nancy as a courtesy that he had a son. Martin knew they hovered in wait to see Crook and, even more so, Kirby. At least Nancy would now believe Crook was real, as real as Kirby.

However, Martin had no intention of discussing either Crook or Kirby. What was Cook or Kirby to Nancy? Martin did not think about what Nancy felt regarding a new baby in the family. He had too much to think about for Nancy to fit inside his head at all.

Christie's birthday marked a near two-year anniversary since the divorce. The divorce was blurry and unimportant in his memory. When he tried to touch it like an old bruise, he felt nothing there. The divorce was necessary because she had to protect financial interest and because she could not stand to be around him. He did not care then, and if the facts be known, he did not care now.

It was three years ago that he sat at his kitchen table and opened the St. Paul newspaper. Before his eyes was the picture of a young man lying dead as the result of a construction accident. The accident occurred in the building of the new Brewer's baseball stadium in Milwaukee.

He was not prepared to see that picture. The angle of the picture was from overhead like looking down from a hay-mound onto the milking-stanchions below.

Within days of seeing that picture he had rolled into a tight ball, a deaf and dumb ball. His next real memory was Crook knocking with his knuckles on Martin's head. Nancy disappeared during that time. He recalled fighting to keep Carmen and Christie in his mind, but

125

he couldn't. He suffered a mental collapse. Only Maureen stayed in his mind because she had always been there. She had been in his life before Joe died.

Martin heard Nancy's voice now and looked up. He forced his thoughts away from his past. Later he would have to think about it, think it all through, but not now. Now was Christie's birthday party. The memories tightened his chest and made his hands shake. It was not so easy to focus away from them once they started.

Suddenly Martin did not want to be around Nancy. She looked skinny and ratchet-faced and nasty, the way she waited to see Crook and Kirby.

He did not want to see Nancy because she was a mirror of his previous self. A surge of rage toward Nancy that he knew to be unreasonable filled his chest and tightened his arms. He stood, left the women as they sat and went to retrieve his daughters for dinner.

"Time to eat," he said to Carmen and lifted her onto a chair.

The five of them sat at the six-foot table. Martin and Christie sat on one side facing Nancy and Maureen who sat in front of the window. Carmen had an end all to herself. Martin felt better, focused on his family. He watched Nancy place cloth napkins neatly under Carmen's and Christie's plates. No one talked other than the careful politeness of "please" and "thank you."

Maureen smiled across the table at Christie. She had suffered from Martin's absence more than Carmen. Sensing that Christie did not enjoy the silence, Maureen said, "It is a big change in the house in four weeks, believe me."

Martin studied his sister. When he saw the love in her eyes a new surge of warmth suddenly closed his throat.

Maureen said, "We should have birthday cake on the porch. It is beautiful."

They talked about the house for a long time. Martin's eyes rested on Maureen who had whimsy in her look, always a little haphazard, always approachable. However, both women had skill at conversation. So, dinner rolled along smoothly and the girls looked happy.

Nancy said, "This table is lovely, Martin. I don't remember this being in the house."

Martin told about the table and its source. Then he said, "Crook did the sanding after I showed him how to run the sander. Actually he did a lot of it by hand."

"Oh, really," Nancy responded. "You let Crook help. I'm surprised as you were always such a perfectionist."

Martin knew there was something wrong with Nancy's tone only because Maureen glanced at Nancy with a quick, worried look. Was it the mention of Crook? He thought it was, so he said, "Crook is a fast learner. He is very scheduled." Martin paused, fork in hand. "He works well with knives."

On the counter behind Martin sat three new chess pieces, all perfectly carved, all finished to a gleaming polish. Crook was trying to broaden his horizons and had created knights.

Maureen softly interrupted, commenting on the roast and potatoes, that they were delicious. Then she stood and walked to stand between Martin and Christie. Maureen lightly touched his shoulder. Her hand felt warm and soothing. Maureen stroked Christie's hair and commented that the girls would do the dishes.

"Where is Crook?" Nancy asked, looking down, hiding her face behind her hair.

"He's in his room, watching Kirby," Martin answered. He showed no anxiety on that topic or interest in pursuing it.

However, the kitchen was suddenly thick with silence. Martin had said aloud the word "Kirby" and he saw Nancy stiffen like a post in her chair. Nancy's reaction baffled him. He said, "Does it matter to you that I have a son?"

Nancy glared at him. She said, "Of course it matters, Martin. It matters to Carmen and Christie." She paused, breathing slowly. "I didn't know you had a girlfriend."

"I didn't," Martin answered.

At that moment Christie returned. "You can sit in the windows, Momma," she said. Nancy made no answer.

Maureen said, "Show me."

Martin and Nancy sat looking at each other in the silent kitchen. Nancy said, "Join the real world for a minute, Martin." She slammed her fist on the table and Martin jerked upright. She had his attention.

She said, "It all matters. Your lawyer will not allow a final financial settlement until you are capable of input." She spoke slowly and distinctly, accenting each word. Martin felt offended by her manner.

Nancy continued, "As it stands now I am guardian of your money though your lawyer watches like a hawk. If there is another woman in your life and if there is a new child in your life, that matters. Think about the money!"

"Oh," Martin said. He sat back in the chair and tried to think about the money. He thought Kirby would soon need a real crib. He thought Crook would need some new clothes. He dressed very hospital. Martin nearly reached for his pocket to pull out the spiral notebook to make a list, but he did not. Nancy meant something more in her words.

"How much," he asked.

"Millions," Nancy said. "Between the money you made and the way I invested it we are comfortable. It is complicated to separate yours from mine. The lawyers are licking their lips."

Martin found it extremely difficult to continue with this conversation. He had one point to settle; after that the lawyers could take care of it. "None of this includes the farm?" he asked.

Nancy shook her head. "Not other than the inordinate amount of money you're spending on it."

"I have money to spend," Martin said.

Nancy nodded. She pushed away from the table.

Martin also stood. His head hurt. He walked slowly through the house, preferring to think about his work. Only the porch, kitchen and a new bathroom where the laundry used to be were actually livable. The children could run under the scaffolding through the living room and dining room, or up and down the staircase in the foyer. Crook's room upstairs was the one formerly occupied by Joe because of the door to the bathroom. Martin installed a semi-kitchen with a hot plate and refrigerator and sink. It was temporary, until Martin could re-do the walls, but it was clean and functional.

After a minute, Martin heard Nancy say, "Be careful climbing around, Christie, you will get dirty, and watch your sister."

"Not likely she will get dirty," Martin answered to no one. "Crook is a compulsive neat-nik. Everyday he cleans through those rooms like they were a surgery." A vision of Crook removing beer cans, grumping and swearing, crossed his mind. Martin smiled. He wanted his coat and thought to go upstairs and get it when Christie found him and took his hand.

Martin took the girls for a walk. The grove was turning colors, and Martin showed them the old garden spot and apple orchard. He showed them the tree and the bench and his hiding place.

Martin thought as they walked through the high, scratchy weeds around the orchard how Nancy had loved him when they were both newly out of school. He had completed graduate work and she had her Bachelor's degree. Hadn't she loved him? "No," he said aloud, "She loved how slick and beautiful I was."

Realizing he said the words aloud he glanced about for the girls. They looked at him from the apple tree and then returned to their work at hand which was throwing rotten apples at each other.

Martin and the girls returned to the house with quiet feet. All three of them knew their raggedy appearance would not go unnoticed. They entered the kitchen to see Maureen and Nancy facing each other at the kitchen sink. Had they not seen them walking to the house?

The women were engrossed with their own words. Nancy said with cold scorn, "That was the man I married. I do not know this ridiculous man with his pencil and notebook and lists."

Martin saw the insult on Maureen's face. Did Nancy not realize calling Martin ridiculous would hurt his sister? Maureen said nothing. She would not argue. Martin and Christie and Carmen remained frozen still.

"Although," Nancy said in a quieter, reserved tone, "Martin did always have lists. On his desk right now is a list written on a yellow legal pad. It is a list of the most prominent names in St. Paul, a waiting list of people who want Martin to build their homes. When I get home, I will have to start calling them. Martin will never build their homes, nor would they any longer want him to." Nancy appeared satisfied with that, like this was Martin's punishment for changing.

"They have already moved on," Maureen said as she turned away and saw Martin standing at the door. Nancy's voice continued behind her.

"Martin did not father a baby nine months ago. Nine months ago Martin was impotent and sick. I don't believe there is a baby." Nancy turned toward Maureen and also saw Martin and her daughters. Her face blanched, but then she shrugged. "Show me the baby," she said.

Martin sat the girls down at the table. Martin wanted a cup of coffee so he poured a cup. He poured juice for the girls in coffee cups. While he did this the only sound in the room was the low rumble from the new energy-efficient dishwasher.

Maureen sat at the table as well, holding a wet wash cloth and looking gray under her red-blond hair. Maureen looked at the two little girls. She said softly, "The barn, that old building outside, is where your Uncle Joe died. That is why Daddy is sad and Mommy is angry. It was a long time ago before you were born. None of it is your fault. The adults around here still have to deal with it." At this Maureen gave Martin a reproachful look.

Martin knew his brother Joseph was dead. He had come that far. He knew that was why he feared the barn. Then he thought that he had to be careful. Exhaustion made him unfocused.

Nancy turned around and said, "Joseph died in the barn? Martin never talked about it. It was like it didn't happen."

Martin looked at his daughters with their wide eyes and pinched cheeks. He said, "Can you go play now? This is not for children."

Christie took Carmen's hand. She pulled the younger girl through the arch into the big entry way and staircase. She said, "We can climb, and they won't care."

Maureen said, "Martin was with him and could never tell exactly what happened. Somehow, Joe fell. All I remember is running in the mud. I couldn't get my feet to move, and I was desperate to call an ambulance. It was a nightmare." Maureen let her voice trail off. "Telling the story still makes me sad and afraid."

Maureen, with tears on her cheeks, said to Martin. "I think I can say it now."

Martin nodded. He wanted to comfort her. "I'm sorry," he said.

Nancy looked confused. She said rather stiffly, "So long ago. How does this all still matter?"

Maureen stood and walked to the porch. Martin said, looking directly at Nancy, "Not to you, but to us. It is why I am sick."

Then Martin glanced down and spoke toward his hands. "Joe died first. He was seventeen and I was sixteen. After Joe died I never again went to the barn. Dad sold his dairy operation. Maureen helped him until it was all settled. My mother died seven years later. I was twenty-three when my mother died. My father died when I was thirty years old. He left the farm to me."

Martin looked up at Nancy but could not really see her more than a colored blur in front of the window. "You and I came to visit my dad several times over the years. After he died I never set foot on the place again. The girls have never seen this house. I've known for a very long time that there was something wrong with me. I just kept on going until I saw that picture in the Milwaukee paper. Then I could not continue with my life. From before Dad's funeral and until I returned, I have never admitted inside of me that Joe is dead."

His voice stopped working. He knew he was crying. He was afraid to see a sneer on Nancy's face so he did not look at her. Then Martin felt Nancy's chin on his head, a gesture she used to do when he was sitting down at his drafting board. The pressure on his head felt familiar and he reached up to pat her hair.

"It is all in the past now," Nancy said. "We have to move forward."

Then Crook's voice drifted down the back stairs to the kitchen. Martin hoped that Crook was in a better mood than he had been earlier in the day. This was not the day for Crook to be silent and brooding and tired. Martin did not have the time or the energy today to wonder what was bothering his friend.

Chapter Seventeen

"Happy Birthday, Christie," Crook said as he stepped from the enclosed stairway and into the kitchen. His eyes sought Christie and found her. He smiled. He carried Kirby on his shoulder. The baby held his head erect while clutching Crook's shirt, and Crook patted Kirby's back in an attempt to keep the tension in the kitchen from making the baby cry.

Martin looked pale but at the same time less sick. Crook paused to study his friend. Yes, he was sad in his heart but more alert in his eyes. He looked Nancy over, who in turn was gaping at him. Her mouth held a sneer, but her eyes held shock. Crook moved his eyes to Maureen who filled the doorway from the porch to the kitchen. With the afternoon light outlining her shape, she looked stunning. Crook felt his heart stop.

He moved to the refrigerator and opened it in search of Kirby's bottle. Two sets of female eyes were boring holes in his back. He wondered if smoke would soon curl away from his shirt. He turned around and as Martin held out his arms Crook handed over the baby while he went to warm the bottle.

He caught Nancy. Her mouth gaped open and her eyes bulged. Crook followed her line of sight right to Martin holding Kirby, tummy down on Martin's knee while jiggling his leg as he always did.

With tremendous effort, grasping the edge of the counter, Nancy croaked, "Where did that baby come from?"

Crook saw Martin look up but he knew Martin did not see Nancy, did not see her knees shaking. Crook hesitated, wondering if he should answer and with what words when Martin said, "This is Kirby. I told you about him. He came home from the bin the same day as Crook."

Maureen, who had not moved from the doorway, now walked slowly, stiffly, around the table. She lifted Kirby from Martin's knee. She came near Crook and took the bottle from the microwave. She felt the outside of Kirby's diaper and wrapped tighter his blanket, then she removed the baby from the kitchen.

After a full minute of watching Nancy gulp air and Martin look at his hands, Crook said, "We need plates and napkins for the party."

"When I have my birthday," Crook told Martin, "I want fifty candles."

Martin looked tired.

"Are we on the porch for cake?" Crook asked, glancing at Nancy who looked at him but did not answer. This kind of behavior was fine with Crook. He was completely comfortable. When Maureen answered from the porch, however, there was no more comfort. She was beautiful and whole and healthy.

Martin said that he would find the girls. Crook heard laughter from what sounded like the ceiling. The place echoed. Nancy walked very carefully onto the porch without carrying a single thing with her, not the juice, not the glasses, nothing.

Crook first carried Kirby's seat to the porch so Maureen had a place for Kirby. Then the two of them opened the tables and laid out paper Barbie table clothes and napkins. Crook handed Nancy a bag of balloons and gestured for her to blow them up.

Martin carried out the sheet cake with dancing Barbie Dolls and supervised Christie as she punched the candles through the frosting. Carmen tried to help her mother blow up balloons.

Crook heard Martin say to his sister, "No one would accuse Crook of being handsome, but he is cool all the same. Don't you think so?"

He saw Maureen blush and laugh. She did not glance at him. He could not think about a woman, not now. But the thought of Maureen lingered all the same.

Maureen said to Martin, "You should introduce me since we are both in your house."

Martin said, "This is Crook. Crook say hello to my sister, Maureen."

"Hello," Crook said.

"I saw you every time I visited Martin," Maureen said. "I did not know for sure that you were the person Martin talked about."

"I am that person," Crook said. He could not control his stare. For Christ's sake what was wrong with him?

He knew himself to be lean and lithe. He practiced a type of over-bearing confidence, complete control. He felt his control slip a fraction as he looked into those round, green eyes. Not happening, he thought.

Martin said, "We called Crook Steve McQueen in *Great Escape*."

Maureen said, "Martin, stop it." Then she looked at Crook and said. "Martin can't help himself. He is always trying to fix me up. He thinks it is my place in life to be married."

Crook allowed himself to feel good about that. Maureen was not married.

A few minutes later everything was nearly ready. Christie held the cake knife and Carmen the ice cream scoop. Maureen happened to stand shoulder to shoulder with Crook at the long edge of the table.

Maureen said quietly to Crook, "I did not trust you because Martin seemed so dependent upon you. I heard your name a hundred times every time I visited."

Maureen paused for several seconds before adding, "I suppose I have you to thank for Martin's vast improvement."

Crook understood that Maureen was hurt by this. He said, "It is too hard for family. Family is not mean enough."

Crook saw a brief look of surprise hit and leave her eyes. He said with intensity, "Just because I enjoy visitor day and flit around do not mistake me for a nice person. Flip the coin and I am a mean son-of-a-bitch."

Maureen's eyes widened. Then for the first time in his memory, an actual surprise happened; Maureen laughed. The sound sparkled and tinkled around him like crystal.

"Was I funny?" he asked.

"Yes," she said.

To cover the new feeling of confusion, Crook picked Kirby up from his seat and showed him the cake, talking to him easily and naturally. He could not allow anything more in his life, especially not now.

Nancy sat in the chair by the window facing Crook. She appeared to consider him a four-eyed monster. This was water off a duck's back to Crook. He did think that Martin should show more respect to the mother of his children, at least in regards to some plausible explanation of a new sibling. However he did not tell Martin this opinion. Martin would do as he had to do.

"How does it feel to be out?" Nancy asked Crook.

"I like it," Crook answered. "The main difference so far is that Martin is the only other nut I see. We have not been off the farm much. Bill and I go fishing on Saturdays." Crook's voice was calm with an odd, quiet cadence that he assumed when speaking with unknown parties or authority figures.

"At least you can walk around outside, look at the trees changing color," Nancy said. Crook, who generally spotted phony, was unsure of Nancy. He thought perhaps his equilibrium was off-kilter. He decided to treat her as a visitor.

"Strange thing about that, now that I can walk outside whenever I want, I don't want to except at the same time of day that we always were allowed outside. Just two days ago I took Martin's watch and timed myself. I had to make myself stay outside five minutes longer than our allotted time at the bin. I'm a creature of habit now." His face parted in his huge smile.

"I never believed you were real," Nancy said.

"You never came to the hospital," Crook answered.

The words burst from her. "Tell us about Kirby," she demanded. "He did not just come home from the bin." She looked at the baby in Crook's arms as though neither Crook nor the baby belonged on this porch or on this earth. Kirby yawned and smacked and stretched turning his strong, little body in Crook's arm.

Crook had a more realistic understanding of Nancy's position than Martin did or likely than Nancy realized. He started to answer something of no meaning when Martin answered. Nancy obviously did not understand that Martin was better. Every time Martin spoke it seemed to take her by surprise.

Martin said, "It doesn't matter, Nancy. Not to you. He is my son. You have to accept that and move on." Martin sat on a wicker chair near the kitchen door and held Carmen on his knee.

Crook, like Martin and Bill, would protect Sandra's secret no matter what that meant. They had been there, witnessing the price she paid. Kirby had not been born alone. Along with Kirby was born a loyalty to him and to his mother that no one would speak of, least of all Crook.

"Where did he come from?" Nancy persisted with passion.

Without moving, without standing, Martin looked steady at his ex-wife. Crook felt his pulse quicken. He had never known a well Martin, and he did not know this man of steel, who said, "His mother died in labor, and I claimed him as his father."

Crook held Kirby against his shoulder and stepped slightly to allow a clear line of site between Nancy and Martin. He rooted for Martin and could not show it. Martin was fragile in his recovery, and Crook understood his influence. Any gesture from him and Martin would stop talking. Softly on his heels, he rocked Kirby.

Crook thought he would drop the subject if he was Nancy. But the woman did not drop it. The children hid their faces.

Nancy said, "I could have blood test run to disprove you are the father." A flush climbed up Nancy's neck and across her face. It looked hot and painful.

Martin said, "Do you as please." He said it so calmly and with such poise that Nancy had no choice but to back off.

"Please, mommy, stop fighting," Christie said.

"I wasn't fighting." But she sat back and calmed herself.

Crook moved to sit by Maureen. He laid Kirby in his seat and watched as Carmen tried to put Kirby's fingers around a rattle. Maureen was staring at her brother, and she was smiling. Suddenly she jumped up from her seat. "The presents," she said. She left the porch followed by the girls. For a minute it was silent on the pastel-painted porch. Crook watched Kirby.

The birthday party was held with balloons and party favors and presents. This particular group of adults was likely never to be gathered again, but for this one time and for this little girl, they would be together. Christie opened her presents, and Carmen opened some presents as well.

Christie opened the present from Crook last. "Thank you very much, Mr. Crook," she told him as she held onto the chess piece. This piece was a Queen, the last Queen that Crook carved.

"It's for a game," Crook told her. "For chess."

"Where is the rest of it?" Christie asked.

"It will come, eventually," Crook told her.

It was after 4:00 pm, and six hours of driving lay between Martin's place in South Dakota and Maureen's apartment in St. Paul. Crook did not go outside with Martin and his guests. He watched from the porch window as everyone settled into their places. A genuine stab of pity cut his chest as he watched Christie clutch her daddy. The child did not cry. Martin likely promised to see her soon, for Christmas, for T-ball. Her dad was much, much better.

Chapter Eighteen

Martin knew that Nancy did not believe it when she said to Martin, "Well, maybe you will come out of this a better person."

"I want the girls to live here," Martin told her.

"Not a chance," Nancy answered.

"Summers," Martin responded. "I would never miss a T-ball game again."

"Deal," Nancy said. "I like to travel in the summer."

"I hope we are not interrupting something here," Maureen's voice caught them both off-guard.

"We're finished," Nancy answered and rolled up the window.

Maureen approached her brother. She reached around him and gave him a tight hug with all her strength.

"I hope you find a husband," Martin told her while he patted her back.

Maureen laughed, "I grew up with standards that ordinary mortals cannot possibly meet."

"In that case you have to go with something completely different so they can't be compared." Martin smiled at her.

Nancy again rolled down the window and added, "I think Crook is incomparable."

Maureen bent to snap Carmen into her seat. She was laughing with her head high and hair lightly blowing across her face.

Martin considered this a successful past social event considering he had nothing to compare it too. He felt good, happy. He stood in front of the porch and watched as Maureen pulled her car into the grass to allow Bill's pick-up room to pass. Even from this distance he felt alarm in Bill's expression. He felt urgency in the way Bill drove without stopping to chat with Maureen.

Bill exited the pick-up hollering for Martin and shut the door with a hard shove. The color of Bill's skin was pale green.

"What!" Martin asked, his face stiff, almost frozen. Bill strode past Martin and onto the porch. Martin shut the door behind them, his heart thundering between his shoulders.

"Crook," Bill continued to yell, pacing back and forth. Crook ran onto the porch from the kitchen. He had been clearing away party leftovers and looked distracted as he returned to the porch. Kirby slept in his seat by the kitchen door.

"Jesus, man," he said. "What is the problem?"

Bill reached for a cigarette from a pack he bought an hour ago. Martin was too stiff to move or talk. He watched Bill with barely a breath. The men sat, Bill and Crook on the wicker chairs and Martin on a kitchen chair. They sat in a circle with Kirby in his seat at Crook's feet. They were three owls in a tree.

Finally Bill rubbed his face. "I don't know how to tell you this."

"Not Sandra." Martin barely forced the words through stiff lips. Has Hauk hurt her?

"No," Bill jerked his head up. He inhaled. "Somebody murdered Hauk. Now we have a mess!"

Crook leaned back and Martin came forward. "Who?" they asked almost simultaneously.

"Do I look like a mystic?" Bill's anxiety put a biting sound in his voice.

"It would seem to me that this loss is a betterment for the world at large," Crook said in his calm manner, resting against the back of the chair.

"However that may be," Bill answered, picking up on Crook's calm demeanor, "somebody is going to pay for this improvement. I hope the whole thing is cut and dried and none of Hauk's escapades get brought into the picture. How likely is that?"

"What exactly do you think might happen, Bill?" Martin fought the darkness by speaking deliberately.

"A big deal investigation," Bill answered with more passion in his voice than he intended. "They'll dig up what Hauk was doing in order to find motives. Likely, they will find Sandra."

"No way," Crook answered. "Only the four of us know about Sandra. They can't trace her to Kirby, to pregnancy, to rape, to Hauk. There is no trail. What would bring Sandra to mind at all?" He sounded like he had given this some thought.

"Nothing," Martin's hands shook, "unless she did it."

"No, no, no," Bill shook his head. "Sandra's disappearance was the last case Hauk worked on. That's why they'll talk to her. If she sticks to her story, she'll be fine. But she might get scared."

"If they ask her about her disappearance, she doesn't have to answer. That case is closed." Crook looked and sounded like the old Crook Martin knew so well. He showed neither worry nor fear.

Bill said, "Hauk was a big man, nearly three hundred pounds. He wasn't tall, like Martin, but he was huge and strong like a bull. He had a thick neck. Who could kill him? I mean who would dare?"

Martin said, "Perhaps someone he was extorting. I couldn't be his only intended victim." Instantly Martin froze and closed his mouth. He didn't mean to say that. Bill and Crook gaped at him. He closed his eyes.

"You better tell us, Martin." Bill said. "Damn," he said under his breath.

Crook said nothing. When Martin opened his eyes Crook was looking at him with hardness in his eyes and around his mouth.

Martin told them about the visit. He told them that he expected Hauk or Carl on the first of October to collect but that he wasn't paying them anything.

"Who is Carl?" Crook said.

"Dumb ass deputy," Bill answered. He put his head down toward his knees.

Crook looked carefully at Martin. Then he asked slowly, "Did they act as though this was a routine type of visit for them, practiced?"

"Yes," Martin said. "I'm not their first trip around the block."

"This is good news and bad news," Crook said. "On the good side, the cops will find more motives than they expect. On the bad side, Martin is the new guy. He is the one that changed the equation."

"I didn't kill Hauk," Martin said.

"I know you did not kill Hauk. It only matters what the cops think," Crook said. Then almost to himself but Martin heard him, Crook said, "Maybe the bastard did not keep book."

Bill looked stunned by this turn of the conversation. He said, "Carl would know about his side money. But it doesn't matter as far as Martin is concerned. Martin was with me last night getting stuff for his party.

"Would Carl dare tell if he was also involved?" Crook said.

"How was he murdered?" Martin asked. Specifically he wanted to know if a knife was used. "When?"

Bill told what he knew. "According to Tillie's cousin, a patrolman in Minnehaha County, Hauk was found dead in his home early Saturday morning. That would be this morning. The patrolman told Tillie that Hauk was stabbed in the back of his neck, though the rumor factory had many causes of death and many suspects. Not a single person who actually saw or heard a thing."

Martin felt his heart stop. He could not draw a breath. For the first time in days, he used his hands to push away the darkness. Hauk had been stabbed.

Neither Bill nor Crook moved. They knew to wait. It was not such a deep darkness as sometimes and it dissolved through Martin's swimming fingers. After a few minutes Martin said, "I hope it will be resolved in a matter of days. It might not involve us at all."

Bill said, "No matter who did it, we are involved."

Crook said, "The best we can hope for is that the case goes unsolved."

"I don't want to know," Martin said.

"Sorry, Martin," Bill said. "It doesn't work to pretend things didn't happen."

Martin looked at Crook. He said, "Is Sandra safe?"

When Crook did not answer, a chill ran from Martin's neck to his toes. He could not speak.

Finally Crook said, "Who found him?"

Bill told them about Carl, the Deputy. "Carl found the body in Hauk's house early this morning, and he went bonkers. He can't stop talking about it. He goes from the pub to the gas station to the court house. He insists he is the primary investigator. He is like a rooster with his head cut off."

All three of them laughed at the little Barney Fife. Relief rose in Martin's heart as he thought of Carl investigating. That is until Crook said, "A fool is dangerous. He doesn't need evidence to persecute."

Bill said, "Two detectives from Pierre will be in Wheaton tomorrow. Hauk, after all, was a County Sheriff."

A tight, consuming fear fell upon the small circle. For several minutes, each man considered things in his own way.

At last Crook said, "They may never figure it out." Then Crook rubbed his forehead in a visible gesture of worry. No one ever saw a visible gesture of worry from Crook. This single movement frightened Martin more than anything.

Martin abruptly stood. "We need to get a TV so we can watch the news."

Chapter Nineteen

Martin lay in the early morning darkness. Hauk was murdered on Friday night. Martin hosted Christie's birthday party on Saturday. Today was early Sunday morning. Carl would likely start the process for removing Kirby from Martin on Monday. Carl told him a week ago after church in the pub that if anything happened to Hauk, he would make absolutely, positively sure that Martin lost Kirby the next business day. Those were Carl's words and why would Carl lie?

The sun rose bright in a clear sky. It edged its way over the horizon and through the trees and into Martin's east window. Martin considered that Carl was pre-occupied today with a murder to solve. But he knew regardless of how busy Carl was on the outside, on the inside he was thinking about him and about Kirby. Carl would be happy to hurt him in revenge for Hauk whether Martin had anything to do with Hauk's death or not. That was the way of the sane world.

Martin slept in the front corner bedroom that had four windows, two sets of two. It was the same room Sandra chose earlier because there was a bed in it. Martin chose this room because he enjoyed the sunrise, and he did not want to have windows facing the barn.

Martin considered that the house was a devil to shingle. He thought, No more rain drops plopping on the hallway floor. But today it did not work to think about the house. For some reason he could not escape his worry by focusing on his work: not on this morning.

He looked out of the window at the sky and the gold, rust leaves. For an hour he sat on the side of his bed. He knew it was time to face the barn. He would not be able to do his work until he was whole. He would not survive the coming storm unless he fixed himself. The young man on the bus told him "murder and mayhem." Was the kid psychic? Had he known? Martin wondered about the kid dealing cards at a casino in Spearfish. Someday, Martin thought, he would tell him that it was mayhem and murder. The mayhem did come first.

He loved Kirby. Kirby came from chaos and was good and clean and new. Martin sighed. First he watched the light creep into his room until he could distinguish his shoes and then the lines of the hardwood floor beneath them. Nothing, yet, had been done to the inside of this room except to throw out and burn the old mattress and store the cast iron bed frame.

The only furniture in the room was the new bed on which he sat. His gym bag stood along the inside wall by the closet door. Crook folded Martin's clean clothes and stacked them into the gym bag. The hundreds of hangers that once filled the rod in the closet had vanished; only one hanger in the closet now. That hanger held his coat. The closet door was shut and his door to the hall was shut.

Most days, after Martin was up and dressed, Crook came into the room, re-made his bed, swept the floor and ran a damp cloth over the twelve inch woodwork. Martin studied the woodwork. He thought the fine wood could be saved if he wanted to contribute that kind of effort to an upstairs. His work would not hold his thoughts. He had no escape.

He did not move. He moved his gaze to the lawn. Through the windows the lawn was visible, sadly overgrown. He would ask Bill to make a few rounds with his tractor mower. That would at least make it easier to clear in the spring.

No curtains hung on his bedroom windows, or shades. The sun became warm on his head. Salvaging this old house, what was it for, what did it matter?

He knew the time had come, but he did not want to know. It was not enough to understand what he had to do at some point in the day. It was not so easy to *just do it.*

He considered Carmen and Christie; reason enough. He saw Christie's tears on her small, serious face. He thought of Sandra. He visualized her fierce, cold eyes and her tall, strong body. His heart hurt for her. For several minutes his thoughts lingered on the young woman who bonded them, who gravitated them all. He felt the touch of her hand and heard the sound of her voice. A knife like pain stabbed into his chest and he shuddered. Had Sandra killed Hauk?

Maureen entered his thoughts and he smiled. His sister was the closest to unconditional love that he knew to exist. When he called, she came without question. Did he want to never be able to return in kind her consistent, loving presence? He found he wanted to, yes, he did, merciful God, want to respond to his sister if she called upon him. He looked again to the window, to the sky, and felt the sting of tears on his dry lips.

What about Crook? What would happen to Crook? He could not allow for Crook to face the consequences of all their actions without him. He would be no help to anyone until he faced the barn. If he turned back now he would never reach this point again. Very slowly and with stiff joints, he stood.

He thought of Joseph and his heart hurt, but he smiled. So funny, always fun. Everyone wanted to be around Joe. One time long ago Joe built a real gong by hanging a tractor rim on a homemade hangman's tower he had welded together. He hit it with a sledge hammer and the noise reverberated for a mile. When Mom ran onto the porch, her face white, Joe bent double with laughter.

The gong lasted nearly a month before Dad had enough. One day after school it was gone. So many things, so much riches inside of him, such quick wit and then one day Joseph was gone.

It was Crook's morning to care for Kirby. Right now, Crook was reading the newspaper to the baby, inserting editorial comments and eliciting gurgles. Martin recalled how Kirby rolled over a few days ago and Crook's astonishment at this never seen before feat of agility.

Martin began to move about, preparing. He grew up in a religious household, and religion stayed with him always. He knelt by the south window and closed his eyes, bringing his knuckles to his mouth. "Help me, Jesus Christ, to get through this," he prayed over and over for several minutes. Then he mumbled every childhood prayer he could remember. At last, he stood and strode to the door.

He wondered again how Sandra was involved. Who drove? Crook couldn't drive. Crook said she could not have done it, nor did Bill think she could do it. But Martin remembered her face as she told about Hauk. He remembered vividly the hard lines of her mouth and eyes as they passed the warm soda back and forth. If Sandra helped to kill Hauk, she would need him to understand.

Martin dressed for the occasion. He showered and shaved. When he emerged from the bathroom, his new growth of beard was gone. Carefully, he parted his hair down the middle and combed it back behind his ears. Martin frowned at his image. He could not face Joe with his hair like that. He found a headband in his TWINS bag. The headband crossed his forehead and looked athletic. That worked.

He dressed in the tan pants and the Docker's shirt. Tennis shoes were okay. He was almost ready. He opened the closet door with a hard yank. The door had a tendency to stick. He wanted to wear the coat. Martin hung the coat, home from the cleaners, wrapped in cellophane, and hanging crisp on a hanger. He knew the exact spot he hung it. Only the coat was not there. He looked at the empty spot on the closet rod and breathed deeply, in and out several times.

This was no time for adversity. He waved it off. He would have to go without the coat. Better anyway to face the battle without amour, to face Joe as he had been twenty-five years ago.

When Martin crossed through the kitchen, Crook's mouth opened and closed without any sound like a fish in water. Martin did not dare to waiver. So he did not stop. He observed the surprise and a little fear on Crook's face and strode on. He did not even stop to say "hello" to Kirby.

Martin noticed the Sunday newspaper adds all over the table. He checked for his coat spread out on the floor under Kirby. Not there. No time to waiver. Opened the kitchen door, he crossed the porch, down the steps and down the path between the weeds to the barn. He did not stop at the pump.

Immediately inside the barn Martin stopped dead still. It was pitch dark until his eyes adjusted. His heart pounded so hard that nothing else worked, almost nothing else existed but his racing heart and his paralyzing fear.

With stiff legs, he moved to the vertical wood slabs nailed to the 2x4's and crossed with narrow wood pieces to form a ladder rising into the hayloft. Like monkeys, he and Joe and Maureen climbed that ladder countless times. As Martin ascended the steps, he felt the past coming upon him. He smelled it in the scent of the wood. He felt the feelings he used to know. He recalled the well-being and vitality and happiness that defined him twenty-five years ago.

The hayloft floor slanted and was no longer safe for a man's weight. To his right some hay, moldy and decaying, rose in mounds along both walls by the hayloft door. To his left the empty space around the basketball hoop was filled with dust swirling in the shafts of light.

Always, Joe swept this space clean with patience and care. Now the rust-orange hoop nailed to the north wall leaned forward. The whole wall leaned dangerously forward. Martin could not imagine what kept it from falling in on itself. A good third of the roof was gone from the long side facing west. Still, enough remained to be The Place and Martin saw it as it was twenty-five years ago.

Staring at the hoop, breathing in the smell of damp hay and cattle and barn, Martin talked out loud but he talked to himself.

It rained so hard the noise on the roof was a constant roar, so constant that we no longer noticed it. And Joe. Joe the Great. If I got an A, Joe got an A+. If I got an A+, Joe got one first. But we played basketball. We were All State players in a state where boy's basketball was an obsession and high school sports fed life into this town.

Joe made All State as a sophomore, unprecedented. The next year, so did I and the town went crazy. Individually we were good. Together we were great. We could not be beaten. We played basketball together every possible minute of every day. We could pass blindfolded.

We lost the championship game of the Class B State Tournament when Joe was a Junior and I was a Sophomore. Remember, Joe, you fouled out with two minutes to go. We were down by two points. I had a chance to pass for a good shot to tie it. But I couldn't see the new kid, I couldn't find his hands. I threw it away. Threw the ball to no one! Remember that, Joe?

"Next year," the coach told us.

"Next year," Dad said.

"You did fine," Mom said with tears still on her eyelashes.

Only there wasn't a next year for Joe. Where was Joe? Joe was dead.

Martin still stood motionless by the entry point of the ladder, literally frozen in time. His fingers became fists. He remembered the plays, he remembered the missed shots. He remembered the shots that fell, that got the roll. He remembered the rebounds in Joe's soft

152

hands, and the bounce pass blind to where Joes's hands would be. Even now, even in his torment, it gave Martin pleasure to remember how they played basketball.

Martin's head began to pound, his face, his neck, his arms became rigid with determination. *It rained that day. We were playing basketball. HORSE. I never won at HORSE against Joe. But on this day, with rain enclosing us in a place distant from all reality, it was important, urgent, more important than anything to finally beat Joe.*

"I am going to beat you, Joe. Yes, yes, yes, I am. Make that. Don't laugh. Make that. Is that so funny? You think I can't beat you?"

With the rain, the mold and the damp in the hayloft, I had to wipe snot from my face with the back of my hand. The memory filled Martin's sinuses as he stood ramrod straight, stiff, staring at the crooked, lopsided, rusty orange basketball hoop with the net reduced to gray threads along the rim.

The ball did not bounce well in the damp. That was why we played HORSE. Just one game, then we would finish the chores. A game of HORSE could take a long time when we really tried. On this day, we tried hard, focused, intent, and competitive beyond reason.

I had the "S." I won't miss. I will not get the damn "E." How did you make that? How did you do that? Did you cheat? I don't know how you could cheat! I can do it. I can do it if you can. Yes! Did you see that, Joe? Did you see that?

Martin's voice rose, "Why should I have to shoot left handed just because you did? Why should I? It is from the spot, it can be any hand. I am NOT scared. What is so funny? So what if my face is red and I have snot on my lip? What is so damn funny?"

Why on that day did it matter so much? Hundreds of days, thousands of hours, it was always fun. Joe was supposed to win. He was the center. I was a guard. Why on that particular rain soaked day did it matter so much?

The tears stung Martin's sensitive cheeks, his nose ran, and on his forehead, the sweat band dripped. Through his raw throat, he mumbled again, "Why?" His head dropped to his chest. It was as it was. At that particular moment his body, mind, and heart were consumed with one thing. He would finally beat Joe at one game of HORSE.

All the hot summer drought made the grass brown in July, and we did not need to mow. Hot, dry and dusty until that day in August when the sky split open and rain poured out all day long. Joe with his long, handsome face, straight hair in his eyes, standing under the hoop, the rebound off the rim in his long fingers, walked away.

I ran over, crazy with anger and shame, to push you with all my strength. But you said, "Next time you'll get me. You are getting that good."

You said those words and I stopped. I stopped right here. The floor was damp. It was damp and slippery by the hole and you sang, "But not yet, but not yet," and danced, your stupid version of a moonwalk. You slipped and disappeared down that hole.

You stumbled and you fell through the hole in the floor. We knew that hole was there. We pitched hay down that hole into the cattle-stanchions below every day of our lives. We knew that hole. We played around that hole and stepped around that hole in the floor everyday. Why did you fall through that hole? Did I push you?

"Come on, Joe, are you too tough to yell? Did you break a finger on your left shooting hand? Come on, Joe, why aren't you yelling? Oh, my God!"

Martin screamed. He did not climb down the ladder, he jumped. He ran for the house. He ran for help. He ran up and down the driveway, soaking wet, screaming for the ambulance. And then he forgot.

Until this very moment, he did not remember what he saw when he looked down that hole in the hay-mound floor. The memory brought him to his knees.

Martin leaned like a rag doll on the far, sloping wall of the hay-mound. He wished for his coat because chills shook his shoulders. Sobs sliced his throat. He wished he had not forced this memory. He wished he had allowed the darkness.

"Joe," Martin's voice raw and whispering, "Dad told you to put that pitch fork away. Dad told you to put it away. Why didn't you? How many times did Dad have to tell you to put that damn pitchfork away?"

Suddenly Martin felt warmth on his shoulders as Crook laid a blanket across him, and he heard Crook's voice. "That is enough for today, man," Crook said. "You are one brave crazy. Come back to the house now."

"Have you seen my coat?" Martin asked as he followed Crook down the ladder.

"Yes," Crook said.

The two men leaned on the pump jack. "It wasn't as bad as I feared," Martin told Crook, his voice still raw.

"You have to be kidding," Crook answered. "I've never seen anything worse, and I've seen a lot."

The two men stood, leaning their weight against the pump, breathing quietly and looking toward the pasture to the west, recovering. Crook leaned so as not to bump the baby he carried in a sling.

Kirby looked at Martin with big eyes from the pouch that Tillie brought over. The pouch was too tight to fit Martin, but it fit Crook perfectly. Crook had the habit of carrying Kirby around with him all day long.

Martin said, "Kirby will never learn to crawl if his legs are bunched in that pouch all day." He reached to lift Kirby. His arms felt weak and trembling, but he lifted Kirby all the same. The three of them started for the house. Martin felt the sun hot through the blanket, and it felt good.

"I tell you, Crook," Martin spoke over his shoulder, "It is not as bad as I expected, or I should say feared. I thought I killed my brother on purpose. I did want to push him, but he danced away. We played with such passion. The game was everything."

Martin had never known such pain as though it happened yesterday.

"It looked bad to me," Crook answered, following the path in Martin's footsteps.

"You could see it," Martin asked, amazed.

"Not it, but I could see you," Crook said.

"I did not push him. I would rather be dead myself and that is the truth. I did not push Joe. I planned to push Joe, but I did not. I didn't mean to hurt him," Martin repeated filled with wonder at the strange relief, light-headed relief that mixed inside with grief like mixing paint colors. He wondered if his legs would work for the remaining steps to the house.

Martin continued to talk. He stopped and turned and talked. For several minutes he talked about Joe, but knew he could not convey the person of Joe or the meaning of Joe. Still, he told what he could, told what happened, told about basketball. He tasted salt on his lips.

Crook did not interfere and he did not say a word. When, at last, they reached the house and Martin was quiet, Crook mumbled, "First the man wouldn't talk, and then he wouldn't quit." He smiled.

 Once inside the kitchen, Martin put Kirby on the floor.

"Floor's cold," Crook said. He moved Kirby to the blanket. "It takes him twelve minutes to wiggle off it."

"I know at noon it is my day to watch Kirby, but I can't today," Martin said. Then, as usual, he took the back stairs up to the hallway. He lay on his bed and went immediately to sleep.

Not until the light was softly fading from Martin's bedroom did the sound of Crook's pounding on his door bring consciousness. Martin felt tired and wobbly. He thought he should eat. Finally he answered the insistent sound at his door.

"What?" he said, but could not muster real strength to his voice.

"Time to eat," Crook said through the wood, "and we have company."

Chapter Twenty

Martin heard the voices in the kitchen as he descended the stairs slowly and carefully. He heard Tillie's laugh and Bill's quiet voice. Sandra, too! Maureen's voice drifted up the stairs and Martin was happy to hear his sister. He could tell her about Joe. Crook's voice did not carry and he was not one to talk much. Kirby rarely cried, but of course, he was in the kitchen, too.

Martin grieved for Joe. As he stood at the door, his hand on the knob, he tried to smile and could not. He opened the door and everyone stopped talking or moving. Maureen came first and hugged him. "I'm sorry you had to see what happened to Joe," she whispered. Martin's throat tightened and tears slid down his cheeks.

He looked up and saw that Crook and Kirby had decorated. They had balloons along the walls and fresh flowers from town.

Martin said, "Crook loves Visitor Day."

"We all helped," Maureen said. "I thought it was too much for what is actually for you a wake. But everyone else thought it was a great victory for you and we should celebrate that. What do you think?"

"I think I am happy to see you," Martin said. He raised his voice and repeated, "Thank you, thank you for coming."

Martin moved to the chair of honor and sat down. Not surprised by the electric energy in Crook as he motioned to the chair, Martin said, "A visitor for you this time, Crook."

"First time," Crook answered.

Martin nodded. Saying more would not be appreciated by Crook who busied himself lining cookies in a perfect row on white paper on the table. Crook was not a talker. He was a listener. Martin saw him turn now to listen to Sandra. Martin said to Sandra, "Please take Kirby out of that pouch." She did not lift Kirby so Tillie handed the little boy to Martin.

Martin thought Sandra favored her right arm. He would ask her about it later. Then Martin saw a look pass between Sandra and Crook. The expression on Sandra's face startled him. She looked triumphant. Martin thought, What have they done? They murdered Hauk.

He did not know if that solved a problem or started a new, equally terrifying one. He would have to prepare for Carl.

Crook did not have a split personality, but he did have compartments. When he needed to use one compartment or the other, he opened that door and stepped in. Still, one thing ran the width and length of his personality, and that was a magnetic presence. Tonight his small, agile frame vibrated with life and good will. Killing Hauk did not change that.

Martin sat, smiling and nodding. He had no appetite but took a coffee. Bill pulled up a chair beside him. Bill watched Crook with confusion in his eyes. Finally, without looking at Martin but keeping his eyes forward, Bill said quietly, "I must be wrong."

Understanding what Bill meant, Martin said, "I think you are not wrong. I think he did it. You will never see it in him."

"What is his story?" Bill asked.

"Don't know," Martin said. "He is whatever he has to be. He is bald as an egg and vain in his clothes. His mouth changes shapes and we want him as a friend. He can look like a garden gnome or a cold-blooded killer, whatever the day requires."

Right now the day required beer on ice. Everyone held a beverage. The smell of Tillie's rooster full of chicken began to waft through the room. The six adults pulled up chairs in a loose circle and looked at one another. It was not exactly carefree. Martin saw that murder weighed them down.

He said, "Maureen have you been introduced to Sandra?"

"Hello," Sandra said, trying a smile.

Martin felt a quick, thick tension. He saw the question in Maureen's eyes. She would not say, "Who is this girl in her jeans and sweatshirt?" But Martin felt the question as if she had spoken aloud.

Martin said, "We have secrets from the hospital that you do not want to know. She plays basketball and I help her with that. She is a part of our," he paused, not wanting to say the word 'revenge.' He said, "Group."

"How have you been?" Martin turned to Sandra and when he did she was immediately his total focus. When Martin and Sandra talked together, no one else existed and much of what they said was without words. Sandra looked wonderful. Her hair pulled back from her face in a ponytail which highlighted her strong features and deep brown eyes and flawless skin.

The strain of her past year showed in the lines around her mouth and under her eyes. He also saw relief, a release from a burden. Hauk was dead. Was she beginning to see that Hauk's death would not turn back time? He took her hand and held it loosely. How guilty was she? She did not look to have guilt in her heart. "How did you hurt your arm?" Martin said.

"I'm fine," she answered, "but the question of the day is how YOU are?" She reached to touch his face, feeling with her fingertips. She smiled at him, her eyes wet. She whispered, "You are the man, Martin."

The late September air held a chill and Crook closed the porch door to stop the draft from reaching Kirby. Martin again looked about at his friends. They had no weak link. They would hold together. Martin again turned to his sister. He felt irresistibly drawn to her company. "I did not push Joe," he said.

Maureen smiled. She had recovered or she covered her confusion regarding a teenager holding Martin's hand. She said, "I can not tell you how relieved I am to know that. I was never sure."

Maureen wore jeans and a white blouse tucked inside her jeans and a gold link belt. Her shoulders, neck and head were straight and graceful, her hair curled around her pale freckled cheeks. When she smiled at Martin, he saw her as lovely. Stunning. He said, "I am so sorry."

"Everyone loved Joe, Martin, but you were connected to him in a way no one else could ever touch. I am so sorry." She put her hands to her face. The room was silent.

Martin said, "Wearing out the tires on your car?"

"I am on vacation, much deserved," she smiled at his light tease. "I'm staying with Tillie for a few days. I just couldn't resist coming back to see you guys, and the house, too."

"Good," Martin answered. He felt his face loosen. His skin did not feel like a mask.

"Gang's all here," Crook announced. "Let's eat."

Bill raised his glass, and everyone stood. "A toast to Martin. Today Martin went to the barn."

Everyone cheered, each person hugged him, and Sandra kept his hand in hers. Martin saw the set of Maureen's chin in a disapproving line. He couldn't help that Maureen disapproved. Maureen didn't know. He thought Tillie should prepare for Maureen's questions. It would be okay. Tillie could tell Maureen about Sandra, about Hauk and about Kirby. Maureen should know. He looked at Sandra. It was her secret and, yet, Maureen should know.

He said to Sandra, "We will need Maureen to help."

Sandra looked confused. "Help with what?"

"You and Crook cannot carry this alone. It is not just you. You cannot just keep on keeping on."

Sandra looked shocked and bewildered. She said with agitation, "I am keeping on just fine."

"You think you are," Martin said. "Later Tillie can explain to Maureen about Hauk and what he did so that she knows what is at stake. But only if you agree."

"When the whole f'n world knows, I can just shoot myself," Sandra said. Again the room was so intensely silent that Sandra's voice almost echoed.

Martin said quietly, "Only the people in this room will know the whole story. There is no weak link."

"No one can ever know the whole story," Sandra said, her face so hard she looked like stone. Martin had no answer for that. It was true.

The woman and the girl stared at each other for some seconds in a hushed room. Then Maureen extended her hand and Sandra took it. "I will get the scoop from Tillie," she whispered. "Let's not talk any more right now."

162

Bill said into the silence, "Our problems should be solved but they don't feel solved. I, for one, am scared. However, what is the old saying, 'Eat, drink and be merry for tomorrow we may die.' And I'm hungry."

When everyone gaped at him, he added, "I'm happy for Martin's improved condition and Crook's new social life but I'm worried now what the price tag is gonna be, that's all. Stop looking at me."

Indulging in his renewed habit of smoking, Bill leaned toward the open window above the sink. He sat the chair legs down hard onto the floor.

Crook set his chair by Maureen. Kirby moved to Crook's lap and then moved to different laps and finally to his seat with a bottle. Tillie sat beside Bill and Martin and Sandra sat along the windows. When the words came, they would talk. When no words came, being together was enough.

"Well, Martin," Tillie's voice floated in the circle. "You have been getting mixed reviews in town."

"What is there to say about me?" Martin asked. He considered his arrival as well as Crook and Kirby to be of no great interest or concern to anyone.

"To begin,--" Tillie leaned forward and took upon herself the confidential air of sharing gossip, "--some people are appalled at your behavior in getting somebody pregnant other than your wife, of course. But there is a growing group who can't help but admire your willingness to give up your whole life just to keep the baby. And, trust me, no one could help but be impressed when you walked into church carrying Kirby without the slightest hint of any embarrassment."

"Oh, my gosh!" said Maureen's astounded voice. "You carried Kirby into church! Good for you. How did anyone even pretend not to notice?"

"I had to carry him, he can't walk," Martin answered, picking up and enjoying the nuance and innuendo that even one day ago was beyond his comprehension. However, talking about Kirby put a weight on his heart. Would Carl come to take Kirby? What would he do?

Bill entered the conversation with his story from the poolhall. The general consensus saw little wonder in Martin's condition, what with losing his marriage and his job. They decided it was still better than being addicted to some drug which was the previous diagnosis. And there was some sympathy for Martin in the death of the baby's mother and some admiration in keeping the baby. Sandra again slid her hand into Martin's without a trace of self-consciousness.

"How did you come to name him Kirby Pucket?" Maureen asked.

Martin leaned on his knees, his one hand dangling between his legs and the other lightly holding Missy's fingers. "It just popped out. The radio announcer always says, 'touch 'em all," when one of the *Twins* hit a home run. 'Touch 'em all, Brian Harper' or Touch 'em all, Kent Hrbeck' but the best one is the way he says, 'Touch 'em all, Kirby Pucket!' It has a ring to it."

"Did you hear that, Kirby," Tillie leaned toward the infant in his seat, "you could have been named 'Touch Em All'." She lightly pinched the tiny fingers. "Well, touch them all, Kirby Pucket Webster."

Maureen said, "Martin, I have to tell you how much better you look. I know you are sad, but that soft, puffy edge along your cheeks and chin is gone. You don't look slack any more."

"The sliver is out," Martin said.

Crook said, "It was not easy. That old barn is haunted."

"Yes, it is," Martin agreed. "Tearing it down is officially on the list."

"Tuesday night is our first game," Sandra said.

"Are you ready?" Immediate interest lifted Martin's voice and put a lively spark in his eyes. "How does the team look? I have a great fake for the bucket to teach you.

"I am personally not ready. Everyone thinks I am recovering from a camping accident, you know. I missed the first week of practice. I'm out of shape and behind schedule, but the team looks outstanding. We have a chance at State, I think." Her voice, as always, mesmerized him.

Then he asked what he asked every time he saw her, but this time he understood her answer. "How is school?" he asked. "How are your parents?"

"School is moving along. I'm living on reputation. I actually miss how it used to be with my mom and dad, but Mom especially. They hover and they wait for me to speak."

Martin could see her tough exterior soften slightly when she talked to him. "You have to stop trying to regain your past. It will never be the same," Martin said, his voice near her ear.

"I want my old life back." Sandra said. Everyone looked at her. Like Martin, they all took a drink or a bite and looked away.

After a few minutes, Martin asked her, "Are you going to tell me about Hauk?"

Sandra studied him for what seemed a long time. Then she said, "You know what, Martin? It is harder to tell you secrets now that you are well, or close to well. It was easier when you were lost like me."

"I know," Martin answered.

"I can't tell you," Sandra whispered, putting her hands on her thighs and staring at her fingers. "Except to say that we executed Crook's plan, and it worked perfectly."

"When you are ready, you can tell me," Martin said. "What did Hauk say when you saw him?" Martin asked. He had moved to a different time and Sandra looked confused.

"What?" Sandra's head came up, startled.

"What did Hauk say?" Martin repeated. He studied her. "Didn't Hauk check on you after all that searching for nothing?"

"Oh, then." The relief so obvious she looked like a balloon releasing air. "I wouldn't come out of my room. My dad had to deal with him. He told Hauk I had gone camping by myself and that had to satisfy him. That's the story the paper printed." Shaking her head, she added, "I never thought people would get into such a dither."

Martin shrugged, "You're important. I hoped you would break down and tell your mom the whole story. None of us will ever tell it for you."

"Can't do that to her. It's better if she doesn't know what happened to me." Thoughtfully, Sandra added, "What would she do if she knew she had a grandson? It's one more reason I hate Hauk. He destroyed the closeness I had with my Mom. I hate him for that almost as much as for what he did to me."

"Hauk is dead," Martin said.

"It doesn't change the hate," Sandra said.

Sandra, usually energy wrapped in tight skin, sat passive and thoughtful. "Isn't it odd," she questioned Martin, "that I still want to play basketball. I really wonder about that. I want to play harder and faster and better than ever. I want it more than I did before this happened. Does that make me a monster of some kind?"

"It's the last strand of a previous life and no one can take it from you," he answered.

Martin waited for her to say more about the other secret. The secret she kept from him. The secret she shared with Crook. But she didn't say anything more, and he did not ask. For now, it was enough to know that Sandra was not alone with it. He trusted Crook to handle it.

"Will you be able to play on Tuesday with your hurt arm?" Martin said.

Sandra nodded.

Martin watched Bill grab a piece of pie and a fork and look at his plate with relish. Then he set it down on the table. If Bill couldn't eat they were in serious trouble. Even Crook, who had company of his own for the first time in his adult life, sat motionless.

"Is something wrong with the pie?" Maureen asked.

"Why are we suddenly so glum?" Sandra asked.

Bill answered, "It's this Hauk thing that has me in a big worry. We can't pretend it didn't happen. I can't think about anything else. We could all be in jail by next week."

"Should we just go to the detectives and tell our story? It's the cover-up that always makes it worse." Tillie appeared tentative as she talked.

Crook said, "We hang tough and we hang together."

"For now we are here to celebrate the trip to the barn," Maureen reminded everyone. "Or the removal of the sliver."

"The removal of Hauk," Crook mumbled, but everyone heard.

"The season opener," Sandra said.

"A boyfriend for Maureen, finally," Martin tried to speak in the same tone as the others, but he could not quite pull it off and laughed, glancing at his crimson sister.

Martin glanced at Crook, but he did not appear the least disturbed by the teasing. In fact, there was the slightest glimpse of pleasure in his eyes.

"A girlfriend for Crook would be more reason than anything. Now we have to drive back to Lincoln to tell that receptionist she is out of luck," Bill said, taking a forkful of apple pie.

"She was always after me," Crook said.

"I think it was Clara who was after you, Crook," Martin said.

"Who was Clara? I forgot," Tillie asked her husband.

"You would not want to meet Clara," Martin said.

"Clara was just hideous," Sandra started to tell Tillie. "She had tufts of hair like Harpo Marx, and she delivered Kirby."

Martin looked at his sister who appeared stunned. Her mouth gaped slightly and a white rim circled her eyes. He said to her, speaking quietly, "It is not easy to be a part of this. No one will question it if you want to go home now."

Maureen said, "How did this happen, Martin?"

"I don't know," Martin said. "I found Sandra hiding in the house. That's the beginning for me."

Maureen did not leave. Martin knew her chance to leave would soon be gone. He did not want her to leave, but he would not stop her. He saw her study Kirby. He saw her sit back in her chair and try to focus on the words flowing around them.

"This is not a game. There is danger here," Bill suddenly said, his voice loud, flat and stern. "We all had motive of one kind or another. Hauk would be extorting Martin soon enough if he wasn't already. He would make Crook miserable for the fun of it once he realized Crook was here. He would hurt Sandra again. He even told me last Sunday in the pub that people were wondering how I came to find Sandra. To top it off, I finally have the perfect, silent fishing partner, and I'm going to loose him."

Martin said, "Hauk threatened to take Kirby and now Carl will carry that out."

"Carl wants more than to take Kirby. He wants to hang you for this murder." Bill appeared so genuinely upset that Martin handed him another beer.

168

Silence surrounded them like physical weight. This was life and death and it centered on a young lady not yet eighteen.

Kirby lay on Martin's thigh. His little arms circled Martin's knee half way around, and his ear rested on the denim of Martin's jeans. Martin jigged his knee in a constant slow motion, and Kirby slept.

Absently, Martin checked the clock above the table. It would not be long before Kirby was hungry, and it was his night to keep the baby. Kirby was not as regular in his eating habits as Bill, but close.

A tired Martin drifted from the conversation. He patted Kirby's strong back. Kirby was a night baby, awake and eager to play from one AM until two or three in the morning. This didn't bother Martin who followed no schedule whatsoever. If Kirby wanted to play at one in the morning, Martin played.

Crook on the other hand, required sleep through the night. If Kirby wanted to play, wide-awake, in the dark, fine. Crook fed him, changed him, shut off the light and went to sleep. Sometimes he dozed to the sounds of gurgles and thumping. Kirby did not cry.

It was Kirby who adjusted. When in Crook's room, Kirby slept through the night. When in Martin's room, he heard stories, played finger games and book games and had a party. Now he slept soundly, preparing. Martin smiled, then Martin pulled himself back to the conversation.

Tillie was talking, "Hauk's murder is the only topic of conversation. So, Martin is off the gossip hook, and Sandra. Hauk is all anyone can talk about. So many stories of who did it from mobsters to husbands to angry people he ripped off for extortion money. So much nasty stuff coming out about Hauk now that he is dead."

Tillie told some of the stories circulating that included corruption beyond belief. Hauk engaged in many sordid little side ventures. Tillie's permed, gray-black hair moved with her head when she talked and nodded. Not a single strand had a life of its own.

Bill looked relieved to talk about it. He told about Carl's story of finding the body. Bill heard that Carl told everyone and anyone who would listen, how Hauk's body was stretched out full on the bed, wearing the same clothes he wore all day. No blood on the bed or anywhere in the house as far as Carl could see. There wasn't even any blood on Hauk's shirt. At first Carl didn't realize Hauk was dead. Not until he stepped closer and saw that Hauk wasn't breathing. He had to turn the body to see the wound. Carl went running from the house, screaming, "Cop down, Cop down" into his radio.

Then Bill added, shaking his head, his old gray eyes filmed with worry, "Carl is a fool, but the men in town to investigate the case look to be nobody's fools. The Governor appointed them special to solve this case. Hauk was a County Sheriff, after all." Bill's expression looked older than a day ago; worry clung to him like mist in rain.

"Sandra has to be ready, they will seek her out," Bill added.

All six adults, with chairs in hand, proceeded into the informal dining area off the kitchen and on the same side of the house. The north wall consisted of a brick fireplace long since unused. When the insurance codes changed regarding fireplaces, Martin's father actually bricked it shut. Renovating the fireplace was on the list, but still far down, after lawn and possibly after razing the barn. The old, cracked plaster walls stood the same and the hardwood floor remained the same, swept clean but in desperate need of work.

In this room, sitting on a packing crate and connected through the window to an antenna, stood the new Sony TV. Two bean bag chairs squatted beneath it. All three local channels out of Sioux Falls led off the news with the murder of Sheriff Leroy Benjamin Hauk. Each person watched Carl spill his guts on TV. Each person thought their own thoughts, but no one laughed because each person sensed danger in Carl. Martin voiced it for them all, "Nothing more dangerous than a fool out of control."

And Crook added softly, "But is he a fool?"

Part Two

Chapter Twenty-One

On Sunday afternoon, Detectives Larry Vilhallen and John White of the Governor's Special Task Force assigned to the McCook County Sheriff murder case, drove a new black Ford Escort past the cemetery and the golf course on Highway 38 heading into Wheaton. After turning right onto Highway 81, the men asked directions at the gas station for Center Lane Apartments, their temporary home away from home. The car clock indicated 4:00 pm. A cool evening breeze bent the grass by the swimming pool and a smell of burning leaves hovered in the air.

Vilhallen and White constituted a special unit assigned by the Governor, personally, to solve the murder of the McCook County Sheriff. Vilhallen had sandy hair and wire rim glasses and a widening middle. At the slightest hint of sunshine, his fair skin turned red and painful. He was the older detective and experienced in homicide; he would take the lead.

The thirty-seven-year old White possessed thick, brown hair, cut short, and a long narrow face. It required a second look to notice the intelligence. White's bland appearance was the perfect camouflage for his work. No one saw him or cared about him until too late.

Without difficulty, the detectives found the government-subsidized housing unit, the beige brick showing some wear. The apartment was not furnished, so McCook County Deputy Carl Banks had been assigned in advance to collect sufficient furniture for the detectives to live with some comfort while stationed in Wheaton. The detectives found the door key held with masking tape to the front door. There was no accompanying note or greeting.

When the two men opened the door, a haphazard heap of furniture allowed only a very narrow entrance. It looked like the deputy had robbed the dump. Obviously any piece of junk was acceptable to Carl.

Vilhallen said, "All the personnel reports from Sheriff Hauk regarding Deputy Carl Banks indicated a dedicated, detailed enforcer of the law."

White sighed, closed his eyes and said, "I think that tells us something about the deceased sheriff, don't you? It looks like a scavenger hunt from his mother-in-law's basement or maybe the back room of the bar."

"He may have saved some poor slob the fee for hauling his junk to the dump." Vilhallen was tired and angry. With a hanky from his pocket, Vilhallen wiped perspiration from his face.

"He seems to have everything we require for comfortable living," White said as he pulled from the stack a lamp with the top hanging by the wire and no bulb. In one swift motion, he threw the lamp against the wall. The round red plaster bottom did not break.

"From this scene, I'm guessing he hated finding us furniture." Vilhallen kicked the deep green couch cushion.

White added, "I am guessing that Deputy Carl is nobody's servant, especially not big town detectives coming to solve his case. I suspect he is a dumb ass."

Vilhallen laughed. "Carl had sense enough to be far away when we opened that apartment door." The two detectives stared with restraint at the heap of junk topped with a three-legged TV stand like a Christmas ornament.

Vilhallen could not look away from the garbage piled in the living room. His eyes bulged and the veins in his neck pumped purple, but he managed to reconcile the situation. Vilhallen considered Carl to be their one connection with the people in town. He was not ready to completely alienate the bastard, not yet. White wanted a hotel room for the night.

It was supper time following a six hour drive from Rapid City. Vilhallen hoped for a quick shower and a sandwich before visiting the crime scene. White planned to read the crime scene reports. Instead both men silently planned revenge as they began to separate pieces of a bed frame from chair legs.

What was too broken to use, they discarded in the hall. They listened to a drunk singing as he came home and to a woman doing laundry. The six o'clock whistle blew and the sun set invisible behind the church steeple. When the apartment manager stopped by, the detectives commandeered his help. Within the hour decent beds and bedding appeared in each of the two small bedrooms with appropriate billing to the State.

By ten o'clock, the two men sat on the green, sagging sofa, pizza in front of them on the blond veneer coffee table, and waited for the local TV news. The one thing that worked was the TV. They had to look down because the TV sat on a kitchen wire rack that sat on the floor.

Just as Vilhallen and White were feeling better, the TV showed pictures of news crews moving at random through Hauk's house.

White began to punch the channel selector. Each of the three local news channels showed footage regarding Hauk's murder. White's face turned an ugly gray. As pictures of the bedroom where Hauk was found changed to pictures of the dishes in Hauk's sink, both detective's felt sick. On that channel, the reporter picked up a folder from the counter and asked everyone in TV-land if something as simple as this folder might help the police solve this crime.

"Tell me this is not happening." Vilhallen threw his uneaten pizza onto the cardboard box. The third channel presented a piece on all the possible ways into and out of the house. An agile cameraman followed his reporter through every doorway and several windows.

The 24-inch TV screen introduced the detectives to Carl Banks. His eager, hyper-excited face appeared on every channel. He spilled his guts, pointing his finger and nearly yelling that Hauk's killer would pay. "Somebody, and I know who you are," Carl said, his face contorted in emotion, "murdered the best sheriff this state's ever had, and the *beep beep* will pay." On another channel Carl wiped his eyes before saying in all seriousness that this was more tragic than the shooting of JFK.

Vilhallen and White stared at one another, disbelief repeated and magnified in each other's expression. They had a big problem in Carl. When Carl told the concerned-looking reporter that "Whoever stabbed Hauk stabbed us all," White had to leave the room. He had to walk. From the doorway, he said to Vilhallen, "This is no longer a two week case with a nice tidy confession. This is a nightmare."

White left, missing one final shot of Carl with tears in his eyes and his arm around his wife as the camera blacked out. Vilhallen managed to mumble, "God, I want to arrest that man."

John White returned an hour later. He was trying for composure, but his hands still shook. "Somebody should have been here from Sioux Falls guarding that scene," White tried, but he had little voice.

"We were here within forty-eight hours of the crime," Vilhallen said, his tone defensive. "How could we know Deputy Carl Banks was a moron beyond definition? We do know that Hauk was not a well-liked man." Vilhallen tried desperately to put the TV disaster behind him and work with what he had.

"How do we know that?" Anger still laced White's tone.

Vilhallen sat on the couch and put his feet on the bowed coffee table, pushing the pizza box to one side with his shoe. "If Sheriff Hauk was loved by somebody or even respected we would have arrived to a place ready to be occupied. People would want to help in any way they could. Look at who he chose as a deputy. Does any of this indicate genuine grief to you? Not a bit. Another thing - no one is going to want to help us out. Every man, woman, and child with any information is going to be on vacation. Trust me on that. I can feel it. Everybody in town knows we are here, and not one person has offered to help. We are in trouble on this one."

As disheartened as Vilhallen felt and sounded, to talk restored an outer calm to the frantic John White.

"You're right," White said. "We saw only one face talking to those TV cameras. No one wants anything to do with this. Hauk was no friend of theirs."

The report by the attending deputy, in this case Carl, would be absolutely worthless. The crime scene would be contaminated beyond use. They had to hope for something in the autopsy, some credible witnesses, something in Hauk's files. They knew Carl sent the body to the police morgue in Sioux Falls. That was verified. To the two detectives in their dumpy apartment, that single normal procedure seemed now to be a small miracle. Likely they would know the murder weapon.

Early the next morning, Monday, the two detectives supervised the unloading and placement of equipment shipped from Sioux Falls. Their headquarters was the empty and dusty back room of City Hall. The delivery truck, parked by the back door, waited on them at 7:30 am. Parked behind the delivery truck was the local telephone van. One worker leaned against the back fender. He did not speak and seemed a little edgy. Vilhallen made a point to address the local man directly but received only a nod or a grunt in response.

With the installation of computers and phones completed and inspected, Vilhallen nodded toward White indicating he should make an effort at communicating with the local telephone man.

"Do you live in Wheaton?" White asked.

The rotund man who looked to be thirty something answered with obvious unwillingness. "Lived here all my life."

"Who were Hauk's friends?" White asked, assuming as low key demeanor as possible. He pulled papers from his brown brief case, while hiding his interest in the young man's obvious discomfort.

After a few seconds, he straightened his shoulders and gave White a direct and straightforward look. "Hauk had his cronies, but I'm not one of 'em. I can't wish you any luck. I'm glad the sonofabitch is dead and wish well to the man who did it." Clear enough.

Without another glance or word, he picked up his equipment and worked his way to the door. He turned back into the large, square off-white room. "Somewhere in Hauk's stuff you might find that he harassed my wife for over a year, driving by twenty times a day, calling during the night, stopping her on the road for any trumped up reason. I doubt he recorded that, but in case you find it and consider me a suspect I will save you taxpayer money by letting you know I have an alibi for whenever it happened. I was in Pierre all week-end at a fishing tournament."

Rob Thether, telephone installer, became the first entry of hundreds entered into Vilhallen's computer. Somewhere, sooner or later, he would get some interesting matches. In a town this size, there were no secrets. Somebody in town already knew who stabbed the sheriff. Generally, the poor bastard confessed.

Detective Vilhallen did all the grunge work, writing down and entering detail after detail until something matched. He believed in stereotypes, and that single exception to every rule. He was forty-seven years old and a professional.

What Vilhallen lacked in intuition and brilliance, he compensated in relentless pursuit. He began to enter his notes into the computer under name, location, and motive. At the touch of a key the computer would cross-reference and bring to the screen connections he had not noticed. He entered everything, no matter how meaningless.

Vilhallen's partner, John White, liked to draw graphs on yellow legal pads. He worked in circles, putting the victim in the middle and working outward through motive, means and opportunity. The crime represented the finished work. From the crime he could find the criminal. He also liked to start with family. In this case any significant relationships were unknown.

All the resources of the State of South Dakota were made available to them. Vilhallen lived in Rapid City and White lived in Pierre. For this high-profile case, they would, above all, have the assistance of Deputy Sheriff Carl Banks.

By ten AM, Carl had still not arrived. They speculated that the Deputy had an inkling his face suffered from over-exposure. Perhaps he had a clue that the big boys were a bit peeved over their sleeping quarters.

As they would soon discover, Vilhallen and White were wrong in both of these assessments. Carl sauntered into the temporary headquarters in the City Hall, saying, "I had those media goons eating out of my hand. I did a fine job with those boys. You can thank me later."

As Vilhallen and White gaped at him, Carl added, "I spent valuable time gathering furniture. Figured you wouldn't mind arranging it."

"You figured wrong, Carl," Vilhallen told him. "We need the crime report."

"When I'm ready," Carl answered. "This is my case. I know who did it. I paid him a brief visit yesterday just to let him know his clock is ticking."

When both Vilhallen and White remained silent, Carl continued, his thumbs in his belt and rocking slightly on his heels. "When I can round up a few trustworthy helpers I'll go get the bastard. Only one thing has changed in town, only one new arrival, only one crazy from the nut bin. Only one man ever told the Sheriff to f-off. Not exactly those words, but the same meaning. He is the perpetrator of this dastardly crime and that is Martin Webster. None of this other shit matters a lick. I've done your job, and the governor can pat you on the back."

"Who did you say did it?" White asked tightly.

"Martin Webster," Carl answered.

"White kind of vehicle does Martin Webster own?" Vilhallen asked, looking up at Carl.

"None. His friend drives him around like the whipped chauffer he is." Carl rolled his eyes.

"What's a whipped chauffer?" White asked.

Carl did not deign to answer.

"Did you ask where he was on Friday night? That is the time of death, correct? You found the sheriff on Saturday morning?" Vilhallen forced his voice to be casual.

"I did not ask any questions of that nature. None of it matters. We just have to go get him." Carl gestured with his hands in front of him as though he was sick of stating the obvious.

"Evidence matters, Carl," White said.

Carl rolled his eyes again. This was becoming a gesture extremely annoying to Vilhallen, who turned away, saying casually, "We've had some reports of Sheriff Hauk bullying people." Vilhallen assumed that White observed Carl carefully.

"Has nothing to do with it," Carl said too quickly and too intensely. "Speaking of evidence, you've got nothing on the sheriff. Hauk has a fine reputation, untarnished. And I will assume the duties until the voters decide."

Carl turned to leave in a sudden, startling movement. He stopped and ordered the detectives to remain working at headquarters. "Don't go through that scene without me," Carl said as he paused at the door.

Vilhallen noted an anxious look on Carl's face as the deputy left at a run.

White said, "He just thought of something he forgot to do."

Vilhallen nodded. "What would be so important as to make him run? We were talking about negative reports regarding the victim.

A few seconds later, White said, "He forgot something in Hauk's house. Did you see him jiggling keys in his pocket?"

Vilhallen said, "We have files somewhere in that house."

"It was such a shock for Carl, finding the body, that the deputy forgot about those files." White reached for his jacket. Vilhallen was already at the door.

"Do we stop Carl or go to Hauk's house?" Vilhallen asked.

"Hauk's house," White said. "That's where Carl is heading and that's where we will find the smoking gun."

Chapter Twenty-Two

The detectives had little trouble finding Hauk's house. Pointless as visiting the crime scene felt to be last night, Vilhallen felt a sense of expectation now. Something lurked inside that house that Carl wanted out.

Carl had certainly behaved suspiciously. It did not take a Masters Degree in Criminal Behavior to know that Carl had secrets. He was wired tighter than a wind-up toy. Nor did it take much experience in law enforcement to know patterns of criminal behavior. If Hauk was crooked, he would have two sets of files. That was still a big if, but could not be discounted.

Vilhallen had not recovered from the unbelievable incompetence in allowing the reporters to destroy any possible physical evidence. Everything at the scene was tainted, even the taste in his mouth, but it was possible something lay hidden that could solve this. He said, "What might we find of interest?"

As the two men walked to the front door of Hauk's single story ranch style house with an attached garage, White said, "One thing we need is Hauk's case files, his most recent cases, notes, arrest reports. Carl will have to provide access to all of that. Those records are at the court house. If Hauk was on the take, those records would be here."

Vilhallen nodded.

If Sheriff Hauk was on the take, he didn't broadcast it by living well. The house was in need of paint and lacked any attempt at maintenance of the exterior or the yard. The house looked to be thirty years old, maybe a government low-income housing project. Vilhallen scribbled notes. Obviously it was too late to be taped off, pointless now: the brown grass was crushed flat by the hundreds of feet that trod upon it. White wondered aloud if Carl had never watched *Law and Order*. He had to know to tape off the scene and allow no access.

The two detectives turned toward the sound of a siren coming toward them. "What an idiot," White muttered as a vehicle belonging to the County Sheriff's Department slammed to a halt, siren wailing, and lights flashing. Carl pushed the gear into park, rocking the vehicle within inches of the rear bumper on Vilhallen's Escort wagon. Carl looked disapprovingly at them over the roof of his car. The TV screen had not done him justice. In person he was wired, strung tight and high pitched.

Carl slapped his palm on the roof of his police car. His voice was an octave higher than earlier and strung-out, ready to crack. He said, "I will have a lot to tell the citizens at the bar after work, a lot to tell. Couldn't you wait for my report on finding the body? You had to come here without me?" Carl was so livid with rage that his body moved in spasmodic, uncontrolled gestures.

When neither detective responded, Carl calmed himself sufficiently to walk toward the house. Carl talked while he walked, his voice getting louder and louder with each step. "If you just let me handle it the whole thing would be solved and done in days. Why can't you leave me alone to take care of this?"

Vilhallen glanced at White and the two men stood calmly watching Carl. Carl jiggled the keys on his key ring out in front of him. "I have the keys right here. I'll let you see it when I finish with the Sheriff's confidential and personal files."

Vilhallen grasped his notepad so tight the cardboard backing bent in his hand. He glanced at White who stood utterly motionless like a big cat ready to strike. Deputy Carl found the correct key and started to work it from the ring. He gestured for the detectives to wait where they stood.

As soon as Carl had the door open Vilhallen and White stepped inside on Carl's heels. Carl paused, removed his hat and shut his eyes. His lips moved in prayer. When he opened his eyes he appeared calmer, more resigned to the disrespect.

Carl said, "I couldn't understand why Hauk wasn't answering his radio." His speech had the pattern of well-rehearsed lines. Still, it was the first time the detectives heard it and they listened carefully.

"Hauk did that sometimes if he was away from his vehicle, but generally not for more than an hour." Carl stopped walking and turned to the two men behind him.

"Did what, exactly?" Vilhallen asked, notepad in hand.

Carl repeated, "Not answer his radio. My instructions were to keep trying until he did answer. We had a procedure. When Hauk was on patrol, I was to check-in every hour or so. It was our safety precaution." He rolled his eyes to indicate that he should not have to be repeating himself.

"On Friday night, the night in question, he did not answer his radio all night long, and that was strange, to say the least." Carl spoke slowly so they could catch his drift. "I was on duty at the courthouse until midnight then the calls shift to my house. So, I just kept trying to raise him. When I left the courthouse, I drove passed his place. Everything looked quiet. I could see his pick-up and the patrol car in the garage, so I went home."

"The garage door was open?" White asked him.

"No, I ran my search beam across the windows in the garage door and saw both vehicles," Carl said.

"Exactly what time did you see both vehicles?" Vilhallen asked.

"To me that was still Friday night," Carl said. "I drove by at 12:30 AM on Saturday morning. Then I went home. Later, I woke up with a nagging feeling about the sheriff. Hauk always checked for any calls or messages. The man was a maniac about keeping his finger on the pulse of things. So I rushed, I mean I didn't even brush my teeth or drink my coffee, I was here before daylight on Saturday." His words and his continence assumed a more genuine aspect.

"Besides," Carl continued, "I didn't want the sheriff mad about anything, nothing worse than a bulldog that's pissed." Carl took a deep breath and the three men faced the kitchen, open from the living room.

Carl started fussing with his keys, pursing his lips, and the single minute of redeeming sincerity vanished. Carl paused. "Go ahead," he said. "The bedroom is straight back."

Vilhallen said, "We will do this by the book, front to back."

Carl turned ashen gray. His thin lips worked without sound. Finally, he nodded.

"We need a list of every person you've allowed inside the house." Vilhallen's voice assumed authority and Carl shrugged, almost pouting. With both detectives looking at him, he finally pointed to his head and said, "Up here."

As the men began to step through the living room, the carpet bending stiff beneath their feet, Vilhallen asked, "So what was the cameraman's name who climbed through that kitchen window?" He pointed into the kitchen.

"I can call the station if you need to know that. They know me there." Carl's voice was taking on a rebellious edge.

White patted Carl's shoulder. "Show us what you saw," he said and waved Carl ahead of them through the living room and into the hallway that led to the bedrooms. John White apparently wanted a happy Carl, a talking Carl.

"I came in the garage door." He pointed toward the door off the kitchen that led to the garage. Vilhallen made notes and drew a quick diagram. "I stepped into the kitchen and yelled for Hauk right from where I stood. I yelled his name two or three times. When he didn't answer or throw anything against the wall as usual when he's hung-over, I nearly left. It was real quiet and I hesitated to be the one to wake him up. No way, if he was hung-over or if he had company." Carl smiled and shook his head in obvious fond memory. "The man was a mean bastard when he was hung-over."

"So what changed your mind?" White questioned, gently.

"Too quiet, something not right in the smell. So, I walked real careful across the kitchen and down this hall."

"Did you call for him from here?" White asked.

"No, I was suspicious of something, so I was real quiet," Carl answered, nearly whispering now. Then he said, "I've been in law enforcement a long time and I can tell the difference between quiet and too quiet."

"Comes from all those years in law enforcement." Larry Vilhallen's voice was calm, matter-of-fact, covering his sarcasm.

"Darn right." Carl nodded emphatically, still wary of Vilhallen.

Again John encouraged him to continue. Carl wiped his forehead with his sleeve. "So, I walked on tiptoe down this hall to Hauk's bedroom door." The Deputy slunk along.

White and Vilhallen followed Carl down the short hallway to the master bedroom. "I knocked real light on his door. But, of course, he didn't answer. If he had, you fellas wouldn't be in town." Carl smiled and looked to see if they caught his joke. John White smiled back. Vilhallen glared.

Carl licked his lips and continued. "I opened the door and saw him stretched out on his bed, clothes and all, even his shoes. First, I quick shut the door." Carl looked into the bedroom and quick shut the door exactly as he had done on Saturday morning.

"If it was that bad of a night for the Sheriff, I didn't even want to be on the property when he opened his eyes. I went two or three steps back this way and caught myself." Carl pointed to show his route. "I realized he wasn't snoring. I went back and tiptoed to the bed and looked at him real close. He was cold and dead. So, I called it in."

Carl actually ran screaming from the house, but that wasn't a detail that needed description as both Vilhallen and White had listened to the 911 call while waiting on Carl. The detectives studied Deputy Carl. He was full of details right up to finding the body and then case closed.

"How did you get into the garage?" Vilhallen asked.

"I bent down and opened the door," Carl answered with a roll of his eyes.

"Did you see blood, or a weapon or anything that struck you as odd?" White asked, still being careful not to step on Carl's toes, playing the good cop.

"Nothing," Carl answered, suddenly stiff and defensive. "No blood anywhere, not a drop. I had to turn him a little to see the wound in the back of his neck, right above his shoulder blade.

That gave me a jolt, I can tell you. Before that I considered it a heart attack." Carl swallowed down a lump in his throat.

The bedroom stank, and Larry covered his face with his handkerchief. The smell was dirty socks and old vomit and spilled booze and death. John White pulled on his surgical gloves and began to take pictures of everything in the room. Among the dozens of fingerprints in this room, his would not be one of them.

Neither detective could be certain if the pulled out drawers and clothes in stacks were original to the scene or the work of curious, unsupervised reporters. Inside the closet White found three police uniforms in the plastic wrap from the cleaners.

The detectives visually examined the kitchen, dining area, living room, hallway, and the second bedroom, and bath. The second bedroom appeared fairly intact. White photographed a locked storage cupboard and a locked desk. The detectives touched nothing and said nothing.

They returned with Carl to the kitchen. The sink and the counter were littered with tidbits of sandwiches and French-fries from the local pub. It looked familiar. The TV cameras did not lie: on the counter lay the infamous folder. Scrawled across the tab in black magic marker was the name Cassandra Peters.

Vilhallen, his own gloves on, bagged and tagged the folder. He could use it for his own information though it was worthless as evidence. Nothing they found inside or outside the house would ever be clean evidence, except possibly, inside the second bedroom.

"Do you have more keys for anything inside that second bedroom?" Vilhallen asked.

Carl took his time in answering. He toyed with a salt shaker from the counter. He looked out the kitchen window onto Hauk's bleak backyard.

"Carl?" John White managed a pleasing tone. "We don't want to be forced to break them open."

"Hauk carried those keys on him at all times." Carl continued to look outside. "I have them, hid away at my house." Of course Carl was lying. Vilhallen saw that Carl could barely restrain himself from touching the keys inside his pocket.

"Did you remove the keys from the body?" Vilhallen was beyond shock.

"Yes, I did," Carl answered with grave seriousness. "I thought to remove them before anybody like you could do it."

"You didn't look for a weapon, but you thought to remove those keys?" White looked steadily at Carl.

"I thought it was a heart attack at that time, and I knew first and foremost Hauk would not want those keys in any hands but mine. Then I turned his body and that was it for me. I couldn't think after that."

Vilhallen considered Carl's attitude to be odd. He could not stop talking about the murder, but he was afraid to say even one word about that second bedroom. At some point, Hauk put the fear of God into Carl regarding whatever the room held.

White said, "We'll need manpower from Minnehaha County to put a twenty-four hour guard on this house."

Vilhallen could not seriously consider Carl a suspect, not for the murder. However, the man's behavior was so odd that he was certainly guilty of something.

Carl squared his thin shoulders and looked hard into White's face. "I don't want anybody poking into Hauk's private affairs, and that includes you." Carl came dangerously close to a sneer. "Hauk is the victim here. He's not the criminal."

"Really," Vilhallen thought.

"I'd like to have a look in that room." John White spoke casually, man to man, law enforcement to law enforcement. "There might be something in there that will help us get a handle on this thing and find whoever did this. You know that."

"I'll do it," Carl said. "I'll bring you the stuff."

Vilhallen took a step back, seriously eyeing Carl. "No," he told him. "You are not to enter this house without one of us with you."

Crimson rose up Carl's long neck and across his face like a visible wave. He blinked and swallowed and then said, "Fuck you."

The three men now stood in the narrow hallway outside of Hauk's bedroom. Vilhallen said, "Let's finish the tour of the rest of the house. We will come back to this room." He nodded toward the closed door of the second bedroom. The men walked away from the closed door after White put an evidence tag on the knob.

Vilhallen thought, we need a look at Carl's vehicle. Somewhere is a large amount of blood and it is not here. He glanced at his partner and saw a quick nod in return. White was on the same page.

They entered the garage through the kitchen. Carl flipped on the light switch. John and Larry stood still for a minute, absorbing the scene. Except for the two vehicles the garage was empty. They would never know what might have been here twenty-four hours ago before the assailant could have walked in and away with anything incriminating.

Hauk had no tools, no lawn mower, no junk in his garage, not even garbage cans or shelves with motor oil, no garden rake or fishing pole or old batteries. It was the most barren garage either detective ever saw.

"Where's his stuff?" Vilhallen asked.

"Hauk never used this garage except to park his patrol car and his truck. He pretty much hired everything done. His whole life was his job, nothing else," Carl answered reluctantly. He was cautious now, wary.

"How many people would you guess came through this garage in the last twenty-four hours?" John's cordial tone sounded forced.

"Let's see," Carl rubbed the black stubble on his chin. "The reporters set up some stuff in here. And my wife brought us some coffee and donuts. Some of the guys from the bar wanted to see, so I brought them inside through here so they wouldn't mess up anything. I told them not to touch anything or move any stuff around. The neighbors came over wondering if they should clean the place, you know, in case Hauk had family coming. I told them to wait. They stayed in the garage. That's it, I'm pretty darn sure." Carl shut his lips tight and rested his hands on his hips. He added, "Only Hauk could have done it better."

"That's it?" Larry made no effort to hide his sarcasm

Pursing his lips and thinking, Carl nodded his head. "Pretty sure," he said.

White asked, "Did you keep a register of everyone who entered?"

"Look, I was in demand. TV people and a newspaper guy, two of them, kept pestering me about this and that. I told those guys not to take anything. That's all I could do. I don't have eyes in the back of my head like you do."

John White moved away quickly. He walked around Hauk's vehicles and opened the passenger door of the patrol car. "When do the lab boys get here?" he asked Carl.

"When you call 'em and tell 'em to come," Carl said.

"Well, Carl," John stood erect and pushed his voice through clenched teeth. "Go right now to your car and radio for the lab boys from Sioux Falls to come right now and for a back-up team to watch this house. But first, did Hauk lock his patrol car when he wasn't in it?"

Carl smirked, "Hell no. Nobody in their right mind would touch anything in Hauk's cop car." He made no move toward his vehicle.

"Make those calls you should have made on Saturday, per procedure and do it now!" Vilhallen had enough. This time Carl left, opening the garage door with more force than necessary and striding under it like he had burrs in his boots.

Inside the sheriff's vehicle, Vilhallen could see no obvious signs of struggle or blood. However, when he bent to look under the front seat from the passenger side door, he did see something interesting and he did not want Carl to know.

It could be meaningless or it could be the one detail that solved the case. In his notepad, Vilhallen described the baby bottle exactly as it lay under the seat. White snapped pictures.

Vilhallen joined Carl who stood by the driver's door of his car, radio in hand. A good, professional deputy in this case would be invaluable, a liaison to the community, a resource of cases and innuendo. Carl was none of that. He was a worried little henchman of a questionable sheriff.

White joined Vilhallen and the three men stayed right there. Vilhallen could not allow Carl to leave on pretense of getting keys that Carl already carried in his pocket. Nor could he or White leave the scene until it was taped off and in the hands of professionals. So, they stood. Eventually, White asked Carl about the town and Carl told them different things. He told them about Sandra Peters going missing and Martin Webster coming back to town. He described the local pub as the main place of information along with the ladies prayer chain.

Vilhallen asked about the coroner photos before the body was moved. Carl had them at his home as well. "We need those, Carl. Why did you take them home? Don't you have an office?"

"Too many Nosy Nordicas around my office," Carl answered. Then he said, quietly but with conviction, "We don't need all this official shit. Like I already told you, I know who killed Hauk. I don't need your help to know that." Only the pitch of Carl's voice indicated how wired he was, coiled like a snake.

Vilhallen and White exchanged glances and then studied Carl as though he were a prize exhibit at the fair.

John White asked, "Who?"

"That crazy guy who just moved back to the area. That's who. Quite a coincidence, him moving back and Hauk being killed. Quite a coincidence."

"That would be the Martin Webster you spoke of?" Vilhallen leaned casually on the passenger door of Carl's county vehicle.

"Yes, it is."

"Why would he do that? Did he have any encounters with the Sheriff?" White spoke from beside Carl's elbow.

"Crazy doesn't need a reason."

Vilhallen watched Carl's expression and knew the man believed it. Carl did not kill the sheriff, but Vilhallen suspected something a little evil inside of Carl.

"How about proof? We need proof, don't we?"

"We bring him in and get a confession. I planned to do it today, but I need back-up. He's not alone out there." Carl warmed to his plan as he told it.

"Remind me again what kind of vehicle he drives?" Vilhallen asked.

"I don't believe he has a vehicle of any kind. His neighbor, Bill Bendix, drives him around." Carl stopped just short of an eye roll. "Like I told you previously."

"You think his neighbor drove him to town, he stabbed Hauk while his neighbor waited for him and, being crazy, he sucked up all the blood and then his neighbor drove him home?" Vilhallen maintained a serious expression

Carl paused a minute. "Don't jerk me around," he said.

White explained to Carl that actual proof, physical evidence, motive, access to the victim were all required. So, they needed the crime scene photos, the weapon, motive and ability, the files of recent and past cases, and the keys to check whatever was locked up inside that second bedroom.

"So you guys are gonna try the victim just like always. It'll be Hauk on trial." Anger blazed from Carl's eyes.

"We need to know the victim to find who did this," White answered.

Vilhallen moved away from Carl's vehicle leaving White to keep watch on Carl. It wouldn't be long before a unit arrived from Sioux Falls. Vilhallen passed the time looking at the layout of the neighborhood. Hauk's house was isolated from his neighbors. For one thing, the house sat further back on the corner lot. Out-of-control lilac bushes covered the corner, preventing passersby from seeing the house from the west or the south.

Three evergreens marked the property line to the south and also blocked the view from the road. A driver could see Hauk's house on the street directly in front of the house and that was it. Vilhallen walked down the street and looked at Hauk's house. For Carl to see inside the garage, he must have driven slowly and maybe pulled into the driveway. Two houses across the street to the east faced Hauk's house.

Vilhallen noted to assign officers to knock on doors and interview neighbors, canvassing for witnesses. It annoyed him that this wasn't already done.

He was beginning his survey from the north side of the house, the garage side, when two Minnehaha county sheriffs department vehicles pulled to a stop in front the house. They came quietly, without sirens, lights or fanfare. He looked at Carl to see if the deputy noticed that. A few minutes later the lab van stopped, and suddenly the place felt like a proper crime scene.

Later that afternoon, Vilhallen and White sat at their makeshift desks in their makeshift office. They looked at the coroner's photos and report on the cause of death. They studied the pictures of the body, slightly turned as Carl admitted doing. They discussed the possible weapon. When the phone rang that the technicians finished their work at the crime scene, they ran for the car. It was time to check that spare bedroom.

Carl was assigned to return to his normal duties and to not mention or interfere with this investigation. When told that he was no longer a part of the investigation into Hauk's murder, Carl had merely nodded. Vilhallen knew Carl had no intention of obeying this order. Carl would follow his own private agenda. Vilhallen could only hope that Carl would cause no harm.

As Vilhallen drove to Hauk's house, White pointed out Carl's county vehicle parked behind the pub. "I hope Carl doesn't have a few beers and share his theory of who killed Hauk."

"That is exactly what he is doing," Vilhallen said. "We have to hope no one listens to him or we could have a vigilante nightmare."

195

Chapter Twenty-Three

At the house, Vilhallen and White found the lab Technicians loading their van. They had bagged and tagged only three items from the house, garage and vehicles. Vilhallen noted the baby bottle in a clear plastic bag, two kitchen knives and a large bag of bedding. They wouldn't take from the scene anything more unless requested.

A technician met them at the front door. "Interesting stuff," he said. "You'll have my full report in the morning. We have some knives, but I doubt they are your murder weapon. We have the baby bottle you found and we'll check that out. Of course, we took the bedding to see what we see, but no visible sign of blood. In fact, we checked everywhere and didn't find blood. We did find a lot of footprints and fingerprints, and we have them photographed and can check for matches if you need."

"In that second bedroom?" White asked.

"Only one set of prints on a cabinet and desk, likely the victim's. We did not force open the cupboard or the desk drawers. Let me know if you find something you want tested." He was a clean-shaven, blond-haired man in his forties, slim and professional. He wore his gloves and carried a black case.

Vilhallen stepped to one side to allow him to exit, but the man stopped and faced him. "One more thing, that little wired deputy, Banks, stopped by to ask some questions. We didn't him anything, but he was a very anxious fellow."

"Did he come inside?" White asked.

"No," the technician answered. "He wanted too. Said he was told to start checking those files and needed to get on it. His name is on the authorized entrance list, but we were not finished with our part and told him to come back later."

"Thanks, Doc," Vilhallen said, and the man left. Two uniforms out of Sioux Falls remained on duty guarding the entrance. The first thing White did was to remove Carl's name from authorized entry. Not removing Carl's name was an oversight and such carelessness could not be repeated. The first thing Vilhallen did was jog to that second bedroom office.

The light was poor in the small room with dusk long since past. The overhead bulb created more shadows than light. Vilhallen put on his gloves and pulled his penlight from his pocket. White entered and stood by the desk. It was an old wood teacher desk with two front drawers that stuck.

"What do you expect to find?" Vilhallen asked.

White said, "I hope for nothing more than letters from an old girlfriend. But I have a creepy feeling. Carl is worried about something."

White looked pale and grave as he took pictures of the desk. He pulled from his jacket pocket a black pouch containing screwdrivers and thin tools. They could no longer wait for Carl to give up the keys.

The first drawer contained four neatly stacked bundles of cash bound with rubber bands and a second locked box, a small metal box like a miniature fishing tackle box. Vilhallen thought that Hauk would not give this particular key to Carl. White took pictures of everything exactly as it was then Vilhallen reached to remove the box from the drawer. He reached but pulled back. "For pity sake," he said. Was he afraid of a box? He removed it and set it on top of the clean desk. The thought ran swiftly, "this box is a classroom study come to life." He glanced at White and saw his complexion blanch. "We'll look later."

Vilhallen moved on. The second drawer held more cash and a small spiral notebook. That was it for the desk. The cupboard was a steel type cupboard designed originally as a gun safe. The detectives expected to find guns inside, and they did. Two shotguns stood in their slots. However, the guns were not the first thing that caught the eye. From bottom to top in two rows were vanilla folders. The shelf designed to hold ammunition contained more folders and the drawer at the bottom was on a separate lock.

The key to the bottom drawer was taped inside the door. When Vilhallen opened it, it contained ammunition and a cleaning kit and two knives in sheaths. These knives were too long and deep to be the murder weapon. These knives were for cleaning deer hide.

The detectives looked at the files, thick and thin, and knew every single page would have to be studied. At this point they could only speculate what the files contained. The actual case files for the County of McCook should be in the court house. White called the uniforms and instructed one of them to carefully box theses files and take the files to their temporary office in City Hall.

Vilhallen and White stared at the flat tin box that came from the desk drawer. White said, "Was Carl after the money, the files or this box?"

"I doubt Carl knew about this box," Vilhallen said.

A small screwdriver opened the box with little damage to the lock. Vilhallen could not help the sudden tightness in his chest as he looked at the contents. His mouth went dry on the instant. Beside him White gasped and stepped back.

Inside the box were a dozen small plastic capped compartments. Inside six of the compartments were small clear plastic evidence bags. White took pictures and Vilhallen used his penknife to light each compartment. For some reason, both detectives hesitated to touch it.

White finally said what they both feared, "It is a trophy box."

Vilhallen nodded.

Each plastic bag was numbered in order. Neither detective knew what the numbers meant. Each bag contained a piece of jewelry or a button or a hair ribbon. One bag contained a lock of hair, black hair held with a paper clip.

"I'll get the lab tech back here," White said. His voice held a slight tremble, and the color was gone from his face. He seemed to force his eyes away from the box and left the room. Vilhallen waited for the lab tech to return, and bag and seal the box. He felt sick.

The file on the kitchen counter was different than the files in the cabinet. It was a heavy folder with wire edges for hanging in a drawer. "Property of McCook County Sheriff's Dept." was stamped on the front. This was a case file that Hauk must have brought home from the office. Vilhallen noted the name on the file, glanced through it briefly and bagged it to take to their headquarters.

Vilhallen said to his partner, "Carl talked about this girl. And I saw the name on an amber alert."

"Cassandra Peters," White read the label aloud. "We should talk to her today."

"Not before I've studied the situation. I have to know more before I interview her." Vilhallen was still shaken by their discovery of the box and its contents.

Vilhallen was too restless to focus, his thoughts churning. He tried to rein them in. His modus operandi was one detail at a time, and he was struggling to find his balance. The lab technician joined the detectives in the kitchen. The three men, shoulder to shoulder, looked at the tin box inside the plastic bag. The technician removed the tin box from the bag and placed it on the counter.

Vilhallen silently hoped that the technician would find it trivial and only reluctantly take it for further processing. Such was not the case. If anything, the blond haired man with his white jacket and gloves appeared more fascinated than either detective. He used tweezers to lift each bag and study it in the flashlight. Then suddenly, the doctor in forensics put each piece exactly as it was, shut the case, re-bagged it with deliberate care, labeled it and prepared to exit.

"I'll be in touch," he said.

"What do you think about it?" Vilhallen asked.

"Well, it is a trophy case. I have no doubt of that. I will get you what info I can, but it is up to you guys to find the connections. I am guessing somewhere out there you have six victims of something." He gave a grudging, tiny twitch to his mouth.

It was late, and though neither Vilhallen nor White felt hungry, eating was required. The only place open that served food was the Pub. As the men parked in back, White mentioned that Carl's vehicle was gone. Vilhallen would have a talk with the man about his use of the County vehicle for his personal business. And White informed Vilhallen that help was coming from the Minnehaha County sheriff's office. Four officers would be there in the morning.

The place was empty and the detectives each took a stool along the bar. Vilhallen said, "I suspect that Hauk is not so much a victim as a perpetrator."

"This case is a Pandora's box," said White. "I have a feeling this investigation is not going to end well, at least not for us."

"What does Carl know about his boss? We have to seriously confront the little weasel first thing in the morning."

A sign on the mirror stated that the kitchen closed at 11:00 PM. They had fifteen minutes and motioned the bartender. The fry cook apparently was not thrilled with their business, but she did her job and they heard the sizzle of hamburger on the grill and fries in the grease. The only voice was Jay Leno.

The bartender plopped mustard and ketchup in front of them and filled their glasses of beer from the tap. He was obviously not the talking kind of bartender, at least not with them. He busied himself with tallying their bill.

"Quiet in here," White said to his back.

"Yup," he answered without turning.

"Always this quiet?" White continued.

"Nope," the bartender answered.

Judging from the tall stack of green slips pushed down on a small spike it certainly was not always this quiet. "Where did everybody go?" Vilhallen asked

The bartender turned to face them at last. He looked them over and then decided to say, "Two rowdies left with Carl. Everybody else has work in the morning."

Vilhallen did not give the food a glance; his eyes were on the bartender. "Where were Carl and friends headed?" Vilhallen asked, already getting up from his stool.

"Do you know the old Webster place?"

Vilhallen remained calm as he glanced at White who was standing and ready. "Better bag our order. We'll take it to go."

Chapter Twenty-Four

"Who went with Carl? What are we up against?" Vilhallen asked as the two detectives raced south out of town.

"It could not have been easy to find men to come with him. Nobody wants anything to do with it. But he is persistent if nothing else," White said while checking his weapon.

"The bartender said two *rowdies* went with Carl," Vilhallen said. "It could be highly dangerous."

"They have a half-hour head start," White said. "I hate gunfire, especially unpredictable, half-drunk gunfire."

Vilhallen did not like to use his flashing light, but he did. His Ford was not intended for speed, it was intended for some comfort and to save tax payer money, but he still hit ninety on the three-mile stretch of highway 81.

On the gravel, he slowed down, turned off the flashing lights, and proceeded cautiously. At Martin's driveway, the two detectives left their vehicle and walked up the slight curve to the house. Voices carried in the cool night air, someone angry working into passion and someone not angry at all. They mixed indistinguishable, at first and then clarified into two separate parties.

Carl's voice, high pitched and bordering on hysteria, screamed, "You crazy nut case, you killed him, you did it!" Then an odd silence just as Vilhallen and White emerged from the lane with the protective high grass and weeds. They stepped into the clearing in front of Martin's porch. The only light came from Carl's headlight beams and a softer light through the closed blinds on the porch windows.

The smaller guy on the ground by the steps noticed them but did not blink an eye or move a muscle. Vilhallen and White took in the scene, accounting for all parties. Vilhallen did not know the small man in the shadow. From his positioning he had to presume he was with Martin.

Carl waved a rifle of all things. No other weapons were visible, though maybe the unknown party had a knife, judging by the way he held his hand. The tall man had to be Martin Webster. He stood on the bottom step from the house and held a bundle in the curve of his arm.

In the few seconds they had to assess the scene, Vilhallen noted what Carl and company did not. The little man in the shadow was coiled taut and leaned with a deceptive purpose. He was the one to watch. Martin, in his aspect and stance appeared more befuddled than dangerous.

Carl screamed, "I told you yesterday that I would be back."

Webster said, "I had a hard day yesterday. I don't remember that."

"He drove around the yard honking. I couldn't decipher his words," said a voice like soft rain.

In a suddenness that surprised the detectives, the heavy rowdy on Carl's right lunged for the little guy. Barely changing his stance, the little guy put out his elbow and the big guy ran into it. It was a carefully aimed blow all the same, in a spot on his jaw to knock his assailant flat but not kill him. The man fell like fluid to the ground as Carl swung his rifle and pulled the trigger. The shot went high.

Vilhallen and White bolted forward. Carl had lost his mind, swinging his cocked rifle toward Martin.

Martin turned his back to the rifle, protecting his bundle. Martin's friend did not move, but yelled the words, "Hurry-up, he's going to shoot."

In a flash, the young hooligan to Carl's left took off running into the grass.

In seconds, Vilhallen and White grabbed Carl from each side, removed the rifle from his hand. The detectives scanned about them for any more signs of trouble. Vilhallen's heart pounded. Only Carl's erratic shot saved them from a murder scene. As he breathed slowly for several seconds, Vilhallen noted the small man's motion of hand to pocket. Everything else was utterly still.

Vilhallen heard White telling Carl that he was a lucky man. Only then did Vilhallen look at the former deputy. Carl stayed on his feet between them, his body wired like an over-heated engine. His eyes were huge and glistening. Not even a breeze cooled their faces, and the overcast night sky held the threat of rain.

"To add insult to injury, you used your county vehicle." White sounded cool and calm.

Vilhallen watched the lithe motion of the unknown man as he climbed the porch steps and took the infant from Martin Webster. They both turned to watch, but neither of them said a word. Vilhallen wondered why neither man was screaming angry. Why were they so calm?

Vilhallen called for an ambulance for the motionless form on the ground and for back-up. A highway patrolman responded within minutes. Carl sat in the back seat of the patrol car, his sullen attitude like a visible black cloud around him.

The medics had Carl's crony up and walking, holding his jaw and cursing. He declined a ride to the emergency room. A county deputy from Davidson County pulled into the yard just as the medics left. He would take Carl and friend to the county lock-up in Wheaton.

The deputy registered shock when he saw Carl in custody. Carl greeted the man by name through the vehicle window.

"Do your job, deputy," Vilhallen told him.

So it was that Vilhallen and White met Martin and Crook and Kirby. Before a word could be exchanged, pickup truck lights appeared in the small curve to the house. A gray-haired farmer leaped from the truck and looked around. Only after the man was satisfied that no one was hurt did he turn to Vilhallen and say, "I'm Bill Bendix from down the road."

It was twenty-seven minutes since Vilhallen and White left the pub. Vilhallen wondered if his food was cold.

Martin gestured for the detectives to come inside. They sat at the kitchen table while the unknown man brought mugs of coffee. Now in the warm kitchen light White recognized Martin from a long ago State B basketball tournament and they discussed that briefly.

White then noted Martin's name and address and Kirby's name. Then White turned his attention to the small bald guy.

"Name?" White said.

The man appeared to hesitate so Martin said, "This is Jeremy Sabo. We call him Crook but he is not a real crook. He was framed."

White gaped at Martin while Vilhallen took new interest in the man called Crook. Vilhallen had never met anyone quite like Crook, but he knew there was more to the man than met the eye. Outside he had behaved like a trained combat professional. Here in the kitchen he held his mug and sat quietly like a harmless almost sad, little fellow.

Bill provided his name and address with the calm confidence of a man who owns land and knows his place. Vilhallen liked the farmer.

Vilhallen said, "You are Martin's only transportation?"

"Yes," Bill said.

"Did you take Martin anywhere on Friday night?"

"Yes. We went into Sioux Falls for last minute birthday party stuff. I dropped him off at home about eleven PM." Bill answered calmly but Vilhallen noted that he glanced often at his friends, possibly looking for reassurance.

"And you, Mr. Sabo? Where were you on Friday night?" White asked.

"I was here with Kirby," Crook said.

Vilhallen said, "Why are you called Crook?"

"Because I am not one," Crook said.

Of course, everyone at the table knew the detectives would be checking on that.

Vilhallen clarified all means of transportation: no car, no truck, no tractor, no lawn mower, only Bill Bendix.

Crook provided the description of what happened earlier with the siren and lights and pounding on the door. Carl screamed for them to come outside, making his accusations.

That was it. Vilhallen and White stood to leave. "One more thing." Vilhallen turned around to ask, "Is your little fellow there missing a bottle?"

Martin shrugged, perplexed at the question. Crook answered, "Not that I know of. Why do you ask?"

"We found a baby bottle under the seat of Hauk's vehicle," Vilhallen told them, watching them carefully, hoping for some telltale reaction. He was disappointed. The men gathered in the kitchen, looked back at him with complete puzzlement. Maybe Crook blinked, but Vilhallen was not sure. He had gambled with the question and now feared he had divulged evidence and got nothing for it.

Vilhallen and White hashed it all over long into the morning hours. One point of interest clung to both detectives: Martin's baby. The baby bottle under the seat took on renewed significance. After dealing with Carl, they would check the last time that vehicle was cleaned and who sat inside. The lab report was due tomorrow. The murder of Sheriff Hauk appeared planned, but may not have been initially. The clean-up was the work of a real pro.

Chapter Twenty-Five

Early the next morning, Vilhallen and White drove the few blocks to the county court house located on a full block of lawn between Highway 81 and Main Street. Inside his cell Carl Banks appeared a different man. He was a bag of bones inside a loose sack of skin.

"Good morning, Mr. Banks," Vilhallen said. "Deputies from Minnehaha County are bringing over boxes of Hauk's files and contents from his desk, as well as the case files located right here. We are going to an interview room and you are going to tell us everything you know about your former boss. Does that work for you?"

The only response from the man sitting on the cot was a slight nod.

"Mr. Webster is declining to press charges despite the endangerment to his infant son. That doesn't mean you will not do jail time, Mr. Banks, but it does mean we can work through this with your cooperation." Vilhallen stood stiffly along the jail bars and spoke through them.

"No jail time," Carl said. It was the last vestige of a cocky little fool.

The tape recorder did not make any noise at all as it recorded the words of Carl and Vilhallen and White. A stenographer took notes and four assistants from the Minnehaha District Attorney's office moved in and out of the conference room as the stack of folders counted down. Each file had to be examined. Hauk kept impeccable records of his illicit dealings. There were forty seven individual cases of extortion.

By noon a story of corruption emerged that astounded the detectives. Vilhallen shook his head again and again, and White stopped talking except for sparse, intermittent clarifications.

Sheriff Hauk garnered about four thousand a month in cash from protection money, pay-offs, gambling, and harassment. It was not vast sums but this was a farming county of forty-five hundred people not a city. Always careful in his victims, he kept each thing small and separate. He made it easier to pay than to fight, especially when the victims believed they were alone. Carl described one instance in which he had a major role. Carl shot two head of prime beef cattle. After that, the owner paid Hauk three hundred a month for protection.

White asked, "How did this start, Carl?"

"DUI's first. Then it moved to the truckers, hairdressers, businesses, extra-marital affairs."

"I don't see a file for the local telephone man," Vilhallen said.

"Messing with the women don't pay so they don't get a file."

"What about Cassandra Peters? She has a legal file but no extortion file." White was talking more to himself than to Carl but Carl rolled his eyes.

"Sandra Peters was a missing person," Carl said. "She had nothing to do with Hauk."

"So why," Vilhallen asked, "did Hauk have her file in his kitchen.."

Carl shrugged.

It was time to break for lunch. The two detectives sitting at the table closed their notepads and the final folder and sat back. Carl hunched at the table, his elbows on the table and his hands holding up his head. Vilhallen studied Carl for a few seconds and said, "Misery, thy name is Carl."

White appeared to find no understanding for the greedy little man. "Why, Carl, with all this in Hauk's life did you suspect Mr. Webster, the one person without a single connection?"

"He has a connection. Hauk was going to send social services to take that baby he has. He didn't write it down because that loony-toon told Hauk to get out," Carl said.

"When was this?" Vilhallen made exact notes. He thought it strange that Martin had not mentioned this last night.

"A few weeks ago," Carl said. "Martin Webster refused to pay. But that's not the reason I know he did it. Martin Webster is the only thing that's changed in this town in all the years Hauk was sheriff. Nothing changed for six or seven years, why would it now? It has to be him. Hauk's backed away from any new clients. It's all status quo but for the nut job." Carl remained convinced.

That afternoon a delivery arrived from the lab in Sioux Falls. White carried the evidence box and the written report into the conference room and set it on the table.

Vilhallen said, "Before we examine the lab report, I have one other question. Where is the money?" Vilhallen had Hauk's ledger open on his desk. "The funds from the desk drawer are a small fraction of Hauk's bottom line."

When Carl returned to the conference room, the detectives decided to finish with the money first and then the contents of the trophy box. Carl stated simply that Hauk knew nothing was noticed faster or caused greater suspicion than money he shouldn't have. Carl's take was twenty-five percent and he put that in a bank account in Sioux Falls. Hauk's money was Hauk's private concern and he never told Carl anything about it.

White nodded and looked at his partner. Vilhallen set the ledger aside and heaved a big sigh. "What we have to talk about now, Mr. Banks, is ugly, real ugly. It makes me sick."

Detective White put the tin box in the center of the table and opened it. Both detectives watched the color drain from Carl's face as though he had a spigot on his neck.

"What do you recognize in here, Carl?" White asked. He had moved his chair slightly away from the table as though he had to make some distance.

Carl could not speak. His eyes bulged and he swallowed several times before he could point to the homemade hoop ear rings. "Those belonged to Allyson Darby," Carl said.

Speaking to the recorder, Vilhallen said, "Mr. Banks is referring to the earrings numbered four on the evidence bag."

Vilhallen checked through the investigator reports. "Allyson Darby is the teenager found dead along a fence line in April two years ago."

Carl said, "Allyson wore those on Safety Day at school. I only noticed because they looked ridiculous. I still remember them. Her death was ruled a suicide by exposure. The suicide part was never released to the public."

Carl did not recognize the other five souvenirs, but his hands shook and he could not look at the box or its contents. "Tell us what you know, Carl. Tell it all," White told him with a cold tone that surprised Vilhallen.

"Hauk liked girls. That's all I know." Carl showed new signs of excitement in his expression, and animation in his body. "I worried about Allyson because she lived down the block from me and I saw her walking to school or the pool or whatever. I took it personal when she disappeared. And I didn't like it when Hauk buried the case. He didn't even try to find her.

But Cassandra Peters disappears and Hauk is like gangbusters looking for her. That's how I knew . . . " Carl stopped himself, closing his lips tight.

"That's how you knew Cassandra Peters was alive. Is that what you were going to say, Carl?" Vilhallen asked.

Carl nodded.

The tin tackle box with its contents was wrapped and re-tagged. The report contained DNA from two of the objects: the hair and one ring. For now, the investigators would continue meticulous research into past cases. Both detectives knew the box had a connection. Of course, it had a connection. Hauk was a serial rapist and a probable murderer.

"Thank you, Mr. Banks," White said, and he left.

Vilhallen stayed behind with the States Attorney and worked through Carl's agreement.

Tomorrow, they would start checking out every name from the files. Vilhallen would also look deeper into Hauk's last case, Cassandra Peters. It all had to be done. What had changed to motivate murder? What point had been reached or line crossed? Why now? Carl was correct in one thing: Martin Webster was the only change in town. He was the only known prospective new name for a private extortion file.

Chapter Twenty-Six

When Maureen crossed Martin's porch on Tuesday morning at seven AM, the rarely used door to the foyer stood open. The light whooshing sound of a paint sprayer as well as the smell of paint met her before she saw Martin on the scaffolding, painting the foyer walls above the staircase. Her first thought was for Kirby but of course Martin did not have Kirby with him on the scaffolding or exposed to the paint fumes.

The plastic tarp under her feet covered the hardwood floor from front door to the far wall. The banister was wrapped with newspaper and duct tape. The old glass chandelier was covered with a sheet and looked like a huge Halloween ornament. The plaster dust from the old torn down walls put a dry, sticky taste in her mouth and plugged her nose.

Martin painted with focus and did not hear her, so she reached backwards to rap her knuckles on the door. Martin looked down, shut off his sprayer and said, "What do you think of this color?" His voice echoed in the empty space around the high stairwell corner.

Maureen, concerned primarily with Carl's visit the previous night, had to re-focus her attention. Martin waited, sprayer in hand, for her to answer his question. Maureen tried to visualize the entire space in the warm pale peachy color that covered several feet along the ceiling. Martin was a genius. It was lovely against the dark woodwork. "Perfect," she answered. He nodded.

"How are you?" she asked, sending her voice toward the ceiling. "Did Carl give you a scare?"

"Fine, now," Martin said. "Yes, he gave me a scare. I first thought he came to get Kirby."

Maureen noticed that all of the woodwork was gone. The place looked naked. Normally the wide, high doorframes consisted of several layers of separate pieces of wood, but the doorframes as well as the floorboards and window trim was removed.

Martin told her he was hoping to have it finished in time for Kirby's baptism. Maureen nodded. She would not express her skepticism about the time this would take. Martin would do what he set out to do. If Kirby wasn't baptized until he was ten, so be it.

"I wanted to know what the detectives were like," Maureen said, her neck starting to ache.

"Crook can tell you," Martin answered. He put his paint mask over his nose and resumed his work. Martin had an air of contentment and satisfaction about himself that made the house seem peaceful. Despite the tension in the town and inside her, Martin seemed peaceful. She watched her brother for several minutes. He was a handsome man, tall and lean and in control.

"Don't forget to stop and eat," she called up to him.

"Don't worry." His voice was muffled with the mask. "My crew takes a two hour lunch if I'm not there." He laughed.

Maureen went in search of Crook. She found him in the newly designated family room off the kitchen. From end to end in straight rows across the floor laid the woodwork pieces. Two sawhorses were placed in front of the window and a long piece of doorframe lay across them. This room held the new TV. The bean bag chairs were pushed almost flat against the wall. The only floor space was a semi-circle of dust in front of the closed-up fireplace. A fan in the window blew the fumes out.

Maureen's eyes smarted instantly. She said, "Oh my gosh, where is Kirby?"

Crook knelt in front of the doorframe brushing on a coat of varnish remover. His head looked to be only inches above the wood and his painstaking, meticulous labor was slow. Across the back of his bald head stretched two thin lines of a surgical mask. Two clean pieces of molding stood in a corner. Crook looked like a little boy playing with toys.

Maureen did a quick sweep for Kirby. Crook looked up and gestured toward the kitchen where Maureen found the baby. Kirby slept in his small bed. His fingers curled around the satin trim of his blanket. He also wore a surgical mask and lay beneath a tent. A baby monitor and an air monitor were hooked to his crib.

Despite the fan in the kitchen window blowing in, the radio on classical music and the air monitor hooked to the bed clearly on the blue *good*, Maureen did not like it. She would talk to Martin about day-care for Kirby if he planned on working. He always planned on working.

From behind her came Crook's voice. "I'm glad you came early. We have extremely important errands to do today."

"How did you know I was coming at all?" she asked him, surprised.

"I knew Bill would tell you and Tillie about our late night visitors and you would come. I'm glad to see you. I need your help." He said this in his habitual matter-of-fact tone. To Maureen he sounded presumptuous.

"Hey," she answered, glaring at him, "your will is not my command."

Crook gaped back at her. He didn't understand and confusion actually crossed his features. Seeing this, Maureen relented. More gently she said, "It is different asking for favors from people who can, if they choose, say 'no.'"

Crook nodded. Maureen said, "In the outside world, the command structure is handled differently and it is not straightforward."

Crook changed his tone. "I need your help, Maureen, with some errands, and I need for you not to ask any questions about it."

Maureen thought about this. She did not flinch nor did she jump onboard. She thought about it, looking at Crook.

"Is this related to Hauk?" she asked.

"That is a question," he said.

She said nothing more and she did she move until Crook understood he had to answer her.

"Yes."

Maureen knew that few people had ever withstood his aura of command, but she felt immune. Underneath, she thought that he somehow did not really mean to be so bossy.

"What errands?" Maureen asked. She stepped away from the baby bed, as her voice made Kirby squirm.

"I need a fire to burn some clothing and I need to replace Kirby's formula." Crook met her eyes and knowledge passed between them.

"What you are asking could put me in jail," Maureen whispered her words because she was going to cry and did not want Crook to know it. Like Martin, Maureen did not willingly show emotion. Being vulnerable was one thing, letting on was another thing entirely. Her heart clenched with fear. Crook was in serious trouble and maybe Martin as well. Her lips felt too stiff to form words and her hands felt cold.

Crook stepped toward her and put his hands on her shoulders. An intense spark lit his sea blue eyes. "It is better if you do not know," he told her. "The law is a line and some of us are on the wrong side of that line without meaning to be. I've learned to live with that. I do what I have to do to protect what is important to me and what is fair to me. I do it, no matter where it falls. I know how to protect you."

Then Crook added as an afterthought, "Damn, a fellow lets one friend inside and the whole world comes storming along for the ride. It makes me a bit angry, but it's too late now to change things. Besides, I owe Martin, he was my last chance to ever see the outside, and he did not let me down."

"Sort of the frying pan to the fire for you," Maureen said, trying to be level, fighting to get a grip on what had changed in the last minutes from suspicion to fact.

With a cock of his head and a thin half-smile, Crook said, "Martin made me laugh."

Maureen's father called her stubborn. Martin called her determined. No one ever called Maureen impulsive. Maureen struggled with a blind leap of faith.

"I'll do it," she said. "I know a good lawyer."

Without another word, Crook grabbed two garbage bags by the kitchen door and took them to Maureen's fire red Mustang. "Not exactly a low-key vehicle," he said as Maureen opened her trunk.

He tossed the bags into the trunk. Then he went inside, followed by Maureen. He told Martin to come down from the scaffolding. It was a blustery day, chilly and windy with occasional rain. The trees dropped their remaining leaves in swirls of wind and the leaves rustled across the driveway. It was too cold for Kirby.

Crook gave Martin the baby-care update. Kirby had two bottles made in the fridge. That was it. He would be fine for a few hours. Crook said, "I will bring back new formula."

Martin stood in the kitchen. Kirby opened his eyes and Martin bent to lift the baby into his arms. Kirby hunkered down into Martin's arm perfectly. "Crook," Martin said, "I don't want Maureen to be involved in this." He was still the soft-spoken, gentle man, but there was new awareness in him, an intelligence and strength. His gaze was level and without emotion.

"I know," Crook answered, "but she already is. The thing is, the cops will find me. Likely they have my file on their desk right now. They will discover that I have a previous violent act. They already know that I have the skills used in this crime. They may have me on their minds as a person of interest, but they can't prove it. It is always the cover-up that gets people. So we have to be very careful in our cover-up."

Maureen did not interrupt the conversation. She thought that Crook had completely given up any pretense of innocence, at least to Martin and now to her.

Martin scratched his head and thought about this. "Well," he said, "there are six people directly or indirectly involved. Any one of us might make a mistake and say something incriminating. That can happen and probably will."

"That is the bottom line. The absolutely only way they will ever prove anything is if one of us gives ourselves away. But I think we can do it. Say nothing to no one. I think we can do that. What do you think, Maureen?" Both men looked at her; the blush rose on her cheeks and neck.

Maureen said, "You mean if the police ask me questions, I refuse to answer at all? Isn't that worse than answering something?"

Crook looked at her for a few seconds, glancing at Martin. "It is uncomfortable to say nothing, but it is best. When you lie, they gotcha. When you try to out-smart them, they gotcha again. Say not one word if asked anything pertaining to anything. Not one word."

Martin said, "These detectives seemed like the real deal to me. When we talked last night I was nervous."

"You didn't look nervous," Crook said.

Martin said to Maureen, "You have no connection."

"I will," Maureen said. The truth of this sunk deep like a lead weight.

Martin patted Kirby's back. He said, "It all depends on the cops doing the investigation, on their own personal agenda, on the victim. In this case, the cops are the real deal. The victim is supposedly one of their own. So this could be one of those cases that never goes away. On the other hand, sometimes it does go away. 'The victim deserved it' kind of thing and the evidence is not there, no physical evidence."

Martin abruptly stopped talking. He looked at his sister, and shrugged. "In for a penny, in for a pound," he said. Martin took two long strides to the window and shut off the fan. He bent down and pulled Kirby's blanket out of the bed. The room was chilly.

"Where is my coat?" Martin said.

Crook continued as if Martin had not asked about the coat. "If it is more detrimental to the law to solve the crime than to leave it unsolved, they might choose to leave it. That could happen."

"Dream on," Martin said.

Maureen almost repeated the question regarding Martin's coat, but she looked at Crook and held her tongue. She would ask later when Martin could not hear.

Martin told them he was taking Kirby to the first game that Sandra would play. "If I'm not here that's where I am." It wasn't even eight o'clock in the morning and the game started at seven that night. No one expected to be gone all day.

Outside, Maureen studied the grove of trees. Now some were dead and most had dead branches, but in her youth on many winter mornings those trees covered in frost were clouds of diamonds. Crook had said he needed a fire. As they sat in the front seat of the car thinking of where to go, Maureen told Crook of the picnic area at the Lake Vermillion State Park. The park was abandoned this time of year. And with this weather, likely not a single person would be there. She described the brick grilling pits. Crook nodded.

"Okay," she said. "We will have a picnic. First stop is the grocery store. We need charcoal." The danger made her giddy. They were like Bonnie and Clyde. For a woman who always stayed safely within the rules, she felt a rush of freedom, but only briefly. The excitement was replaced with gut-clenching fear before they reached the highway.

Maureen parked her shinny red Mustang in front of the grocery store windows. Crook said, "Maybe park down the block."

Through the windows Maureen could see the middle-aged clerk at the cash register. "Leave me alone, Crook. I can do this. I know these people."

It was a two check-out store, but there were long aisles of food and a crisp business. "Hello Maureen, long time no see," the clerk said as soon as Maureen was through the front door. Elsie was the mom of one of Maureen's classmates. She, like everyone, knew everyone in town or from town. She glanced at the car and the man inside it. "I heard you were on vacation," Elsie said, in a friendly tone but blatantly nosy.

Understanding immediately that she and Crook were anything but inconspicuous, she decided to do as she would anytime. "Hello, Elsie," she smiled warmly, "I am on vacation, helping Martin, you know." Since Martin's return had taken second place behind Hauk's murder, Elsie had bigger fish to fry.

"You see that fella there?" Elsie pointed down the second aisle. Maureen saw an unimposing brown-haired man reading the label on laundry detergent. "He is one of those big shot detectives in town investigating Hauk's murder." Elsie had lowered her voice to a near whisper. Maureen fought the temptation to run.

Maureen grabbed a cart, forced a parting smile at Elsie and started after her own groceries. She couldn't think of what it was she wanted. She pulled the sleeves of her sweater over her shaking fingers and tried a couple deep breaths to still her hammering heart. "Focus," she told herself. She found the new baby formula. Was it Enfamil? No, that was the kind Crook had to throw out. She grabbed Similac. She found the charcoal and lifted two big bags into her cart.

She was rushing now, nearly trotting. She grabbed canned vegetables, pastries and some brats. She backtracked for stick matches and again for charcoal lighter. She put on a lot of miles for a few things. The sauerkraut was in the aisle were the detective now stood with his cart neatly organized. She felt an aversion to meeting him as he glanced her way.

She pretended to think, her finger to her chin. She moved around the canned items in her cart. Still he stood there. She could hardly go past the aisle again. Suddenly sauerkraut did not sound good at all. She asked herself what she would do if she didn't know who he was. She didn't know the answer to that. She thought, at the rate I am going, he will never forget me. She decided to check out, now. He came up behind her at the checkout.

Maureen did not glance toward the car. It took every ounce of self-discipline but she stayed focused on Elsie. Maybe Crook would run. This detective would recognize him from last night.

The detective was distracted, checking his watch. Standing behind Maureen, he watched impatiently as Elsie keyed in each item that Maureen took from her cart. A kid appeared from no where and grabbed the heavy bags of charcoal. Maureen forced herself to watch the digital display of prices, not that she saw a single one, and Elsie chatted while she keyed. Maureen handed Elsie cash and waited to be told if she needed more, but Elsie handed change back.

"See ya, Elsie," Maureen said and then moved as quickly as her frozen limbs allowed. She forced a quick smile at the man behind her, trying to give the impression that she did not want to keep him waiting.

"Enjoy your vacation," Elsie answered as she turned her attention to her next customer. When Maureen glanced back she saw his eyes followed her, but he did not turn to look through the windows. She heard the detective say. "It's a chilly day for grilling." The carry-out stood with the charcoal waiting for her to open her trunk and she nearly did.

"Back seat," she told him and he obeyed.

Crook did not move a muscle. He seemed frozen. He had pulled Martin's baseball cap down over his face and sat low in the passenger seat staring straight ahead. He looked like a boy.

Maureen started for the driver's door when she realized she left her keys on the checkout while reaching for her change. Without a word she ran back inside. Maureen smiled and reached across the detective and picked up her keys.

"Big game tonight," Elsie was saying as Maureen forced her legs to walk slowly from the store.

In the car, Maureen backed out and took off. Crook said, "Cops are the luckiest people on the face of the earth. The good news is they don't know it."

Maureen glanced at him and saw the same relief she felt. He sat back and appeared to watch the fall countryside move swiftly past his window. She felt the hammering in her chest slow.

The State Park was abandoned as expected. The public picnic area was desolate, and the lake water rough and snapping in the wind. Hard almost horizontal rain pelted the windshield. Maureen parked close to the picnic shelter and shut off her car. Even in her beige sweater and the warm socks from Tillie, Maureen felt chilled just looking at the place.

The shelter gave little protection, but a near-by cluster of evergreens provided a wind break. Out of the wind, the temperature was maybe forty degrees. The cookout pits consisted of cement ovens built up from the ground with a grill across the top. In minutes, Maureen had the charcoal glowing red. She hovered over the heat while Crook continued to bring everything from the car. He ate a pastry with a lemon center and handed one to Maureen. They watched the charcoal heat and drank orange juice. The wind carried the smoke away in a straight line.

"Why didn't you do this in the burn pit at the farm?" Maureen asked.

"The first place the cops would look, that and the garbage. Better to be away from there." He lifted the first bag, opened it and then appeared to hesitate.

"What's wrong?"

Crook said, "I have all of the clothes except for Martin's coat. I can't burn Martin's coat. That coat is so thick and heavy it would take a blaze. I will have to do something about that and soon."

"You ruined Martin's coat?" Maureen's face was too stiff to talk. She had to force her words.

"Yes," Crook said. "If that is found, it could fry us all."

"Where is it?" Maureen did not really want to know. She felt sick.

"Hidden for now, but the cops will come with a search warrant. I have to think what to do with it. It would take a bigger fire than we can light to touch that coat."

A minute passed in stunned silence. Then Crook said, "If you close your eyes, Maureen, you can always say you didn't see a thing." Crook pulled from the bag a gray athletic warm-up suit with WHS in black letters across the front. Maureen closed her eyes so tight she saw lights then opened them again.

Crook loosely piled the material onto the coals. As he did so Maureen saw blood spatter across the front in a line from shoulder to hip. She looked away. Crook used a pair of pliers from her trunk to turn the clothing like cooking meat until the material burst into flame.

Maureen stepped back, grateful for the wind that carried the smoke and the smell away from her hot face. The fire was too big for the oven and they stood back, allowing it to consume the clothing, watching bits of burned fabric break free and fly into the cold dead grass where the rain killed the red edges. Nausea climbed into Maureen's throat. She gagged and could not speak.

Crook added a pair of socks, panties, bra and light canvas shoes. Maureen added more charcoal and lighter fluid. The wind lessoned and the rain changed from drizzle to a steady beat on the shelter roof.

"I have one more sack," Crook said. Maureen wanted to cry.

"Hurry up," she said. "Park Maintenance drives through here on random checks." Wet to her skin despite the roof of the shelter, her teeth began to chatter. She turned to see Crook running, head bowed, with one more garbage bag in his hand. The rain felt like tears on her cheeks and her hair curled flat on her forehead. She thought they looked like what they were: criminals. When she rubbed her eyes and cheeks she felt black smudges that followed the curve of her cheek in black lines.

Quickly working with the wet plastic, Crook emptied the last of it onto the sizzling coals. He described his favorite jeans, the pair he wore his last day at the hospital. Sliding from the bag and landing in a sloppy stack on top of the jeans, his navy ribbed shirt, his socks and briefs and t-shirt. He removed a pair of his shoes and looked at them closely. He threw them on the pile as well. .

Next came a sheriff's uniform stiff with dried blood, briefs and socks. The fire pit was too small to adequately burn the sheriff's clothes. Crook checked the charcoal and lighter fluid. He dumped a few briquettes on the flame.

Maureen watched Crook, his expression hard. Fear tickled her spine. Not fear of Crook but fear for him. Crook looked up and caught her expression. He said to her, "I don't want to loose the years I have left. I'm risking it all to get away clean. Can you understand that?"

"That's why I am here," Maureen said. She shivered in the cold and whispered around the lump hurting her throat. "I want my chance at life, too." She stepped toward him, put her arms around his neck and kissed his cold, trembling lips.

Suddenly the clothes caught flame and the two wet, trembling figures stepped back from the pit and watched. Maureen untangled herself from Crook's arm and ran to the car. She ran from the cold and from the intensity of the situation and the intensity of Crook. She started the engine and turned the heat on full blast. One thing about her Mustang, the heater worked. Still, it took several minutes before she could stop shivering.

She watched Crook tend the flames. When he took one of the bags and started picking up bits of cloth and tennis shoe from the grass, Maureen once again braved the weather and ran to help him. When the fire burned down, he used a stick to stir through it, picking out buttons and zippers and the remnants of a wallet. He opened the wallet and laid out on the embers each recognizable item in the wallet, even the cash. The remaining piece of leather wallet would not burn, so he put that in the garbage bag of scrap pieces.

A sudden gust of wind caught Maureen on the side of her face and caused a sharp pain in her ear. She hunched her head and kept going, working like a fiend until not a single scrap of material remained on the grass. "That has to be it," she shouted at him. "I can't stand this a second longer." He nodded and started for the warm car.

The next stop was the Food Pantry in Sioux Falls. On the way Crook tossed bits from the window. At the Food Pantry, Maureen deposited the unused cans of baby formula in the designated box outside while Crook ran to the garbage dumpster with the remaining garbage including the plastic bags and every empty formula can he could find.

"If it ever comes to searching this dumpster we are done anyway," he told Maureen, looking sick. "The same with the formula. I left a bottle of Kirby's in Hauk's car. I just can't risk it making a difference."

His color was flushed and his lips white. As Maureen started for home, she asked him how he felt. Crook said nothing.

Maureen maneuvered her vehicle through the streets. Noting Crook's shivering, she risked a McDonald's drive-thru for hot coffee. Handing him the coffee, she said, "This would be the time to have Martin's coat."

"I think I will return the coat to where I killed Hauk. That way all the evidence is in one place. The cops either find it or they don't." Crook held the hot cup in both his hands.

"That coat ties Martin to the murder."

"I know, but those detectives have no reason to search where I am going to put it, not yet. We have a little time. I would confess before anyone charged Martin."

Crook said nothing more and Maureen did not ask. Eventually Crook would tell her. For right now it was more than enough to get through the next minute.

For a half hour Maureen drove and Crook rode in silence, not even music on the radio, only the wipers in soft swooshes on the windshield. Their clothes began to dry and the shivers stopped, color returned to Crook's lips and the red flush cooled on his cheeks.

He looked straight ahead and not at all toward Maureen. The rain enclosed them and the wipers moved it away and Crook reached for her hand and held it tight.

It was after noon when they entered Martin's house. Maureen went straight for the bathroom. On one side was a state of the art laundry. She shed her clothes and put them in the washer. Then she crossed the divide from laundry to bathroom and ran hot water into the claw-footed tub. Everything was new but the tub itself. She took a few minutes to revel in the clean lines and the tile floor and the big, soft towels. Then she climbed into the hot water and allowed herself to float away.

Chapter Twenty-Seven

In his final written statement to Villhalen and White the former deputy, Carl Banks, wrote:

"On Friday morning, the last Friday of Sheriff Hauk's life, I was excited. All I could think about was the planned visit to Martin Webster. I pictured Hauk showing Webster who was boss. I could hardly wait.

"Hauk promised that I could drive his county vehicle while he drove his sheriff's vehicle. The first visit when Hauk informed Martin Webster that he would need to pay money to Hauk each month, Webster did not appear to understand. He did not know that the Sheriff was talking to him. Webster looked stupid. Hauk would start the process to remove Webster's baby from his custody. That was the threat.

"No one ever refused Hauk's protection. They were normal people. I thought Webster might need some additional convincing. I once saw Hauk hit a trucker in the face with steel knuckles. I hoped for something like that.

"Sheriff Hauk promised a return visit. This was the visit I was to join the sheriff. And this was the visit I looked forward to. I expected Hauk and I would drive to Webster's farm on Saturday morning.

"I was unaware of a man called Jeremy Sabo at the farm. Sabo was not there at the time of our first visit. Sheriff Hauk didn't know about him either. Had Hauk known another nut-case was living at that house, he would have had a field day with that little creep. I did find an unopened letter from a doctor in Nebraska, but I did not open Hauk's mail.

"On the final day of his life Hauk was still in a knot over Cassandra Peters. I was frustrated with him for that reason. I thought he should move on from the case. It was finished, done. Hauk needed to let it go. I wanted Hauk to focus on Webster. However I could not reason with him about this. Hauk had reached a point of stubborn, hard-headed obsession with Cassandra Peters. On that Friday, I could think only of Martin Webster. I had made up my mind that Webster would show proper respect and pay his money and shut his mouth. That was the rules set by Hauk and me.

"Hauk may have made a return visit to Martin's place on Friday night. He may have driven to his death unaware that Jeremy Sabo set an ambush. I can't help you with that. I don't know.

"My main duty on that Friday was to keep constant updates with Hauk. As I mentioned earlier, Hauk was in a bad mood. It was difficult to speak with him. He seemed real pissy. He insisted on hourly updates. Yet, he made no response to my updates unless I was late. At the time I figured his mood would pass. I was not worried when Hauk failed to respond to my Friday night radio calls. He would be fine for our Saturday morning errand.

"On my final drive around town I spotted Hauk's vehicle turning down the block to Cassandra Peter's house. At that time Hauk was fine and seeing to his sheriff work. I made one last stop at the court house, did my messages and clocked out.

On Saturday morning I drove to Hauk's house and discovered his body. That statement is already on file.

Carl Banks"

Chapter Twenty-Eight

On the last evening of Hauk's life, Sandra was in the gym. She stayed after practice to work on a new left-handed lay-up that Martin taught her. She worked without speaking much to the assistant coach who rebounded for her and passed the ball. When the coach had to go home for supper, Sandra declined a ride and told him that she would rather walk the four blocks to her house.

She did not shower in the locker room because she felt anxious to get home. This was the night she would begin to play bait to Hauk. She knew Hauk was coming. She spotted him every afternoon driving slow on her street. She felt it as a tingle down her spine and a squeezing in her stomach. Hauk would come for her, and she would be ready.

As she made her way from the gym she felt her usual clutch of anger tighten her stomach. No one seemed to believe that Hauk wanted to kill her. Martin could not believe the fact of it. He had no comprehension of evil. Bill could not believe her because to him it did not make sense. Only Crook understood to prepare for the possibility, to make a plan. Sandra took that plan to heart and would use it. They would all believe when she was dead.

As Sandra walked home dusk lay lazily over the streets. She shivered and wrapped her jacket tighter around her. She watched everything as she walked, allowing only a hazy day-dream about using her left-handed shot at the perfect time in the state tournament. A car crossed the intersection at her block and she stopped, standing still, heart pounding until she recognized the car as her neighbors'. This fear was crazy in a small town like this where she knew almost everyone. Picking up her pace, she moved quickly down the final block. Hauk was not out prowling tonight as he had every night since she returned to town.

Upon seeing her two-story white house, no lights in the window except the lamp in the living room her mother always left on, she remembered her mother telling her they were going out for supper with friends. She went through the back door into the kitchen. This door was never locked. She dropped her gym bag and opened the refrigerator. Balancing a bag of chips, a sandwich and soda, she trotted up the steps to her room.

A light shown under her bedroom door and she thought she must have left it on this morning, which was a bit odd. Still she turned the knob on the white wood door and stepped inside. Simultaneously she screamed and dropped the things she carried, turning to run from the sight of Hauk lying on her bed playing with her underwear. He was fast for a big man and caught her. He twisted her arm behind her back.

"Stand still and I won't break your arm," he told her. She did this, fighting to breathe and fighting to find control. "Okay, now clean up your mess before your mother gets home." His voice was calm on the outside but Sandra felt his excitement.

Sandra shook the pain from her arm and bent to pick up her sandwich and chips and the rolling bottle of Coke. As she did this, she thought of Crook. During her recovery and before she went home, Crook educated her on many things. One of the things he told her was not to show fear. "It is the fear in their prey that turns on the predator," he told her. "It is not the sex, it is the power."

They passed two afternoons practicing survival skills while Martin cared for Kirby and made notes about his house. Crook made her role-play different, dangerous situations. It seemed ridiculous and insipid at the time. But it was there in her mind, what she had to do.

Crook told her she had to face what happened, to look at it and accept it. Denying something horrible is what Martin tried to do. Martin focused on other stuff and lived in a world of denial for more than twenty years and see what happened; it catches up later.

Crook told Sandra his own story of betrayal that took away thirty years of his life on the outside. "But," he told her, "I still lived. Strange as it may sound to you, crazy people have a life. We like dessert after supper just like you do." When she recalled these words Sandra smiled. Her fear moved away from her, lingering at the tip of her fingers, ready to enclose her at the first sign of weakness.

In the amount of time it took Sandra to snatch a rolling soda bottle and set it on the dresser, she repeated inside her head the Wednesday plan. She would not be a victim. She would likely end up dead, but she would not be Hauk's victim. Sandra controlled her panic.

"I guess you know about the money," she said, putting resignation in her voice.

Hauk not only took the bait, he leaped at it. "What money, and tell it all." He commanded her to talk, taking her arm to twist it behind her with one hand and touching her with the other. Even with her sports bra on, it hurt when he fondled her. He seemed to mistake her pain for the anguish of spilling the beans.

"I thought you already knew." Sandra talked through clenched teeth. "The money in the barn."

He twisted a little harder.

"The suitcase of money is in the barn on the Webster farm." She yelled and he released her. She fell to the floor. The triumph in her heart outweighed the searing pain in her shoulder and upper arm. Tears ran down her cheeks from the pain but she knew Hauk no longer wanted to touch her. Greed consumed his eyes.

"Webster didn't bring money with him from the loony-bin you lying sack of shit." Hauk curled his lips as he stood above her.

"Yes, he did," Sandra said forcing her voice to stay low and calm. She hung her head. "He kept it in a suitcase the whole time, hiding it from his ex-wife." Careful, she thought, not too much. She shut her lips.

Hauk said, "You hid out on the Webster farm. I didn't think you would hide there." He sneered at her. "You and the rats and the mold, perfect." Hauk appeared to ponder this. She saw him making connections as he stared down at her. "That bastard baby is mine. I'll make Webster's life so miserable he'll give me that farm." He was gleeful, pleased. Now Sandra saw crazy. Crazy was not Martin or even Clara, the mid-wife. Crazy was Hauk.

"Did you tell the fool about me?" Hauk glared at her.

"No." Sandra lied.

"Your story about camping never cut it with me. But I have to tell ya, I never saw you with the crazy guy. Learn something new everyday."

Sandra almost said, "Martin is not crazy," but she shut her lips and said nothing. She sat on the floor caressing her shoulder.

"Let's go." Hauk nudged her with the point of his boot. His demeanor was that of a co-conspirator. She did not allow herself for even a second to waver in her belief that Hauk was not human. He planned to kill her.

As Sandra's fast pace slowed in the kitchen, she felt Hauk's breath on her hair. She leaned on the bar stool which faced the island counter. Hauk ran his fingers down her back. Sandra put her face into the island sink and threw up. The nausea was not due to Hauk's touch though the touch did make her sick. It was partially due to the pain in her shoulder, but mostly due to her fear. Do not panic, she said to herself. Do not panic.

That money seed planted in Hauk's sick mind could grow into danger for Martin and Kirby. This realization frightened her. But Hauk constituted danger for as long as he lived, not just for tonight. Her hope for survival rested on Crook, and that Hauk did not know about Crook.

She forced herself to breathe. She drank some water. Hauk waited for her, standing behind her, close but not touching.

Hauk indicated the garage door and Sandra went that way without question. Hauk's police vehicle was parked inside her dad's garage. He lifted the door while wordlessly, Sandra climbed inside. Hauk backed out, stopped and appeared to be waiting. Sandra understood that she was expected to get out and close the door. She considered getting out of the car and running. That would not fix tomorrow. She did not budge. Finally, Hauk backed out of the driveway with the garage door left open.

He pushed her shoulder as a suggestion that she slide down in her seat. Someone would spot her inside the vehicle through the streets or on the highway. Friday evening traffic was consistent, several cars parked at the gas station, their owners filling up their ride and buying beer. The site of Hauk's vehicle put the fear of God into them.

As the moonlit fields passed her window, she remembered that Martin was not home. He'd gone with Tillie and Bill into Sioux Falls shopping for something his ex-wife wanted for Carmen. At least for tonight Martin was safe. Crook would be watching Kirby.

Hauk turned on the gravel and drove fast, faster than the gravel road allowed. She thought to turn the wheel in one quick grab and then run for Crook. She started to position herself when Hauk brought the vehicle to sudden and complete stop. They were just past Bill's place and down the slight hill to Martin's house.

"Here is the plan, Carl." Hauk turned toward her and stopped. Apparently realizing she was not Carl, he started again. "The plan is to drive right to the barn, lights off. Show me the money. We take it and leave. Simple. We will not hear one single complaint about it." He laughed a horrible half-silent sound.

She nodded.

He turned off the lights and drove slow to Martin's driveway. She wondered why would he need her once he had the money. "You plan to kill me in the barn." It was a statement, not a question.

"You know, you royal pain in my ass, that is a brilliant idea. The crazy guy would be blamed and I could laugh all the way to the bank." He spoke in an exaggerated thoughtful tone. It was at that point Sandra took comfort in Hauk's failure to know about Crook. He knew everything about everybody, but he didn't.

The vehicle slowly crunched down the road and into Martin's driveway. As they rounded the slight curve and saw the house, it was completely dark. Sandra's heart clenched. No one was home. Crook must have gone with Martin.

She said, "The crazy guy has an alibi if he is not at home."

With a nasty laugh, Hauk said, "I don't think that is a problem."

"People won't always lie for you," she said.

"Yes, they will."

As the vehicle, lights off, rolled past the house, Hauk looked straight ahead toward the sloping barn roof outlined against the night sky. Sandra saw a rectangle patch of light waving in the wind on the tall weeds. Hope blossomed. She was excruciatingly careful not to look up at the bedroom window on the north side of the house facing the barn. In his room, Crook would have the radio on low so Kirby could learn country music. She forced her eyes forward.

Hauk stopped with the bumper nearly against the water tank. Suddenly Carl's voice blasted into the silence. Sandra screamed, and Hauk smirked.

"Checking in, Bossman. Quiet night." Carl sounded hesitant. Hauk ignored the radio and Carl. Sandra thought to grab the radio and scream for help, but Hauk called her Carl, so she did not. If Hauk called her Carl while planning his crime, Carl must be his partner. Screaming for help to Carl might bring help, but not for her.

The house was dark, but Sandra knew Crook's room was on the barn side of the house. He and Kirby were upstairs for the night. Hauk did not look back at the house once he drove passed it.

For the four miles to Martin's, Sandra had studied the configuration of the dashboard. She had spotted a worn button near the wheel and determined that was the siren. With her left hand she reached out, quick, and pushed it. She was rewarded with a squeak of siren sound and a backhand from Hauk. As her head spun she glimpsed the light in Crook's window go out. Crook was coming.

Sandra straightened herself in the seat and looked through the windshield at the moonlit night. "It will be pitch dark inside the barn," she said. He grabbed a flashlight from its casing attached to the dashboard.

"Let's go," he said.

"No," Sandra said, quiet but firm. "If you are going to shoot me you will have to do it now, here in your car. Then lie your way out of that."

In the backsplash of light she saw his features contort in fury. She prepared for pain, but none came. Instead he opened his door and the interior light burned her eyes. He started around the front of the car. She fumbled to lock her door but he held his keys and unlocked it at the same time ripping her door open. He grabbed her by her right arm and pulled her from the car with as little effort as grabbing a stuffed doll.

Sandra cried out as the pain in her shoulder seared through her neck and down to her fingers. He let go of her and waved his flashlight for her to precede him through the weeds to the side door of the barn.

Slowly Sandra led the way. Never having been inside the barn, Sandra stepped slowly, thinking of something to do, anything. Once inside, she would be lost. She stopped still about two feet from the door. The flashlight exposed the rusty latch and door pull. "It pulls hard," she said.

"So what," he said.

She took a deep breath and reached for the latch and at that moment she heard a slight crunch in the dry weeds like a footstep. She dared not stop her motion and let on that she heard anything, but Hauk held her arm for her to stop. He obviously heard the sound. He waved the flashlight across the weeds in a sweeping motion but nothing appeared from the darkness but the budding tops of ragweed.

He pushed for her to go on, but he was wary now, alert, and took his weapon from the holster. She heard a click and started to pray. Just as she expected, stepping into the interior of the barn was stepping into a black hole with rough, hard-packed earth beneath her feet. She felt the scamper of feet across her tennis shoes. Martin had not cleared the rats from the barn.

"Find the money," Hauk ordered her and then he handed over to her the flashlight. The weight was substantial in her hand. He read her thoughts and said, "Don't think about it. You find the money and I might let you live. You try anything and you are dead as you stand, and I will find the money myself." He had no need to raise his voice; the low deep sound was enough to create prickles down her spine.

She moved the flashlight in a slow arch across whatever was in front of her. They moved cautiously across a wide walkway with storage rooms and a milk room, then black emptiness on one side and a feeding trough and stanchions on the other. Sandra spotted a makeshift ladder. She brought the light back to it and started that way.

During these minutes the only thing that prevented Sandra from propelling herself into a dead run into the blackness of the barn was Crook. She trusted Crook to keep his word.

She had to use the light to mark her footing. The old dirt floor was lumpy under her feet. She heard Hauk breathing behind her. She tried to appear confident of the way, stepping carefully but without hesitation. She listened for any sound other than her own and Hauk. She listened and she begged God for His mercy.

Once at the ladder, she turned and handed Hauk the flashlight, astounded that he took it from her hand without question. She pointed up and glanced at his face. His whole face, not just his eyes, but every plane and crevice was filled with greed, money-lust. He had a tiny speck of saliva on his lips, which he licked away.

Sandra thought, I am a dead girl walking. But she climbed, one rung at a time, reaching with her left arm and stepping up. Her sweat pants caught on the slivered wood and she continually had to yank the material free. Nine long steps and her head poked above the hole in the hay-mound floor. Up here was light. With a good third of the roof leaning inward, the moonlight created shadows and dark places.

Sandra stepped through, Hauk quickly climbing after her. She ran, suddenly bolting without purpose for the old basketball hoop leaning toward her like a grinning face. She lost her footing on the slope of the floor and rolled until the wall beneath the hoop stopped her. She covered her face in her arms, waiting for death. When nothing happened she looked up to see Hauk searching the old hay toward the hay-mound door. She pulled out some desperate courage and started crawling uphill to the ladder. Crook would not get here in time, she had to reach the ladder. Then she would drop down and run.

The flashlight swept across the mounds of moldy dry hay and into the space beyond the open hay-mound door. She held her breath as she crawled, closer and closer, but he suddenly whirled the light upon her.

"Where is it?" In five steps he was upon her, on his knees, holding her down, with the flashlight raised, poised to strike.

Then a different voice, a near whisper, said, "Sandra, when he lets go of you, roll away." Hauk did let go, and Sandra did roll away. Before Hauk could regain his feet, Crook buried his carving knife in Hauk's neck, in and out quick as lightening. Hauk's body continued to stand for two or three endless seconds and then he dropped the flashlight and he fell heavy to the floor.

The flashlight rolled down the sloping floor, *thunk, thunk, thunk, thunk* until it stopped at Sandra's shoulder.

No sound at all, not even a breath entered the hay-mound. Then a chilly blast of wind suddenly cracked through the slanting roof and shook the hay-mound floor. Sandra felt nothing. She knew only that she lived. Crook knelt beside her, caressing her hair and face. He said, "It's over, at least this part. Are you hurt?"

She shook her head beneath Crook's hand. When he helped her to stand, the pain in her shoulder brought a gasp.

Crook picked up the flashlight. Hauk's unmoving body lay diagonal across the slope of the floor. The two of them turned the 250-pound dead-weight to the slope and rolled him to the rectangle hole along the far wall and pushed him through. Sandra and Crook heard the thud as Hauk hit the stanchions below.

Crook waved her around the huge puddle of blood soaking the floor. The splatter from when Crook stabbed Hauk reached Sandra's sweatshirt and dotted the letters spelling WHS Athletic Dept. He ran the light across her face. Sandra looked into the light with dry eyes and tight lips. Her heart did not race. She felt no more regret for Hauk than she felt for the rats. She felt a tremendous sense of relief.

"We need to get him to the water tank," Crook told her.

"Wheel barrow?" Sandra whispered.

"We can't leave a trace of blood on anything," Crook answered.

It was an extraordinarily difficult task. After a half hour the two of them together had barely managed to extract the body from the stanchions. They stood panting in the darkness with the rats smelling blood around them.

"Sandra," Crook said quietly and gently, "go to the house and bring Martin's coat and the garbage bags under the sink and check on Kirby. I had to leave him in my room. He generally sleeps through the night for me, but check on him, please." She nodded and left the darkness. He tried to light her passage to the side door but it was an odd angle. She had to feel her way out.

Chapter Twenty-Nine

It seemed a long time to stand with the ghosts of the dead, but Crook did, thinking and planning. He ran through his mind what they had to do, and at last Sandra returned.

"Kirby?" he asked.

"Sleeping like a baby," she answered.

With effort, they managed to get Hauk onto the coat and then the two of them pulling together managed to drag the coat and the body out of the barn into the moonlight. They were careful to drag him along the path already there, but nonetheless they damaged and broke a wide swath of weeds.

At the pump, Crook used the new electric pull switch and directed the flow to the nearly empty cattle tank. Crook completely undressed the corpse. Revulsion turned in his stomach, but he continued without hesitation. Then he and Sandra lifted the body, first the head and shoulders onto the rim and then the torso splashed into the deepening water.

It was no easy task.

Sandra grimaced with obvious pain but did not refrain from lifting. Crook said, "Is anything broken in your arm or shoulder?"

Sandra shook her head. Crook did not believe her but he dropped it.

"Let it fill," Crook told her. He bunched Hauk's blood drenched-clothes into a garbage bag, keeping out his belt, weapon, holster, boots and badge. He did not know if Hauk had another pair of boots. He would see. Then he followed the path to the house.

He carried Hauk's things to the house. He had to have light. Sandra would wait outside because Crook worried about the transference of Hauk's blood into the kitchen. He had blood on himself, his shirt, and his jeans. He took his clothes off outside and put them into a clean garbage bag that Sandra held for him. He removed his shoes and worked in his stocking feet.

Inside the kitchen, he poured an entire bottle of vinegar into Martin's beautiful new stainless steel sink and ran water into the deep side. Using a sponge, Crook carefully cleaned the wet blood from each of Hauk's possessions. He wore rubber gloves as he cleaned. Crook used the damp sponge to wipe Hauk's gun off, then once the holster was clean he put the weapon back.

Methodically, he cleaned each item with the vinegar until the water was crimson. Not a visible sign of blood remained on boots, badge, belt, or holster. If Hauk carried a wallet, that was with his clothes and beyond repair. A technician could test to his heart's content but would find nothing but degraded signs of Hauk's own blood which could be from any time and any place. At last satisfied, Crook placed the items into a new garbage bag.

He cleaned the sink with bleach and let the hot water continue to run. He poured bleach down the drain. He made two bottles for Kirby and went upstairs. Crook dressed and then lifted a sleeping Kirby from his playpen and into his infant seat. He wrapped blankets across the baby, and carried the infant seat to the kitchen. He set Kirby by the door, checked again that he slept comfortably, grabbed the garbage bag, and left the house. He would grab Kirby on the way out.

As the two of them walked back to the pump, Crook said, "I could leave Hauk to rot where he laid and let the rats clean up, but Martin would find him sooner or later and we can't have that. So, now we do this."

"We could call the cops, the real ones in Sioux Falls." Sandra made this suggestion with obvious hesitation. "It was self-defense."

"Or entrapment," Crook said.

"He came to me," Sandra said.

Crook knew the questions that would be asked. He said, "Too late, and we don't have a phone." Then he added as an afterthought, "It is all or nothing for us now, but I will keep you out of it."

"You can't keep me out of it because I won't allow it." Then they said nothing more. The sound of running water carried in the night air. When they reached the tank, it was running over. They could not see the color of the water and they could not see Hauk.

Sandra stripped off her sweats and climbed into the cold water. It circled her to her hips. "I have him," she said. "I am kicking him to the edge."

Again they had to lift and shove the body over the edge where Crook guided the body's fall onto Martin's coat. Sandra climbed out, shivering in her underwear and quickly putting back on her sweats. She moved to turn off the pump. Crook said, "Let it run."

A brisk wind blew from the west, and they worked as quickly as possible with the cold stiffening their fingers. Of course the blood on Martin's coat would again transfer to the body, but Crook would take care of that later. For now they wrapped the huge, naked dead man in Martin's coat and lifted and hefted and moved it slowly bit by bit into the back seat of his police vehicle.

Crook indicated for Sandra to drive. He found a hat in the back seat window and put it on her head. Passing motorists would only see the cop hat and not notice Sandra's face. Again Sandra did as she was asked without hesitation or complaint. Crook used a valuable second to study the girl. Sandra could be in shock. He knew she worked through pain. He thought, I must tell Martin to make sure she sees a shrink.

Sandra backed up and turned around. Crook thought to stop her and then realized it was no time to worry about tracks. Sandra stopped at the house where Crook ran inside and grabbed Kirby, clean diapers and two bottles tucked into the side of his seat. Kirby, seat and all, rode on Crook's lap because Hauk occupied the back seat. Not only did the huge bulk of Hauk's body seem to fill the vehicle, but so did Hauk's evil aura fill the air. Crook covered Kirby's little face with a light blanket.

Crook said, "Even dead the man gives me the creeps."

Sandra said, "Not so much now."

It was the longest four miles in the lives of either of them. For a few seconds, Crook feared they would meet Bill bringing Martin home, but they did not. It was nearly nine o'clock at night, three hours since Sandra left practice. Bill and Tillie and Martin must be eating out in Sioux Falls before bringing home Martin's new stash of stuff.

Carl's nagging insistent voice came through the radio just as they neared the lights of town. Sandra shook her head at Crook's look of alarm. "Hauk didn't answer," she said.

"Take back roads," he said.

The endless blocks finally ended at Hauk's. He had a garage door opener and Sandra pushed it and drove inside. She pushed to shut the door, shut off the engine and sat there. She made a gasping sound with each breath.

"Are you all right?" Crook asked.

"How are you?" Sandra asked, not turning her head.

Crook observed the layout of the house and the garage. Through the window he observed the corner lot and the lilac bushes. The streetlight cast shadows across the street, but the garage was in darkness. The wind blew in clouds and the night was no longer lightened by the moon. Crook judged this to be good.

Once inside the garage, they kept the lights on. Crook had to see exactly what he was doing. He handed Sandra gloves, told her to not touch or move anything, no matter what she saw, and to fetch a container with warm water and soap. Crook walked behind her, using the flashlight until he found Hauk's bedroom. He found a clean uniform in the plastic wrap from the cleaners. He found briefs and socks. Once back in the garage, he and Sandra again struggled to remove Hauk from his car, but it was getting easier as they developed technique. They drug him to the back of the garage where a passer-by could not see them from the garage door windows.

Crook told Sandra to walk home. Stay in the shadow, but walk as she normally would, wave at passers-by. Get a car and come back. Sandra told him that her father's car was gone, but she had the keys for her mother's black Mazda.

"It's nearly a mile from here," Sandra said. Her house was across the highway on the east side of town.

"Be quick then," Crook said. "Take off the gloves as soon as you are outside. Bring back a change of clothes. Do not change at home, bring it with you."

"What about the blood on my clothes?" she asked.

"Think of it as ketchup and stay in the shadow." Crook was brusque. He knew Sandra was reaching her physical limit, and he needed her to do this one more thing.

Chapter Twenty-Seven

Sandra left via the side door. She considered taking the alleys between the houses, but decided it looked more suspicious to be walking the alleys alone at night than walking the streets. With her underwear still damp and no jacket, she shivered uncontrollably after two blocks. Her shoulder settled into numbness.

The wind blew her hair forward onto her face. At first she used both hands to hold it back. She hunched her shoulders and gave up on her hair. She looked at her feet, and forced her hands through crusted blood and inside the front pockets on her sweatshirt. Her words came stronger and her legs moved faster.

"We had hard running drills at practice. Hauk knocked my food to the floor. I haven't eaten since sloppy-joes at school. Hauk yanked my arm right from the socket."

Car lights turned onto the block ahead of her and she paused. The car passed by without slowing.

"That was before the conspiracy to commit murder which was necessary for survival, if I survive. Cover-up after the fact, toting around three hundred pounds of ugly, pushing the body through cold water in bare legs. What else? Oh yeah, come within a millimeter of major head trauma, walk a mile and bring back the car, take off my plastic dish washing gloves, freeze my ass off, and act normal."

Sandra crossed highway 81. She could see some headlights in the distance but not close enough to make her anything more than a shadow under the streetlights. Only Wheaton closed down on a Friday night by ten o'clock. Everyone was somewhere else.

The stinging salt on her lip was her own tears. She used her sleeve to wipe her mouth and nose as she at last entered her kitchen. She moved as though walking through water. She could not find the keys and then found them on the hook where they belonged. She could not find a new set of clothes. Everything looked strange, out-of-place. She grabbed a shirt and jeans from her hamper, dropping the keys and again finding them. She found clean, dry socks and underwear from a drawer. It all seemed to belong to someone else.

She picked up an apple from the counter and bit into it. It hurt to chew and swallow.

Finally, after what seemed like hours, she was inside her mother's little Mazda and driving to Hauk's house. She parked along the north side, not in the front. She put the gloves back on, circled the lilac bushes and entered the same way she left.

At the rear of the garage, Hauk lay on a blanket, his arms folded across his chest. His uniform appeared pristine including holster and weapon, badge and boots. His ugly face looked asleep. Sandra floated in her body, rocking on her feet, ready to fall.

"Good girl," Crook said. "Can you help lift Hauk to his bed?"

The two of them pulled the blanket through the doorway into the kitchen. With his gloved hand, Crook reached to flip off the garage light. They pulled Hauk through the kitchen and down the hall. On the count of three, they swung him onto the bed. Sandra's stomach lurched and black dots swam in her eyes as she swung.

Crook straightened the blanket and tidied Hauk's hair. Then the two of them stood in the room with the light from the hallway and looked down at the body stretched out on the bed.

"Rest in Peace," Crook said.

"Go to hell," Sandra said.

"Sandra."

"Okay," she amended. "Go where you deserve to be with the mercy of God."

"Good," Crook told her, "well said. Now let's get out of here."

They retraced their steps. In the garage Crook lifted Kirby's seat from Hauk's vehicle, but he grabbed hold of the handle off-center and the seat pivoted, nearly spilling the baby. He carried Martin's coat in a ball under one arm and held onto Kirby's seat with his other hand.

The two of them fought the bitter wind to Sandra's car. Again Crook held Kirby, seat and all on his lap inside the cramped front seat. "He needs to be changed and have his 10:00PM bottle. Do you want to spend the night?"

Sandra declined. "I'll make it to my own bed. My parents have worried enough." She paused for a second and swallowed through a sore throat. "Thank you, Crook. You saved my life, again."

Once at the house, Crook told her, "You have to change before you go home and give me the sweat suit." Crook set Kirby, sleeping in his seat, in the bathroom while Sandra showered. He tossed in a garbage bag and called, "I'm going to shut off the pump."

Sandra did as she was told, numb now with fatigue. She managed the drive home but everything looked different. The fence lines seemed new and the curve in the road was new. The streets and buildings looked like the fake fronts of a movie set.

Her parents were not home yet. After parking her mother's car in the same spot she followed the same path she used five hours earlier, the same food, the same steps, the same bedroom, but everything was completely different. She barely recognized her room. But tonight she was too tired and sore to think about it. She slept for twelve hours without fear.

Chapter Thirty-One

On Tuesday evening, twenty hours after Carl's visit to the farm, Martin, Kirby, Bill and Tillie, entered the lobby of the Armory where the high school teams played their games. The sounds lifted Martin's spirit, putting a smile on his face and a lilt in his step. He considered it great while the balls bounced on the court in warm-up drills, and the band played a marching song he did not recognize. The wonderfulness came simultaneously with the pain. He could not remember one without the other, but for now he allowed only the excitement in a visceral wave of pleasure.

He paid his two dollars; the price had gone up. In the program he found Sandra's name. He held the program in front of his face to hide his ridiculous tears. Then he ducked into the bathroom.

"They should put a changing table in here," Martin said to a young stranger standing at the sink. The young man chuckled a bit and hurriedly left. "I guess a changing table is nothing to cry about," Martin told Kirby before a flush told him he was not alone.

A high school kid appeared beside Martin at the sink and offered to hold Kirby, reaching for the seat. Martin handed Kirby to the young man, then bent his head and splashed water on his face. Glancing at his reflection, he had to wonder if he would ever be normal. He thanked the teenager and took the handle of Kirby's seat. The young man held the door for him. Bill and Tillie waited for him in the lobby.

He wondered if the excitement would be like this when his daughter played ball. He hoped with all his heart that for Christie it would come with much less struggle than it came for Sandra, at least this year. It was being here at all that lit the fire of his pride in Sandra. Joe did not make it to have that "SR" behind his name, but Sandra did.

As the group loitered in the lobby, Tillie spotted the two detectives standing at the other end. They stood at the door traditionally used for the visiting team. She elbowed Bill and pointed for confirmation in their identity. He nodded.

The talk of the crowd milling around them was, of course, that Carl was in jail. On this topic even Martin paid attention to the rumors flowing like hot syrup over pancakes. No one seemed upset with that event. In fact, the opposite was true.

The band stopped playing and the bouncing balls receded into the locker rooms. It was time to find their seat. Martin waved for Tillie and Bill to go ahead and save him a place. He held back, wanting to calm himself. He bent at the water fountain and stood up to find Sandra standing at his elbow.

"I have to go right now," she talked fast, "but I saw you, and I wanted to say hello and to tell you that I won't get to start tonight because I wasn't up to speed at practice. So don't be disappointed." Her face, flushed with adrenalin, looked so pretty that Martin smiled at her despite the disappointment.

"How is your arm?" Martin said.

"What arm?" Sandra said. "I'll get to play, probably a lot. My shot is better than last year. I've worked my left-handed put back. You'll like it. But it really isn't fair for me to start when I didn't practice the whole time like everybody else." She was trying to comfort him, and he felt better.

"Focus," Martin advised with intensity in his face. "Make adversity your right hand man. Focus through it." His final words bounced off Sandy's retreating figure as she jogged to join her team. Martin knew she broke protocol to run to the lobby. She better be in line for the Anthem.

The seating in the armory ran along the west wall while the teams sat along the east wall and the baskets were placed at the north and south ends. Tillie nudged Bill who nudged Martin as Vilhallen and White climbed the packed bleachers and sat four rows above them.

Martin held Kirby through the entire game. Sometimes Kirby looked out over Martin's shoulder and sometimes he sat on Martin's lap and watched the game. Martin was a calm parent. Kirby felt like an extension of Martin's own body. Kirby was not a handsome baby. He was, however, a very unique baby. Kirby's wise little face with his clear, intelligent eyes brought almost as much entertainment to the people sitting behind Martin as did the ball game.

Martin watched Sandra play. He focused on the game. He did not talk. Martin did not yell or cheer because he did not want to alarm Kirby. Instead he made mental notes to tell Sandra for next time.

This was a big game because the opponents were the one adversary that could beat Wheaton in their district. With three minutes remaining, the score was tied. Martin noted exhaustion in Sandra. Her legs looked like Jell-O. He glanced to the bench to see if the coach was preparing to send in the player who actually started the game at post. He could see no intention of benching Sandra for a minute of rest.

He saw Sandra's face take on that hard edge of concentration. "That's right," he mumbled. "Work through it." On court, Sandra received a nice feed from her teammate and missed a three-foot shot. Martin winced. "One minute of rest might have paid off," he said aloud, but no one cared, the whole gym was focused on the game, even Kirby.

With eight seconds left, the team had one more chance to win the game. Everyone stood, including Martin which made it difficult for those behind him to see. "Go left, Sandra," Martin yelled and his voice caught a higher decibel than the crowd. He saw Sandra's quick nod. Kirby cried and Martin patted the baby into quiet.

"Get the ball inside, get the ball inside." Martin whispered. The man behind and to his right yelled for the outside shot. Time out.

The high inbound pass went from point guard to Sandra. She executed her pivot, exchanged the ball to her left hand, went up and banked it home. It brought the house down. Now Martin said nothing, remembering his determination to be calm. Sandra looked white. He noted the fatigue around her mouth as though she were only inches away from him. The final second ticked away to cheers.

"Nothing new for Sandra in making the winning shot," Bill said. Martin nodded but he knew she had not been quite in this place before. Until now her talent and the fun of it carried her. This time, her game was more. This time she reached inside and found strength, found the will.

Martin watched Sandra join the line to slap hands with the opposing players and then jog off the court. The crowd began to file out. Bill continued to talk about the game but Martin didn't hear him until Tillie said, "Remember, it's only a game." To this Bill answered, "Bullshit." And Martin nodded agreement.

As Martin and group maneuvered their way down the bleachers they reached Sandra's parents who remained sitting. Tillie saw and recognized the couple and stopped to congratulate them on Sandra's game. While Martin waited patiently for Tillie to move along, he studied the couple. He thought, "What you don't know can hurt you."

He could say nothing, not about their daughter nor their grandson. He would push Sandra to talk to her parents. He could see that they loved her. As Martin stood on the bleachers, Vilhallen and White stepped down to where he stood.

Vilhallen said, "Hello, Mr. Webster. This must bring back memories."

"It does," Martin said.

Since Vilhallen continued to stand there, Martin felt obligated to say something. "Carl isn't in jail for his visit to me, is he?"

"Which visit?" Vilhallen said. "Are your referring to the visit to extort or the visit to arrest you?"

"I was referring to the second visit," Martin said. "I assume he will not be filing paperwork with social services. Is that right?" Martin could not help the lurch of his heart.

"The first visit could be a motive for wanting the previous sheriff dead," Vilhallen said.

"Yes," Martin said, "Yes, it could." He could not agree more.

Vilhallen smiled. "Carl Banks is in jail for other activities of an illegal nature not related to you. Did you change your mind about pressing charges?"

Martin shook his head. He could guess the nature of the illegal activities. He waited for the crowd to move along. He adjusted the handle of Kirby's infant seat in his hand. When he looked up the detectives had moved ahead several feet. He could see only the back of

257

Vilhallen's beige jacket. He had a funny feeling that the detectives were watching him. He thought, Good. The more they watch me the less they watch Sandra or Crook.

Chapter Thirty-Two

As Larry Vilhallen and John White stood to the side of the crowd milling through the gymnasium entrance, they watched the conversation between Martin Webster and Sandra Peters with undisguised fascination. Vilhallen insisted the two detectives attend the game because he wanted to see Cassandra Peters. It was an added bonus to see Martin Webster, and not only to see him, but to see him talking to Sandra. He was not sure what it meant.

Back at his office, three files sat on his desk. The file of Hauk's last case was Cassandra Peters. The second folder was Jeremy Sabo. A Dr. Duerkson forwarded a large folder of Crook's years in the Hospital and the proceedings that put him there. The third file was thin and flat with one sheet inside. That was Martin's folder. A note in Hauk's hand on the inside cover of the file stated, "Check this out."

The list of persons of interest was long indeed. However experience and intuition put these three files on their desk while the long list was assigned to their helpers on the case. White snapped a continuous flow of pictures from his inconspicuous camera that looked like a phone.

Neither detective believed that Martin was guilty of murder, but both believed he knew something about it. Both detectives seriously considered Crook as a man capable of a professional hit like this crime appeared to be. Sandra was that last case worked and a likely victim of Hauk's predatory ways. Experience told them that motive almost always came sooner rather than later. The missing link, the connections to Hauk did not exist and for that reason there was no case, no cause for a search warrant. Carl's ranting did not constitute evidence.

White said, "Cassandra Peters could be our link."

The detectives knew they were missing something, some link that would tie it all together. Thus the two detectives watched the brief conversation between Martin and Sandra with keen interest. This was the first indication of a connection. While Martin gently swung the infant seat containing his son, Sandra gave only nominal attention to the baby. Of course, the connection could be basketball, but both detectives knew it ran deeper than that.

Vilhallen wanted to tail both Sandra and Martin but had only one vehicle and decided to follow Martin. This they did.

White said, "Martin is a care-giver, a protector. I can't see him for murder."

Vilhallen said, "We are missing the link that ties it all together. They'll trip up. Somebody who knows something will give it all away. They always do."

They discreetly followed Bill's big Lincoln right to Martin's driveway. The hope was for some interaction between their suspects. Vilhallen wished that Martin would take care of his yard. Once the Lincoln pulled past the mild curve to the front of Martin's house, they could not see a thing above the rampant grass and weeds stretching twenty yards to the road.

They continued on the gravel road, turned around and waited in the grass driveway to a field for Bill's car to emerge. About an hour later, Bill and his wife exited Martin's driveway and went home. They watched the taillights disappear over the hill. They stayed put for another two hours but no figure emerged from the parting in the weeds to walk down the road. Vilhallen did not know what he expected to see. He thought perhaps Jeremy Sabo would emerge, or Cassandra Peters would visit.

White said, "Martin Webster leads a quiet life."

"On the surface," Vilhallen said.

They left their vehicle and walked up the driveway to check the house. Only one shaded light was on upstairs in a corner room facing north toward the barn. It was so quiet that the dead leaves rustling along the gravel path chatted and danced with the wind. The detectives called it a night.

They discussed at length the relationship between Martin and Sandra and what it could mean. Of course, they considered that Sandra had been pregnant when she ran. That would make her the best at keeping a secret of anyone, ever. But it had to be considered. Martin could not be the father, but Hauk could. Was that a key? Possible? How did Martin end up with the baby? Was Sandra the mother? Complete conjecture.

The lab results on the baby bottle provided zero. They had the formula brand and the bottle brand. Hundreds of people right here in town used that formula and that baby bottle. The prints on the glass were too smudged for identification. It was more likely it rolled from a blanket or a bag than dropped by a hand. They had no physical evidence.

They discussed the fact that neither Martin nor Crook had a vehicle of any kind. That meant that Hauk had to come to them, and maybe he did as per Carl's statement. Crook obviously had a prior, hence his stay at the hospital. Martin did too in a way. His brother died in a mysterious accident. Maybe Hauk came out to give Crook grief and inquire as to protection money and that was the last crime of Hauk's life. Possible. But Hauk did not appear to be aware of Jeremy Sabo. The initial letter from the hospital in Omaha had gone unopened. The large file sent from Dr. Duerksen was received only a day ago.

Tomorrow they would start digging. Somewhere was the link. They had Hauk to Sandra and Sandra to Martin and Martin to Crook. It was weak. They had to keep looking; they were on the right trail.

For two days Vilhalen and White worked through files and reports. The autopsy report concluded the cause of death to be a single knife wound to the back of the neck. The weapon used was a four inch, narrow, sharp blade consistent with a pocket knife or paring knife. The wound was inflicted at an angle consistent with the perpetrator standing above the victim, and it did not require more than average strength.

The wound caused immediate death due to the location. The autopsy listed the likelihood of deliberate placement to be at ninety percent, while accidentally hitting that location to be at ten percent. The conclusion of this indicated a highly skilled attack.

Also the victim bled a great deal. The victim bled on himself, the perpetrator and the surrounding area. In addition the body had fourteen bruises, scratches, bite marks and gouges in various stages of healing. These previous wounds were consistent with fighting a person of less strength or in a manor consistent with the care of wild animals.

On the forensics report only minute traces of blood were found on the victim's bed, bedding or in either of his vehicles. These blood specks could be from any time.

White sent the photographs taken at the ball game of Martin Webster and Sandra Peters to a criminal psychologist. Her report indicated the two adults in the photo were emotionally intimate but not physically intimate. They did not touch each other. The body language indicated a type of relationship that, when not family, was reminiscent of the relationship between survivors of some catastrophe or when one has saved the life of the other.

Then the criminal psychologist added: "This could also be a sharing of mutual interest like a coach and player. Keep in mind this report is not evidence. The conclusions are fifty percent probability."

The female in the photo is likely not the mother of the infant. In none of the photos does she indicate protection or even awareness in her body language that the infant is there. On the other hand, the male in the picture is likely the father. He continued to hold the infant seat in his hand while his posture leaned protectively. At all times he was aware of the infant even as he is focused on the female.

The detectives read the reports from the other officers investigating the list of extortion victims. No one without an alibi had the skills or opportunity. There was no where a triggering event that changed the status quo. So at noon on the second day, the detectives narrowed their search to the three files on their desk. They had Carl's statement of Hauk's extortion visit to Martin but that was weak.

It had to be a combination. Knowing the victim as the detectives now did, they knew Hauk would plan a second visit to Martin, though that visit was only conjecture. Lucky for Martin, Hauk was a very busy man those first days after his return.

The detectives determined two steps. They would start the process for a warrant to visit Mr. Webster and Mr. Sabo. It could not be based on existing physical evidence, but it could be based on the likelihood of finding the evidence. It could be based on previous violent acts by Crook, the skills to do the crime and a likelihood that the sheriff went to the residence.

The second step was to interview Cassandra Peters. Vilhallen would interview the young lady while White convinced a judge to issue the search warrant. Then both detectives along with their assistants would make a visit to the farm.

It was a school day, but Vilhallen made arrangements to meet Sandra and her parents at her home after lunch. For this, Ms. Peters could miss Study Hall and Algebra II, her mother could miss work and her father, the dentist, could change his appointments for the afternoon. This was, after all, a murder investigation by Special Appointment of the Governor himself. This case had to be resolved.

As Vilhallen prepared for the interview, he made careful notes. He noted first the facts of the case. Then he noted his assumptions. He noted what he hoped to discover, and his planned approach.

Normally, the dogged Vilhallen conducted a tough and thorough interview, verifying all of the facts. Before entering the interview he generally had a clear picture of what went down. This case was different from any previous case. It bothered him that the victim was no victim, but an actual criminal conducting brazen criminal activity under the power and protection of his office.

It bothered him more that the young lady in question could be the owner of a souvenir in Hauk's box. This was an assumption based primarily on instinct but also on the fact of her going missing and on Carl's statement regarding Hauk's intense search to find her. Also, Carl said he last saw Hauk's vehicle proceeding down Sandra's block.

Vilhallen did his preparation. He knew the family; father, local dentist; mother, billing clerk for an insurance office; two children, both daughters. He knew the dentistry practice thrived financially. The couple belonged to the community with deep roots including grandparents and a wide circle of community involvement. He had one burning question. If Sandra was a victim, had it been her dad who killed the bastard? Or was it even possible that

Sandra had not told her parents?   Vilhallen was certain that the killer of Hauk was connected to Sandra.

Vilhallen felt no enthusiasm for what he was about to do. He had never been less sure of what he was going to hear, or see. He did not like facing the unknown.

Chapter Thirty-Three

Vilhallen checked out the souvenir box from the other-wise empty evidence locker. It was important to the case to know for sure if Sandra was a victim. It went to motive. Of course, this case suffered from way too much motive.

Vilhallen ate a light lunch, decided on his approach as a warmer, gentler person, checked his recorder, talked with White regarding the search warrant and left for the white house belonging to Sandra's family.

He expected tears and protests from all three of them. He expected emotion on every level. No seventeen year old girl could go through what he suspected Sandra went through and not be vulnerable, exhausted and ready to spill her story. One more time, he went over every thing he had. Again, he noted the four points he had to clarify: transportation, location, opportunity and ability.

Vilhallen had second thoughts regarding confronting Sandra with the souvenir box. He struggled with his conscience on this point. Could solving this case justify the potential to do more damage to a victim? He was supposed to serve and protect. The whole case made Vilhallen sick. He knew White had similar misgivings, but White was determined to get to the bottom of Hauk's murder. Vilhallen had reached a stage where the end did not always justify the means.

As he drove to the Peter's house, he decided to move forward. He knew the worst possible approach to an interview was hesitation. As he exited the vehicle, he squared his shoulders and assumed an attitude of knowledge and power.

Vilhallen's carefully planned approach lasted as long as it took to be seated at the kitchen table with coffee and cookies. The white square table with four cushioned white chairs in a clean, pretty kitchen was as far removed from an interview room as conceivable. And that was just for starters. None of the three faces looking at him held a single trace of agitation or worry. He could cross off the emotional factor.

"Good game last night," he said to Sandra.

"Thank you," she answered and smiled.

"I watched Martin Webster play at the state tournament years ago. It was a huge deal back in the day. I'm surprised he didn't play college ball." Vilhallen watched Sandra's face. She had no response to Martin's name.

Sandra's dad nodded. "Martin is a real hometown hero. Rumor had it that he didn't play college ball because of the tragedy with his brother. Joe was my classmate in school." Mr. Peters had more to say, but Vilhallen cut him off with a curt nod. Containment was important.

"How do you know Martin Webster?" Vilhallen asked Sandra.

"He works with me on basketball strategy," Sandra said.

Sandra's parents appeared surprised at this, but remained silent.

"How did you meet?"

Sandra said nothing. Vilhallen realized she was a tough cookie, possibly coached. His thoughts went to Jeremy Sabo but he forced himself to focus.

If Sandra made no answer her parents said nothing as well.

"Why did you run away?"

Again Sandra said nothing. This time her dad answered. "That case is resolved."

"Have you been inside Martin Webster's house? Have you been inside Hauk's police vehicle? Do you know the man referred to as Crook? Do you own a knife?"

Sandra remained unmoved and mute. Her mother finally said with a soft hesitancy, "Sandra is not required to answer your questions."

"It would help us all if she cooperated," Vilhallen said. He was feeling anger began to churn his stomach. He was beginning to wonder if this girl was a victim. He decided to use his final weapon.

Vilhallen pulled from his briefcase the small, flat tackle box taken from Hauk's locked desk drawer. He removed it from the plastic bag with gloved hands. He shuddered inwardly, and looked up to find three pairs of eyes staring at the box. Carefully and deliberately, he opened the lid and pushed it forward so Sandra could see the contents.

"This is important, Sandra," he said quietly. "These things were found inside Hauk's house. Do you recognize anything?" Vilhallen paused and waited, intently watching Sandra's expression.

The girl turned pale. While her parents did not understand what they looked at, Sandra knew. After a few seconds, Sandra nodded. "The green hair-tie is mine."

She did not look to anyone. Her lips trembled and her hands locked together on top of the table. "I recognize the earring. That was Allyson's." She still did not look up. She could not take her eyes from the small things in small compartments.

Vilhallen regretted his decision to show the box. The girl could not look away from it. Did it take such an action to break a child? Did he even need it to solve the case? Nevertheless, he continued.

"What else?" Vilhallen's voice was respectful.

"Angelina used to wear blue butterfly clips like that," she whispered. Then she looked up. "Hauk hurt all these girls." She said this with a shock so genuine that her mother gasped, and her father pushed back.

Vilhallen carefully initialed the tag and put the evidence away. He wanted to verify what he and White already knew. The tackle box was a trophy case. He also wanted to verify Sandra as a victim. "I'm sorry," he said.

When Vilhallen looked up he did not see a trembling teenager ready to spill her guts. He saw a young lady with steel eyes and an iron jaw. Both parents studied her just as he did. They obviously did not understand what they had just witnessed.

Vilhallen sighed, closed his eyes for a second and then continued. "How do you know Martin?" he asked.

"He comes to the games, gives me pointers on how to play even though he was a guard and I play center." She looked deathly pale, but far from vulnerable.

"How did you meet him?" Vilhallen asked again.

"Why?" she asked back. Her game face could not be broken.

Vilhallen glanced briefly at Sandra's mother. For some reason, he expected her to tell Sandra to answer the question. He was grasping at straws. Her father stood now, leaning his thin body against the counter. Her parents knew she had secrets and they did not want to know the answers, not in front of a stranger. She was home and safe and that was everything.

Vilhallen said, "It is important to our investigation to understand the dynamic of what happened to Sheriff Hauk. We believe your relationship with Martin Webster is a part of what happened and we need to know about it." He sounded sterner than he wanted.

"Then it is enough for you to know that Martin Webster is my friend," Sandra answered.

"And how did you meet him?" Vilhallen asked again, softening his tone.

"Martin has nothing to do with Hauk and what Hauk did to people," Sandra said.

Vilhallen knew from Sandra's expression that it was pointless to continue. Further harassment would only alienate everyone in the room. But he could not help himself. He was driven to know the truth and patient reason had no hold on his actions.

He asked one more question. "And how about Mr. Sabo, do you know him?"

"Who?" Sandra asked.

"You know him as Crook?" Vilhallen said.

Before Sandra could speak her father said, "Who is that?"

Vilhallen gave a brief explanation as to Crook's presence at the Webster farm.

Sandra sat mum. Her colorless lips compressed in a line outlined in white. Nothing would break the girl's composure. Unless. He tried one more question.

"Have you ever been pregnant?" he asked her, studying her expression. She did not blink.

Her mother again gasped and stared at Vilhallen. Her father said through stiff lips, "We will ignore that question. What else?"

Vilhallen laid it out. He threw away his last vestige of common sense. "We think Hauk raped Cassandra, and Cassandra assisted in his murder."

He remembered the criminal psychologist did not believe Sandra to be the mother of the baby in the picture, but Vilhallen thought she was. It was a wild strike, a fighter's useless flailing. He did not speak those thoughts. It was too much of a stretch.

He looked at three stunned faces, stunned into utter silence.

Mr. Peters leaned down to the tape recorder, close, and said, "This interview is over. The detective is crazy." He then shut if off, handed it to Vilhallen and escorted him to the door.

Except for confirmation that the murder victim was an evil man, and Cassandra identified her hair ribbon in the trophy box, Vilhallen had nothing. He knew he had nothing. He did not get transportation, location, who and with what. He did not get any verification of his theory as to the dynamic between Martin, Crook and Sandra. He certainly had no answer as to why Martin would take upon himself an infant not his own.

Vilhallen walked to his car feeling defeated. More than defeated, he felt sad, sad for everyone involved. Cruelty was justified in identifying a murderer. It was not justified in the devastation of a teenage girl. He thought, we could be wrong about this. We could be wrong. He secretly blamed Carl. If not for Carl, they would never have looked at Martin. Now the case was like a fire that ravaged all in its path. Now the truth would be known regardless the price that had to be paid. And for what?

271

Chapter Thirty-Four

Sandra could not breathe. She saw the little, once pretty things in tiny plastic bags that belonged once to her or to other girls like her. For the first time it crossed her mind that she should die. I am nothing, she thought. I am a green hair-tie in a plastic bag.

"It hurts," she whispered to her mother who had taken her hand.

"Who should I call for help?" her father asked as he paced without purpose. Then he knelt before his little girl. "Why didn't you tell us? You could tell us anything."

First she said, "I thought you would be ashamed of me." Then seeing the wounded expression on her mother's face Sandra said, "If I told I would have to admit what happened to me. I would know that you knew. I just could not do that."

Her mother gasped. She said, "Sandra Ann Peters!"

The anger in her mother's eyes felt wonderful to Sandra. Her mother was angry that she would think such a thing as shame to be possible. The comfort that brought to Sandra's heart was amazing, a literal weight taken from her.

"I want to quit basketball. I can't play any more," Sandra whispered. "I'm beaten. It's over."

"You are not beaten," her father said.

"Look what he did. Did you see what he did? Each of those little things in that box was a life that he took. Well, I took his." Sandra paused. The room spun. She clutched the table with her free hand. "Did you understand me? I took his, but it was too late. It didn't save me or any of those girls."

Her mother cradled her like a baby. Then her father pulled up a chair close to her mother. He did not say, "Basketball is your ride through college." He did not say, "It can't be that bad." Mostly he did not say, "It will be all right."

Sandra looked at him and saw that he was so white his face seemed separate from his hair, like a mask. He said, "It is too late for me to kill him with my bare hands. That is the only thing that is too late."

Her mother, who looked ready to faint, rocked in her chair like she held an infant. One hand held Sandra's hand and the other clutched her stomach. She appeared to understand at last what the box meant.

She said, "Why didn't you let us help you?"

Her dad said, "She is telling us now. We will help now."

"I couldn't admit it to myself. I just wanted to get my old life back."

Then after a minute, Sandra looked up at her parents. She said, "This will take awhile."

"We have all the time you need," her dad said.

Chapter Thirty-Five

The search warrant allowed a search and seizure for any physical evidence relating to the murder of Sheriff Hauk. It covered the house, the outbuildings, the property, and the persons of Martin Webster and Jeremy Sabo.

Vilhallen and White used all of their considerable expertise in organizing the search. It included three cars from the Minnehaha County Sheriff's Department as well as their own and a CSI crew. It was not the biggest search either detective ever participated in, but it was considerable. The scheduled departure from the courthouse in Wheaton was 3:00 pm. The briefing was scheduled for 2:30.

Vilhallen and White had twenty minutes for one final interview with Mr. Carl Banks. Carl actually posted bail that morning but would not be released until after the execution of the search warrant. A far different Deputy Banks waited in the conference room than the detectives previously encountered or expected. He was not the wired, inept, arrogant Carl of the TV fame, nor was he the bag of bones, deflated Carl from the plea agreement.

Dressed in pressed khaki pants and striped shirt, tucked and belted, Carl showed neither fidgety nerves nor desperation. Carl Banks appeared completely balanced.

Vilhallen and White greeted Carl with civility if not warmth. They sat across the table from Carl and placed yellow legal pads on the table for notes, no recorder. "What we want to

274

clarify with you, Carl, is a few points related to solving the murder of your Sheriff. It is outside of your full disclosure relating to your plea agreement," White said.

Carl nodded, calm and agreeable.

Vilhallen studied Carl as White talked. He doubted that Carl could help them. He said, "What we need to establish is a relationship between Cassandra Peters and Martin Webster."

Carl gaped at them.

"Think about it for a minute, Mr. Banks."

Carl said, "Only the timing puts them together. Sandra Peters would not associate with Webster."

White slid a photograph of Martin and Sandra standing together in the armory lobby. Carl looked at it with wide eyes. He said, "Damn."

"Why is this so surprising?" White's intelligent eyes burned with intensity.

"Because Cassandra Peters is a respected young lady and Martin Webster is a nut case."

"Can you look past your own prejudice for a minute and think of any possible connection beyond their obvious interest in basketball?" White was icy calm.

Vilhallen waited, watching Carl's brow furrow in concentration.

"The kids used to use the Webster house to party," he said.

Vilhallen switched topics while White noted this information. "After reported missing, Cassandra Peters was never actually found. How did she get home?" Vilhallen watched Carl shift his thoughts.

"Bill Bendix brought her home on Tuesday morning. He just dropped her off at her house. Her mom was home, unable to work with her daughter missing and all," Carl said. He appeared confused by the switch in topics from the relationship between Martin and Sandra to Bill Bendix.

"What was her story?" Vilhallen asked quickly.

"Sandra told her parents, her parents told Hauk and Hauk told me that Bill Bendix found her at the state park campsite. Odd though because the campsite was searched without finding a sign of her."

"Did that seem odd to you that Bill Bendix, Martin's neighbor, brought Sandra home?" White asked.

"Sure it did, but I was just relieved it was over, so I didn't care how she got home."

"What about Hauk? What was his reaction to Bill Bendix bringing Sandra home?" White asked and Vilhallen watched.

Carl's brow furrowed in concentration. "Hauk was finishing his report. Read to me what he wrote and then threw his pen across the room."

Vilhallen thought that Carl Banks possessed an amazing ability of recall. Vilhallen said, "Did you think it was a coincidence that Martin's friend and neighbor found Cassandra?"

"Didn't think of it at all," Carl answered.

Vilhallen considered it an extraordinary coincidence.

"On the search report in Hauk's office he listed all of the places that required searching. The list included 'abandoned farm buildings.' Did you search the Webster house?" White asked.

"I planned to, even before I knew about Martin. But Sandra's friends told me she wouldn't go to the old party haunt because of the rats. She was terrified of them. I believed them, so I crossed it off." Carl looked at them with a slight smile. He was apparently becoming accustomed to the topic switching technique.

"Rats!" Vilhallen uttered under his breath. She stayed with the rats, and she was afraid of them. What drove this girl? Did it go to motive? Of course it did. On his pad he printed: We are here to find Hauk's killer.

"Yes, a lot of them. That was why the kids didn't go near there anymore."

Carl paused then he added, "Hauk was odd these last months, scarier. With hindsight, I think he knew he should have left Sandra alone. The fact that she didn't say a word to anyone about what he did, I mean what we know now that he did because of the trophy case, scared Hauk. I suspect he wanted to find her himself and maybe find her body." Carl said this with trembling lips, tears in his eyes.

"You think Hauk did to Sandra what he did to Allyson?" Vilhallen tried to temper his voice.

Carl nodded.

"We call Hauk's actions 'escalation.'" White had gone pale.

Carl said nothing that they did not already know or suspect but to hear it from a man who allowed it to happen was shocking. Vilhallen knew Sandra had admitted no such actions on the part of Hauk. She admitted only that her hair tie was included inside his trophy box.

And you did nothing about that?" White asked.

"I said with hindsight. At the time I just thought Hauk was getting weird. When Sandra disappeared, I worried about it, but not really. It nagged me, that's all."

"And you felt Sandra was alive because Hauk was looking for her?"

"Yes."

"So, Hauk did not say he visited Mr. Webster on the Friday night of his murder. You have only intuition that he drove to the farm?" White returned to his agenda.

"Any disturbance calls for Martin's place or anything like that on Friday night?

"No."

"Why did you mess up the scene, Carl? You are a smarter man than you wanted us to believe, so why?" White asked with ice in his eyes.

"I mistakenly thought I could get those records out of the house. If I made the scene useless to you, I thought you would not care about anything in the house," Carl said quietly, looking at the table.

"Why didn't you take Hauk's extortion files out right away?"

"I wish I had, but I didn't think of it right away. Then I couldn't get ten minutes to myself. So, I devised the plan to ruin the scene. I wasn't myself." He smiled a crooked, self-effacing grin.

Vilhallen said, "It wasn't that you spent a good deal of time furnishing our place."

Carl chuckled but said nothing.

The detectives quickly covered the exact time Carl last saw Hauk. He told them he saw Hauk driving down Sandra's block at 4:30 pm. And the last time he heard his voice was a half hour earlier at 4:00.

"But you suspect that Hauk would have driven to the Webster's farm alone, maybe to check it out, maybe to impart some fear into Martin Webster?" White clarified one more time.

"He would," Carl answered.

That was it. No more questions. Time to go.

Chapter Thirty-Six

As it happened, Martin and Crook rose early that morning. Martin was a little behind schedule and he wanted to work. The problem they encountered was Kirby. Kirby screamed at the sound of the power sander on the wood banister in the hallway. So, the men took turns running the sander and playing with Kirby on the porch with the doors to the house closed.

Martin and Crook had lunch at 11:30 when Martin took Kirby upstairs for his nap, sometimes Martin slept too. Crook returned to his carving spot on the porch where he worked on a chess set for Dr. Duerksen. He examined his attempt at carving a knight and thought the knight looked rather queenly. As he turned the piece in his fingers, he saw through the window police vehicles parking in a semi-circle facing the porch.

"Shit," he said. He grabbed his carving knife from the table, retracting the blade as he ran upstairs. He burst into Martin's room without knocking. Kirby slept on his tummy with his butt in the air. Crook, as close to panic as he had ever known, unhooked Kirby's sleeper and slid the knife into the baby's diaper. He adjusted the positioning of the heavy, steel knife so as not to make Kirby uncomfortable. Then while whisper-yelling at Martin he re-hooked the sleeper. Martin did not see that Crook slid the murder weapon into the baby's diaper. Kirby rolled over wide awake. All three of them went downstairs.

Crook reached the front door just after Vilhallen knocked hard.

"Whoa," Crook said as he swung the door open. "What's up?" On the inside, his heart pounded, on the outside he put on his blank, distant expression like a mask.

He read slowly every word of the warrant as the detectives and company stood on the stoop, not choosing to force their way past him, at least not yet. Crook felt a surge of relief and struggled not to show it at the listing for personal search. Kirby was not named on the warrant. Good boy, Mr. Kirby, he thought, and he stepped aside.

An officer immediately placed himself at Crook's side, and Vilhallen opened the door to the kitchen. Kirby began to wail. A female technician reached to take the baby from Martin, but Crook said, "Please don't touch the baby." The young woman stepped back.

Martin shifted Kirby to his shoulder and patted him into quiet. While Crook stood, composed and still, breathing quiet, Martin carried Kirby toward the changing table against the far kitchen wall. Crook froze. Slowly and carefully, he said, "Martin, give Kirby to me. You need to read the search warrant."

With no objection, Martin handed over the baby. Crook handed Martin the search warrant. During these seconds no one else moved. Crook felt frozen in time. The cops were an audience at a play.

Now Vilhallen began directing traffic. Crook lifted the infant to his shoulder and rocked him from heel to toe. Kirby shut his eyes. Vilhallen walked a perplexed looking Martin out to the porch. Crook followed. He could not allow himself to look at his chess pieces. Anyone with a brain could see someone had been carving. But when? They could not know when he last carved. They might ask with what knife.

The blocks of wood and the shavings lay on a portable tray at the north end of the porch. No knife lay by the carving. When asked the location of the knife, Crook decided he would say nothing.

Martin walked to that end of the porch and stood in front of the tray while Vilhallen directed his crew. Vilhallen pointed here and there like a maestro leading the band. Crook moved to stand by Martin, out of the way, not daring to move his hands. The other detective, White, watched him like a hawk. Still, when two officers came to search Martin and Crook from top to bottom the shavings had disappeared from the table.

While standing against the table Martin had rubbed the wood shavings with his hands onto the back of his jeans. Shavings stuck to the back of Martin, but the pieces of wood did not seem out of place on Martin, and the chess pieces appeared to be a neglected hobby. Admiration for Martin surged in Crook's heart. Always the small detail was the big difference.

From Martin's clothing they extracted his pad with his list, the square completely degenerated letter from Christie, twelve two-penny nails, a finger nail clipper and a yellow, cloth type tape measure. From Crook they extracted absolutely nothing.

Another loud knock on the door and both Martin and Crook hesitated, looking at John White. The detective opened the door and a bustling, upset Tillie stepped right past him and looked at Martin.

"I'll take Kirby home with me," she announced, turning to glare at White. The detective had nearly as good a game face as Crook, but Tillie did not wait for assent or decline. She took the baby in his Vikings blanket and purple stretch beanie. If she felt anything unusual in his diaper, she did not indicate it. "That is, unless you believe this baby rolled into town and stabbed

Hauk." Anger oozed from her. It was wonderful for Martin and Crook to see. She knew no fear.

However when she started toward the kitchen to fetch bottles and diapers, White blocked her way. He indicated with his head for a female officer to get the things, check them and bring them to Tillie. Crook noticed that Vilhallen studied everything about Kirby that he could without touching the baby.

Vilhallen said to White, "We should have included someone from Social Services. For now, it's best to allow the neighbor lady to take the infant." Crook smiled at this.

The female officer returned with the diaper bag, bottles and cereal and handed it to Tillie who disappeared as quick as she came, carrying Kirby, the diaper bag and Crook's carving knife. No one on the porch said a word. The two male officers asked for Martin's and Crook's shoes and socks. The officers handed them to a lab technician who sprayed them with something. She shook her head in the negative to White who nodded. The lab technician handed the shoes and socks back to the Officers who then handed them to Martin and Crook.

Crook saw Martin fighting laughter. It was too deadly a game for laughter.

"These Officers will wait outside with you," White told Martin and Crook.

"It's cold out," Martin said.

White had the lab tech fetch two jackets from the van. Within another minute, Martin and Crook sat on the front steps with two highly alert Officers of the Minnehaha County Sheriff's Department leaning on the railing behind them. No one said a word as the afternoon wore on and the chill air picked up a breeze. Crook watched a few clouds gathering along the eastern horizon beyond the yellow and orange grove.

He thought, *I've survived this long by adapting to change, but this is different. If there is a god, I ask him to reach through those clouds and save me. Don't let them go to the barn and find that coat.*

Chapter Thirty-Seven

At 3:10 pm, Bill stood in his farmyard, cap over gray hair, and watched the caravan go by. No sirens or lights were necessary to convey the power of the law. As he strode to the house, tasting the road dust in his teeth, his muscles were strangely stiff. He fought his way the ten yards from his work area to his kitchen door.

Inside, Maureen and Tillie sat at the kitchen table. Maureen had white soap on her face and Tillie painted Maureen's nails. For the first second, they looked charming and sweet to Bill, but only for that second. He lumbered to the table and sat heavy in the kitchen chair. "Did you see?" he asked, a slight tremble in his fingers as they lay flat on the table.

"What?" Alarm sounded in Tillie's voice.

He described the caravan of six vehicles headed down the hill to Martin's. "Cop cars," he said. "Coming for Martin and Crook."

Maureen emitted a little scream and Tillie tightened the caps on the polish.

"Tell me everything, Maureen, everything that Crook told you. No secrets," Bill said. And Maureen did. She knew the exact location of the coat that Crook could not burn and the location of the blood stains under the basketball hoop on the wide hay-mound boards.

"The cops will find it," Bill said. "It doesn't seem fair. When the law goes bad, we have to do the same." It was not easy for a man, sixty-five years old, who never broke the law in his life and never considered doing so, to contemplate a crime. Yes, he complained about taxes and he complained about conspiracies to keep farm prices down, but he never considered thievery of any kind or anything else for that matter.

"Okay," he said to Tillie. "You take the Lincoln and go get Kirby out of there. I have a plan of my own regarding that damn coat."

Bill went to his garage and plugged in his portable twenty volt heat lamp for the battery to charge. The gauge was right in the middle, a good battery, and would take a half hour, forty-five minutes to have a full charge. He returned to the house and found black clothes to wear. He knew black would hardly conceal him in the day, but it was his trip back in the night he was thinking about.

He watched Tillie put sandwiches, chips, an apple, and a coffee thermos in a knap sack. Then she sliced a wedge of pie and put it into a pie piece-shaped Tupperware and slid the container and a fork into the sack.

Maureen prepared to come with him, but he shook his head no and meant it.

"I can help you."

"No, you can't," Bill said.

He slid on his black parka, and he left for the garage, his face pale and his shoulders bent. He mumbled, "How does a Korean Veteran of the U.S. Army Corp of Engineers reach this point of law breaking?"

He stood aside as Tillie backed the Lincoln out of the garage. She lifted dust as she turned in the driveway.

The portable heater looked like a desk lamp. The head was long and narrow inside a teepee-shaped core. The pole bent easily with a strong grip. The contraption was powered by the battery. Bill used the lamp for countless animals born too early or too late in the year, even a litter of farm kittens. Well, Tillie used it for the kittens.

Bill found that his perception was strangely magnified which again reminded him of his days in Korea. He did not have time to think about it. He had time only to move along, faster if possible.

He found a sharp wire cutter. It would not work well for his purposes, but he didn't have time to dig through his tools. He put the heavy, awkward tool into the knapsack along with his lunch. He carried the knapsack over his shoulder. The portable heat lamp weighed close to thirty pounds. Bill carried it in a sling across his back.

Pulling his gloves from his coat pocket, he put them on as he walked the driveway, across the road, through the ditch and into the picked corn field belonging to his neighbor. He followed the row of bare corn stalks to the fence line at the other end and then followed the fence west to Martin's wasted and empty pasture land.

Chapter Thirty-Eight

After an hour of sitting on the cold cement steps, Martin requested permission to get a chair. The officers guarding them allowed Martin to carry outside two wicker chairs from the porch. Martin positioned the chairs on the gravel alongside the steps and motioned for Crook to have a seat.

Crook had retreated into a distant place that Martin could not reach. Martin knew it was Crook's defense mechanism. He also knew that Crook's thin butt had to be cold whether Crook admitted it or not. The two men sat side-by-side without speaking.

Martin was losing patience with the time used by the cops. He also feared they were damaging his work. He was considering what action was possible on his part when Vilhallen exited the porch door and sat on the steps.

"Busy little bees inside the house. I keep imaging how Cassandra Peters hid up there, pregnant and alone." Vilhallen sounded casual.

Martin's heart skipped a beat, but he made no response. Crook moved his fingers slightly on his leg. Martin noticed but he felt confident Vilhallen did not see Crook move. Neither Martin nor Crook said a word.

"Of course, it is not the same place and nothing remains of how it was, from what I've learned. From foundation to roof, the house is clean and solid. No rodents," Vilhallen said, continuing his monologue.

Martin and Crook continued to listen. Martin's mouth went dry. He wanted to ask for water. Instead he said to Vilhallen, "Do you have any gum?"

Vilhallen fished gum from his pocket and handed the package to Martin. "The girl went through a lot. It wouldn't be hard to imagine justifiable homicide." Vilhallen looked at Martin. "As a general principle, do you believe in justifiable homicide? Let's say if someone was avenging a rape, would that make homicide justifiable?"

Martin came within a hair's breath of saying, "Saving a life would." He stopped himself, shutting his lips, seeing Crook's fingers flutter. Martin said instead, "I can't talk theory with you, Mr. Vilhallen. I'm worried about the damage to my house."

"What about you, Mr. Sabo? Do you think homicide is justifiable at certain times?" Vilhallen looked at Crook, not with hard eyes.

Crook did not say a word nor move a muscle. Vilhallen looked away. While looking down at the ground, his elbows on his knees, Vilhallen said, "What sent you up in the first place, Jeremy?"

Martin wanted to lash out at the detective sitting safe and calm three feet away, but he did not move. Something in the manner of Vilhallen's speech, his casual approach made Martin think of fishing. The man was guessing. That he guessed correctly made no difference. Sandra had told him nothing.

Crook continued to look at his hands laying flat on his legs, so Martin said, "If you don't already know that, then you have some work to do."

"I just wanted to chat a bit while we finish up inside the house," Vilhallen said. He smiled at Martin. "I noticed one playpen for the baby in each of the two occupied bedrooms. In one room we have a few books and one teddy bear sitting neatly by the play pen. While in the other room, we have a mass of books and toys littering the otherwise spotless room. Fairly diverse parenting styles, but nothing suspicious. I noted the baby bottles and the formula. I was trying to get the feel of things, where everybody was and what they did, when Hauk drove up to the house on Friday night."

Martin fought glancing at Crook because he wondered this, too. Then he caught the trick. He said, "Why would Hauk drive out here?"

Before Vilhallen could answer, John White exited from the porch, allowing the door to slam. He strode down the steps, his hands in his pockets and an angry set to jaw. "The house is clean, the cleanest house I've ever seen. No one was murdered inside this house."

White turned from Vilhallen to Crook. "So where did it happen? Outside someplace, in the garage, in the barn? Where? That much blood can't be hidden."

It was only because of Crook's utter stillness that Martin knew. He recalled the make-shift plan with Sandra. *Tell Hauk about the money, the money in the barn.*

Neither Crook nor Martin said anything to White's outburst. Vilhallen said, "Calm down, John. Gather everybody and look at the out-buildings. Look for tire tracks in the weeds. We should have thought about the dogs."

"Let your people know I haven't cleared the rodents from those structures," Martin said. "They should be prepared."

This time the detectives had no words. White looked at his watch, less than an hour until sunset. He strode back inside yelling for everybody to come outside.

Vilhallen joined his team on the steps. "We look outside," he said. "Be prepared to encounter rodents. Look for any signs of struggle, vehicle tracks, anything out of place. Look for blood."

"By rodents he means rats. Be prepared for rats," White said.

Martin risked a quick look at Crook. To the untrained eye, Crook looked calm, collected and patient. To Martin, he looked depressed.

"Don't despair," Martin whispered to him.

"It's all over," Crook said.

Chapter Thirty-Nine

Bill knew the tree with the bench and hidden drawing paper. Joe and Martin thought he couldn't see them hiding in the branches. It was true, he couldn't see them. He knew they were there, and he pretended to see them so they would come down and get back to work. The memories ran like cool water through his mind as he walked toward the tree.

He liked Joe. In fact Joe had been his favorite because he smiled and laughed a lot and joked with Tillie. Now, he expected some help from Joe. He could feel the boy's presence beside him. Martin was the more gifted of the two, sensitive and moody. Joe was balanced, at ease with himself. Joe was fun, and Martin was fun when he was around Joe. Those boys would have made any parent proud. They made an old neighbor proud.

Bill felt foolish tears, and he quickly brushed hard at his face.

Standing under the tree in the late afternoon light, he removed his wire cutter and dropped the knapsack to the ground. He surveyed his route to the barn. Bill said, "Your mission, Joe, should you choose to accept it, is to make sure nobody comes to the barn. We may be too late already for all I know. They may have come and gone." Talking out loud was his custom from too much time spent working alone on the farm.

From where he stood the dilapidated barn was between him and the house. He would take the path from the tree and go around to the side door of the barn, walking upright most of the way. The day held bright sunshine, maybe forty degrees, cold wind. Unusual for the wind to be cold coming from the south-west; must be looping around in a circle.

Only when he stepped past the corner of the barn, did he become visible from the house. The ragweed stood tall on both sides of the narrow path. From the corner, Bill crawled on his hands and knees with the heat lamp on his back and the wire cutter in his hand. For about three feet, someone standing by the north side of the house and looking exactly that way toward the barn could see him. He scuttled fast.

Not a sound carried to him. All those people must be inside the house. He knew there was nothing inside the house; let them look long and hard. "Right, Joe?" he said.

He reached up from his crouching position and pulled open the side door to the barn. Pulling against the wind, he had to use force to swing it open enough for him to shimmy through. He closed it behind him. For a few seconds, he sat on his haunchesl and closed his eyes, breathing hard. The crawl was not easy for an old man. Then he pulled himself up and looked through the dim light.

From the caved-in part of the roof, light filtered through the hay-mound floor in square shafts squirming with dust mites visible in the light. He walked past the storage rooms and spotted the old ladder. Both Bill and the heat lamp did not fit through the opening, so he had to balance himself, remove the heat lamp from the sling, and push it over his head through the hole.

It dropped, crashing to the barn floor twelve feet down. Bill froze. He listened. Only silence hovered around him like a cloak.

"Better it than me," Bill said, climbing down after it. Nothing could break the heat lamp, but the long thin bulb was a different story. He checked it before taking it back up the ladder. In the hay-mound the slant of the floor under his feet felt pronounced so he sidled sideways until he reached the pile of alfalfa hay. The last hay put up by the old man, Martin's dad. The stuff looked too decayed to burn; he ran his fingers through it and pulled to the surface some dry, brown lumps.

Unpacking the heat lamp, he positioned the bulb exactly as the sunshine hit the pile through the roof. He placed the bulb about four inches from the mound of hay and cranked it to the highest setting for heat. Then he walked to the big hay-mound door and peered through the cracks toward the house. It was 4:15 pm and he could not see any movement. Vehicles parked in a semi-circle across the front of the house, noses facing the porch, but he could not see the front steps.

"Okay, Joe, we need to work fast. We need a flame and we can not use accelerant, it has to be natural, an Act of God." He continued a flow of words, talking as he worked. He found Martin's great coat exactly were Maureen told him Crook put it. The coat lay covered loosely with hay, or more accurately mulch. Anyone with an eyeball would have seen that in the first minute. The coat lay stretched out full, buttoned and sleeves across the breast, respectful. Bill shook his head. It was only a coat.

The rats had helped him out some. Smelling the blood, they had tried to find the flesh. They succeeded only in eating or clawing away bits of the tough material and exposing tufts of white colored stuffing.

"It won't burn. Crook was right about that. He couldn't burn this coat," he mumbled while he pushed the big, black buttons through their holes. Once unbuttoned, he tried to open it, but the front stuck to the back, thick material. Fetching the wire cutter, he attempted to cut the material. He needed the material to be loose enough to burn. Intact and folded, the whole barn could burn to cinders, but the coat would still be there, evidence and all.

The material just bent between his cutter blades and would not cut. Finally, he carried it to the heat lamp and pried open the front, gagging from the stench. Putting one foot on each side, he straddled the coat, holding the material taut. He finally pulled increasing the holes made by the rats. Once started, Bill was able to gouge the lining. The stuffing had rotted little over its fifty years of existence. Bill did as much damage as possible to open the heavy duty material. He knew he would never be able to cut through the seams or the collar so he did not try.

He spread the coat belly down on top of the hay and to one side. Tendrils of smoke rose softly from the hay where the heat hit it directly. "We have smoke," he announced. But he needed something more. The whole moldy stack could smolder for days and go out without ever catching the floor boards.

He stood, thinking about this, then walked to the barn door and peered through the cracks. No action on the southern front. As he turned back, his eyes followed the line of the old pulley system used to hoist the hay into the loft. The cable hung loose from the center joist of the roof because the rough-edged boards from the caving section of roof sliced it through.

But he remembered, along that wall to the west, by the cable box and end pulley was a crate of rags and a tin cupboard with grease. The roof along that edge was sagging low. Blue sky leaked among the broken boards and shingles. He had about two feet of height between the floor and the rough edge of sagging roof, right there at its lowest point. He circled around, sliding against the slant. Bill went down on his knees and then on his belly, crawling beneath the sagging section of roof.

He saw the crate. The cupboard stood upright, nailed to the wall and was out of his reach, but he could get the crate. He reached out and grabbed between the wood slates and jerked it hard toward himself. With the jerk of his arm, a six-inch roofing nail protruding from a broken slat gouged through his coat sleeve and into his right forearm. The gouge went with the momentum of his pull and cut his arm for eight or nine inches.

Bill, with great presence of mind, did not jerk his arm up. His arm was caught between the side of the crate and broken edge of sagging roof. His gloved fingers entwined in the space between the crate slats. He had only one choice, to keep pulling

Sliding backwards on his knees, he jerked the crate to him. Damn, that hurt. Blood dripped from his gloved fingers. Tillie would fix it later; for right now he had to keep going. Inside the crate was an answer to prayers: greasy, half-rotted rags.

Smoke curled to the open roof and vaporized in the wind. Quickly, Bill began to spread the rags along the floor and then turned the crate upside down and dumped the rest over the large pool of dried blood beneath the sagging basketball hoop. The floor had to catch. He loosened the rags with his hands.

Then he went back to the heat lamp. He needed to see an actual flame. The smoke hurt his eyes and throat while he positioned the greasiest of the rags loosely between the dry hay, and repositioned his lamp close over the spot. Again he walked to the big hay-mound u-shaped door and peered out. Now he saw activity; his stomach squeezed. A group of men stood in a semi-circle on his side of the house. The head honcho was giving them instructions. As Bill watched, the men broke into groups and started walking in different directions away from the house. These men would check the scattered outbuildings and the burn pit on their way to the barn. They were coming.

Chapter Forty

Crook said to Martin, "It smells like someone is burning leaves."

"That is the smell of a smoldering haystack."

Crook said, "I should tell you now why I was sent to the bin."

"Okay," Martin said. "You are under no obligation to ever tell me."

"Is it okay if I tell you?" Crook did not look at Martin.

Martin said, "I am honored to be your confidant." He hoped it would not be too sad.

Crook looked toward the growing dusk as he talked. He said, "I lived with my mom in a sagging old apartment building in Omaha. On the ground floor, corner apartment lived an old, crippled man. Now days we would call him a pedophile; back then we called him a dirty old man. Me and my friends thought he was funny. Every time one of my friends had cash we said, 'You've been to visit the dirty.'

"When I was seventeen my mom got sick. I couldn't fix it. I couldn't stand to be around it because it angered me. I was immature and self-centered at the time. My mother asked me to read to her, but I wouldn't. I got the neighbor lady to read to my mother.

"I was past the age for the old man. He liked little boys, six or seven. One morning, I came down the steps late for school and in no mood to be polite. I saw the old man talking to a kid outside his door. The kid had a back pack on for school. The kid was crying and the old man was shoving a ten dollar bill into his hand and trying to pull the kid into his room.

"I always had a knife in my pocket, even then. I went up to the two of them and I grabbed the ten from the old man's hand, but he wouldn't let go of the kid, so I pulled out my knife and told him to let go of the kid. He wouldn't let go so I stabbed his hand. The kid ran, and I went to school.

"When the cops found him he had twenty-seven knife wounds. The cops said I killed him for ten dollars. They tried me as an adult. My attorney said temporary insanity and a plea arrangement for the mental hospital. Enough people came to my sentencing for the judge to have a clue.

"The judge told me after a year in the hospital, my mother could get me out. But my mother died, and I was forgotten. I couldn't get myself out. In a way I didn't want to. I did the time for walking away from my mother."

Martin said, "Life isn't fair."

Crook sat back, apparently watching three officers systematically searching the grove.

Martin said, "You don't have to be so all or nothing. There is a middle ground, sometimes."

"I know. I can't help it."

Vilhallen called everybody to meet near the steps. It was five thirty and chilly. The wind from the south-east calmed as the sun rolled to the western horizon, but the air cooled quickly. The Officers and technicians stood in a loose semi-circle facing the detectives and waiting on orders. Vilhallen and White stood some twelve paces from the corner of the house and to Crook's left toward the barn.

"We only have the barn left to search. I think we can finish this before dark. Any volunteers?" Vilhallen sounded half-hearted.

White said, "Let's do this! Or we can come back at first light." To Martin's ear, he sounded determined – a dangerous man.

The policeman standing nearest Martin said quietly to the man beside him, "I hope whoever is burning has a permit and knows what they are doing."

A thin haze began to cover the dusk.

White began to walk slowly toward the barn. Martin could not see the path from his position, so he rose and walked a few steps to watch the proceedings.

Crook said, "Say good-bye for me to Maureen."

Martin did not answer.

Crook said, "My new friends possess far more issues than the nuts I left behind."

Martin said, "You walked out of that hospital by the front door. Don't walk back inside, not yet."

Chapter Forty-One

The light faded fast in the hay-mound as the sun sank beneath the roof line. "Flame, Joe. We need flame now," Bill said. He also knew he had to get out before one of those groups came walking to the barn.

First he heard it, then he saw it; the crackle of flame as it caught the rag. The wind worked as a draft, igniting the flame and lifting the smoke.

Still, he waited. He wanted to see the floorboards catch. While he waited, he shut off the heat lamp, and tried to hold his breath. Even with a rag over his face, the smoke was dense and dangerous. With deft motion, he pushed the hot lamp down into its casing, carried it down the slanted floor and dropped it through the hole above the stanchions.

Realizing he left the wire cutter lying by the coat, he started toward them. Too late; blue flame rolled along the coat lining and the tool was beneath the coat. Darn it, he liked those wire cutters.

Time to make his exit. A steady line of fire came from the original source at the hay pile and moved across the row of rags to the basketball hoop. The slanting, cracked floorboards showed red slivers of wood. Then he realized the row of burning rags blocked him from the ladder. He could still leap over it, but the jagged edge of board on the sagging section of roof also glowed red and flame began to curl up the boards and under the shingles.

Too late for the ladder; he would have to jump the hole above the stanchions. Now he felt Joe. He honest to goodness felt him like a hug, propelling him to the opening in the floor and a gentle shove to the hard packed black earth twelve feet down. His sixty-five year old body landed with a jolt, miraculously right between the thick wood of the stanchions on either side. His heat lamp lay about a foot from his head.

Bill gave his condition some thought. The wind was knocked out of him, but his coat padded the landing enough to save his bones. He could move. His jaw felt tender and his ears rang a little, but overall not a bad landing. First he crawled and then he stood. Picking up the heat lamp, he found his way past the storage rooms and to the side door.

He remembered the men walking around outside and wondered how close they might be. It would not do for him to be spotted exiting the burning barn. He opened the door a crack and looked out. Dusk gave some cover, but he heard voices coming from the yard.

"He who hesitates is lost," he said, going to his knees. The thick air spun, and he wobbled forward on his arms. He paused for balance and gritted his teeth against the pain, reaching for the lap. With his last strength he hoisted the lamp onto his back and wound the flexible head over his shoulder. He crawled, mouth dry and heart pounding wildly. He crawled through the door and onto the path. He kicked shut the door behind him and paused until he heard the latch catch hold.

One arm throbbing, he crawled painfully along the path between the weeds. He reached the path that headed either to the house or to the tree. Bill clenched his teeth and listened. He would again be visible for three feet or so. He heard voices but saw nothing moving. Rising to his knees, he peered across the top of the weeds. He saw a man in a police jacket using a flashlight to check the stock tank.

Lowering himself, he scurried like the rats holding the head of the damn heat-lamp with his chin and feeling the casing slide on his back. His mouth was too dry to cry out. He moved forward on the path feeling nothing but the necessity to move.

He moved forward until he was clear of sight. He still crawled until he rounded the corner of the barn and several feet past it. Once in the thistles, he slowly stood, straightening his body, clearing his head. He cradled the lamp in his good arm as he tread the narrow path through the thistles and up the slope to the tree. He sat on "the bench" and breathed in and out, in and out many times, slowly and carefully waiting for his heart to slow.

When he looked up, flames across the area of sagging roof reached for the evening sky. He couldn't believe it, and he could not look away. He heard the fire and nothing else. The wind died with the sunshine, and quiet darkness began to envelope him. He was too tired and hurt to walk home, so he found the knapsack, sat on his smooth seat, drank coffee and ate.

When he heard the sirens above the sound of the fire, he decided it was time to go. Darkness was no hindrance in retracing his steps. However climbing between the barbed wire fence challenged his now stiff bones. He caught on the barbs and had to tear himself free, leaving pieces of coat behind. His black parka was ruined, his wire cutters gone forever, his arm hurt and so did his jaw and every bone in his body, but Bill felt very, very good. He walked the corn rows, through the ditch, down his driveway and into his warm, well lit kitchen.

Chapter Forty-Two

When the yelling began, Crook hung his head into his hands, but briefly. He would face his fate like a man. He walked slowly, looking toward the barn. His steps had no direction; he moved numbly toward the law. When he looked down he saw his hands in front of him, ready for the cuffs. Crook thought, "I only did what I had to do."

He stopped ten steps past Martin and again looked to the barn. In that moment Crook got religion.

Crook saw flames shoot from the barn along the caved roof line. He would remember that instant for the rest of his life and refer to it in his thoughts as the moment he learned to pray. Now, his mouth opened and he gaped. "Thank you, thank you, thank you," he said, lips moving but no sound emerging.

Chapter Forty-Three

Detective White stood by the pump-jack looking into the stock tank. The ground beneath his feet felt stiff and gave slightly under his weight as wet ground would when it was trying to freeze. The stock tank was yellow-gray, cracked and dry. He thought perhaps it was recently drained. He considered the advisability of testing the tank bottom or the earth for traces of blood and determined it to be pointless. If blood had mixed with this water last Friday, it would no longer be viable.

He ran his flashlight along the weeds between the pump and the barn and saw the path outlined by broken and crushed yellow weeds. Suddenly his heart churned hard. This was it. They used the barn. He ran heedless down the path toward the side entrance to the barn. He heard the yelling behind him and did not hear it. It was not for him. A foot from the door, Vilhallen grabbed him around the shoulder and locked his fist across his chest.

"Not worth it, John," Vilhallen said. White struggled because he still did not understand. He saw two rats squirm around loose rocks in the foundation, running pall-mall into the weeds. Then with the smell and the haze and sting in his throat he understood. The damned barn was burning.

"The evidence." White could barely speak the words, still facing the barn door now with smoke exiting around the edges.

"Likely nothing," Vilhallen answered, shaking his head. "We have to let it go. The fire department is on its way."

As the detectives walked back toward the house, the sirens already sounded in the distance. The technicians covered their noses and mouths with cloth. White looked up to see the tall, lean Martin standing near the house. Martin stood still, hands loose at his sides, staring at the barn. He moved his gaze to Jeremy Sabo who was covering his face with a white dish towel.

White said to Vilhallen, "How did they do it?"

Chapter Forty-Four

Vilhallen, White, and Jerome Mathis, the local Fire Chief, stood near the police vehicles and watched the barn burn.

"Shouldn't you do something more?" White asked, but he talked with little energy. "Important evidence could be burning before our eyes."

Jerome Mathis said, calm and quiet, "You should thank your lucky stars if that is true."

"How so?" Vilhallen said.

"This case is the biggest embarrassment to law enforcement ever known in the State of South Dakota. Hopefully the guy who did it won't bill you for cleaning up your mess. If the rumors are even half true, Hauk hurt a lot of people. Where were you when the citizens needed you?" Jerome Mathis rocked on his heels and looked toward the flames against the night sky.

Vilhallen stared at the man. He was a bit too heavy. His coat buttoned over his belly and left about three inches of stomach hanging between the coat and his belt buckle. But the man had a point. A good defense attorney would wreak havoc on law enforcement gone bad. The actual crime may have been in defense of life. He began planning his report to the governor.

However, even if nothing could be proved, he wanted to know. He almost had to know. He stood and watched while the fire fighters contained the flames and made no effort to save the barn. Person by person Vilhallen and White sent their team home until only the fire fighters remained with them and Martin and Crook

Martin and Crook loitered several feet away from the detectives. They seemed unsure of their standing. Vilhallen sidled closer to hear their conversation.

"It is odd that Bill is not here. I expected his pick-up truck to come racing up the drive at the first spark of flame against the sky," Martin said.

Crook said, "Maureen and I had a movie date tonight. Even Tillie could come over and bring Kirby."

"Kirby has to stay with Tillie until the house is cleaned," Martin said.

Vilhallen walked up to Martin. "Martin, the men need to use your restroom. Is there a way to restore the plumping and turn the water on?"

Crook stared at him. "Not too embarrassed to ask? That is a cop for ya." Then Crook stepped back, shutting his lips tight.

"Are we friends now?" Martin asked, looking down at the man who was tall but still four inches shorter than Martin.

"We can be," Vilhallen answered, "if that will fix the plumping."

Martin turned toward the house, Crook on his heels. Vilhallen kept some distance, but not out of range to hear their words. He briefly considered a visit to Bill Bendix. Then decided it was time to give it up. They had no evidence.

Martin restored the pipes and Crook cleaned the bathrooms. Crook made coffee in the big pot. Upon seeing Vilhallen hovering in the kitchen, Crook said, "The coffee is for the firefighters saving Martin's property, not for the detectives who tried to ruin it."

Vilhallen wanted some coffee so he ignored Crook's words. He watched Crook efficiently move a card table and folding chairs outside. Crook put the coffee urn on the table and poured a few mugs. He did not have disposable cups. Crook found hamburger and made sloppy-joes. Vilhallen could not stop watching the small man.

A tent appeared over them as Crook put food on the table, made more coffee and found juice. The firefighters worked through the night as did Crook. Martin entered the tent. He said to Crook, "I've made my bed and now I am going to sleep in it."

Crook said, "Sleep good."

As dawn rode up the trees to the east only six one-foot square charred timbers stood in two rows of three to represent the barn. The stanchions still stood, black skeletons. The fire chief and a newly arrived fire investigator combed the ashes. Vilhallen, White, and Crook sat in a row on folding chairs by the pump. The weeds were trampled to ground, black with soot and singed with burn, no longer blocking their view. They watched.

Martin came along, looking fresh saved and showered and toting a chair. Unfolding his chair, he sat by Crook. The four fans in a row watched the Fire Chief and the Fire Investigator confer for several minutes. The two firemen picked up and carried over a three-foot square box with a wire mesh bottom. They set the box on the ground in front of White and Vilhallen and everyone bent to look inside.

The exhausted Fire Chief said, "Hello, Martin, how are you?" Martin looked past the grime and the black uniform and recognized Jerome. "Fine," he answered. "I presume I owe you some money for all this commotion."

"That you do," Jerome answered, "but the building is no loss. It was a fire hazard and needed to come down." The two men continued to chat as though at a church breakfast.

Vilhallen thought, everything and everyone is connected in a small town. How did Hauk get away with his schemes for so long? He was careful in his victims. That is until he ran into Cassandra Peters. The wrong girl and his escalating sickness ended his life.

The Fire Chief informed Vilhallen that no evidence of arson existed, and he would have the full report within a few days. "We are calling it an Act of God," he said. "A coincidence for sure, but who knows about these things. That box is all that remains."

Remembering something, Jerome held out his hand containing a black wallet. "Found this by the stanchions," he told Martin. John White, snatched it from Jerome's hand, "I have to check everything first."

Vilhallen saw that Crook did not flinch. This wallet did not belong to Hauk. The wallet appeared old and inexpensive even in its current half-melted condition. White opened it carefully while everyone present positioned to see what the wallet might contain.

Fully intact, inside clear plastic on the front pocket was a driver's license issued in the name of Joseph Adam Webster. Stashed in the money folder were a one dollar bill and several pictures. The school pictures were of young ladies. Vilhallen saw Martin smile. From behind the school pictures, White pulled a folded newspaper clipping. It was a newspaper photo of Martin and Joe dressed in suit and tie, standing together on the stage.

"This picture was taken at the homecoming festivities following our third place finish at the State B basketball tourney. I was a sophomore year and Joe was a junior," Martin said quietly. He added, "I remember this but I never knew how much that homecoming meant to Joe. He kept this clipping in his wallet." He reached for the clipping with trembling fingers and took it from White's hand. "After all these years Joe is saying good-bye."

Last thing in the wallet was a seventh grade school picture of a smiling red-haired, freckled-faced girl. Martin and Crook laughed, and White wordlessly handed the wallet to Martin.

The fire chief and the investigator left leaving the four men to pour over the contents of the box. Vilhallen leaned back on his chair. His eyes burned, and he wanted rest. Since he could not sleep, he continued to watch. Martin was possibly the most likeable man he had ever encountered on an investigation. Crook, on the other hand was not likeable at all. He was alarming.

Inside the box, resting on the mesh bottom was a wire cutter. Some melted chunks of material lay beside the wire cutter. That was it, the only remaining remnants of the barn.

"Was there anything in that barn we would take an interest in?" White asked Martin and Martin shook his head no.

White, pale with exhaustion, said, "You seem to recognize something."

Martin picked up the biggest chunk of material which was a remnant of a coat collar. He said, "I remember this coat."

"Well then, gentlemen, we will go now. I wish we met under better circumstances, but I wish you both well." Vilhallen reached out a hand and Martin shook it as did Crook.

White managed to nod with civility toward the men, then followed Vilhallen to their Ford Focus. White said, "Poor little town."

Vilhallen said, "Poor us. We did what they let us do."

Chapter Forty-Five

Only when the cloud of dust from the departing vehicle settled onto the driveway did Martin turn toward Crook. "My coat? You used my coat in the removal of Hauk? How was that necessary?" His voice remained calm and quiet as always but his eyes held some fire.

"I tried to save it. I did my best to save it," Crook answered, showing emotion for one time in his life. "I am sorry about the coat, Martin." In living memory no apology had ever issued from his lips before this one.

"Okay, then," Martin said. "Now tell me about it, the short version. I have work to do." Then pausing, he again looked at his friend. "How did you burn the barn?"

"I didn't," Crook answered.

"Well the barn didn't sit there for sixty years and decide to burn last night," Martin said, puzzling this over in his mind. "Bill?" he said. Crook had to agree. It was the only explanation for the man's absence. "We can return his wire cutter," Martin said.

They had no explanation for why Bill needed a wire cutter in his arson, but they had no doubt it was his and served some purpose. For now, Crook needed to sleep and Martin needed to restore his porch and kitchen. If Bill didn't show up by noon, Martin would walk over.

At 12:30 pm, Martin knocked on the front door of Bill's house. When Maureen answered, he hugged her and pecked her forehead. "All okay," he said to her anxious look. Then he saw Bill, lying on the couch, pillows under his head and shoulders. He looked rough, black and blue around his chin and mouth, gauze bandage on his arm, singed hair and red skin and soot outlining the creases of his face like a child outlining a coloring page.

"I see why you didn't come over, Mr. Bill." Martin pulled up a kitchen chair to face the couch as he talked. Before sitting, he found Kirby playing on a blanket on the kitchen floor and he picked the baby up in one low sweep. Kirby laughed.

"You see what I did?" Bill asked.

"We guessed but only because you didn't come over," Martin said.

"I wanted to. I wanted to see the faces on those cops when the barn went up," Bill smiled, delighted with himself.

"It's Crook's face you should have seen," Martin answered. Then added, "So you knew my coat was going up in flame and you left it behind."

Bill looked at him for a second, almost frightened.

"I joke sometimes now," Martin said. Bill laughed.

"I am greatly relieved that no one was hurt in that fire," Bill said. His expression turned grave.

"Even a detective doesn't walk into a burning building," Martin said. "Though one of them almost did."

Martin heard the whole story. He nodded at the part that Joe helped and Joe saved Bill's life. He did not doubt that to be true, but that was for inner life and not for talk past the one telling.

Before Martin left, he told Maureen to pick Crook up at seven or so, the same movie they missed last night showed tonight. Maureen smiled and nodded. Then Martin put his son in his seat and covered him warm, thanked Tillie and was about to leave when Tillie told him to wait.

She handed over Crook's carving knife in a clear plastic baggie. "I cleaned it," she said, "but Crook may need to clean it some more. Kirby Pucket Webster crapped all over it." She bent double with laughter. Then she handed him a second baggie containing the buttons from his coat. "Bill saved the buttons," she said.

As Martin stepped outside, Maureen followed him.

"I plan to propose to Crook tonight," she said.

"Propose what?" Martin studied her pretty face.

"I think I will marry Jeremy Sabo," Maureen said softly.

"Why?" Martin felt a little shocked. "He is not a gentle man."

"He has gentleness somewhere in his heart. But I am going to marry him because I can't stop thinking about him."

That evening Martin felt nervous for Maureen. He could not imagine what Crook would say. They were attending *Mr. Holland's Opus*. They planned to shop. Crook wanted two varnished cedar-lined boxes, one with horses running across a field and one with birds flying across a blue sky. He was specific in this. He had cut the ad for the keepsake boxes from the Sunday paper.

Crook said Martin needed a box for mementoes because he finally removed the square wad of paper that was once Christie's letter from his shirt pocket. Martin planned to put the letter and the newspaper clipping from Joe's wallet and the baggie of coat buttons inside the box with the birds, not the horses.

When at last Crook and Maureen entered the house late that night, Martin waited in the family room with the TV tuned to the news, surrounded by woodwork in sorted stacks. He was drawing plans for the fireplace.

Maureen entered first. Martin thought she looked happy. Crook lingered a little behind. Maureen said, "Our marriage has conditions."

Martin nodded, craning his neck to see Crook who hid in the doorway.

"Jeremy has to find something productive to do with his time. He has to take lessons to become a Catholic, and he has to relocate to Fargo. Unlike you, I am not financially independent. I have a job. In fact, I am back to work on Tuesday."

Martin finally managed to look at Crook's face which was split nearly in two with his smile. Martin laughed out loud. "When?" Martin said.

This took Maureen a bit by surprise and she bent her head in thought. "Let's go with Christmas," she said, turning to look at Crook.

"No," Crook said. "We will play it by ear and see when it feels right. Martin knows a contractor in Fargo who needs a good interior man. The shrink in Yankton will set me up with a shrink in Fargo for my out-patient visits. But most of all, Martin does not need me. He will miss me, but he does not need me."

"All set then," Martin said. He picked up a sleeping Kirby and left the room. He thought, this is real. Maybe some happiness lives on in the world.

Chapter Forty-Six

The following afternoon Martin sat on his front steps. He pushed Kirby back and forth in Kirby's new stroller. He surveyed his yard and considered the best method for fixing the overgrown mess. As he discussed his options, a late model Jeep Tahoe pulled into his driveway and Jarvis Peters DDS stepped from behind the wheel.

Jarvis Peters was tall and thin like his daughter Sandra. Also like Sandra he carried himself with confidence and authority. Martin moved over a few inches to give the man space and Jarvis sat down.

Jarvis said nothing at first, nor did Martin. They sat and looked at Kirby who had his fist in his mouth. Finally Jarvis said, "I came to thank you, but I can't just yet. Now that I am here, I need to ask why you did not bring Sandra home. You should have brought her home first thing and told us what happened."

Martin looked at the man and thought of his own daughters. "Couldn't," he answered. "It wasn't the time. Sandra would not go, and I was not capable of making her. All I could do was move with the flow as it came."

"You befriended her. You were kind to her and cared for her." Jarvis Peter's jaw shook slightly as he talked. Martin looked away.

"I did no more for her than she did for me," Martin answered. "We survived together. I am glad she is home now."

"She wants to quit basketball. After all these years that it meant so much to her, she wants to quit."

"No," Martin said. "This is not the time to quit what she loves." Martin sat for another minute. Then he asked, "How is she doing today?"

Jarvis told Martin about the visit by Detective Vilhallen, the trophy case, and the aftermath.

"Oh," Martin said. "I see why she thinks she wants to quit basketball. I am so sorry."

"I think she wants to die but couldn't. So she wants to quit basketball instead," Jarvis said quietly. He could not seem to look away from Kirby. "Was she very afraid? She claims not to remember exactly how the delivery happened."

Martin said, "She was very brave. Crook found good people to help her." He thought of Clara, but he was talking to Sandra's dad. He added, "It is a hospital so they had all the equipment and professional people there to help."

Jarvis nodded. His jaw no longer trembled. He did not say anything so Martin said, "Can I get you something to drink? I have coffee or lemonade or beer leftover from the sliver party."

Jarvis shook his head. "We can't help with him." He nodded toward Kirby. "I do not know why I can't. I just can not accept him as a grandson. It makes me sick to think of what Sandra went through."

Martin nodded. He said, "I have Kirby."

Jarvis stood and took a few steps toward his vehicle. He turned around, looking at the ground, and said, "Thank you for saving my daughter. It should have been me. I should have known."

"You couldn't know. Sandra would do whatever she had to do so you would not know," Martin said. "It was by the grace of God that she came here and I found her. We saved each other. Now you have the hard part. Tell her I said that I expect to see her play on Tuesday night."

As the Tahoe left, Crook came from the house. He said, "Me and Bill are going fishing."

"Have fun," Martin said. He looked again to his lawn. "I did not thank Sandra for forcing me to function. She should know that she helped me as much as I helped her."

As Martin watched Sandra's father leave the yard, he thought of his arrival. He thought of his bus ride home and the kid who sat beside him. He thought of finding Sandra. Now the time was approaching to say farewell to the teenager. She would have her own bus ride.

Chapter Forty-Seven

Martin did watch Sandra play on Tuesday night. He saw the difference in her. The hyper-passion was gone. She played with detachment, and the perfect game-face, and incredible skill. Emotion had no place in her game.

He watched Sandra and her teammates through the season and through the State Tournament. Finally, he got to welcome home a winning team. He watched Sandra on the stage for the award ceremony and could not help flashing back to two boys who stood in nearly the same place many years before. Unlike Joe, Sandra declined to hold the trophy instead handing it to a teammate.

She smiled, but it was a sad smile. Martin thought, Sandra had not got her old life back.

Martin attended the graduation ceremony and then went to Sandra's house for the reception. Bill and Tillie also attended, but Kirby did not. Kirby had a babysitter. This was Sandra's day. As evening approached, Martin stepped onto the back patio and sat on a deck chair. Most of the guests had left and Sandra should leave also for her class party, but she wanted Martin to go with her.

He sat in the warm spring evening, drinking an iced slushy drink and looking across the green manicured lawn. "I am not going to your class party. It is your decision if you want to go or not. You might enjoy being with your friends."

"I'm too old for them. They're kids." Sandra sounded very much like a child herself, and Martin smiled.

Her mom came onto the deck and offered Sandra a ride. Sandra said, "In a minute," then gave Martin a pleading look.

In answer he smiled at her and said, "It will not hurt to have fun, but not too much fun."

"I know," she choked. "I am a freak."

Martin stood. He took her hand and led her away from any guest. He wanted to sound firm, but he couldn't. He looked into her lovely brown eyes that he once tried to turn green, and felt a choking sensation in his throat.

"You are not a freak." He hugged her to him. "You will not believe this, but you are not the only person to suffer like this. When you go to school in the fall, the University of Minnesota has a rape support group. I have the name of the person you contact. Promise me you will attend the meetings."

"I will promise to go to one meeting if you come to this senior party with me." She tried to look pleading, but it only made Martin laugh.

"I am not going to your senior party." Martin intended to convey to Sandra that he could not be in her social life. She could not be dependent upon him. Instead he saw devastation in her eyes.

He closed his eyes for a few seconds. "You know that we are forever connected. You know that I am your friend no matter what you do. I know, probably better than anyone but Crook, how strong you are. Don't alienate yourself from your friends because they have not been forced to suffer."

Sandra said, looking into his eyes, "Why can't you be my boyfriend?"

For a second Martin was so shocked he almost stepped away from her. He would be grateful the rest of his life that he did not take that single step back. He had not pushed Joe, and he had not stepped away from Sandra.

He couldn't speak at all for several beats of his heart. Then he forced himself to meet her gaze, her teenage face so intent and so pretty. He shook his head. "I didn't know," he whispered. "What made you think I could be your boyfriend?"

"I thought you loved me." Her lips were too tight to form words. "You knew about me and still cared."

Martin stood speechless. He couldn't think of what to say. He bent and kissed the top of her head, and shook his head.

She snatched her hand from his and started to turn away. Martin took hold of her shoulders. Her tears smeared black mascara down her cheeks. "I am so sorry," he said. Then he released her.

Sandra nodded. She turned and strode away with a determined step. She passed her dad on her way out. Martin returned to his chair, and Jarvis sat down by him.

Jarvis said, "What was that about?"

"I won't go to the senior party with her." The words sounded trivial, but Martin knew that Sandra did not cry easily. "Her heart is broken. I hope feeling normal pain means she is healing."

Jarvis looked thoughtful for a few seconds. He said, "Sandra will be okay." He paused. "Some day she will have to meet Kirby to reconcile herself to her past."

"Someday she will," Martin agreed.

Chapter Forty-Eight

On the fourth of August, Martin and Kirby stood on the south steps. Martin watched Carmen and Christie play on the carpet of grass that stretched to the road. Kirby stood beside him, clutching his bottle in one hand and the material of Martin's jeans in the other.

Martin reached down and scooped Kirby into his arms. "Really, son, you have to either not walk so early or trade-in your bottle." In answer Kirby put the bottle to his mouth.

Parked near the house sat a new SUV. Martin purchased the vehicle because he could not ask Bill to drive the girls to town for T-ball. Beside the SUV sat a John Deer pedal tractor. Kirby liked to sit on it while Carmen pushed him around the driveway.

It was nearly a year since Martin had returned to the farm. Kirby would soon be one. Martin thought that he should be at peace but something was wrong. A nagging itch that he could not scratch hampered his contentment.

"Daddy misses Crook," Martin said to Kirby. You are lucky to have him for a godfather. Lucky boy." Martin rocked Kirby and watched the girls play.

"Daddy has to take a trip." He would go alone. Crook was in Fargo, and Bill had work of his own. This time he had private business: one last errand, he needed to go alone.

The following week, Nancy and her new companion came for the girls. Both girls seemed content to return to the city and school. Kirby could not stay with Tillie. It was too much for Tillie to keep track of Kirby for more than a few hours. So Maureen and Crook agreed to drive from Fargo and pick-up Kirby.

Crook and Maureen arrived in the afternoon of the third Saturday in August. Maureen drove the fire-red Mustang into the yard and parked beside Martin's SUV. When she strode toward Martin she looked less sophisticated and more matronly. Martin liked the subtle change. Crook unfolded from the passenger seat and put his arms out to Kirby.

Martin hugged his sister and then he stood back and said, "Kirby can't ride in your car. He has to have a toddler seat."

The three adults strode around the car looking at it as though they could somehow fix that problem. They tried the seat from Martin's SUV, and it would not fit. They briefly considered using only the seat belt but reluctantly decided that Kirby had to have a seat.

"We will have to take your car," Crook said.

"It's not a car," Martin said.

Nevertheless, that was the solution. Martin would drive the Mustang.

The four of them took a walk through the orchard and up to the bench. Crook carried the little boy, and they stood without speaking as they looked toward the house and the burned remnants of the barn. Of course, Martin and Bill had torn down the outbuildings and mowed the weeds. Martin had poured new gravel and fixed the garage.

"You've done a lot in a year, Martin," Maureen said. She had tears on her cheeks.

Crook said, "You can build something there." He gestured to the scarred ground where the barn had stood. "Get Kirby a horse."

Bill and Tillie joined them for supper. They talked about the upcoming wedding. Crook and Maureen would be married in May in Fargo.

"Why so long?" Bill asked.

"Crook has a lot of work to do first," Maureen said.

Martin said, "He has to take church lessons for almost a year. Have you started on that?" Crook nodded.

"He has to build his furniture refinishing business," Maureen said.

"No one will pay him by the hour." Bill said.

"You better change your name to Jeremy. Crook is not a good name for a business man." Tillie looked serious, but Crook smiled and nodded.

Maureen said, "He has to learn how to drive."

Martin thought that his friend, the almost lifer from the bin, looked happy. He could not be sure because Crook showed little emotion. Then Crook lifted Kirby from his high-chair and did a graceful waltz to the sink.

The group talked about Sandra, but Martin would say only that he heard from her about once a week. He had nothing more he could say. Sandra was a work in progress, forming her plans. He did not know.

Maureen asked when he planned on re-finishing the fireplace. Martin shrugged. Then they played cards. Bill and Tillie went home. On Sunday morning, Maureen and Crook packed up the SUV. Kirby reached from Maureen's arms and put his little hands on Martin's face and kissed his cheek.

"Daddy will come for you in one week," Martin said.

Then Martin stood in his driveway. He watched the dust follow his vehicle down the road. The silence and stillness felt physical. He could reach out and touch it.

Chapter Forty-Nine

As Martin turned west onto I-90, he remembered the taillights of the bus moving west in the rain. Martin adjusted the rear-view mirror to see himself. He was clean-shaven. His thick, black hair still curled about his head but in a far more disciplined manner. He had awareness in his eyes behind his new glasses. Nothing about him was frightening. He thought he looked fairly bland.

Rain did not slash the windows, and wind did not rock the vehicle. No one sat beside him. There was nothing lucky about the passenger seat. Martin's heart ached for that sick man riding home. He knew even then that he had to heal or die. Fortunately he had healed, and he had answered one puzzling question. It was mayhem and murder, not murder and mayhem.

He arrived in Rapid City in time for supper. He checked into a hotel and then ate in the dining room. He asked about a casino called Uptown Joe's. The casino was located in Spearfish next to a haunted hotel. As Martin followed his directions he could see that effort had been made to maintain the old west aura of the buildings. The tourist season was ebbing, but even so the streets were crowded. He had to drive around to find a hitching post.

The casino was a few blocks off the beaten path, dealing mostly to regulars. Still, a lively country band played on a small stage and a long buffet was open all night for a one time ticket.

Martin found the young man with the charismatic smile within minutes of entering the establishment. He dealt at the blackjack table. Martin watched the young man's deft hands and careful eyes. Martin stood at the black-jack table. When the young man looked toward him, Martin said, "Do you remember me from the bus ride? I was only a short part of your trip. I wanted to thank you for helping me."

The kid looked at him, wary for a few seconds and then recognition lit his features, and he smiled. "You cleaned up real well," the kid said. "Meat you at the lunch counter in forty minutes."

Martin bought a buffet ticket and sat at the counter eating slowly. He was not hungry. Crook would enjoy the music more than Martin did. It was too noisy.

When the kid tapped Martin's shoulder, he indicated an exit to an outside patio. The noise shut off behind the door and they found a table set apart from the others.

Martin said, "You remember me."

"Not every day, but often, I think of you." The kid's name was Joshua per the tag on his pocket.

"Why do you remember me?" Martin asked.

"You were unique even to someone who sees dozens of new faces in a week."

"Did I scare you?"

"No, you didn't scare me. For some reason I was scared for you. I had this feeling that something was going to happen to you."

"I happened to me. Are you psychic?"

"Since I was little I've tried to be open to cosmic forces greater than me." Joshua shrugged. "It never works."

"You don't know that your intuitive power works, but it does. You deal in chance." Martin reached for his wallet and was about to hand a hundred dollar bill to Joshua.

The young man waved his hand and shook his head. "You can't pay for cosmic forces. And you shouldn't show that kind of money in a casino."

Martin returned his wallet to his pocket. "Thank you helping me when you didn't have to," Martin told him and Joshua nodded.

"Did you come all this way just for this?" Joshua said.

"Yes," Martin said. "I came to thank you, and I had to be sure you were real. At the time, I just couldn't be sure."

"I'm so real, I have to get back to work. It puts me at peace to see you all normal and everything."

Martin studied the young man. Joshua did not know that he had nudged him off the bus, moved him forward, talked to him when few would have. The kid did not know that he was Martin's first push into his real life.

"You were like a guardian angel sitting beside me. I thought I made you up. I had to tell you that in case it mattered to you." Martin spoke calmly, without emotion, stating the facts.

Joshua seemed taken aback but only for a second. Then he said, "Thank you, thank you for coming here and telling me that."

Joshua returned to his job, and Martin left. He thought, fate is a funny thing. Maybe everything would have gone exactly the same if Joshua had not sat beside him on the bus ride. No, he thought, Joshua changed it. He started to wake-up my mind.

Chapter Fifty

Her first year away from Wheaton, Sandra called once a week Mostly she called on Thursday night after her group support meeting. He knew the names of everyone in her group. Sometimes it was late, after a ballgame when she called. It did not matter. Martin answered her calls regardless of where or when.

Martin felt close to Sandra: not like a daughter, not like a sister but more than a friend. He had never before Sandra or since Sandra met someone who connected so strongly to his survival.

Her second year away she called once or twice a month. Martin loved the sound of her voice. He learned a new sound: the sound of her laughter. It was during this time that he began talking a little about Kirby. She would listen but not respond. During her third year away, Martin began to feel a separation. The separation was named Kirby. His son was the cornerstone of his life. His friend should care about his cornerstone.

Even knowing the pain of her past did not always explain her failure to acknowledge their son. During her senior year, Sandra called only a few times. On what would be her last call, Martin said, "You can not pretend that Kirby is not here with me anymore."

Sandra said, "I know." She did not call again.

Martin returned to work doing local residence projects in Sioux Falls or Yankton or Madison. He thought of Sandra every day. He began to think that she would never come.

Kirby grew into a loving, gentle boy with a dog named Bert. He was both a smart child and a strong child. He made friends at day care, and he thrived.

Five years after Martin's return, Kirby started kindergarten. Kirby and Martin had breakfast early that morning. Kirby chatted about some string he found in the grass by the south steps. Kirby was sure that the gold cord came from a treasure chest and wondered if he could dig in the yard after school.

Martin combed Kirby's hair, carefully parting it on the side. He took Kirby's first day of school picture, one with Bert and one without Bert since Bert didn't get to go to school. Martin drove Kirby to the kindergarten entrance, parked his Bronco and stepped into the line with all the other parents. Kirby would not hold his hand, but stood beside him surveying the surroundings and the other kids in silent contemplation.

Kirby's turn came and the teacher bent down to talk with him. He already knew her name and the seat assigned to him from a previous visit and danced in place waiting to get on with it. Martin assured him that he would be back at lunch time to take him home. He was a morning kindergarten kid. Kirby nodded, said, "Bye, Dad," and went to his seat without looking back. When the bell rang he turned to wave goodbye. Martin had no choice but to leave him and go home.

When he drove into his driveway, a car he did not recognize, a black Honda, sat parked in the driveway. A young woman sat on the front steps. Sandra had cut her thick light brown hair short; her flawless skin glowed and her eyes sparked. She stood when Martin stepped from his vehicle, and she walked up to him. She wore a white blouse and blue jeans. Athletic muscle showed even through the jeans. He waited for her to speak, almost holding his breath. He loved the sound of her voice.

"Hello," she said. "I love what you've done with the yard."

He took her hand. "Come inside?" is all he managed to say. She did.

"How is Crook?"

"He goes by Jeremy now. Crook is not a good name for a businessman."

"And Maureen?"

"They have twin daughters."

"Not bald, I hope," she said.

Martin laughed. "Actually, they have Maureen's hair."

He served her coffee and she asked about Tillie and Bill. He told her that Bill planned to sell the farm and move into town maybe next year.

Then she said, "Tell me about Kirby."

He did. He brought out the pictures: baptism pictures, wedding pictures where Kirby wore a white tux, Christie and Carmen teaching Kirby to walk, to play ball, to pet Bert, hundreds of pictures. The albums included pictures of Bill showing him how to put a worm on a fishing hook, and Tillie giving him his birthday cake.

Sandra looked at them all, laughing at some and crying at some.

"Does he ask about his mother?" she said. She looked at the table and not at Martin.

"Yes, but I told him I couldn't tell him yet. I said when he was ten, I might tell him then. I assured him he had a very beautiful mother," Martin said. "To be honest, he doesn't seem to dwell on it much. He accepts his lot in life with wonderful resilience."

Sandra looked at him sharply. "You won't tell him everything! You won't ever tell him he was conceived in a rape!"

"No," Martin answered. "I am his dad, but the story of his mother has yet to be determined. Your mom and dad watch him from a distance. They ask me about him and talk to him after church. But they can't acknowledge him, you know. They have forgiven him because they know it was not his fault."

Sandra nodded. "I have also forgiven him. I want you to tell him that his mother died. I want you to tell him that his mother loved him very much. Can you lie for me?"

Martin could not speak.

"I want Hauk's evil to end with me." Tears slid down her cheeks. "I didn't even know how badly hurt I was by what happened, and what I did. I never told anyone, not even my support group about leading Hauk to the barn. It has taken all this time, years, for me to be reconciled."

"You know your secret is safe," Martin said.

"I want to meet him, but just this one time. I will tell him I am a basketball friend."

At lunchtime Martin parked in the row of parent vehicles. He walked with Sandra to the door. They stood with a loose cluster of moms and day-care providers. The teacher's aid pushed open the door and a line of twenty-two glowing children emerged, having already learned to rejoice at the end of the school day.

"Kirby," Sandra called him as he ran by heading for the Bronco. He stopped and turned toward her. She went up to him and said, "Hello, Kirby, how was school?"

He said, "I am the second oldest in my class. That's because I was on a bubble."

"Let's go for a walk, Kirby," Sandra invited. The boy looked at his dad.

Martin said, "I will walk along. We can just walk around the block."

Sandra started to reach for Kirby's hand and then stopped. Instead she set a slow pace around the school.

"So, are you the smartest kid in your class?" she asked, making conversation.

"Maybe," Kirby answered. "There's a girl in my class who can read. I can't read."

"How do you know she can read?" Sandra asked.

"She told me," he said.

"So, how was it to be on a bubble?" Sandra smiled as she asked.

"It wasn't a real bubble." Kirby stopped and faced her and put his arms out in a gesture of explanation. "That is how my dad says things," he said. "I was too little for school last year."

When they returned to Martin's vehicle Bert occupied the front passenger seat. Sandra opened the door. Kirby climbed on the ledge and petted Bert who licked his face in return. Kirby then climbed in beside the dog leaving Sandra on the side walk.

"Sandra is coming with us," Martin told Kirby. So the boy and Bert climbed between the seats and settled in the back. Martin did not start the engine. He waited until Kirby groaned and buckled his seat belt.

Kirby was required to at least pretend to nap after school. Now he entered the kitchen from the back stairs. He looked at his dad with a puzzled expression.

"Is Sandra your friend?" he said.

Martin said, "Yes."

"Come here, Kirby," Sandra said. When the child stood at her knees, she put her hands gently on his shoulders. "I am your friend, too."

"Good," Kirby said. "Can you stay for supper? My dad will cook whatever you like."

"No," Sandra said. "I have to see my mom and dad, and then I fly to a city called Syracuse."

"I don't have a mom," Kirby said. "My classmate named Todd doesn't have a dad."

Martin could see that Sandra had no answer for this. So he said, "Kirby, you had a mom who loved you very much. Then one day she had to take a bus ride to heaven."

Yes, Martin thought, he could lie for Sandra. Kirby would never know his biological parents, but he was Kirby's dad. He had a birth certificate and a social security card inside a cedar box and the love of this strong boy to prove it.

The End

Printed in Great Britain
by Amazon